PRAISE FOR
NEW YORK TIMES
BESTSELLING AUTHOR

BARBARA DELINSKY

"When you care to read the very best,
the name of Barbara Delinsky should come
immediately to mind."
—*Rave Reviews*

"Women's fiction at its finest."
—*Romantic Times*

"One of this generation's most gifted writers of
contemporary women's fiction."
—*Affaire de Coeur*

"Barbara Delinsky knows the human heart and its
immense capacity to love and to believe."
—*Washington* (PA) *Observer-Reporter*

"Delinsky creates...a remarkably beautiful story."
—*Baton Rouge Advocate*

"An excellent storyteller."
—*Publishers Weekly*

BARBARA DELINSKY

DREAMS

MIRA

ISBN 1-55166-627-8

DREAMS

Copyright © 1999 by MIRA Books.

The publisher acknowledges the copyright holder
of the individual works as follows:

THE DREAM
Copyright © 1990 by Barbara Delinsky.

THE DREAM UNFOLDS
Copyright © 1990 by Barbara Delinsky.

THE DREAM COMES TRUE
Copyright © 1990 by Barbara Delinsky.

Visit us at www.mirabooks.com

Printed in U.S.A.

CONTENTS

THE DREAM 9

THE DREAM UNFOLDS 161

THE DREAM COMES TRUE 303

THE DREAM

1

Jessica Crosslyn lowered herself to the upholstered chair opposite the desk, smoothed the gracefully flowing challis skirt over her legs and straightened her round-rimmed spectacles. Slowly and reluctantly she met Gordon Hale's expectant gaze.

"I can't do it," she said softly. There was defeat in that softness and on her delicate features. "I've tried, Gordon. I've tried to juggle and balance. I've closed off everything but the few rooms I need. I keep the thermostat low to the point of freezing in winter. I've done only the most crucial of repairs, I've gone with the lowest bidders, and even then I've budgeted payments—" She caught in her breath. Her shoulders sagged slightly under the weight of disappointment. "But I can't do it. I just can't do it."

Gordon was quiet for a minute. He'd known Jessica from birth, had known her parents far longer than that. For better than forty years, he had been banker to the Crosslyns, which meant that he wasn't as emotionally removed as he should have been. He was deeply aware of the fight Jessica had been waging, and his heart went out to her.

"I warned Jed, you know," he said crossly. "I told him that he hadn't made adequate arrangements, but he just brushed my warnings aside. He was never the same after your mother died, never as clearheaded."

Jessica couldn't help but smile. It was an affectionate smile, a sad one as she remembered her father. "He was *never* clearheaded. Be honest, Gordon. My father wrote some brilliant scientific treatises in his day, but he was an eccentric old geezer. He never knew much about the workings of the everyday world. Mom was the one who took care of all that, and I tried to take over when she died, but things were pretty far gone by then."

"A fine woman, your mother."

"But no financial whiz, either, and so enamored with Dad that she was frightened of him. Even if she saw the financial problems, I doubt she'd have said a word to him about it. She wouldn't have wanted to upset him. She wouldn't have wanted to sully the creative mind with mention of something as mundane as money."

Gordon arched a bushy gray brow. "So now you're the one left to suffer the sullying."

"No," Jessica cautioned. She knew what he was thinking. "My mind isn't creative like Dad's was."

"I don't believe that for a minute. You have a Ph.D. in linguistics. You're fluent in Russian and German. You teach at Harvard. And you're published. You're as much of a scholar as Jed was any day."

"If I'm a scholar, it's simply because I love learning. But what I do isn't anything like what Dad did. My mind isn't like his. I can't look off into space and conjure up incredibly complex scientific theories. I can't dream up ideas. What I do is studied. It's orderly and pragmatic. I'm a foreign language teacher. I also read literature in the languages I teach, and since I've had access to certain Russian works that no one else has had, I was a cinch to write about them. So I'm published."

"You should be proud of that."

"I am, but if my book sells a thousand copies, I'll be lucky, which means that it won't save Crosslyn Rise. Nor will my salary." She gave a rueful chuckle. "Dad and I were alike in that, I'm afraid."

"But Crosslyn Rise was his responsibility," Gordon argued. "It's been in the family for five generations. Jed spent his entire life there. He owed it to all those who came before, as much as to you, to keep it up. If he'd done that, you wouldn't be in the bind you are now. But he let it deteriorate. I told him things would be bleak if he didn't keep on top of the repairs, but he wouldn't listen."

Jessica sighed. "That's water over the dam. The thing is that on top of everything else, I'm having plumbing and electrical problems. Up to now, I've settled for patches here and there, but that won't work any longer. I've been told—and I've had second and third opinions on it—that I need new systems for both. And given the size and nature of Crosslyn Rise..."

She didn't have to finish. Gordon knew the size and nature of Crosslyn Rise all too well. When one talked about installing new plumbing and electrical systems in a home that consisted of seventeen rooms and eight bathrooms spread over nearly eighty-five hundred square feet, the prospect was daunting. The prospect was even more daunting when one considered that a myriad of unexpected woes usually popped up when renovating a house that old.

Shifting several papers that lay neatly on his desk, Gordon said in a tentative voice, "I could loan you a little."

"A little more, you mean." She gave a tiny shake of her head and chided, "I'm having trouble meeting the payments I already have. You know that."

"Yes, but I'd do it, Jessica. I knew your family, and I know you. I'm the president of this bank, humble though it may be. If I can't pull a few strings, give a little extra for special people, who can I do it for?"

She was touched, and the smile she sent him told him so. But his generosity didn't change the facts. Again she shook her head, this time slowly and with resignation. "Thanks, Gordon. I do appreciate the offer, but if I was to accept it, I'd only be getting myself in deeper. Let's face it. I love my career, but it won't ever bring me big money. I could hurry out another book or two, maybe take on another course next semester, but I'd still come up way short of what I need."

"What you need," Gordon remarked, "is to marry a wealthy old codger who'd like nothing more than to live in a place like Crosslyn Rise."

Jessica didn't flinch, but her cheeks went paler than they'd been moments before. "I did that once."

"Chandler wasn't wealthy or old."

"But he wanted the Rise," she said with a look that went from wry to pained in the matter of a blink. "I wouldn't go through that again even if Crosslyn Rise were made of solid gold."

"If it were made of solid gold, you wouldn't have to go through anything," Gordon quipped, but he regretted mentioning Tom Chandler. Jessica's memories of the brief marriage weren't happy ones. Sitting forward, he folded his hands on his desk. "So what are your options?"

"There aren't many." And she'd been agonizing about those few for months.

"Is there someone who can help you—a relative who may have even a distant stake in the Rise?"

"Stake? No. The Rise was Dad's. He outlived a brother who stood to inherit if Dad had died first, but they were never on the best of terms. Dad wasn't a great communicator, if you know what I mean."

Gordon knew what she meant and nodded.

"And, anyway, now Dad's dead. Since I'm an only child, the Rise is mine, which means that no one else in the family has what you'd call a 'stake' in it."

"How about a fascination? Are there any aunts, uncles or cousins who've been intrigued by it over the years to the point where they'd pitch in to keep it alive?"

"No aunts or uncles, but there's a cousin. She's Dad's brother's oldest daughter, and if I called her she'd be out on the next plane from Chicago to give me advice."

Gordon studied her face. It told her thoughts with a surprising lack of guile, given that her early years had been spent, thanks to her mother, among the North Shore's well-to-do, who were anything but guileless. "I take it you know what that advice would be?"

"Oh, yes. Felicia would raze the house, divide the twenty-three acres into lots and sell each to the highest bidder. She told me that when she came for Dad's funeral, which was amusing in and of itself because she hadn't seen him since she was eighteen. Needless to say, she was here for the Rise."

"But the Rise is yours."

"And Felicia knew we were having trouble with the upkeep and that the trouble would only increase with Dad gone. She knew I'd never agree to raze the house, so her next plan was to pay me for the land around it. She figured that would give me enough money to renovate and support the house. In turn, she'd quadruple her investment by selling off small parcels of the land."

"That she would," Gordon agreed. "Crosslyn Rise stands on prime oceanfront land. Fifteen miles north of Boston, in a wealthy, well-run town with a good school system, fine municipal services, excellent public transportation… She'd quadruple her investment or better." His eyes narrowed. "Unless you were to charge her a hefty sum for the land."

"I wouldn't sell her the land for *any* sum," Jessica vowed. Rising from her seat, she moved toward the window. "I don't want to sell the land at all, but if I have to, the last person I'd sell to would be her. She's a witch."

Gordon cleared his throat. "Not quite the scholarly assessment I'd expected."

With a sheepish half smile, Jessica turned. "No. But it's hard to be scholarly when people evoke the kind of visceral response Felicia does." She slipped her hands into the pockets of her skirt, feeling more anchored that way. "Felicia and I are a year apart in age, so she used to visit when we were kids. She aspired to greatness. Being at the Rise made her feel she was on her way. She always joked that if I didn't want the Rise, she'd take it, but it was the kind of joking that wasn't really joking, if you know what I mean." When Gordon nodded, she went on. "By the time she graduated from high school, she realized that her greatness wasn't going to come from the Rise. So she went looking in other directions. I'm thirty-three now, so she's thirty-four. She's been married three times, each time to someone rich enough to settle a large lump sum on her to get out of the marriage."

"So she's a wealthy woman. But has she achieved that greatness?"

Wearing a slightly smug what-do-you-think look, Jessica gave a slow head shake. "She's got lots of money with nowhere to go."

"I'm surprised she didn't offer to buy Crosslyn Rise from you outright."

"Oh, she did. When Dad was barely in his grave." Her shoulders went straighter, giving a regal lift to her five-foot-six-inch frame. "I refused just as bluntly as she offered. There's no way I'd let her have the Rise. She'd have it sold or subdivided within a year." She paused, took a breath, turned back to the window and said in a quiet voice, "I can't let that happen."

They were back to her options. Gordon knew as well as she did that some change in the Rise's status was necessary. "What are your thoughts, Jessica?" he asked as gently as he could.

She was very still for a time, gnawing on her lower lip as she looked out over the harbor. Its charm, part of which was visible from Crosslyn Rise, not two miles away, made the thought of leaving the Rise all the harder. But it had to be faced.

"I could sell off some of the outer acreage," she began in a dubious tone, "but that would be a stopgap measure. It would be two lots this year, two lots next year and so on. Once I sold the lots, I wouldn't have any say about what was built on them. The zoning is residential, but you know as well as I do that there are dozens of styles of homes, one tackier than the next."

"Is that snobbishness I detect?" Gordon teased.

She looked him in the eye without a dash of remorse. "Uh-huh. The Rise is Georgian colonial and gorgeous. It would be a travesty if she were surrounded by less stately homes."

"There are many stately homes that aren't Georgian colonial."

"But the Rise is. And anything around it should blend in," she argued, then darted a helpless glance toward the ceiling. "This is the last thing I want to be discussing. It's the last thing I want to be *considering*."

"You love the Rise."

She pondered the thought. "It's not the mortar and brick that I love, not the kitchen or the parlor or the library. It's the whole thing. The old-world charm. The smell of polished wood and history. It's the beauty of it—the trees and ponds, birds and chipmunks—and the peace, the serenity." But there was more. "It's the idea of Crosslyn Rise. The idea that it's been in my family for so long. The idea that it's a little world unto itself." She faltered for an instant. "Yes, I love the Rise. But I have to do something. If I don't, you'll be forced to foreclose before long."

Gordon didn't deny it. He could give her more time than another person might have. He could indeed grant her another, smaller loan in the hope that, with a twist of fortune, she'd be able to recover from her present dire straits. In the end, business was business.

"What would you like to do?" he asked.

She started to turn back to the window but realized it wouldn't make things easier. It was time to face facts. So she folded her arms around her middle and said, "If I had my druthers, I'd sell the whole thing, house and acreage as a package, to a large, lovely, devoted family, but the chances of finding one that can afford it are next to nil. I've been talking with Nina Stone for the past eight months. If I was to sell, she'd be my broker. Without formally listing the house, she'd have an eye out for buyers like that, but there hasn't been a one. The real estate market is slow."

"That's true as far as private buyers go. Real estate developers would snap up property like Crosslyn Rise in a minute."

"And in the next minute they'd subdivide, sell off the smallest possible lots for the biggest possible money and do everything my cousin Felicia would do with just as little care for the integrity of the Rise." Jessica stood firm, levelly eyeing Gordon through her small, round lenses. "I can't do that, Gordon. It's bad enough that I have to break apart the Rise after all these years, but I can't just toss it in the air and let it fall where it may. I want a say as to what happens to it. I want whatever is done to be done with dignity. I want the charm of the place preserved."

She finished without quite finishing. Not even her glasses could hide the slight, anticipatory widening of her eyes.

Gordon prodded. "You have something in mind?"

"Yes. But I don't know if it's feasible."

"Tell me what it is, and I'll let you know."

She pressed her lips together, wishing she didn't have to say a word, knowing that she did. The Rise was in trouble. She was up against a wall, and this seemed the least evil of the options.

"What if we were to turn Crosslyn Rise into an exclusive condominium complex?" she asked, then hurried on before Gordon could answer. "What if there were small clusters of homes, built in styles compatible with the mansion and tucked into the woods at well-chosen spots throughout the property?" She spoke even more quickly, going with the momentum of her words. "What if the mansion itself was redone and converted into a combination health center, clubhouse, restaurant? What if we developed the harbor area into something small but classy, with boutiques and a marina?" Running out of "what ifs," she stopped abruptly.

Unfolding his hands, Gordon sat back in his chair. "You'd be willing to do all that?"

"Willing, but not able. What I'm talking about would be a phenomenally expensive project—"

He stilled her with a wave of his hand. "You'd be *willing* to have the Rise turned into a condominium complex?"

"If it was done the right way," she said. She felt suddenly on the defensive and vaguely disloyal to Crosslyn Rise. "Given any choice, I'd leave the Rise as it is, but it's deteriorating more every year. I'm long past the point of being able to put a finger in the dike. So I have to do something. This idea beats the alternatives. If it was done with forethought and care and style, we could alter the nature of Crosslyn Rise without changing its character."

"We?"

"Yes." She came away from the window to make her plea. "I need help, Gordon. I don't have any money. There would have to be loans, but once the cluster homes were built and sold, the money could be repaid, so it's not like my asking you for a loan just to fix up the Rise. Can I get a loan of the size I'd need?"

"No."

She blinked. "No? Then you don't like the idea?"

"Of the condo complex? Yes, I do. It has definite merit."

"But you won't back me."

"I can't just hand over that kind of money."

She slid into her chair and sat forward on its edge. "Why not? You were offering me money just a little while ago. Yes, this would be more, but it would be an investment that would guarantee enough profit to pay back the loan and then some."

Gordon regarded her kindly. He had endless respect for her where her work at Harvard was concerned. But she wasn't a businesswoman by any stretch of the imagination. "No financial institution will loan you that kind of money, Jessica. If you were an accredited real estate developer, or a builder or an architect, you might have a chance. But from a banker's point of view, loaning a linguistics professor large amounts of money to build a condominium complex would be akin to loaning a librarian money to buy the Red Sox. You're not a developer. You may know what you want for the Rise, but you wouldn't know how to carry it out. Real estate development isn't your field. You don't have the kind of credibility necessary to secure the loan."

"But I need the money," she cried. The sharp rise in her voice was out of character, reflecting her frustration, which was growing by the minute.

"Then we'll have to find people who *do* have the necessary credibility for a project like this."

Her frustration eased. All she needed was a ray of hope. "Oh. Okay. How do we go about doing that and how does it work?"

Gordon relaxed in his chair. He enjoyed planning projects and was relieved that Jessica was open to suggestion. "We put together a consortium, a group of people, each of whom is willing to invest in the future of Crosslyn Rise. Each member has an interest in the project based on his financial contribution to it, and the amount he takes out at the end is commensurate with his input."

Jessica wasn't sure she liked the idea of a consortium, simply because it sounded so real. "A group of people? But they're strangers. They won't know the Rise. How can we be sure that they won't put their money and heads together and come up with something totally offensive?"

"We handpick them. We choose only people who would be as committed to maintaining the dignity and charm of Crosslyn Rise as you are."

"No one is as committed to that as I am."

"Perhaps not. Still, I've seen some beautiful projects, similar to what you have in mind, done in the past few years. Investors can be naturalists, too."

Jessica was only vaguely mollified, a fact to which the twisting of her stomach attested. "How many people?"

"As many as it would take to collect the necessary money. Three, six, twelve."

"Twelve people? Twelve strangers?"

"Strangers only at first. You'd get to know them, since you'd be part of the consortium. We'd have the estate appraised as to its fair market value, and that would determine your stake in the project. If you wanted, I could advance you more to broaden your stake. You'd have to decide how much profit you want."

Her eyes flashed. "I'm not in this for the profit."

"You certainly are," Gordon insisted in the tone of one who was older and wiser. "If the Rise is made into the kind of complex you mention, this is your inheritance. And it's significant, Jessica. Never forget that. You may think you have one foot in the poorhouse, but Crosslyn Rise, for all its problems, is worth a pretty penny. It'll be worth even more once it's developed."

Developed. The word made her flinch. She felt guilty for even considering it—guilty, traitorous, mercenary. In one instant she was disappointed with herself, in the next she was furious with her father.

But neither disappointment nor fury would change the facts. "Why does this have to be?" she whispered sadly.

"Because," Gordon said quietly, "life goes on. Things change." He tipped his head and eyed her askance. "It may not be all that bad. You must be lonely living at the Rise all by yourself. It's a pretty big place. You could choose one of the smaller houses and have it custom-designed for you."

She held up a cautionary hand. He was moving a little too quickly. "I haven't decided to do this."

"It's a solid idea."

"But you're making it sound as if it can really happen, and that makes me feel like I'm losing control."

"You'd be a member of the consortium," he reminded her. "You'd have a voice as to what's done."

"I'd be one out of three or six or maybe even twelve."

"But you own the Rise. In the end, you'd have final approval of any plan that is devised."

"I would?"

"Yes."

That made her feel better, but only a little. She'd always been an introverted sort. She could just imagine herself sitting at the far end of a table, listening to a group of glib investors bicker over her future. She'd be outtalked, outplanned, outwitted.

"I want more than that," she said on impulse. It was survivalism at its best. "I want to head the consortium. I want my cut to be the largest. I want to be *guaranteed* control over the end result." She straightened in her chair. "Is that possible?"

Gordon's brows rose. "Anything's possible. But advisable? I don't know, Jessica. You're a scholar. You don't know anything about real estate development."

"So I'll listen and learn. I have common sense and an artistic eye. I know the kind of thing I want. And I love Crosslyn Rise." She was convincing herself as she talked. "It isn't enough for me to have the power to approve or disapprove. I want to be part of the project from start to finish. That's the only way I'll be able to sleep at night." She wasn't sure she liked the look on Gordon's face. "You don't think I can do it."

"It's not that." He hesitated. There were several problems that he could see, one of which was immediate. He searched for the words to tell her what he was thinking, without sounding offensive. "You have to understand, Jessica. Traditionally, men are the investors. They've been involved in other projects. They're used to working in certain ways. I'm...not sure how they'll feel about a novice telling them what to do.''

"A woman, you mean," she said, and he didn't deny it. "But I'm a reasonable person. I'm not pigheaded or spiteful. I'll be open-minded about everything except compromising the dignity of Crosslyn Rise. What better a leader could they want?"

Gordon didn't want to touch that one. So he tried a different tack. "Changing the face of Crosslyn Rise is going to be painful for you. Are you sure you want to be intimately involved in the process?"

"Yes," she declared.

He pursed his lips, dropped his gaze to the desktop, tried to think of other evasive arguments, but failed. Finally he went with the truth, bluntly stating the crux of the problem. "The fact is, Jessica, that if you insist on being the active head of the consortium, I may have trouble getting investors." He held up a hand. "Nothing personal, mind you. Most of the people I have in mind don't know who or what you are, but the fact of a young, inexperienced woman having such control over the project may make them skittish. They'll fear that it will take forever to make decisions, or that once those decisions are made, you'll change your mind. It goes back to the issue of credibility."

"That's not fair!"

"Life isn't, sometimes," he murmured, but he had an idea. "There is one way we might be able to get around it."

"What?"

He was thoughtful for another minute. "A compromise, sort of. We get the entire idea down on paper first. You work with an architect, tell him what you want, let him come up with some sketches, work with him on revising them until you're completely satisfied. Then we approach potential investors with a fait accompli." He was warming to the idea as he talked. "It could work out well. With your ideas spelled out in an architect's plans, we can better calculate the costs. Being specific might help in wooing investors."

"You mean, counterbalance the handicap of working with me?" Jessica suggested dryly, but she wasn't angry. If sexism existed, it existed. She had worked around it before. She could do it again.

"Things would be simplified all around," Gordon went on without comment. "You would have total control over the design of the project. Investors would know exactly what they were buying into. If they don't like your idea, they don't have to invest, and if we can't get enough people together, you'd only be out the architect's fee."

"How much will that be?" Jessica asked. She'd heard complaints from a colleague who had worked with an architect not long before.

"Not as much as it might be, given the man I have in mind."

Jessica wasn't sure whether to be impressed or nervous. The bravado she's felt moments before was beginning to falter with talk of specifics, like architects. "You've already thought of someone?"

"Yes," Gordon said, eyeing her directly. "He's the best, and Crosslyn Rise deserves the best."

She couldn't argue with that. "Who is he?"

"He's only been in the field for twelve years, but he's done some incredible things. He was affiliated with a New York firm for seven of those years, and during that time he worked on PUDs up and down the East Coast."

"PUDs?"

"Planned Urban Developments—in and around cities, out to suburbs. Five years ago, he established his own firm in Boston. He's done projects like the one you have in mind. I've seen them. They're breathtaking."

Her curiosity was piqued. "Who is he?"

"He's a down-to-earth guy who's had hands-on experience at the building end, which makes him an even better architect. He isn't so full of himself that he's hard to work with. And I think he'd be very interested in this project."

Jessica was trying to remember whether she'd ever read anything in the newspaper about an architect who might fit Gordon's description. But such an article would have been in the business section, and she didn't read that—which, unfortunately, underscored some of what Gordon had said earlier. Still, she had confidence in her ideas. And if she was to work with a man the likes of whom Gordon was describing, she couldn't miss.

"Who *is* he?" she asked.

"Carter Malloy."

Jessica stared at him dumbly. The name was very familiar. Carter Malloy. She frowned. Bits and snatches of memories began flitting through her mind.

"I knew a Carter Malloy once," she mused. "He was the son of the people who used to work for us at the Rise. His mom kept the house and his dad gardened." She felt a moment's wistfulness. "Boy, could I ever use Michael Malloy's green thumb now. On top of everything else, the Rise needs a landscaping overhaul. It's been nearly ten years since the Malloys retired and went south." Her wistfulness faded, giving way to a scowl. "It's been even longer since I've seen their son, thank goodness. He was obnoxious. He was older than me and never let me forget it. It used to drive him nuts that his parents were poor and mine weren't. He had a foul mouth, problems in school and a chip on his shoulder a mile wide. And he was ugly.''

Gordon's expression was guarded, his voice low. "He's not ugly now.''

"Excuse me?''

"I said,'' he repeated more clearly, "he's not ugly now. He's grown up in lots of ways, including that.''

Jessica was surprised. "You've been in touch with Carter Malloy?''

"He keeps an account here. God only knows he could easily give his business to one of the bigger banks in Boston, but he says he feels a connection with the place where he grew up.''

"No doubt he does. There's a little thing about a police record here. Petty theft, wasn't it?''

"He's reformed.''

Her expression said she doubted that was possible. "I was always mystified that wonderful people like Annie and Michael Malloy could spawn a son like that. The heartache he caused them.'' She shook her head at the shame of it. "He's not living around her, is he? Tell me, so I'll know to watch out. Carter Malloy isn't someone I'd want to bump into on the street.''

"He's living in Boston.''

"What is he—a used-car salesman?''

"He's an architect.''

Jessica was momentarily taken aback. "Not the Carter Malloy I knew.''

"Like I said, he's grown up.''

The thought that popped into her head at that moment was so horrendous that she quickly dashed it from mind. "The Carter Malloy I knew couldn't possibly have grown up to be a professional. He barely finished high school.''

"He spent time in the army and went to college when he got out.''

"But even if he had the gray matter for college,'' she argued, feeling distinctly uneasy, "he didn't have the patience or the dedication. He could never apply himself to anything for long. The only thing he succeeded at was making trouble.''

"People change, Jessica. Carter Malloy is now a well-respected and successful architect.''

Jessica had never known Gordon to lie to her, which was why she had to accept what he said. On a single lingering thread of hope, she gave a tight laugh. "Isn't it a coincidence? Two Carter Malloys, both architects? The one you have in mind for my project—does he live in Boston, too, or does he have a house in one of the suburbs?''

Gordon never answered. Jessica took one look at his expression, stood and began to pace the office. Her hands were tucked into the pockets of her skirt, and just as the challis fabric faithfully rendered the slenderness of her hips and legs as she paced, it showed those hands balled into fists. Her arms were straight, pressed to her sides.

"Do you know what Carter Malloy did to me when I was six? He dared me to climb to the third notch of the big elm out beyond the duck pond." She turned at the window and stared back. "Needless to say, once I got up there, I couldn't get back down. He looked up at me with that pimply face of his, gave an evil grin and walked off." She paused before a Currier and Ives print on the wall, seeing nothing of it. "I was terrified. I sat for a while thinking that he'd come back, but he didn't. I tried yelling, but I was too far from the house to be heard. One hour passed, then another, and each time I looked at the ground I got dizzy. I sat up there crying for three hours before Michael finally found me, and then he had to call the fire department to get me down." She moved on. "I had nightmares for weeks afterward. I've never climbed a tree since."

She stopped at the credenza, turned and faced Gordon, dropping her hands and hips back against the polished mahogany for support. "If the Carter Malloy I knew is the one you have in mind for this job, the answer is no. That's my very first decision as head of this consortium, and it's closed to discussion."

"Now that," Gordon said on a light note that wasn't light at all but was his best shot at an appeal, "is why I may have trouble finding backers for the project. If you're going to make major decisions without benefit of discussion with those who have more experience, there isn't much hope. I have to say that I wouldn't put my money into a venture like that. A bullheaded woman would be hell to work with."

"Gordon," she protested.

"I'm serious, Jessica. You said you'd listen and learn, but you don't seem willing to do that."

"I am. Just not where Carter Malloy is concerned. I couldn't work with him. It would be a disaster, and what would happen to the Rise, then?" Her voice grew pleading. "There must be other architects. He can't be the only one available."

"He's not, and there are others, but he's the best."

"In all of Boston?"

"Given the circumstances, yes."

"What circumstances?"

"He knows the Rise. He cares about it."

"Cares?" she echoed in dismay. "He'd as soon burn the Rise to the ground and leave it in ashes as transform it into something beautiful."

"How do you know? When was the last time you talked with him?"

"When I was sixteen." Pushing off from the credenza, she began to pace again. "It was the first I'd seen him in a while—"

"He'd been in the army," Gordon interrupted to remind her.

"Whatever. His parents didn't talk about him much, and I was the last person who'd want to ask. But he came over to get something for his dad one night. I was on the front porch waiting for a date to pick me up, and Carter said—" Her memories interrupted her this time. Their sting held her silent for a minute, finally allowing her to murmur, "He said some cruel things. Hurtful things." She stopped her pacing to look at Gordon. "Carter Malloy hates me as much as I hate him. There's no way he'd agree to do the work for me even if I wanted him to do it, which I don't."

But Gordon wasn't budging. "He'd do it. And he'd do it well. The Carter Malloy I've come to know over the past five years is a very different man from the one you remember. Didn't you ever wonder why his parents retired when they did? They were in their late fifties, not terribly old and in no way infirm. But they'd saved a little money over the years, and then Carter bought them a place in Florida with beautiful shrubbery that Michael could tend year-round. It was one of the first things Carter did when he began to earn good money. To this day he sees that they have everything they need. It's his way of making up for the trouble he caused them when he was younger. If he hurt you once, my guess is he'd welcome the chance to help out now."

"I doubt that," she scoffed, but more quietly. She was surprised by what Gordon had said. Carter Malloy had never struck her as a man with a thoughtful bone in his body. "What do you mean by help out?"

"I'd wager that he'd join the consortium."

"Out of pity for me?"

"Not at all. He's a shrewd businessman. He'd join it for the investment value. But he'd also want to be involved for old times' sake. I've heard him speak fondly of Crosslyn Rise." He paused, stroked a finger over his upper lip. "I'd go so far as to say we could get him to throw in his fee as part of his contribution. That way, he'd have a real stake in making the plans work, and if they didn't, it would be his problem. He'd swallow his own costs—which would be a far sight better than your having to come up with forty or fifty thousand if the project fizzled."

"Forty or fifty thousand?" She hadn't dreamed it would be so much. Swallowing, she sank into her chair once again, this time into the deepest corner, where the chair's back and arms could shield her. "I don't like this, Gordon."

"I know. But given that the Rise can't be saved as it is, this is an exciting option. Let me call Carter."

"No," she cried, then repeated it more quietly. "No."

"I'm talking about a simple introductory meeting. You can tell him your general thoughts about the project and listen to what he has to say in return. See how you get along. Decide for yourself whether he's the same as he used to be. There won't be an obligation. I'll be there with you if you like."

She tipped up her chin. "I was never afraid of Carter Malloy. I just disliked him."

"You won't now. He's a nice guy. Y'know, you said it yourself—it drove him nuts that he was poor and you were rich. He must have spent a lot of time wishing Crosslyn Rise was his. So let him take those wishes and your ideas and make you some sketches."

"They could be very good or very bad."

"Ah," Gordon drawled, "but remember two things. First off, Carter has a career and a reputation to protect. Second, you have final say. If you don't like what he does, you have the power of veto. In a sense that puts him under your thumb, now, doesn't it?"

Jessica thought back to the last time she'd seen Carter Malloy. In vivid detail, she recalled what he'd said to her, and though she'd blotted it from her mind over the years, the hurt and humiliation remained. Perhaps she would find a measure of satisfaction having him under her thumb.

And, yes, Crosslyn Rise was still hers. If Carter Malloy didn't come up with plans that pleased her, she'd turn her back on him and walk away. He'd see who had the last laugh then.

2

Jessica had never been a social butterfly. Her mother, well aware of the Crosslyn heritage, had put her through the motions when she'd been a child. Jessica had been dressed up and taken to birthday parties, given riding lessons, sent to summer camp, enrolled in ballet. She had learned the essentials of being a properly privileged young lady. But she had never quite fit in.

She wasn't a beautiful child, for one thing. Her hair was long and unruly, her body board-straight and her features plain—none of which was helped by the fact that she rarely smiled. She was quiet, serious, shy, not terribly unlike her father. One part of her was most comfortable staying home in her room at Crosslyn Rise reading a good book. The other part dreamed of being the belle of the ball.

Having a friend over to play was both an apprehensive and exciting experience for Jessica. She liked the company and, even more, the idea of being liked, but she was forever afraid of boring her guest. At least, that was what her mother warned her against ad infinitum. As an adult, Jessica understood that though her mother worshipped her father's intellect, deep inside she found him a boring person, hence the warnings to Jessica. At the time, Jessica took those warning to heart. When she had a friend at the Rise, she was on her guard to impress.

That was why she was crushed by what Carter Malloy did to her when she was ten. Laura Hamilton, who came as close to being a best friend as any Jessica had, was over to visit. She didn't come often; the Rise wasn't thought to be a "fun" place. But Laura had come this time because she and Jessica had a project to do together for school, and the library at the Rise had the encyclopedias and *National Geographic*s that the girls needed.

When they finished their work, Jessica suggested they go out to the porch. It was a warm fall day, and the porch was one of her favorite spots. Screened in and heavily shaded by towering maples and oaks, it was the kind of quiet, private place that made Jessica feel secure.

She started out feeling secure this day, because Laura liked the porch, too. They sat close beside each other on the flowered porch sofa, pads of paper in their laps, pencils in hand. They were writing poems, which seemed to Jessica to be an exciting enough thing to do.

Carter Malloy didn't think so. Pruning sheers in hand, he materialized from behind the rhododendrons just beyond the screen, where, to Jessica's chagrin, he had apparently been sitting.

"What are you two doing?" he asked in a voice that said he knew exactly what they were doing, since he'd been listening for quite some time, and he thought it was totally dumb.

"What are *you* doing?" Jessica shot right back. She wasn't intimidated by his size or his deep voice or the fact that he was seventeen. Maybe, just a little, she was intimidated by his streetwise air, but she pushed that tiny fear aside. Given who his parents were, he wouldn't dare touch her. "What are you doing out there?" she demanded.

"Clipping the hedges," Carter answered with an insolent look.

She was used to the look. It put her on the defensive every time she saw it. "No, you weren't. You were spying on us."

He had one hip cocked, one shoulder lower than the other but both back to emphasize a developing chest. "Why in the hell would I want to do that? You're writing sissy poems."

"Who is he?" Laura whispered nervously.

"He's no one," was Jessica's clearly spoken answer. Though she'd always talked back to Carter, this time it seemed more important than ever. She had Laura to impress. "You were supposed to be cutting the shrubs, but you weren't. You never do what your father tells you to do."

"I think for myself," Carter answered. His dark eyes bore into hers. "But you don't know what that means. You're either going to tea parties like your old lady or sticking your nose in a book like your old man. You couldn't think for yourself if you tried. So whose idea was it to write poems? Your prissy little friend's?"

Jessica didn't know which to be first, angry or embarrassed. "Go away, Carter."

Lazily he raised the pruning sheers and snipped off a single shoot. "I'm working."

"Go work somewhere else," she cried with a ten-year-old's frustration. "There are lots of other bushes."

"But this one needs trimming."

She was determined to hold her ground. "We want to be alone."

"Why? What's so important about writing poems? Afraid I'll steal your rhymes?" He looked closely at Laura. "You're a Hamilton, aren't you?"

"Don't answer," Jessica told Laura.

"She is," Carter decided. "I've seen her sitting in church with the rest of her family."

"That's a lie," Jessica said. "You don't go to church."

"I go sometimes. It's fun, all those sinners begging for forgiveness. Take old man Hamilton. He bought his way into the state legislature—"

Jessica was on her feet, her reed-slim body shaking. The only thing she knew for sure about what Carter was saying was that it was certain to offend Laura, and if that happened, Laura would never be back. "Shut up, Carter!"

"Bought his way there and does nothing but sit on his can and raise his hand once in a while. But I s'pose he doesn't have to do nothing. If I had that much money, I'd be sittin' on my can, too."

"You *don't* have that much money. You don't have *any* money."

"But I have friends. And you don't."

Jessica never knew how he'd found her Achilles' heel, but he'd hit her where it hurt. "You're a stupid jerk," she cried. "You're dumb and you have pimples. I wouldn't want to be you for anything in the world." Tears swimming in her eyes, she took Laura's hand and dragged her into the house.

Laura never did come back to Crosslyn Rise, and looking back on it so many years later, Jessica remembered the hurt she'd felt. It didn't matter that she hadn't seen Laura Hamilton for years, that by the time they'd reached high school Jessica had found her as boring as she'd feared she would be herself, that they had nothing in common now. The fact was that when she was ten, she had badly wanted to be Laura's best friend and Carter Malloy had made that harder than ever.

Such were her thoughts as the *T* carried her underground from one stop to the next on her way from Harvard Square to Boston. She had a two-o'clock meeting with Carter Malloy in his office. Gordon had set it up, and when he'd asked if Jessica wanted him along, she had said she'd be fine on her own.

She wasn't sure that had been the wisest decision. She was feeling nervous, feeling as though every one of the insecurities she'd suffered in childhood was back in force. She was the not-too-pretty, not-too-popular, not-too-social little girl once again. Gordon's support might have come in handy.

But she had a point to prove to him, too. She'd told him that she wanted to actively head the consortium altering Crosslyn Rise. Gordon was skeptical of her ability to do that. If he was to aggressively and enthusiastically seek out investors in Crosslyn Rise, she had to show him she was up to the job.

So she'd assured him that she could handle Carter Malloy on her own, and that, she decided in a moment's respite from doubt, was what she was going to do. But the doubts returned, and as she left the trolley, climbed the steep stairs to Park Street and headed for Winter, she hated Carter Malloy more than ever.

It wasn't the best frame of mind in which to be approaching a meeting of some importance, Jessica knew, which was why she took a slight detour on her way to Carter's office. She had extra time; punctual person that she was, she'd allowed plenty for the ride from Cambridge. So she swung over to West Street and stopped to browse at the Brattle Book Shop, and though she didn't buy anything, the sense of comfort she felt in the company of books, particularly the aged beauties George Gloss had collected, was worth the pause. It was with some reluctance that she finally dragged herself away from the shelves and set off.

Coming from school, she wore her usual teaching outfit—long skirt, soft blouse, slouchy blazer and low heels. The occasional glance in a store window as she passed told her that she looked perfectly presentable. Her hair was impossible, of course. Though not as unruly as it had once been, it was still thick and hard to handle, which was why she had it secured with a scarf at the back of her head. She wasn't trying to impress anyone, least of all Carter Malloy, but she wanted to look professional and in command of herself, if nothing else.

Carter's firm was on South Street in an area that had newly emerged as a mecca for artists and designers. The building itself was six stories tall and of an earthy brick that was a pleasantly warm in contrast to the larger, more modern office tower looming nearby. The street level of the building held a chic art gallery, an equally chic architectural supply store, a not-so-chic fortune cookie company, and a perfectly dumpy-looking diner that was mobbed, even at two, with a suit-and-tie crowd.

Turning in at the building's main entrance, she couldn't help but be impressed by the newly refurbished, granite-walled lobby. She guessed that the building's rents were high, attesting to Gordon's claim that Carter was doing quite well.

As she took the elevator to the top floor, Jessica struggled, as she'd done often in the five days since Gordon had first mentioned his name, to reconcile the Carter Malloy she'd known with the Carter Malloy who was a successful architect. Try as she might, she couldn't shake the image of what he'd been as a boy and what he'd done to her then. Not even the sleekly modern reception area, with its bright walls, indirect lighting and sparse, avante-garde furnishings could displace the image of the ill-tempered, sleezy-looking juvenile delinquent.

"My name is Jessica Crosslyn," she told the receptionist in a voice that was quiet and didn't betray the unease she felt, "I have a two-o'clock appointment with Mr. Malloy."

The receptionist was an attractive woman, sleek enough to complement her surroundings, though nowhere near as new. Jessica guessed her to be in her late forties. "Won't you have a seat? Mr. Malloy was delayed at a meeting. He shouldn't be more than five or ten minutes. He's on his way now."

Jessica should have figured he'd be late. Keeping her waiting was a petty play for power. She was sure he'd planned it.

Once again she wished Gordon was with her, if for no other reason than to show him that Carter hadn't changed so much. But Gordon was up on the North Shore, and she was too uncomfortable to sit. So, nodding at the receptionist, she moved away from the desk and slowly passed one, then another of the large, dry-mounted drawings that hung on the wall. Hingham Court, Pheasant Landing, Berkshire Run—pretty names for what she had to admit were attractive complexes, if the drawings were at all true to life. If she could blot out the firm's name, Malloy and Goodwin, from the corner of each, she might feel enthusiasm. But the Malloy, in particular, kept jumping right off the paper, hitting her mockingly in the face. In self-defense, she finally turned and slipped into one of the low armchairs.

Seconds later, the door opened and her heart began to thud. Four men entered, engaged in a conversation that kept them fully occupied while her gaze went from one face to the next. Gordon had said Carter Malloy had changed a lot, but even accounting for that, not one of the men remotely resembled the man she remembered.

Feeling awkward, she took a magazine from the glass coffee table beside her and began to leaf through. She figured that if Carter was in the group, he'd know of her presence soon enough. In the meanwhile, she concentrated on keeping her glasses straight on her nose and looking calm, cool, even a bit disinterested, which was hard when the discussion among the four men began to grow heated. The matter at hand seemed to be the linkage issue, a City of Boston mandate that was apparently costing builders hundreds of thousands of dollars per project. Against her will, she found herself looking up. One of the group seemed to be with the city, another with Carter's firm and the other two with a construction company. She was thinking that the architect was the most articulate of the bunch when the door opened again. Her heart barely had time to start pounding anew when Carter Malloy came through. He took in the group before him, shook hands with the three she'd pegged as outsiders, slid a questioning gaze to the receptionist, then, in response to the woman's pointed glance, looked at Jessica.

For the space of several seconds, her heart came to a total standstill. The man was unmistakably Carter Malloy, but, yes, he'd changed. He was taller, broader. In place of a sweaty T-shirt emblazoned with something obscene, tattered old jeans and crusty work boots, he wore a tweed blazer, an oxford-cloth shirt with the neck button open, gray slacks and loafers. The dark hair that had always fallen in ungroomed spikes on his forehead was shorter, well shaped, cleaner. His skin, too, was cleaner, his features etched by time. The surly expression that even now taunted her memory had mellowed to something still intense but controlled. He had tiny lines shadowing the corners of his eyes, a small scar on his right jaw and a light tan.

Gordon was right, she realized in dismay. Carter wasn't ugly anymore. He wasn't *at all* ugly, and that complicated things. She didn't do well with men in general, but attractive ones in particular made her edgy. She wasn't sure she was going to make it.

But she couldn't run out now. That would be the greatest indignity. And besides, if she did that, what would she tell Gordon? More aptly, what would Carter tell Gordon? Her project would be sunk, for sure.

Mustering every last bit of composure she had stashed away inside, she rose as Carter approached.

"Jessica?" he asked in a deep but tentative voice.

Heart thudding, she nodded. She deliberately kept her hands in her lap. To offer a handshake seemed reckless.

Fortunately he didn't force the issue, but stood looking down at her, not quite smiling, not quite frowning. "I'm sorry. Were you waiting long?"

She shook her head. A little voice inside told her to say something, but for the life of her she couldn't find any words. She was wondering why she felt so small, why Carter seemed so tall, how her memory could have been so inaccurate in its rendition of as simple a matter as relative size.

He gestured toward the inner door. "Shall we go inside?"

She nodded. When he opened the door and held it for her, she was surprised; the Carter she'd known would have let it slam in her face. When she felt the light pressure of his hand at her waist, guiding her down a corridor spattered with offices, she was doubly surprised; the Carter she'd known knew nothing of courtly gestures, much less gentleness. When he said, "Here we are," and showed her into the farthest and largest office, she couldn't help but be impressed.

That feeling lasted for only a minute, because no sooner had she taken a chair—gratefully, since the race of her pulse was making her legs shaky—than Carter backed himself against the stool that stood at the nearby drafting table, looked at her with a familiarly wicked gleam in his eye and said, "Cat got your tongue?"

Jessica was oddly relieved. The old Carter Malloy she could handle to some extent; sarcasm was less debilitating than charm. Taking in a full breath for the first time since she'd laid eyes on him, she said, "My tongue's where it's always been. I don't believe in using it unless I have something to say."

"Then you're missing out on some of the finer things in life," he informed her so innocently that it was a minute before Jessica connected his words with the gleam in his eye.

Ignoring both the innuendo and the faint flush that rose on her cheeks, she vowed to state her business as quickly as possible and leave. "Did Gordon explain why I've come?"

Carter gave a leisurely nod, showing none of the discomfort she felt. But instead of picking up on his conversation with Gordon, he said, "It's been a long time. How have you been?"

"Just fine."

"You're looking well."

She wasn't sure why he'd said that, but it annoyed her. "I haven't changed," she told him as though stating the obvious, then paused. "You have."

"I should hope so." While the words settled into the stillness of the room, he continued to stare at her. His eyes were dark, touched one minute by mockery, the next by genuine curiosity. Jessica half wished for the contempt she used to find there. It wouldn't have been as unsettling.

Tearing her gaze from his, she looked down at her hands, used one to shove the nose piece of her glasses higher and cleared her throat. "I've decided to make some changes at Crosslyn Rise." She looked back up, but before she could say a thing, Carter beat her to it.

"I'm sorry about your father's death."

Uh-huh, she thought, but she simply nodded in thanks for the words. "Anyway, there's only me now, so the Rise is really going to waste." That wasn't the issue at all, but she couldn't quite get herself to tell Carter Malloy the problem was money. "I'm hoping to make something newer and more practical out of it. Gordon suggested I speak with you. Quite honestly, I wasn't wild about the idea." She watched him closely, waiting to see his reaction to her rebuff.

But he gave nothing away. In a maddeningly calm voice, he asked, "Why not?"

She didn't blink. "We never liked one another. Working together could be difficult."

"That's assuming we don't like one another now," he pointed out too reasonably.

"We don't *know* one another now."

"Which is why you're here today."

"Yes," she said, hesitated, then added, "I wasn't sure how much to believe of what Gordon told me." Her eyes roamed the room, taking in a large desk covered with rolls of blueprints, the drafting table and its tools, a corked wall that bore sketches in various stages of completion. "All this doesn't jibe with the man I remember."

"That man wasn't a man. He wasn't much more than a boy. How many years has it been since we last saw each other?"

"Seventeen," she said quickly, then wished she'd been slower or more vague when she caught a moment's satisfaction in his eye.

"You didn't know I was an architect?"

"How would I know?"

He shrugged and offered a bit too innocently, "Mutual friends?"

She did say, "Uh-huh," aloud this time, and with every bit of the sarcasm she'd put into it before. He was obviously enjoying her discomfort. *That* was more like what she'd expected. "We've never had any mutual friends."

"Spoken like the Jessica I remember, arrogant to the core. But times have changed, sweetheart. I've come up in the world. For starters, there's Gordon. He's a mutual friend."

"And he'd have had no more reason to keep me apprised of your comings and goings than I'd have had to ask. The last I knew of you," she said, her voice hard in anger that he'd dared call her 'sweetheart,' "you were stealing cars."

Carter's indulgent expression faded, replaced by something with a sharper edge. "I made some mistakes when I was younger, and I paid the price. I had to start from the bottom and work my way up. I didn't have any help, but I made it."

"And how many people did you hurt along the way?"

"None once I got going, too many before," he admitted. His face was somber, and though his body kept the same pose, the relaxation had left it. "I burned a whole lot of bridges that I've had to rebuild. That was one of the reasons I shifted my schedule to see you when Gordon called. You were pretty bitchy when you were a kid, but I fed into it."

She stiffened. "Bitchy? Thanks a lot!"

"I said I fed into it. I'm willing to take most of the blame, but you were bitchy. Admit it. Your hackles went up whenever you saw me."

"Do you wonder why? You said and did the nastiest things to me.

It got so I was conditioned to expect it. I did whatever I could to protect myself, and that meant being on my guard at the first sight of you.''

Rather than argue further, he pushed off from the stool and went to the desk. He stood at its side, fingering a paper clip for a minute before meeting her gaze again. "My parents send their best."

Jessica was nearly as surprised by the gentling of his voice as she was by what he'd said. "You told them we were meeting?"

"I talked with them last night." At the look of disbelief that remained on her face, he said, "I do that sometimes."

"You never used to. You were horrible to them, too."

Carter returned his attention to the paper clip, which he twisted and turned with the fingers of one hand. "I know."

"But why? They were wonderful people. I used to wish my parents were half as easygoing and good-natured as yours. And you treated them so badly."

He shot her a look of warning. "It's easy to think someone else's parents are wonderful when you're the one who doesn't live with them. You don't know the facts, Jessica. My relationship with my parents was very complex." He paused for a deep breath, which seemed to restore his good temper. "Anyway, they want to know everything about you— how you look, whether you're working or married or mothering, how the Rise is."

The last thing Jessica wanted to do was to discuss her personal life with Carter. He would be sure to tear it apart and make her feel more inadequate than ever. So she blurted out, "I'll tell you how the Rise is. It's big and beautiful, but it's aging. Either I pour a huge amount of money into renovations, or I make alternate plans. That's why I'm here. I want to discuss the alternate plans."

Carter made several more turns of the paper clip between his fingers before he tossed it aside. Settling his tall frame into the executive chair behind the desk, he folded his hands over his lean middle and said quietly, "I'm listening."

Business, this is business, Jessica told herself and took strength from the thought. "I don't know how much Gordon has told you, but I'm thinking of turning Crosslyn Rise into a condominium complex, building cluster housing in the woods, turning the mansion into a common facility for the owners, putting a marina along the shore."

Gordon hadn't told Carter much of anything, judging from the look of disbelief on his face. "Why would you do that?"

"Because the Rise is too big for me."

"So find someone it isn't too big for."

"I've been trying to, but the market's terrible."

"It takes a while sometimes to find the right buyer."

I don't have a while, she thought. "It could take years, and I'd really like to do something before then."

"Is there a rush? Crosslyn Rise has been in your family for generations. A few more years is nothing in the overall scheme of things."

Jessica wished he wouldn't argue. She didn't like what she was saying much more than he did. "I think it's time to make a change."

"But condominiums?" he asked in dismay. "Why condominiums?"

"Because the alternative is a full-fledged housing development, and that would be worse. This way, at least, I'd have some control over the outcome."

"Why does that have to be the alternative?"

"Do you have any better ideas?" she asked dryly.

"Sure. If you can't find an individual, sell to an institution—a school or something like that."

"No institution, or school or something like that will take care of the Rise the right way. I can just picture large parking lots and litter all over the place."

"Then what about the town? Deed the Rise to the town for use as a museum. Just imagine the whopping big tax deduction you'd get."

"I'm not looking for tax deductions, and besides, the town may be wealthy, but it isn't *that* wealthy. Do you have any idea what the costs are of maintaining Crosslyn Rise for a year?" Realizing she was close to giving herself away, she paused and said more calmly, "In the end, the town would have to sell it, and I'd long since have lost my say."

"But...condominiums?"

"Why not?" she sparred, hating him for putting her on the spot when, if he had any sensitivity at all, he'd know she was between a rock and a very hard place.

Carter leaned forward in his seat and pinned her with a dark-eyed stare. "Because Crosslyn Rise is magnificent. It's one of the most beautiful, most private, most special pieces of property I've ever seen, and believe me, I've seen a whole lot in the last few years. I don't even know how you can think of selling it."

"I have no choice!" she cried, and something in her eyes must have told him the truth.

"You can't keep it up?"

She dropped her gaze to the arm of her chair and rubbed her thumb back and forth against the chrome. "That's right." Her voice was quiet, imbued with the same defeat it had held in Gordon's office, and with an additional element of humiliation. Admitting the truth was bad enough; admitting it to Carter Malloy was even worse.

But she had to finish what she'd begun. "Like I said, the Rise is aging. Work that should have been done over the years wasn't, so what needs to be done now is extensive."

"Your dad let it go."

She had an easier time not looking at him. At least his voice was kind. "Not intentionally. But his mind was elsewhere, and my mother didn't want to upset him. Money was—" She stopped herself, realizing in one instant that she didn't want to make the confession, knowing in the next that she had to. "Money was tight."

"Are you kidding?"

Meeting his incredulous gaze, she said coldly, "No. I wouldn't kid about something like that."

"You don't kid about much of anything. You never did. Afraid a smile might crack your face?"

Jessica stared at him for a full second. "You haven't changed a bit," she muttered, and rose from her chair. "I shouldn't have come here. It was a mistake. I knew it would be."

She was just about at the door when it closed and Carter materialized before her. "Don't go," he said very quietly. "I'm sorry if I offended you. I sometimes say things without thinking them through. I've been working on improving that. I guess I still have a ways to go."

The thing that appalled Jessica most at that minute wasn't the embarrassment she felt regarding the Rise or her outburst or even Carter's apology. It was how handsome he was. Her eyes held his for a moment before, quite helplessly, lowering over the shadowed angle of his jaw to his chin, then his mouth. His lower lip was fuller than the top one. The two were slightly parted, touched only by the air he breathed.

Wrenching her gaze to the side, she swallowed hard and hung her head. "I do think this is a mistake," she murmured. "The whole thing is very difficult for me. Working with you won't help that."

"But I care about Crosslyn Rise."

"That was what Gordon said. But maybe you care most about getting it away from me. You always resented me for the Rise."

The denial she might have expected never came. After a short time, he said, "I resented lots of people for things that I didn't have. I was wrong. I'm not saying that I wouldn't buy the Rise from you if I had the money, because I meant what I said about it being special. But I don't have the money—any more, I guess, than you do. So that puts us in the same boat. On equal footing. Neither of us above or below the other."

He paused, giving her a chance to argue, but she didn't have anything to say. He had a right to be smug, she knew, but at that moment he wasn't. He was being completely reasonable.

"Do you have trouble with that, Jessica? Can you regard me as an equal?"

"We're not at all alike, you and I."

"I didn't say alike. I said equal. I meant financially equal."

Keeping her eyes downcast, she cocked her head toward the office behind her. "Looks to me like you're doing a sight better than I am at this point."

"But you have the Rise. That's worth a lot." When she simply shrugged, he said, "Sit down. Please. Let's talk."

Jessica wasn't quite sure why she listened to him. She figured it had something to do with the gentle way he'd asked, with the word "please," with the fact that he was blocking the door anyway, and he wasn't a movable presence. She suspected it might have even had something to do with her own curiosity. Though she caught definite reminders of the old Carter, the changes that had taken place since she'd seen him last intrigued her.

Without a word, she returned to her seat. This time, rather than going behind his desk, Carter lowered his long frame into the matching chair next to hers. Though there was a low slate cube between them, he was closer, more visible. That made her feel self-conscious. To counter the feeling, she directed her eyes to her hands and her thoughts to the plans she wanted to make for Crosslyn Rise.

"I don't like the sound of condominiums, either, but if the condominiums were in the form of cluster housing, if they were well placed and limited in number, if the renovations to the mansion were done with class and the waterfront likewise, the final product wouldn't be so bad. At least it would be kept up. The owners would be paying a lot for the privilege of living there. They'd have a stake in its future."

"Are you still teaching?"

At the abrupt change of subject, she cast him a quick look. "I, uh, yes."

"You haven't remarried?"

When her eyes flew to his this time, they stayed. "How did you know I'd married at all?"

"My parents. They were in touch with your mom. Once she died, they lost contact."

"Dad isn't—wasn't very social," Jessica said by way of explanation. But she hadn't kept in touch with the Malloys, either. "I'm not much better, I guess. How have your parents been?"

"Very well," he said on the lightest note he'd used yet. "They really like life under the sun. The warm weather is good for Mom's arthritis, and Dad is thrilled with the long growing season.''

"Do you see them often?"

"Three or four times a year. I've been pretty busy."

She pressed her lips together and shook her head. "An architect. I'm still having trouble with that."

"What would you have me be?"

"A pool shark. A gambler. An ex-con."

He had the grace to look humble. "I suppose I deserved that."

"Yes." She was still looking at him, bound by something she couldn't quite fathom. She kept thinking that if she pushed a certain button, said a certain word, he'd change back into the shaggy-haired demon he'd been. But he wasn't changing into anything. He was just sitting with one leg crossed over the other, studying her intently. It was all she could do not to squirm. She averted her eyes, then, annoyed, returned them to his. "Why are you doing that?"

"Doing what?"

"Staring at me like that."

"Because you look different. I'm trying to decide how."

"I'm older. That's all."

"Maybe," he conceded, but said no more.

The silence chipped at Jessica's already-iffy composure nearly as much as his continued scrutiny did. She wasn't sure why she was the one on the hot seat, when by rights the hot seat should have been his. In an attempt to correct the situation, she said, "Since I have an appointment back in Cambridge at four—" which she'd deliberately planned, to give her an out "—I think we should concentrate on business. Gordon said you were good." She sent a look toward the corked wall. "Are these your sketches, or were they done by an assistant?"

"They're mine."

"And the ones in the reception area?"

"Some are mine, some aren't."

"Who is Goodwin?"

"My partner. We first met in New York. He specializes in commercial work. I specialize in residential, so we complement each other."

"Was he one of the men standing out front?"

"No. The man in the tan blazer was one of three associates who work here."

"What do they do—the associates?"

"They serve as project managers."

"Are they architects?" She could have sworn the man she'd heard talking was one.

Carter nodded. "Two are registered, the third is about to be. Beneath the associates, there are four draftspeople, beneath them a secretary, a bookkeeper and a receptionist."

"Are you the leading partner?"

"You mean, of the two of us, do I bring in more money?" When she nodded, he said, "I did last year. The year before I didn't. It varies."

"Would you want to work on Crosslyn Rise?"

"Not particularly," he stated, then held up a hand in appeasement when she looked angry. "I'd rather see the Rise kept as it is. If you want honesty, there it is. But if you don't have the money to support it, something has to be done." He came forward to brace his elbows on his thighs and dangle his hands between his knees. "And if you're determined to go ahead with the condo idea, I'd rather do the work myself than have a stranger do it."

"You're a stranger," she said stiffly. "You're not the same person who grew up around Crosslyn Rise."

"I remember what I felt for the Rise then. I can even better understand those feelings now."

"I'm not sure I trust your motives."

"Would I risk all this—" he shot a glance around the room "—for the sake of a vendetta? Look, Jessica," he said with a sigh, "I don't deny who I was then and what I did. I've already said that. I was a pain in the butt."

"You were worse than that."

"Okay, I was worse than that, but I'm a different person now. I've been through a whole lot that you can't begin to imagine. I've lived through hell and come out on the other side, and because of that, I appreciate some things other people don't. Crosslyn Rise is one of those things."

Jessica wished he wasn't sitting so close or regarding her so intently or talking so sanely. Either he was being utterly sincere, or he was doing one hell of an acting job. She wasn't sure which, but she did know that she couldn't summarily rule him off the project.

"Do you think," she asked in a tentative voice, "that my idea for Crosslyn Rise would work?"

"It could."

"Would you want to try working up some sketches?"

"We'd have to talk more about what you want. I'd need to see a plot plan. And I'd have to go out there. Even aside from the fact that I haven't been there in a while, I've never looked around with this kind of thing in mind."

Jessica nodded. What he said was fair enough. What wasn't fair was the smooth way he said it. He sounded very professional and very male. For the second time in as many minutes, she wished he wasn't sitting so close. She wished she wasn't so aware of him.

Clutching her purse, she stood. "I have to be going," she said, concentrating on the leather strap as she eased it over her shoulder.

"But we haven't settled anything."

She raised her eyes. He, too, had risen and was standing within an arm's length of her. She started toward the door. "We have. We've settled that we have to talk more, I have to get you a plot plan, you have to come out to see Crosslyn Rise." Her eyes were on the doorknob, but she felt Carter moving right along with her. "You may want to talk with Gordon, too. He'll explain the plan he has for raising the money for the project."

"Am I hired?" He reached around her to open the door.

"I don't know. We have to do all those other things first."

"When can we meet again?"

"I'll call you." She was in the corridor, moving steadily back the way she'd come, with Carter matching her step.

"Why don't we set a time now?"

"Because I don't have my schedule in front of me."

"Are you that busy?"

"Yes!" she said, and stopped in her tracks. She looked up at him, swallowed tightly, dropped her gaze again and moved on. "Yes," she echoed in a near-whisper. "It's nearly exam time. My schedule's erratic during exam time."

Her explanation seemed to appease Carter, which relieved her, as did the sight of the reception area. She was feeling overwhelmed by Carter's presence. He was a little too smooth, a little too agreeable, a little too male. Between those things and a memory that haunted her, she wanted out.

"Will you call me?" he asked as he opened the door to the reception area.

"I said I would."

"You have my number?"

"Yes."

Opening the outer door, he accompanied her right to the elevator and pushed the button. "Can I have yours?"

Grateful for something to do, she fumbled in her purse for a pen, jotted her number in a small notebook, tore out the page and handed it to him. She was restowing the pen when a bell rang announcing the elevator's arrival. Her attention was riveted to the panel on top of the doors when Carter said, "Jessica?"

She dared meet his gaze a final time. It was a mistake. A small frown touched his brow and was gone, leaving an expression that combined confusion and surprise with pleasure. When he spoke, his voice held the same three elements. ''It was really good seeing you,'' he said as though he meant it and surprised himself in that. Then he smiled, and his smile held nothing but pleasure.

That was when Jessica knew she was in big trouble.

3

Carter *had* enjoyed seeing Jessica, though he wasn't sure why. As a kid, she'd been a snotty little thing looking down her nose at him. He had resented everything about her, which was why his greatest joy had been putting her down. In that, he had been cruel at times. He'd found her sore spots and rubbed them with salt.

Clearly she remembered. She wasn't any too happy to see him, though she'd agreed to the meeting, which said something about the bind she was in regarding Crosslyn Rise. Puzzled by that bind, Carter called Gordon shortly after Jessica left his office.

In setting up the meeting, Gordon had only told him that Jessica had wanted to discuss an architectural project relating to the Rise. Under Carter's questioning now, he admitted to the financial problems. He talked of putting together a group of investors. He touched on Jessica's insistence on being in command. He went so far as to outline the role Carter might play, as Gordon had broached it with Jessica.

Though Carter had meant what he'd said about preferring to leave Crosslyn Rise as it was, once he accepted the idea of its changing, he found satisfaction in the idea of taking part in that change. Some of his satisfaction was smug; there was an element of poetic justice in his having come far enough in the world to actively shape the Rise's future.

But the satisfaction went beyond that. Monetarily it was a sound proposal. His gut told him that, even before he worked out the figures. Given the dollar equivalent of his professional fees added to the hundred thousand he could afford to invest, he stood to take a sizable sum out of the project in two to three years' time.

That sum would go a long way toward broadening his base of operation. Malloy and Goodwin was doing well, bringing in greater profit each year, but there were certain projects—more artistically rewarding than lucrative—that Carter would bid on given the cushion of capital funds and a larger staff.

And then, working on the alteration of Crosslyn Rise both as architect and investor, he would see more of Jessica. That thought lingered with him long after he'd hung up the phone, long after he'd set aside the other issues.

He wanted to see more of her, incredible but true. She wasn't gorgeous. She wasn't sexy or witty. She wasn't anything like the women he dated, and it certainly wasn't that he was thinking of dating *her*. But at the end of their brief meeting, he had felt something warm flowing through him. He guessed it had to do with a shared past; he didn't have that with many people, and he wouldn't have thought he'd want it with *anyone*, given the sins of his past. Still, there was that warm feeling. It fascinated him, particularly since he had felt so many conflicting things during the meeting itself.

Emotions had come in flashes—anger and resentment in an almost automatic response to any hint of arrogance on her part, embarrassment and remorse as he recalled things he'd said and done years before. She was the same as he remembered her, but different—older, though time had been kind. Her skin was unflawed, her hair more tame, her movements more coordinated, even in spite of her nervousness. And she was nervous. He made her so, he guessed, though he had tried to be amenable.

What he wanted, he realized, was for her to eye him through those granny glasses of hers and see the decent person he was now. He wanted to close the last page on the book from the past. He wanted her acceptance. Though he hadn't given two thoughts to it before their meeting, that acceptance suddenly mattered a lot. Only when he had it would he feel that he'd truly conquered the past.

Jessica tried to think about their meeting as little as possible in the hours subsequent to it. To that end, she kept herself busy, which wasn't difficult with exams on the horizon and the resultant rash of impromptu meetings with students and teaching assistants. If Carter's phone number seemed to burn a hole in her date book, she ignored the smoke. She had to be in command, she told herself. Carter had to know she was in command.

She wasn't terribly proud of the show she'd put on in his office. She'd been skittish in his presence, and it had showed. The most merciful thing about the meeting was that he had waited until she had a foot out the door before smiling. His smile was potent. It had confused her, excited her, frightened her. It had warned her that working with him wasn't going to be easy in any way, shape or form, and it had nearly convinced her not to try it.

Still she called him. She waited two full days to do it, then chose Thursday afternoon, when she was fresh from a buoying department meeting. She enjoyed department meetings. She liked her colleagues and was liked in return. In the academic sphere, she was fully confident of her abilities. So she let the overflow of that confidence carry her into the phone call to Carter.

"Carter? This is Jessica Crosslyn."

"It's about time you called," he scolded, and she immediately bristled—until the teasing in his voice came through. "I was beginning to think you'd changed your mind."

She didn't know what to make of the teasing. She'd never heard teasing coming from Carter Malloy before. For the sake of their working together, she took it at face value and said evenly, "It's only been two days."

"That's two days too long."

"Is there a rush?"

"There's always a rush where enthusiasm and weather are concerned."

She found that to be a curious statement. "Enthusiasm?"

"I'm really up for this now, and I have the time to get started," he explained. "It's not often that the two coincide."

She could buy that, she supposed, though she wondered if he'd purposely injected the subtle reminder that he was in demand. "And the weather?" she came back a bit skeptically. "It's not yet May. The best of the construction season is still ahead."

"Not so, once time is spent on first-draft designs then multiple rounds of revisions." Carter kept his tone easygoing. "By the time the plans are done, the investors lined up and bidding taken on contractors, it could well be September or October, unless we step on it now." Having made his point, he paused. "Gordon explained the financial setup and the fact that you want sole approval of the final plans before they're shown to potential investors."

Jessica was immediately wary. "Do you have a problem with that?"

"It depends on whether you approve what I like," he said with a grin, then tacked on a quick, "Just kidding."

"I don't think you are."

"Sure I am," he cajoled. "A client pays me for my work, I give him what he wants."

"And if you think what he wants is hideous?"

"I know not to take the job."

"So in that sense," she persisted, not sure why she was being stubborn, but driven to it nonetheless, "you ensure that the client will approve what you like."

"Not ensure—" he dug in his own heels a little "—but I maximize the likelihood of it. And there's nothing wrong with that. It's the only sensible way to operate. Besides, the assumption is that the client comes to me because he likes my style.''

''I don't know whether I like your style or not,'' she argued. ''I haven't seen much of it.''

She seemed to be taking a page from the past and deliberately picking a fight. As he'd done then, so now Carter fought back. ''If you'd asked the other day, I'd have shown you pictures. I've got a portfolio full of them. You might have saved us both a whole lot of time and effort. But you were in such an all-fired rush to get back to your precious ivory tower—''

He caught himself only after he realized what he was doing. Jessica remained silent. He waited for her to rail at him the way she used to, but she didn't speak. In a far quieter voice he asked, ''Are you still there?''

''Yes,'' she murmured, ''but I don't know why. This isn't going to work. We're like fire and water.''

''The past is getting in the way. Old habits die hard. But I'm sorry. What I said was unnecessary.''

''Part of it was right,'' she conceded. ''I was in a rush to get back. I had another appointment.'' He should know that he wasn't the only one in demand. ''But as far as my ivory tower is concerned, that ivory tower has produced official interpreters for assorted summit meetings as well as for embassies in Moscow, Leningrad and Bonn. My work isn't all mind-in-the-clouds.''

''I know,'' Carter said quietly. ''I'm sorry.'' He didn't say anything more for a minute, hoping she'd tell him he was forgiven. But things weren't going to be so easy. ''Anyway, I'd really like to talk again. Tell me when you have free time. If I have a conflict, I'll try to change it.''

Short of being bitchy, which he'd accused her of being as a child, she couldn't turn her back on his willingness to accommodate her. She looked at the calendar tacked on the wall. It was filled with scrawled notations, more densely drawn for the upcoming few weeks. Given the choice, she would put off a meeting with Carter until after exams, when she'd be better able to take the disturbance in stride. But she remembered what he'd said about the weather. If she was going to do something with Crosslyn Rise, she wanted it done soon. The longer she diddled around with preliminary arrangements, the later in the season it would be and the greater the chance of winter closing in to delay the work even more. Instinctively she knew that the longer the process was drawn out, the more painful it would be.

''I'm free until noon next Tuesday morning,'' she said. ''Do you want to come out and walk through Crosslyn Rise then?''

Carter felt a glimmer of excitement at the mention of walking through Crosslyn Rise. It had been years since he'd seen the place, and though he'd never lived there, since his parents had always rented a small house in town, returning to Crosslyn Rise would be something of a homecoming.

He had one meeting scheduled for that morning, but it was easily postponed. "Next Tuesday is fine. Time?"

"Is nine too early?"

"Nine is perfect. It might be a help if between now and then you wrote down your ideas so we can discuss them in as much detail as possible. If you've seen any pictures of things you like in newspapers or magazines you might cut them out. The more I know of what you want, the easier my job will be."

Efficient person that she was herself, she could go along with that. "You mentioned wanting to see a plot plan. I don't think I've ever seen one. Where would I get it?"

"The town should have one, but I'll take care of that. I can phone ahead and pick it up on my way. You just be there with your house and your thoughts." He paused. "Okay?"

"Okay."

"See you then."

"Uh-huh."

Jessica couldn't decide whether to put coffee on to brew or to assume that he'd already had a cup or two, and she spent an inordinate amount of time debating the issue. One minute she decided that the proper thing would indeed be to have it ready and offer him some; the next minute it seemed a foolish gesture. This was Carter Malloy, she told herself. He didn't expect anything from her but a hard time, which was just about all they'd ever given each other.

But that had been years ago, and Carter Malloy had changed. He'd grown up. He was an architect. A man. And though one part of her didn't want to go out of her way to make the Carter Malloy of any age feel welcome in her home, another part felt that she owed cordiality to the architect who might well play a part in her future.

As for the man in him, she pushed all awareness of that to the farthest reaches of consciousness and chose to attribute the unsettled feeling in her stomach to the nature of the meeting itself.

Carter arrived at nine on the dot. He parked his car on the pebbled driveway that circled some twenty feet in front of the ivy-draped portico. The car was dark blue and low, but Jessica wouldn't have known the make even if she'd had the presence of mind to wonder—which she didn't, since she was too busy trying to calm her nerves.

She greeted him at the front door, bracing an unsteady hand on the doorknob. Pulse racing, she watched him step inside, watched him look slowly around the rotundalike foyer, watched him raise his eyes to the top of the broadly sweeping staircase, then say in a low and surprisingly humble voice, "This is...very...weird."

"Weird?"

"Coming in the front door. Seeing this after so many years. It's incredibly impressive."

"Until you look closely."

He shot her a questioning glance.

"Things are worn," she explained, wanting to say it before he did. "The grandeur of Crosslyn Rise has faded."

"Oh, but it hasn't." He moved toward the center of the foyer. "The grandeur is in its structure. Nothing can dim that. Maybe the accessories have suffered with age, but the place is still a wonder."

"Is that your professional assessment?"

He shook his head. "Personal." His gaze was drawn toward the living room. The entrance to it was broad, the room itself huge. Knee-to-ceiling windows brought in generous helpings of daylight, saving the room from the darkness that might otherwise have come with the heavy velvet decor. Sun was streaming obliquely past the oversized fireplace, casting the intricate carving of the pine mantel in bas-relief. "Personal assessment. I always loved this place."

"I'm sure," she remarked with unplanned tartness.

He shot her a sharper look this time. "Does it gall you seeing me here? Does it prick your Victorian sensibilities? Would you rather I stay out back near the gardener's shed?"

Jessica felt instant remorse. "Of course not. I'm sorry. I was just remembering—"

"Remembering the past is a mistake, because what you remember will be the way I acted, not the way I felt. You didn't know the way I really felt. *I* didn't know the way I really felt a lot of the time. But I knew I loved this place."

"And you hated me because I lived here and you didn't."

"That's neither here nor there. But I did love Crosslyn Rise, and I'd like to feel free to express what I'm thinking and feeling as we walk around. Can I do that, or would you rather I repress it all?"

"You?" she shot back, goaded on by the fact that he was being so reasonable. "Repress your feelings?"

"I can do it if I try. Granted, I'm not as good at it as you. But you've had years of practice. You're the expert. No doubt there's a Ph.D. in Denial mixed up with all the diplomas on your wall.'' His eyes narrowed, seeing far too much. ''Don't you ever get tired of bottling everything up?''

Jessica's insides were beginning to shake. She wanted to think it was anger, but that was only half-true. Carter was coming close to repeating things he'd said once before. The same hurt she'd felt then was threatening to engulf her now. ''I don't bottle everything up,'' she said, and gave a tight swallow.

''You do. You're as repressed as ever.'' The words were no sooner out than he regretted them. She looked fearful, and for a horrifying minute, he wondered if she was going to cry. ''Don't,'' he whispered and approached her with his hands out to the side. ''Please. I'm sorry. Damn, I'm apologizing again. I can't believe that. Why do you make me say mean things? What is it about you that brings out the bastard in me?''

Struggling against tears, she didn't speak. A small shrug was the best she could muster.

''Yell at me,'' Carter ordered, willing to do anything to keep those tears at bay. ''Go ahead. Tell me what you think of me. Tell me that I'm a bastard and that I don't know what I'm talking about because I don't know you at all. Say it, Jessica. Tell me to keep my mouth shut. Tell me to mind my own business. Tell me to go to hell.''

But she couldn't do that. Deep down inside, she knew she was the villain of the piece. She'd provoked him far more than he'd provoked her. And he was right. She was repressed. It just hurt to hear him say it. Hurt a lot. Hurt even more, at thirty-three, than it had at sixteen.

Moving to the base of the stairs, she pressed herself against the swirling newel post, keeping her back to him. ''I've lived at Crosslyn Rise all my life,'' she began in a tremulous voice. ''For as long as I can remember, it's been my haven. It's the place I come home to, the place that's quiet and peaceful, the place that accepts me as I am and doesn't make demands. I can't afford to keep it up, so I have to sell it.'' Her voice fell to a tormented whisper. ''That hurts, Carter. It really hurts. And seeing you—'' she ran out of one breath, took in another ''—seeing you brings back memories. I guess I'm feeling a little raw.''

The warmth Carter had experienced the last time he'd been with Jessica was back. It carried him over the short distance to where she stood, brought his hands to her shoulders and imbued his low, slow voice with something surprisingly caring. ''I can understand what you're feeling about Crosslyn Rise, Jessica. Really, I can.'' With the smallest, most subtle of movements, his hands worked at the tightness in her shoulders.

"I wish I could offer a miracle solution to keep the Rise intact, but if there was one, I'm sure either you or Gordon would have found it by now. I can promise you that I'll draw up spectacular plans for the complex you have in mind, but it doesn't matter how spectacular they are, they won't be the Crosslyn Rise you've known all your life. The thought of it hurts you now, and it'll get worse before it gets better." He kept kneading, lightly kneading, and he didn't mind it at all. Her blouse was silk and soft, her shoulders surprisingly supple beneath it. His fingers fought for and won successive bits of relaxation.

"But the hurt will only be aggravated if we keep sniping at each other," he went on to quietly make his point. "I've already said I was wrong when I was a kid. If I could turn back the clock and change things, I would." Without thinking, he gathered a stray wisp of hair from her shoulder and smoothed it toward the tortoiseshell clasp at her nape. "But I can't. I can only try to make the present better and the future better than that—and 'try' is the operative word. I'll make mistakes. I'm a spontaneous person—maybe 'impulsive' is the word—but you already know that." He turned her to face him, and at the sight of her openness, gentled his voice even more. "The point is that I can be reasoned with now. I couldn't be back then, but I can be now. So if I say something that bugs you, tell me. Let's get it out in the open and be done."

Jessica heard what he was saying, but only peripherally. Between the low vibrancy of his voice and the slow, hypnotic motion of his hands, she was being warmed all over. Not even the fact that she faced him now, that she couldn't deny his identity as she might have if her back was still to him, could put a chill to that warmth.

"I'd like this job, Jessica," he went on, his dark eyes barely moving from hers yet seeming to touch on each of her features. "I'd really like this job, but I think you ought to decide whether working with me will be too painful on top of everything else. If it will be," he finished, fascinated by the softness of her cheek beneath the sweeping pad of his thumb, "I'll bow out."

His thumb stopped at the corner of her mouth, and time seemed to stop right along with it. In a flash of awareness that hit them simultaneously came the realization that they were standing a breath apart, that Carter was holding her as he would a desirable woman and Jessica was looking up at him as she would a desirable man.

She couldn't move. Her blood seemed to be thrumming through her veins in mockery of the paralysis of her legs, but she couldn't drag herself away from Carter. He gave her comfort. He made her feel not quite so alone. And he made her aware that she was a woman.

That fact took Carter by surprise. He'd always regarded Jessica as an asexual being, but something had happened when he'd put his hands on her shoulders. No, something had happened even before that, when she'd been upset and he'd wanted to help ease her through it. He felt protective. He couldn't remember feeling that for a woman before, mainly because most of the women he'd known were strong, powerful types who didn't allow for upsets. But he rather liked being needed. Not that Jessica would admit to needing him, he knew. Still, it was something to consider.

But he'd consider it another time, because she looked frightened enough at that minute to bolt, and he didn't want her to. Slowly, almost reluctantly, he dropped his hands to his sides.

A second later, Jessica dropped her chin to her chest. She raised a shaky hand to the bridge of her nose, pressed a fingertip to the nosepiece of her glasses and held it there. "I'm sorry," she whispered, sure that she'd misinterpreted what she'd seen and felt, "I don't know what came over me. I'm usually in better control of myself."

"You have a right to be upset," he said just as quietly, but he didn't step away. "It's okay to lose control once in a while."

She didn't look up. Nor did she say anything for a minute, because there was a clean, male scent in the air that held her captive. Then, cursing herself for a fool, she cleared her throat. "I, uh, I made coffee. Do you want some?"

What Carter wanted first was a little breathing space. He needed to distance himself mentally from the vulnerable Jessica, for whom he'd just felt a glimmer of desire. "Maybe we ought to walk around outside first," he suggested. "That way I'll know what you're talking about when you go through your list. You made one, didn't you?"

She met his gaze briefly. "Yes."

"Good." He remembered the feel of silk beneath his fingers. She was wearing a skirt that hit at midcalf, opaque stockings and flat shoes that would keep her warm, but her silk blouse, as gently as it fell over her breasts, wouldn't protect her from the air. "Do you want a sweater or something? It's still cool outside."

She nodded and took a blazer from the closet, quickly slipping her arms into the sleeves. Carter would have helped her with it if she hadn't been so fast. He wondered whether she wanted breathing space, too— then he chided himself for the whimsy. If Jessica had been struck in that instant with an awareness of him as a man, it was an aberration. No way was she going to allow herself to lust after Carter Malloy—*if* she knew the meaning of the word *lust*, which he doubted she did. And he certainly wasn't lusting after her. It was just that with his acceptance that she was a woman, she became a character of greater depth in his mind, someone he might like to get to know better.

They left through the front door, went down the brick walk and crossed the pebbled driveway to the broad lawn, which leveled off for a while before slanting gracefully toward the sea. "This is the best time of year," he remarked, taking in a deep breath. "Everything is new and fresh in spring. In another week or two, the trees will have budded." He glanced at Jessica, who was looking forlornly toward the shore, and though he doubted his question would be welcome, he couldn't pass by her sadness. "What will you do—if you decide to go ahead and develop Crosslyn Rise?"

It was a minute before she answered. Her hands were tucked into the pockets of her blazer, but her head was up and her shoulders straight. The fresh air and the walking were helping her to recover the equilibrium she'd lost earlier when Carter had been so close. "I'm not sure."

"Will you stay here?"

"I don't know. That might be hard. Or it might be harder to leave. I just don't know. I haven't gotten that far yet." She came to a halt.

Carter did, too. He followed her gaze down the slope of the lawn. "Tell me what you see."

"Something small and pretty. A marina. Some shops. Do you see how the boulders go? They form a crescent. I can see boats over there—" she pointed toward the far right curve of the crescent "—with a small beach and shops along the straightaway."

Carter wasn't sure he'd arrange the elements quite as she had, but that was a small matter. He started walking again. "And this slope?"

She came along. "I'd leave it as is, maybe add a few paths to protect the grass and some shrubbery here and there."

They descended the slope that led to the shoreline. "You used to sled down this hill. Do you remember?"

"Uh-huh. I had a Flexible Flyer," she recalled.

"New and shiny. It was always new and shiny."

"Because it wasn't used much. It was no fun sledding alone."

"I'd have shared that Flexible Flyer with you."

"Shared?" she asked too innocently.

"Uh, maybe not." He paused. "Mmm, probably not. I'd probably have chased you into the woods, buried you under a pile of snow and kept the Flyer all to myself."

Wearing a small, slightly crooked smile, she looked up at him. "I think so."

He liked the smile, small though it was, and it hadn't cracked her face after all. Rather, it made her look younger. It made him feel younger. "I was a bully."

"Uh-huh."

"You must have written scathing things about me in your diary."

"I never kept a diary."

"No? Funny, I'd have pegged you for the diary type."

"Studious?"

"Literary."

"I wrote poems."

He squinted as the memory returned. "That's...right. You did write poems."

"Not about you, though," she added quickly. "I wrote poems about pretty things, and there was absolutely nothing pretty about you that I could see back then."

"Is there now?" he asked, because he couldn't help it.

Jessica didn't know whether it was the outdoors, the gentle breeze stirring her hair or the rhythmic roll of the surf that lulled her, but her nervousness seemed on hold. She was feeling more comfortable than she had before with Carter, which was why she dared answer his question.

"You have nice skin. The acne's gone."

Carter was oddly pleased by the compliment. "I finally outgrew that at twenty-five. I had a prolonged adolescence, in *lots* of ways."

The subject of why he'd been such a troubled kid was wide open, but Jessica felt safer keeping things light. "Where did you get the tan?"

"Anguilla. I was there for a week at the beginning of March."

They'd reached the beach and were slowly crossing the rocky sand. "Was it nice?"

"Very nice. Sunny and warm. Quiet. Restful."

She wondered whether he'd gone alone. "You've never married, have you?"

"No."

On impulse, and with a touch of the old sarcasm, she said, "I'd have thought you'd have been married three times by now."

He didn't deny it. "I probably would have, if I'd let myself marry at all. Either I knew what a bad risk I was, or the women I dated did. I'd have made a lousy husband."

"Then. What about now?"

Without quite answering the question, he said, "Now it's harder to meet good women. They're all very complex by the time they reach thirty, and somehow the idea of marrying a twenty-two-year-old when

I'm nearly forty doesn't appeal to me. The young ones aren't mature enough, the older ones are too mature.''

"Too mature—as in complex?"

He nodded and paused, slid his hands into the pockets of his dark slacks and stood looking out over the water. "They have careers. They have established life-styles. They're stuck in their ways and very picky about who they want and what they expect from that person. It puts a lot of pressure on a relationship."

"Aren't you picky?" she asked, feeling the need to defend members of her sex, though she'd talked to enough single friends to know that Carter was right.

"Sure I'm picky," he said with a bob of one shoulder. "I'm not getting any younger. I have a career and an established life-style, and I'm pretty set in my ways, too. So I'm not married." He looked around, feeling an urge to change the subject. "Were you thinking of keeping the oceanfront area restricted to people who live here?"

"I don't know. I haven't thought that out yet." She studied the crease on his brow. "Is there a problem?"

"Problem? Not if you're flexible about what you want. As I see it, either you have a simple waterfront with a beach and a pier and a boat house or you have a marina with a dock, slips, shops and the appropriate personnel to go with them. But if you want the marina and the shops, they can't be restricted—at least, not limited to the people who live here. You could establish a private yacht club that would be joined by people from all along the North Shore, and you can keep it as exclusive as you want by regulating the cost of membership, but there's no way something as restrictive as that is going to be able to support shops, as I think of shops." As he talked, he'd been looking around, assessing the beachfront layout. Now he faced her. "What kind of shops did you have in mind?"

"The kind that would provide for the basic needs of the residents— drugstore, convenience store, bookstore, gift or crafts shop." She saw him shaking his head. "No?"

"Not unless there's public access. Shops like that couldn't survive with such a limited clientele base."

Which went to show, Jessica realized in chagrin, how little she knew about business. "But I was thinking really *small* shops. Quaint shops."

"Even the smallest, most quaint shop has to do a certain amount of business to survive. You'd need public access."

"You mean, scads of people driving through?" But that wasn't at all what she wanted, and the look on her face made that clear.

"They wouldn't have to drive through. The waterfront area could be arranged so that cars never cross it."

"I don't know," she murmured, disturbed. Turning, she headed back up toward the house.

He joined her, walking for a time in silence before saying, "You don't have to make an immediate decision."

"But you said yourself that time was of the essence."

"Only if you want to get started this year."

"I don't *want* to get started at all," she said, and quickened her step.

Knowing the hard time she was having, he let her go. He stayed several paces behind until she reached the top of the rise, where she slowed. When he came alongside her, she raised her eyes to his and asked in a tentative voice, "Were you able to get the plot plan?"

He nodded. "It's in the car."

"Do you want to take it when we go through the woods?"

"No. I'll study it later. What I want is for you to show me the kinds of settings you had in mind for the housing. Even though ecological factors will come into play when a final decision is made, your ideas can be a starting point." He took a deep breath, hooked his hands on his hips and made a visual sweep of the front line of trees. "I used to go through these woods a lot, but that was too many years ago and never with an eye out for something like this."

She studied his expression, but it told her nothing of what he was feeling just then, and she wanted to know. She was feeling frighteningly upended and in need of support. "You said that you really wanted this project." She started off toward a well-worn path, confident that Carter would fall into step, which he did.

"I do."

"Why?"

"Because it's an exciting one. Crosslyn Rise is part of my past. It's a beautiful place, the challenge will be to maintain its beauty. If I can do that, it will be a feather in my cap. So I'll have the professional benefit, and the personal satisfaction. And if I invest in the project the way Gordon proposed, I'll make some money. I could use the money."

That surprised her. "I thought you were doing well."

"I am. But there's a luxury that comes with having spare change. I'd like to be able to reject a lucrative job that may be unexciting and accept an exciting job that may not be lucrative."

His argument was reasonable. *He* was reasonable—far more so than she'd have expected. Gordon had said he'd changed. *Carter* had said he'd changed. For the first time, as they walked along the path side by side, with the dried leaves of winter crackling beneath their shoes, she wondered what had caused the change. Simple aging? She doubted it. There were too many disgruntled adults in the world to buy that. It might have been true if Carter had simply mellowed. But given the wretch of a teenager he'd been, mellowing was far too benign a term to describe the change. She was thinking total personality overhaul— well, not total, since he still had the occasional impulsive, sharp-tongued moment, but close.

For a time, they walked on without talking. The crackle of the leaves became interspersed with small, vague sounds that consolidated into quacks when they approached the duck pond. Emerging from the path into the open, Jessica stopped. The surface of the pond and its shores were dotted with iridescent blue, green and purple heads. The ducks were in their glory, waiting for spring to burst forth.

"There would have to be some houses here, assuming care was taken to protect the ducks. It's too special a setting to waste."

Carter agreed. "You mentioned cluster housing the other day. Do you mean houses that are physically separate from one another but clustered by twos and threes here and in other spots? Or clusters of town houses that are physically connected to one another?"

"I'm not sure." She didn't look at him. It was easier that way, she found. The bobbing heads of the ducks on the pond were a more serene sight. But her voice held the curiosity her eyes might have. "What do you think?"

"Off the top of my head, I like the town house idea. I can picture town houses clustered together in a variation on the Georgian theme."

"Wouldn't that be easier to do with single homes?"

"Easier, but not as interesting." He flashed her a self-mocking smile, which, unwittingly looking his way, she caught. "And not as challenging for me. But I'd recommend the town house concept for economic reasons, as well. Take this duck pond. If you build single homes into the setting, you wouldn't want to do more than two or three, and they'd have to be in the million-plus range. On the other hand, you could build three town house clusters, each with two or three town houses, and scatter them around. Since they could be marketed for five or five-fifty, they'd be easier to sell and you'd still come out ahead."

She remembered when Gordon had spoken of profit. Her response was the same now as it was then, a sick kind of feeling at the pit of her stomach. "Money isn't the major issue."

"Maybe not to you—"

"Is it to you?" she cut in, eyeing him sharply.

He held his ground. "It's one of the issues, not necessarily the major one. But I can guarantee you that it *will* be the major issue for the people Gordon lines up to become part of his consortium. You and I have personal feelings for Crosslyn Rise. The others won't. They may be captivated by the place and committed to preserving as much of the natural contour as possible, but they won't have an emotional attachment. They'll enter into this as a financial venture. That's all.''

"Must you be so blunt?" she asked, annoyed because she knew he was right, yet the words stung.

"I thought you'd want the truth."

"You don't have to be so *blunt*." She turned abruptly and, ignoring the quacks that seemed stirred by the movement, headed back toward the path.

"You want sugarcoating?" He took off after her. "Where are you going now?"

"The meadow," she called over her shoulder.

With a minimum of effort, he was by her side. "Y'know, Jessica, if you're going ahead with this project, you ought to face facts. Either you finance the whole thing yourself—"

"If I had that kind of money, there wouldn't *be* any project!"

"Okay, so you don't have the money." He paused, irked enough by the huffy manner in which she'd walked away from him to be reckless. "Why don't you have the money? I keep asking myself that. Where did it go? The Crosslyn family is loaded."

"Was loaded."

"Where did it go?"

"How do *I* know where it went?" She whirled around to face him. "I never needed it. It was something my father had that he was supposedly doing something brilliant with. I never asked about it. I never cared about it. So what do I know?" She threw up a hand. "I've got my head stuck in that ivory tower of mine. What do I know about the money that's supposed to be there but isn't?"

He caught her hand before it quite returned to her side. "I'm not blaming you. Take it easy."

"Take it easy?" she cried. "The single most stable thing in my life is on the verge of being bulldozed—by *my* decision, no less—and you tell me to take it easy? Let go of my hand."

But he didn't. His long fingers wound through hers. "Changing Crosslyn Rise may be upsetting, but it's not the end of the world. It's just a house, for heaven's sake."

"It's my family's history."

"So now it's time to write a new chapter. Crosslyn Rise will always be Crosslyn Rise. It's not going away. It's just getting a face-lift. Wouldn't you rather have it done now, when you can be there to supervise, than have it done when you die? It's not like you have a horde of children to leave the place to.''

Of all the things he'd said, that hurt the most. The issue of having a family, of passing something of the Crosslyn genes to another generation had always been a sensitive issue for Jessica. Her friends didn't raise it with her. Not even Gordon had made reference to it during their discussion of Crosslyn Rise. The fact that Carter Malloy was the one to twist the knife was too much to bear.

"Let me go," she murmured, lowering both her head and her voice as she struggled to free her hand from his.

"No.''

She twisted her hand, even used her other one to try to pry his fingers free. Her teeth were clenched. "I want you to let me go."

"I won't. You're too upset."

"And you're not helping." She lifted her eyes then, uncaring that he saw the tears there. "Why do you have to say things that hurt so much?" she said softly. "Why do you do it, Carter? You could always find the one thing that would hurt me most, and that was the thing you'd harp on. You say you've changed, but you're still hurting me. Why? Why can't you just do your job and leave me alone?"

Seconds after she'd said it, Carter asked himself the same question. It should have been an easy matter to approach this job as he would another. But he was emotionally involved—as much with Jessica as with Crosslyn Rise—which was why, without pausing to analyze the details of that emotional involvement, he reached out, drew Jessica close and wrapped her in his arms.

4

When Carter had been a kid, he'd imagined that Jessica Crosslyn was made of nails. He'd found a hint of give when he'd touched her earlier, but only when he held her fully against him, as he did now, did he realize that she was surprisingly soft. Just as surprising was the tenderness he felt. He guessed it had to do with the tears he'd seen in her eyes. She was fighting them still, he knew. He could feel it in her body.

Lowering his head so that his mouth wasn't far from her ear, he said in a voice only loud enough to surmount the whispering breeze, "Let it out, Jessica. It's all right. No one will think less of you, and you'll feel a whole lot better."

But she couldn't. She'd been too weak in front of Carter already. Crying would be the last straw. "I'm all right," she said, but she didn't pull away. It had been a long time since someone had held her. She wasn't yet ready to have it end, particularly since she was still in the grip of the empty feeling brought on by his words.

"I don't do it intentionally," he murmured in the same deeply male, low-to-the-ear voice. "Maybe I did when we were kids, but not now. I don't intentionally hurt you, but I blurt out things without thinking." Which totally avoided the issue of whether the things he blurted out were true, but that was for another time. For now there were more immediate explanations to be offered. "I'm sorry for that, Jessica. I'm sorry if I hurt you, and I know I ought to be able to do my job and leave you alone, but I can't. Maybe it's because I knew you back then, so there's a bond. Maybe it's because your parents are gone and you're alone. Maybe it's because I owe you for all I put you through."

"But you're putting me through more," came the meek voice from the area of his shirt collar.

"Unintentionally," he said. His hands flexed, lightly stroking her back. "I know you're going through a hard time, and I want to help. If I could loan you the money to keep Crosslyn Rise, I'd do it, but I don't have anywhere near enough. Gordon says you've got loans on top of loans."

"See?" The reminder was an unwelcome one. "You're doing it again."

"No, I'm explaining why I can't help out more. I've come a long way, but I'm not wealthy. I couldn't afford to own a place like Crosslyn Rise myself. I have a condo in the city, and it's in a luxury building, but it's small."

"I'm not asking—"

"I know that, but I want to do something. I want to help you through this, maybe make things easier. I guess what I'm saying is that I want us to be friends."

Friends? Carter Malloy, her childhood nemesis, a friend? It sounded bizarre. But then, the fact that she was leaning against him, taking comfort from his strength was no less bizarre. She hadn't imagined she'd ever want to touch him, much less feel the strength of his body. And he was strong, she realized—physically and, to her chagrin, emotionally. She could use some of that strength.

"I'm also thinking," he went on, "that I'd like to know more about you. When we were kids, I used to say awful things to you. I assumed you were too stuck-up to be bothered by them."

"I was bothered. They hurt."

"And if I'd known it then," he acknowledged honestly, "I'd probably have done it even more. But I don't want to do that now. So if I know what you're thinking, if I know what your sore spots are, I can avoid hitting them. Maybe I can even help them heal." He liked that idea. "Sounds lofty, but if you don't aim high, you don't get nowhere."

"Anywhere," she corrected, and raised her head. There was no sarcasm, only curiosity in her voice. "When did you become a philosopher?"

He looked down into her eyes, dove gray behind her glasses. "When I was in Vietnam. A good many of the things I am now I became then." At her startled look, he was bemused himself. "Didn't you guess? Didn't you wonder what it was that brought about the change?"

She gave a head shake so tiny it was almost imperceptible. "I was too busy trying to deny it."

"Deny it all you want, but it's true. I'll prove it to you if you let me, but I can't do it if you jump all over me every time I say something dumb." When she opened her mouth to argue, he put a finger to her lips. "I can learn, Jessica. Talk to me. Reason with me. Explain things to me. I'm not going to turn around and walk away. I'll listen."

Her fingers tightened on the crisp fabric of his shirt just above his belt, and her eyes went rounder behind her glasses. "And then what?" she asked, still without sarcasm. In place of her earlier curiosity, though, was fear. "Will you take what I've told you and turn it on me? If you wanted revenge, that would be one way to get it."

"Revenge?"

"You've always hated what I stood for."

He shook his head slowly, his eyes never once leaving hers. "I thought I hated it, but it was me I hated. That was one of the things I learned a while back. For lots of reasons, some of which became self-perpetuating, I was an unhappy kid. And I'm not saying that all changed overnight. I spent four years in the army. That gave me lots of time to think about lots of things. I was still thinking about them when I got back." His hands moved lightly just above her waist. "That last time when I saw you I was still pretty unsettled. You remember. You were sixteen."

The memory was a weight, bowing her head, and the next thing she knew she felt Carter's jaw against her crown, and he was saying very softly, "I treated you poorly then, too."

"That time was the worst. I was so unsure of myself anyway, and what you said—"

"Unsure of yourself?" His hands went still. "You weren't."

"I was."

"You didn't look it."

"I felt it. It was the second date I'd ever had." The words began to flow and wouldn't stop. "I didn't like the boy, and I didn't really want to go, but it was so important to me to be like my friends. They dated, so I wanted to date. We were going to a prom at his school, and I had to wear a formal dress. My mother had picked it out in the store, and it looked wonderful on her, but awful on me. I didn't have her face or her body or her coloring. But I put on the dress and the stockings and the matching shoes, and I let her do my hair and face. Then I stood on the front porch looking at my reflection in the window, trying to pull the dress higher and make it look better...and you came around the corner of the house. You told me that I could pull forever and it wouldn't do any good, because there was nothing there worth covering. You said—"

"Don't, Jessica—"

"You said that any man worth beans would be able to see that right off, but you told me that I probably didn't have anything to worry about, because you doubted anyone who would ask me out was worth beans. But that was no problem, either, you told me—"

"Please—"

"Because, you said, I was an uptight nobody, and the only thing I'd ever have to offer a man would be money. I could buy someone, you said. Money was power, you said, and then—"

"Jessica, don't—"

"And then you reached into your pocket, pulled out a dollar bill and stuffed it into my dress, and you said that I should try bribing my date and maybe he'd kiss me."

She went quiet, slightly appalled that she'd spilled the whole thing and more than a little humiliated even seventeen years after the fact. But she couldn't have taken back the words if she'd wanted to, and she didn't have time to consider the damage she'd done before Carter took her face in his hands and turned it up.

"Did he kiss you?"

She shook her head as much as his hold would allow.

"Then I owe you for that, too," he whispered, and before she could begin to imagine what he had in mind, his mouth touched hers. She tired to pull back, but he held her, brushing his mouth back and forth over her lips until their stiffness eased, then taking them in a light kiss.

It didn't last long, but it left her stunned. Her breath came in shallow gasps, and for a minute she couldn't think. That was the minute when she might have identified what she felt as pleasure, but when her heart began to thud again and her mind started to clear, she felt only disbelief. "Why did you do that?" she whispered, and lowered her eyes when disbelief gave way to embarrassment.

"I don't know." He certainly hadn't planned it. "I guess I wanted to. It felt right."

"You shouldn't have," she said, and exerted pressure to lever herself away. He let her go. Immediately she felt the loss of his body heat and drew her blazer closer around her. Mustering shreds of dignity, she pushed her glasses up on her nose and raised her eyes to his. "I think we'd better get going. There's a lot to cover."

She didn't wait for an answer, but moved off, walking steadily along the path that circled the rear of the house. She kept her head high and her shoulders straight, looking far more confident than she felt. Instinct told her that it was critical to pretend the kiss hadn't happened. She couldn't give it credence, couldn't let on she thought twice about it, or Carter would have a field day. She could just imagine the smug look on his face even now, which was why she didn't turn. She knew he was following, could hear the crunch of dried leaves under his shoes. No doubt he was thinking about what a lousy kisser she was.

Because he sure wasn't. He was an incredible kisser, if those few seconds were any indication of his skill. Not that she'd liked it. She couldn't possibly *like* Carter Malloy's kiss. But she'd been vulnerable at that moment. Her mind had been muddled. She was definitely going to have to get it together unless she wanted to make an utter fool of herself.

How to get it together, though, was a problem. She was walking through land that she loved and that, a year from then, wouldn't be hers, and she was being followed by a demon from her past who had materialized in the here and now as a gorgeous hunk of man. She had to think business, she decided. For all intents and purposes, in her dealings with Carter she was a businesswoman. That was all.

They walked silently on until the path opened into a clearing. Though the grass was just beginning to green up after the winter's freeze, the lushness of the spot as it would be in full spring or high summer was lost on neither of them. They had the memories to fill in where reality lay half-dormant.

Jessica stopped at the meadow's mouth. When Carter reached her side, she said, "Another grouping of homes should go here. It's so pretty, and it's already open. That means fewer trees destroyed. I want to disturb as little of the natural environment as possible."

"I understand," Carter said, and walked on past her into the meadow. He was glad he understood something. He sure didn't understand why he'd kissed her—or why he'd found it strangely sweet. Unable to analyze it just then, though, he strode along one side of the four-acre oval, stopping several times along the way to look around him from a particular spot. After standing for a time in deep concentration at the far end, he crossed back through the center.

And all the while, with nothing else to do and no excuse not to, Jessica studied him. Gorgeous hunk of man? Oh, yes. His clothes—heathery blazer, slate-colored slacks, crisp white shirt—were of fine quality and fitted to perfection, but the clothes didn't make him a gorgeous hunk. What made him that was the body beneath. He was broad shouldered, lean of hip and long limbed, but even then he wouldn't have been as spectacular if those features hadn't all worked together. His body flowed. His stride was smooth and confident, the proud set of his head perfectly comfortable on those broad shoulders, his expression male in a dark and mysterious way.

If he felt her scrutiny, it obviously didn't affect him at all. But then, she mused, he was probably used to the scrutiny of women. He was the type to turn heads.

With a sigh, she turned and started slowly back on the path. It was several minutes before Carter caught up with her. "What do you think?" she asked without looking at him.

"It would work."

"If you'd like more time there, feel free. You can meet me up at the house."

"Are you cold?" he asked, because she was still hugging the blazer around her.

"No. I'm fine."

He glanced back toward the meadow, "Well, so am I. This is just a preliminary walk-through. I've seen enough for now. What's next?"

"The pine grove."

That surprised him. "Over on the other side of the house?" When she nodded, he said, "Are you sure you want to build there?"

She looked up at him then. "I need a third spot. If you can think of someplace better, I'm open for suggestion."

Drudging up what he remembered of the south end of the property, he had to admit that the pine grove seemed the obvious choice. "But that will mean cutting. The entire area is populated with trees. There isn't any sizable clearing to speak of, not like at the duck pond or in the meadow." He shook his head. "I'd hate to have to take down a single one of those pines."

Jessica took in a deep breath and said sadly, "So now you know what I'm feeling about this project. It's a travesty, isn't it? But I have no choice." Determined to remain strong and in control, she turned her eyes forward and continued on.

For the first time, Carter did know what she felt. It was one thing when he was dealing with the idea—and his memory—of Crosslyn Rise, another when he was walking there, seeing, smelling and feeling the place, being surrounded by the natural majesty that was suddenly at the mercy of humans.

When they reached the pine grove, he was more acutely aware of that natural majesty than ever. Trees that had been growing for scores of years stretched toward the heavens as though they had an intimate connection with the place. Lower to the ground were younger versions, even lower than that shrubs that thrived in the shade. The carpeting underfoot was a tapestry of fine moss and pine needles. The pervasive scent was distinct and divine.

I have no choice, Jessica had said on a variation of the theme she'd repeated more than once, and he believed her. That made him all the more determined to design something special.

Jessica was almost sorry when they returned to the house. Yes, she was a little chilled, though she wouldn't have said a word to Carter lest, heaven forbid, he offer her his jacket, but the wide open spaces made his masculinity a little less commanding. Once indoors, there would be nothing to dilute it.

"You'll want to go through the house," she guessed, more nervous as they made their way across the back porch and entered the kitchen.

"I ought to," he said. "But that coffee smells good. Mind if I take a cup with me?"

She was grateful for something to do. "Cream or sugar?"

"Both."

As efficiently as possible, given the awkwardness stirring inside her, she poured him a mugful of the dark brew and prepared it as he liked it.

"You aren't having any?" he asked when she handed him the mug.

She didn't dare. Her hands were none too steady, and caffeine wouldn't help. "Maybe later," she said, and in as businesslike a manner as she could manage, led him off on a tour of the house.

The tour should have been fairly routine through the first floor, most of which Carter had seen at one time or another. But he'd never seen it before with a knowledge of architecture, and that made all the difference. High ceilings, chair rails and door moldings, antique mantelpieces on the three other first-floor fireplaces—he was duly impressed, and his comments to that extent came freely.

His observations were professional enough to lessen the discomfort Jessica felt when they climbed the grand stairway to the second floor. Still she felt discomfort aplenty, and she couldn't blame it on the past. Something had happened when Carter had kissed her. He'd awoken her to the man he was. Her awareness of him now wasn't of the boy she'd hated but of the man she wished she could. Because that man was calm, confident and commanding, all the things she wanted to be just then, but wasn't. In comparison to him, she felt inadequate, and, feeling inadequate, she did what she could to blend into the woodwork.

It worked just fine as they made their way from one end of the long hall down and around a bend to the other end. Carter saw the once-glorious master bedroom that hadn't been used in years; he saw a handful of other bedrooms, some with fireplaces, and more bathrooms than he'd ever dreamed his mother had cleaned. He took everything in, sipping his coffee as he silently made notes in his mind. Only when he reached the last bedroom, the one by the back stairs, did his interest turn personal.

"This is yours," he said. He didn't have to catch her nod to know that it was, but not even the uncomfortable look on her face could have kept him from stepping inside. The room was smaller than most of the others and decorated more simply, with floral wallpaper and white furniture.

Helpless to stop himself, he scanned the paired bookshelves to find foreign volumes and literary works fully integrated with works of popular fiction. He ran a finger along the dresser, passed a mirrored tray bearing a collection of antique perfume bottles and paused at a single framed photograph. It was a portrait of Jessica with her parents when she was no more than five years old; she looked exactly as he remembered her. It was a minute before he moved on to an old trunk, painted white and covered with journals, and an easy chair upholstered in the same faded pastel pattern as the walls. Then his gaze came to rest on the bed. It was a double bed, dressed in a nubby white spread with an array of lacy white pillows of various shapes and sizes lying beneath the scrolled headboard.

The room was very much like her, Carter mused. It was clean and pure, a little welcoming, a little off-putting, a little curious. It was the kind of room that hinted at exciting things in the nooks and crannies, just beyond the pristine front.

Quietly, for quiet was what the room called for, he asked, "Was this where you grew up?"

"No," she said quickly, eager to answer and return downstairs. "I moved here to save heating the rest of the house."

The rationale was sound. "This is above the kitchen, so it stays warm."

"Yes." She took a step backward in a none-too-subtle hint, but he didn't budge. In any other area of the house, she'd have gone anyway and left him to follow. But this was her room. She couldn't leave him alone here; that would have been too much a violation of her private space.

"I like the picture," he said, tossing his head toward the dresser. A small smile played at the corner of his mouth. "It brings back memories."

She focused on the photograph so that she wouldn't have to see his smile. "It's supposed to. That was a rare family occasion."

"What occasion?"

"Thanksgiving."

He didn't understand. "What's so rare about Thanksgiving?"

"My father joined us for dinner."

Carter studied her face, trying to decide if she was being facetious. He didn't think so. "You mean, he didn't usually do it?"

"It was hit or miss. If he was in the middle of something intense, he wouldn't take a break."

"Not even for Thanksgiving dinner?"

"No," she said evenly, and met his gaze. "Are you done here? Can we go down?"

He showed no sign of having heard her. "That's really incredible. I always pictured holidays at Crosslyn Rise as being spectacular—you know, steeped in tradition, everything warm and pretty and lavish.''

"It was all that. But it was also lonely.''

"Was that why you married so young?'' When her eyes flew to his, he added, "My mother said you were twenty.''

She wanted to know whether he'd specifically asked for the details and felt a glimmer of annoyance that he might be prying behind her back. Somehow, though, she couldn't get herself to be sharp with him. She was tired of sounding like a harpy when his interest seemed so innocent.

"Maybe I was lonely. I'm not sure. At the time I thought I was in love.''

Obviously she'd changed her mind at some point, he mused. "How long did it last?''

"Didn't your mother tell you that?''

"She said it was none of my business, and it's not. If you don't want to talk about it, you don't have to.

Jessica rested against the doorjamb. She touched the wood, rubbed a bruised spot. "It's no great secret.'' It was, after all, a matter of public record. "We were divorced two years after we married.''

"What happened?''

She frowned at the paint. "We were different people with different goals.''

"Who was he?''

She paused. "Tom Chandler.'' Her arm stole around her middle. "You wouldn't have known him.''

"Not from around here?''

She shook her head. "Saint Louis. I was a sophomore in college, he was a senior. He wanted to be a writer and figured that I'd support him. He thought we were rich.'' The irony of it was so strong that she was beyond embarrassment. Looking Carter in the eye, she said, "You were right. Bribery was about the only way I'd get a man. But it took me two years to realize that was what had done it.''

Carter came forward, drawn by the pallor of her face and the haunted look in her eyes, either of which was preferable to the unemotional way she was telling him something that had to be horribly painful for her. "I don't understand.''

"Tom fell in love with Crosslyn Rise. He liked the idea of living on an estate. He liked the idea of my father being a genius. He liked the idea of my mother devoting herself to taking care of my father, because Tom figured that was what I'd do for him. Mostly, he liked the idea of turning the attic into a garret and spending his days there reading and thinking and staring out into space.''

"Then you tired of the marriage before he did?''

"I...suppose you could say that. He tired of me pretty quickly, but he was perfectly satisfied with the marriage. That was when I realized my mistake.''

There was a world of hurt that she wasn't expressing, but Carter saw it in her eyes. It was all he could do not to reach out to help, but he wasn't sure his help would be welcome. So he said simply, "I'm sorry.''

"Nothing to be sorry about.'' She forced a brittle smile. "Two years. That was all. I was finishing my undergraduate degree, so I went right on for my Ph.D., which was what I'd been planning to do all along.''

"I'm sorry it didn't work out. Maybe if you'd had someone to help with the situation here—''

"Not Tom. Forget Tom. He was about as adept with finances as my mother and twice as disinterested.''

"Still, it might not have been so difficult if you hadn't been alone.''

She tore her eyes from his. "Yes, well, life is never perfect.'' She looked at the bright side, which was what she'd tried hard to do over the years. "I have a lot to be grateful for. I have my work. I love that, and I do it well. I've made good friends. And I have Crosslyn—'' she caught herself and finished in a near whisper "—Crosslyn Rise.'' Uncaring whether he stayed in her room or not, she turned and went quickly down the back stairs.

When Carter joined her, Jessica was standing stiffly at the counter, taking a sip of the coffee she'd poured herself. Setting the mug down, she raised her chin and asked, "So, where do we go from here as far as this project is concerned?''

Carter would have liked to talk more about the legacy of her marriage, if only to exorcise that haunted look from her eyes. His good sense told him, though, that such a discussion was better saved for another time. He **was** surprised that she'd confided in him as much as she had. Friends did that. It was a good sign.

"Now you talk to me some more about what you want,'' he said. "But first I have to get my briefcase from the car. I'll be right back.''

Left alone in the kitchen for those few short moments, Jessica took several long, deep breaths. She didn't seem able to do that when Carter was around. He was a physical presence, dominating whatever room he was in. But she couldn't say that the domination was deliberate—or offensive, for that matter. He was doing his best to be agreeable. It wasn't his fault that he was so tall, or that his voice had such resonance, or that he exuded an aura of power.

"Do you have the list?" he asked, striding back into the kitchen. When she nodded and pointed to a pad of paper waiting on the round oak table nearby, he set his briefcase beside it. Then he retrieved his coffee mug. "Mind if I take a refill?"

"Of course not." She reached for the glass carafe and proceeded to fix his coffee with cream and sugar, just as he'd had it before. When he protested that he could do it, she waved him away. She was grateful to be active and efficient.

Carrying both mugs, she led him to the table, which filled a semicircular alcove off the kitchen. The walls of the alcove were windowed, offering a view of the woods that had enchanted Jessica on many a morning. On this morning, she was too aware of Carter to pay much heed to the pair of cardinals decorating the Douglas fir with twin spots of red.

"Want to start from the top?" Carter asked, eyeing her list.

She did that. Point by point, she ran through her ideas. Most were ones she'd touched on before, but there were others, smaller thoughts— ranging from facilities at the clubhouse to paint colors—that had come to her and seemed worth mentioning. She began tentatively and gained courage as she went.

Carter listened closely. He asked questions and made notes. Though he pointed out the downside of some of her ideas, not once did he make her feel as though something she said was foolish. Often he illustrated one point or another by giving examples from his own experience, and she was fascinated by those. Clearly he enjoyed his work and knew what he was talking about. By the time he rose to leave, she was feeling surprisingly comfortable with the idea of Carter designing the new Crosslyn Rise.

That comfort was from the professional standpoint.

From a personal standpoint, she was feeling no comfort at all. For no sooner had that low blue car of his purred down the driveway than she thought about his kiss. Her pulse tripped, her cheeks went pink, her lips tingled—all well after the fact. On the one hand, she was gratified that she'd had such control over herself while Carter had been there. On the other hand, she was appalled at the extent of her reaction now that he was gone.

Particularly since she hadn't liked his kiss.

But she had. She had. It had been warm, smooth, wet. And it had been short. Maybe that was why she'd liked it. It hadn't lasted long enough for her to be nervous or frightened or embarrassed. Nor had it lasted long enough to provide much more than a tempting sample of something new and different. She'd never been given a kiss like that before—not from a date, of which there hadn't been many of the kissing type, and certainly not from Tom. Tom had been as self-centered in lovemaking as he'd been in everything else. A kiss from Tom had been a boring experience.

Carter's kiss, short though it was, hadn't been boring at all. In fact, Jessica realized, she wouldn't mind experiencing it again—which was a *truly* dismaying thought. She'd never been the physical type, and to find herself entertaining physical thoughts about Carter Malloy was too much.

Chalking those thoughts up to a momentary mental quirk, she gathered her things together and headed for Cambridge.

The diversionary tactic worked. Not once while she was at work did she think of Carter, and it wasn't simply that she kept busy. She took time out late in the afternoon for a relaxed sandwich break with two male colleagues, then did some errands in the Square and even stopped at the supermarket on her way home—none of which were intellectually demanding activities. Her mind might have easily wandered, but it didn't.

No, she didn't think about Carter until she got home, and then, as though to make up for the hours before, she couldn't escape him. Every room in the house held a memory of his presence, some more so than others. Most intensely haunted were the kitchen and her bedroom, the two rooms in which she spent the majority of her at-home hours. Standing at the bedroom door as she had done when he'd been inside, sitting once again at the kitchen table, she saw him as he'd been, remembered every word he'd said, felt his presence as though he were there still.

It was the recency of his visit, she told herself, but the rationalization did nothing to dismiss the memories. By walking through her home, by looking at all the little things that were intimate to her, he had touched her private self.

She wanted to be angry. She tried and tried to muster it, but something was missing. There was no offense. She didn't feel violated, simply touched.

And that gave her even more to consider. The Carter she'd known as a kid had been a violater from the start; the Carter who had reentered her life wasn't like that at all. When the old Carter had come near, she'd trembled in anger, indignation and, finally, humiliation; when the new Carter came near, the trembling was from something else.

She didn't want to think about it, but there seemed no escape. No sooner would she immerse herself in a diversion than the diversionary shell cracked. Such was the case when she launched into her nightly workout in front of the VCR; rather than concentrate on the routine or

Barbara Delinsky

the aerobic benefits of the exercise, she found herself thinking about body tone and wondering whether she looked better at thirty-three for the exercise she did, than she'd looked at twenty-five. And when she wondered why she cared, she thought of Carter.

When, sweaty and tired, she sank into a hot bath, she found her body tingling long after she should have felt pleasantly drowsy, and when she stopped to analyze those tingles, she thought of Carter.

When, wearing a long white nightgown with ruffles at the bodice, she settled into the bedroom easy chair, with a lapful of reading matter that should have captured her attention, her attention wandered to those things that Carter had seen and touched. She pictured him as he had stood that morning, looking tall and dark, uncompromisingly male, and curious about her. She spent a long time thinking about that curiosity, trying to focus in on its cause.

She was without conclusions when the phone rang by her bed. Startled, she picked it up after the first ring, but the sudden stretch sent the books on her lap sliding down the silky fabric of her gown to the floor. She made a feeble attempt to catch them at the same time that she offered a slightly breathless, "Hello?"

Carter heard that breathlessness and for an awful minute wondered if he'd woken her. A glance at his watch told him it was after ten. He hadn't realized it was so late. "Jessica? This is Carter." He paused. "Am I catching you at a bad time?"

Letting the books go where they would, she put a hand to her chest to still her thudding heart. "No. No. This is fine."

"I didn't wake you?"

"No. I was reading." Or trying to, she mused, but her mind didn't wander farther. It was waiting for Carter's next words. She couldn't imagine why he'd called, particularly at ten o'clock at night.

Carter wasn't sure, either. Nothing he had to say couldn't wait for another day or two, certainly for a more reasonable hour. But he'd been thinking about Jessica for most of the day. They had parted on good terms. He wanted to know whether those good terms still stood, or whether she'd been chastising herself for this, that and the other all day. And beyond that, he wanted to hear her voice.

Relieved now that he hadn't woken her, he leaned back against the strip of kitchen wall where the phone hung. "Did you get to school okay today?"

"Uh-huh."

"Everything go all right? I mean, I didn't get you going off on the wrong foot or anything, did I?"

She gave a shy smile that he couldn't possibly see, but it came though in her voice. "No. I was fine. How about you?"

"Great. It was a really good day. I think you bring me good luck."

She didn't believe that for a minute, but her smile lingered. "What happened?"

Carter was still trying to figure it out. "Nothing momentous. I spent the afternoon in the office working on other projects, and a whole bunch of little things clicked. It was one of those days when I felt really in tune with my work."

"Inspired?"

"Yeah." He paused, worried that she'd think he was simply trying to impress her. "Does that sound pretentious?"

"Of course not. It sounds very nice. We should all have days like that."

"Yours wasn't?"

She thought back on what she'd done since she'd seen him that morning. "It was," she said, but cautiously. "It's an odd time. I gave the final lecture to my German lit class, and I was really pleased with the way it went, but the meetings I had after that were frustrating."

Carter was just getting past the point of picturing her with her nose stuck in a book all day. He wanted to know more about what she did. "In what way?"

"At the end of the term, students get nervous. They're realizing that a good part of their grade is going to depend on a final exam, a term paper or both. If they go into these last two weeks with a solid average, they're worried about keeping it up. If they go in with a low average, they're desperate to raise it. Even the most laid-back of them get a little uptight."

"Didn't you when you were in school?"

"Sure. So I try to be understanding. It's mostly a question of listening to them and giving them encouragement. That's easy to do if I know the student. I can concentrate on his strengths and relate the class material to it. If I don't know the student, it's harder, sort of like stabbing in the dark at the right button to help the student make the connection."

Carter was quiet for a minute. Then he said, "I'm impressed. You're a dedicated professor, to put that kind of thought into interactions with students. The professors I studied under weren't like that. They were guarded, almost like they saw us as future competition, so they wanted us to learn, but not too much."

She knew some colleagues who were like that, and though she couldn't condone the behavior, she tried to explain it by saying, "You were older when you started college."

"Not that much. I was twenty-three."

"But you were wise in a worldly way that was probably intimidating."

A day or a week before, Carter might have taken the observation as an offense. That he didn't take it that way now was a comment on how far he'd come in terms of self-confidence where Jessica was concerned. It was also an indication of how far she'd come; her tone was gentle, conversational, which was how he kept his. "How did you know I was world wise at twenty-three?" She'd seen so little of him then.

"You were that way at seventeen, and you were very definitely intimidating."

He thought back to those years with an odd blend of nostalgia and self-reproach. "I tried to be. Lord, I tried. Intimidating people was about the only thing I was good at."

"You could have been good at other things. Look where you are now. That talent didn't suddenly come into being when you hit your twenties. But you let everyone think you had no brains."

"I thought it, too. I was messed up in so many other ways that no brains seemed part of the package."

Jessica wanted to ask him about being messed up. She wanted to know the why and how of it. She wanted to be able to make some sense of the person he'd been and relate it to the person he was now. Because this person was interesting. She could warm to this Carter as she would never have dreamed of doing to the one who had once been malicious.

The irony of it was that in some ways the new Carter was more dangerous.

"Are you still there?" he asked.

"Uh-huh," she answered as lightly as she could given the irregular skip of her pulse.

He figured he was either making her uncomfortable by talking about the past or boring her, and he didn't want to do either, not tonight, not when they finally seemed to be getting along. So he cleared his throat. "You're probably wondering why I called."

She was, now that he mentioned it. A man like Carter Malloy wouldn't call her just to talk. "I figured you'd get around to it in good time," she said lightly. She wanted him to know that she was taking the call in stride, just as she'd taken his kiss in stride. It wouldn't do for him to know that she was vulnerable where he was concerned.

"Well, now's the time. When I was driving back to town from Crosslyn Rise this morning, it occurred to me that it might help both of us if you were to see some of the other things I've done."

"I saw those sketches—"

"Not sketches. The real thing. I've done other projects similar in concept to the one you want done. If you were to see them in person, you might get a feeling for whether I'm the right man for this job."

Jessica felt something heavy settle around her middle. "You're having second thoughts about working here."

"It's not—"

"You can be honest," she said, tipping up her chin. "I'm not desperate. There are plenty of other architects."

"Jessica—"

"The only reason Gordon suggested you was because you were familiar with the Rise. He figured you'd be interested."

"I *am*," Carter said loudly. "Will you please be quiet and let me speak?" When he didn't hear anything coming from the other end of the line, he breathed, "Thank you. My Lord, Jessica, when you get going, you're like a steamroller."

"I don't want to play games. That's all. If you don't want this job, I'd appreciate your coming right out and saying so, rather than beating around the bush."

"I *want* this job. I *want* this job. How many times do I have to say it?"

More quietly she said, "If you want it, why were you looking to give me an out?"

"Because I want you to *choose* me," he blurted. Standing well away from the wall now, he ran his fingers through his hair. "I'd like to feel," he said slowly, "that you honestly want me to do the work. That you're *enthusiastic* about my doing it. That it isn't just a case of Gordon foisting me on you, or your not having the time or energy to interview others."

She was thinking that he wasn't such a good businessman after all. "You're an awful salesman. You should be tooting your own horn, not warning me off. Are you this way with all your clients?"

"No. This case is different. You're special."

His words worked wonders on the heaviness inside her. She felt instantly lighter, and it didn't matter that he'd meant the words in the most superficial of ways. What he'd said made her feel good.

"Okay," she breathed. "I'm sorry I interrupted."

Stunned by the speed and grace of her capitulation, Carter drew a blank. For the life of him, he couldn't remember what had prompted the set-to. "Uh..."

"You were saying that maybe I ought to see some of the things you've done."

Gratefully he picked up the thread. "The best ones—the ones I like best—are north of you, up along the coast of Maine. The farthest is three hours away. They could all be seen in a single day.'' He hesitated for a second. ''I was thinking that if you'd like, we could drive up together.''

It was Jessica's turn to be stunned. The last thing she'd expected was that Carter would want to spend a day with her, even on business. Her words come slowly and skeptically. ''Isn't that above and beyond the call of duty?''

''What do you mean?''

''You don't have to go to such extremes. I can drive north myself.''

''Why should you have to go alone if I'm willing to take you?''

''Because that would be a whole day out of your time.''

''So what else is my time for?''

''Working.''

''I get plenty of work done during the week. So do you, and you said you were coming up on exams. I was thinking of taking a Sunday when both of us can relax.''

That was even *more* incredible. ''I can't ask you to take a whole Sunday to chauffeur me around!''

''Why not?''

''Because Sundays are personal, and this would be business.''

''It could be fun, too. There are some good restaurants. We could stop and get something to eat along the way.''

Jessica returned her hand to her chest in an attempt to slow the rapid beat of her heart.

''Or you could shop,'' he went on. ''There are some terrific boutique areas. I wouldn't mind waiting.''

She was utterly confused. ''I couldn't ask you to do that.''

''You don't have to ask. I'm offering.'' He was struck by an afterthought that hardened his voice. ''Unless you'd rather not be with me for that length of time.''

''That's not it.''

''Then what is?''

''*Me.* Wouldn't you rather not be with *me* for that length of time? You'll be bored to tears. I'm not the most dynamic person in the world.''

''Who told you that?''

''You. When I was ten, you caught me sitting on the rocks, looking out to sea. You asked what I saw, and when I wouldn't answer, you said I was dull and pathetic.''

He felt like a heel. ''You were only ten, and I was full of it.''

''But Tom agreed. He thought I was boring, too. I've never been known as the life of the party.''

"Sweetheart, a man can only take being with the life of the party for so long. Let me tell you, *that* can get boring. You, on the other hand, have a hell of a lot going for you." He let the flow of his thoughts carry him quickly on. "You read, you think, you work. Okay, so you don't open up easily. That doesn't mean you're boring. All it means is that a man has to work a little harder to find out what's going on in that pretty head of yours. I'm willing to work a little harder. I think the reward will be worth it. So you'd be doing me a favor by agreeing to spend a Sunday with me driving up the coast." He took a quick breath, not allowing himself the time to think about all he'd said. "What'll it be—yes or no?"

"Yes," Jessica said just as quickly and for the very same reason.

5

Jessica had a dream that night. It brought her awake gradually, almost reluctantly, to a dark room and a clock that read 2:24 a.m. Her skin was warm and slightly damp. Her breath was coming in short whispers. The faint quivering deep inside her was almost a memory, but not quite.

She stretched. When the quivering lingered, she curled into a ball to cradle it, because there was something very nice about the feeling. It was satisfying, soft and feminine.

Slowly, even more slowly than she'd awoken, she homed in on the subject of her dream. Her reluctance this time had nothing to do with preserving a precious feeling. As Carter Malloy's image grew clearer in her mind, the languorous smile slipped from her face. In its place came a look of dismay.

Jessica had never had an erotic dream before. Never. Not when she'd been a teenager first becoming aware of her developing body, not when she'd been dating Tom, not in the long years following the divorce. She wasn't blind to a good-looking man; she could look at male beauty, recognize it, admire it for what it was. But it had never excited her in a physical sense. It had never buried itself in her subconscious and come forward to bring her intense pleasure in the middle of the night.

Flipping to her other side, she shielded her face with her arm, as if to hide her embarrassment from a horde of grinning voyeurs masked by the dark.

Carter Malloy. Carter Malloy, beautifully naked and splendidly built. Carter Malloy, coming to her, kissing her, stroking her. He'd been exquisitely gentle, removing her clothes piece by piece, loving her with his hands and his mouth, driving her to a fever pitch that she'd never experienced before.

With a moan, she flipped back to the other side and huddled under the covers, but the sheet that half covered her face couldn't blot out the persistent images in her mind. Carter Malloy, kissing her everywhere, *everywhere*, while he offered his own body for her eager hands and lips. In her dream, he was large and leanly muscled, textured at some spots, smooth and vulnerable at others, very, very hard and needy at still others.

Sitting bolt upright in bed, she turned on the lamp, hugged her knees to her chest and worked to ground herself among the trappings of the old and familiar. To some extent she was successful. At least the quivering inside her eased. What she was left with, though, was an undertone of frustration that was nearly as unwelcome.

She couldn't understand it. She just wasn't a passionate person. Lovemaking with Tom had been a part of marriage that she'd simply accepted. Occasionally she'd enjoyed it. Occasionally she'd even had an orgasm, though she could count the number of times that had happened on the fingers of one hand. And she hadn't minded that it was so infrequent. Sex was a highly overrated activity, she had long since decided.

That didn't explain why she'd dreamed what she did, or why the dream had brought her to a sweet, silent climax.

Mortified anew, she pressed her eyes to her knees. What if someone had seen her? What if someone had been watching her sleep? Not that anyone would have or could have seen her, still she wondered if she had made noise, or writhed about.

It was something she'd eaten, she decided. Certain foods were known to stir up the senses. Surely that was what had brought on the erotic interlude.

But she went over every morsel of food that had entered her mouth that day—easy to do, since she was neither a big eater nor an adventurous one—and she couldn't single out anything that might have inspired eroticism.

Maybe, she mused, it had to do with her own body. Maybe she was experiencing a hormonal shift, maybe even related to menopause. But she was only thirty-three! She wasn't ready for menopause!

The hormonal theory, though, had another twist. They said that women reached their peak of sexual interest at a later age than men. Women in their thirties and forties were supposed to be hot—at least, that was what the magazines said, though she'd always before wondered whether the magazines said it simply because it was what their thirty- and forty-year-old readers wanted to hear.

Maybe there was some truth to it, though. Maybe she was developing needs she'd never had before. She had been a long time without a man, better than eleven years. Maybe the dream she'd had was her body's way of saying that it was in need. Maybe that need even had to do with the biological clock. Maybe her body was telling her that it was time to have a baby.

Throwing the covers back, she scrambled from the bed, grabbed her glasses and, barefoot, half walked, half ran down the back steps to the kitchen. Soon after, she was sitting cross-legged on one of the chairs with an open tin of Poppycock nestled in her lap.

Poppycock was her panacea. When she'd been little, she had hidden it in her room, because her mother had been convinced that the caramel coating on the popcorn would rot her teeth. Now that her mother wasn't around to worry, Jessica kept the can within easy reach. It wasn't that she pigged out on a regular basis, and since she didn't have a weight problem, it probably wouldn't have mattered if she had, but Poppycock was a treat. It was light and fun, just the thing she went for when she was feeling a little down.

She wasn't feeling down now, but frustrated and confused. She was also feeling angry, angry at Carter, because no matter how long she made her list of possible excuses for what had happened, she knew it wasn't coincidence that had set Carter Malloy's face and body at the center of her dream. She cursed him for being handsome and sexy, cursed herself for being vulnerable, cursed Crosslyn Rise for aging and putting her into a precarious position.

One piece of popcorn followed another into her mouth. In time, she helped herself to a glass of milk, and by the time that was gone, it was well after three. Having set her mind to thinking about the material she had to cover in her Russian seminar that afternoon, she'd calmed down some. With a deep, steady breath, she rose from the chair, put the empty glass into the sink and the tin of Poppycock into the pantry, and went back to bed.

When Jessica had agreed to drive north with Carter, he had wanted to do it that Sunday for the sake of getting her feedback as soon as possible. She had put him off for a week, knowing that she had far too much work to do in preparation for exams, to take off for the whole day. In point of fact, the following Sunday wouldn't be much better; though she had teaching assistants to grade exams, she always did her share, and she liked it that way.

But Carter was eager, and she knew that she could plan around the time. So they had settled on the day, and he had promised to call her the Saturday before to tell her when he would be picking her up. She wasn't scheduled to hear from him until then, and in the aftermath of that embarrassingly carnal dream, she was grateful for the break. Given twelve days' time, she figured she could put her relationship with him into its proper perspective.

That perspective, she decided had to be business, which was what she thought about during those days when she had the free time to let her mind wander. She concentrated on the business of converting

Crossslyn Rise into something practical and productive—and acclimating herself to that conversion.

To that end, she called Nina Stone and arranged to meet her for dinner at a local seafood restaurant, a chic establishment overlooking the water on the Crosslyn Rise end of town. The two had met the year before, browsing in a local bookstore, and several months after that, Jessica had approached her about selling Crosslyn Rise. Though Nina hadn't grown up locally, she'd been working on the North Shore for five years, and during that time she had established herself as an aggressive broker with both smarts and style. She was exactly the kind of woman Jessica had always found intimidating, but strangely, they'd hit it off. Jessica could see Nina's tough side, but there was a gentler, more approachable side as well. That side came out when they were together and Nina let down her defenses.

Despite her reputation, despite the aggressiveness Jessica knew was there, Nina had never pressured her. She was like Carter in the sense that, having come from nothing, she was slightly in awe of Crosslyn Rise—which meant that she was in no rush to destroy it.

For that reason among others, Jessica felt comfortable sharing the latest on the Rise with her.

"A condominium community?" Nina asked warily. She was a small woman, slender and pixieish, which made her assertiveness in business somewhat unexpected and therefore all the more effective. "I don't know, Jessica. It would be a shame to do that to such a beautiful place."

"Condominium communities can be beautiful."

"But Crosslyn Rise is that much more so."

Jessica sighed. "I can't afford it, Nina. You've known that for a while. I can't afford to keep it as it is, and you haven't had any luck finding a buyer."

"The market stinks," Nina said, sounding defensive, looking apologetic. "I'm selling plenty on the low and middle end of the scale, but precious little at the top." She grew more thoughtful. "Condos are going, though, I do have to admit. Particularly in this area. There's something about the ocean. Young professionals find it romantic, older ones find it restful." She paused to sip her wine. Her fingers were slender, her nails polished red to match her suit. "Tell me more. If this was Gordon Hale's idea, I would guess that it's financially sound. The man is a rock. You say he's putting together a consortium?"

"Not yet, but he will when it's time. Right now, I'm working with someone to define exactly what it is that I want."

"Someone?"

After the slightest hesitation, she specified, "An architect."

Nina studied her for a minute. "You look uncomfortable."

Jessica pushed her glasses up on her nose. "No."

"Is this architect a toughie?"

"No. He's very nice. His name is Carter Malloy." She watched for a reaction. "Ever heard of him?"

"Sure," Nina said without blinking an eye. "He's with Malloy and Goodwin. He's good."

Jessica felt a distant pride. "You're familiar with his work, then?"

"I saw something he did in Portsmouth not long ago. Portsmouth isn't my favorite place, but this was beautiful. He had converted a textile mill into condos. Did an incredible job combining old and new." She frowned, then grinned at the same time. "If I recall correctly, the man himself is beautiful."

"I don't know as I'd call him beautiful," Jessica answered, but a little too fast, and that roused Nina's interest.

"What would you call him?"

She thought for a minute. "Pleasant looking."

"Not the man I remember. Pleasant looking is someone you'd pass by and smile at kindly. A beautiful man stirs stronger emotions. Carter Malloy was ruggedly masculine—at least, in the picture I saw."

"He is masculine looking, I suppose."

Nina came forward, voice lowered but emphatically chiding. "You suppose, my foot! I can't believe you're as immune to men as you let on. One lousy husband can't have neutered you, and you're not exactly over the hill. You have years of good fun still ahead, if you want to make something of them." She raised her chin. "Who was the last man you dated?"

Jessica shrugged.

"Who?" Nina prodded, but good-naturedly as she settled back in her seat. "You must remember."

"It's a difficult question. How do you define a date? If it's going somewhere with a man, I do that all the time with colleagues."

"That's not what I mean, and you know it. I'm talking about the kind of date who picks you up at your house, takes you out for the evening, kisses you when he brings you home, maybe even stays the night."

"Uh, I'm not into that."

"Sleeping with men?"

"Are you?" Jessica shot back, in part because she was uncomfortable doing the answering and in part because she wanted to know. She and Nina had become friends in the past year, but the only thing Jessica knew about her social life was that she rarely spent a Saturday night at home.

Nina was more amused than anything. "I'm not into sleeping around, but I do enjoy men. There are some nice ones around who are good for an evening's entertainment. Since I'm not looking to get married, I don't threaten them."

"You don't want to get married?"

"Honey, do I have the time?"

"Sure. If you want."

"What I want," Nina said, sitting back in her chair, looking determined but vulnerable, "is to make good money for myself. I want my own business."

"I thought you were making good money now."

"Not enough."

"Are you in need?"

"I've been in need since the day I learned that my mother prostituted herself to put milk on our table."

Jessica caught in a breath. "I'm sorry, Nina. I didn't know."

"It's not something I put on the multiple-listings chart," she quipped, but her voice was low and sober. "That was in Omaha. I have a fine life for myself here, but I won't ever sell myself like my mother did. So I need money of my own. I refuse to ever ask a man for a cent, and I won't have to, if I play my cards right."

"You're doing so well."

"I could be doing even better if I went out on my own. But I'll have to hustle."

Jessica was getting a glimpse of the driven Nina, the one who was restless, whose mind was always working, whose heart was prepared to sacrifice satisfaction for the sake of security. Jessica found it sad. "But you're only thirty."

"And next year I'll be thirty-one, and thirty-two the year after that. The way I figure it, if I work my tail off now and go independent within a year, by the time I'm thirty-five, I can be the leading broker in the area, with a fully trained staff, to boot. Maybe then I'll be able to ease up a little, even think of settling down." She gave a crooked smile. "Assuming there are any worthwhile men out there then."

"If there are, you'll find them," Jessica said, and felt a shaft of the same kind of envy she'd known as a child, when all the other girls were prettier and more socially adept than she. Nina had short, shiny hair, flawless skin and delicate bones. She dressed on the cutting edge between funky and sophisticated and had a personality to match. "You draw people like honey draws bees."

"Lucky for me, or I'd be a loss at what I do." She paused to give Jessica a look that was more cautious than clever. "So I've made the ultimate confession. And you? Do you ever think of settling down?"

Jessica smiled and shook her head. "I don't attract men the way you do."

"Why not?" Nina asked, perfectly serious. "You're smart and pretty and gainfully employed. Aren't those the things men look for nowadays?

Pretty. Carter had used that word. *A man has to work a little harder to find out what's going on in that pretty head of yours.* It was an expression, of course, not to be taken seriously. "Men look for eye-catching women like you."

"And once they've done the eye-catching, they take a closer look and see the flaws. No man would want me right now. I'm too hard. But you're softer. You're established. You're confident in ways I'm not."

"What ways?" Jessica shot back in disbelief.

"Financial. You have Crosslyn Rise."

"Not for long," came the sad reminder.

While the waiter served their lobsters, Nina considered that. As soon as he left, she began to speak again. "You're still a wealthy woman, Jessica. The problem is fluidity of funds. You don't have enough to support the Rise because your assets are tied up *in* the Rise. If you go through with the project you've mentioned, you'll emerge with a comfortable nest egg. Besides, you don't have the fear—" she paused to tie the lobster bib around her neck "—of being broke that I have. You're financially sound, and you're independent. That gives you a head start in the peace-of-mind department. So all you have to do—" she tore a bright red feeler from the steaming lobster "—is to find a terrific guy, settle down somewhere within commuting distance of Harvard and have babies."

"I don't know," Jessica murmured. She was looking at her lobster as though she weren't sure which part to tackle first. "Things are never that simple."

"You watch. Things will get easier when this business with the Rise is settled." That said, she began to suck on the feeler.

Jessica, too, paused to eat, but she kept thinking about Nina's statement. After several minutes, she asked, "Are we talking about the same 'things'?"

"Men. We're talking about men."

"But what does my settling the Rise have to do with men?"

"You'll be freer. More open to the idea of a relationship." When Jessica's expression said she still didn't make the connection, Nina said,

"In some respects, you've been wedded to the Rise. No—" she held up a hand "—don't take this the wrong way. I'm not being critical. But in the time I've known you, I've formed certain impressions. Crosslyn Rise is your haven. You've lived there all your life. Even when you married, you lived there."

"Tom wanted it."

"I'm sure he did. Still, you lived there, and when the marriage fell apart, he left and you were alone there again."

"I wasn't alone. My parents were there."

"But you're alone now, and you're still there. Crosslyn Rise is like a companion."

"It's a house," Jessica protested.

But Nina had a point to make. "A house with a presence of its own. When you're there, do you feel alone?"

"No."

"But you should—not that I'm wishing loneliness on you, but man wasn't put on earth to live in solitude."

"I'm with people all day. I like being alone at night."

"Do you?" she asked, arching a delicately shaped brow. "I don't. But then, my place isn't steeped in the kind of memories that Crosslyn Rise is. If I were to come home and be enveloped by a world of memories, I probably wouldn't feel alone, either." She stopped talking, poked at the lobster with her fork for a distracted minute, then looked up at Jessica. "Once Crosslyn Rise is no longer yours in the way that it's always been, you may need something more."

Jessica shot her a despairing look. "Nothing like the encouragement of a friend."

"But it *is* encouragement. The change will be good for you. More so than any other person I know, you've had a sameness to your life. Coming out from the shadow of Crosslyn Rise will be exciting."

The image of the shadow stuck in Jessica's mind. The more she mulled it over, the more she realized that it wasn't totally bizarre. "Do you think I hide behind the Rise?" It was a timid question, offered to a friend with the demand for an honest answer.

Nina gave it as she saw it. "To some extent. Where your work is concerned, you've been as outgoing as anyone else. Where your personal life is concerned, you've fallen back on the Rise, just because it's always been there. But you can stand on your own in any context, Jessica. If you don't know that now, you will soon enough."

Soon enough wasn't as soon as Jessica wanted. At least, that was what she was thinking the following Sunday morning as she dressed to spend the day driving north with Carter. He'd called her the morning before to ask if eight was too early to come. It wasn't; she was an early riser. Her mind was freshest during those first postdawn hours. She did some of her most productive work then.

She didn't feel particularly productive on Sunday morning, though. Nor, after mixing, matching and discarding four different outfits did she feel particularly fresh. She couldn't decide what to wear, because the occasion was strange. She and Carter certainly weren't going on a date. This was business. Still, he'd mentioned stopping for something to eat, maybe even shopping, and those weren't strictly business ventures. A business suit was too formal, jeans too casual, and she didn't want to wear a teaching ensemble, because she was *tired* of wearing teaching ensembles.

At length, she decided on a pair of gabardine slacks and a sweater she'd bought in the Square that winter. The sweater was the height of style, the saleswoman had told her, but Jessica had bought it because it was slouchy and comfortable. For the first time, she was glad it was stylish, too. She was also glad it was a pale gray tweed, not so much because it went with her eyes but because it went with the slacks, which, being black, were more sophisticated than some of her other things.

For a time, she distracted herself wondering why she wanted to look sophisticated. She should look like herself, she decided, which was more down-to-earth than sophisticated. But that didn't stop her from matching the outfit up with shiny black flats, from dusting the creases of her eyelids with mocha shadow, from brushing her hair until it shone and then coiling it into a neat twist at the nape of her neck.

She was a bundle of nerves by the time Carter arrived, and the situation wasn't helped by his appearance. He looked wonderful—newly showered and shaved, dressed in a burgundy sweater and light gray corduroy pants.

Taking her heavy jacket from her, he stowed it in the trunk of the car with his own. He held the door while she slipped into the passenger's seat, then circled the car and slid behind the wheel.

"I should warn you," Jessica said when he started the car, "that I'm a terrible passenger. If you have any intention of speeding, you'll have a basket case on your hands."

"Me? Speed?"

Without looking at him, she sensed his grin. "I can remember a certain squealing of tires."

"Years and years ago, and if it'll put your mind at ease, the last accident I had was when I was nineteen," Carter answered with good humor, and promptly stepped on the gas. He didn't step on it far, only enough to maintain the speed limit once they'd reached the highway, and not once did he feel he was holding back. Sure, there were times when he was alone in the car and got carried away by the power of the engine, but he wasn't a reckless driver. He certainly didn't vent his anger on the road as he used to do.

But then, he didn't feel the kind of anger at the world that he used to feel. He rarely felt anger at all—frustration, perhaps, when a project that he wanted didn't come through, or when one that did wasn't going right, or when one of the people under him messed up, or when a client was being difficult—but not anger. And he wasn't feeling any of those things at the moment. He'd been looking forward to this day. He was feeling lighthearted and refreshed, almost as though the whole world was open to him just then.

He took his eyes from the road long enough to glance at Jessica. Her image was already imprinted on his mind, put there the instant she'd opened her front door, but he wanted a moment of renewed pleasure.

She looked incredibly good, he thought, and it wasn't simply a matter of having improved with age. He'd noted that improvement on the two other occasions when he'd seen her, but seeing her today took it one step further. She was really pretty—adorable, he wanted to say, because the small, round glasses sitting on her nose had that effect on her straight features, but her outfit was a little too serious to be called adorable. He liked the outfit. It was subtle but stylish, and seemed perfectly suited to who she was. He was pleased to have her in the car with him. She added the class that he never quite believed he'd acquired.

"Comfortable?" he asked.

She darted him a quick glance. "Uh-huh."

He let that go for several minutes, then asked, "How are exams going?"

"Pretty well," she said on an up note.

"You sound surprised."

"I never know what to expect. There have been years when it's been one administrative foul-up after another—exams aren't printed on time, or they're delivered to the wrong place, that kind of thing."

"At Harvard?" he teased.

She took his teasing with a lopsided smile. "At Harvard. This year, the Crimson has done itself proud."

"I'm glad of that for your sake."

"So am I," she said with a light laugh, then sobered. "Of course, now the rush begins to get things graded and recorded. Graduation isn't far off. The paperwork has to be completed well before then."

"Do you go to graduation?"

"Uh-huh."

"Must be...uplifting."

Her laugh was more of a chuckle this time, and a facetious one at that. Carter took pleasure in the sound. It said that she didn't take herself or her position too seriously, which was something he needed to know, given all the years he'd assumed she was stuck-up. She didn't seem that way, now. More, she didn't seem conscious of any social difference between them. He was convinced that the more he was with her, architect to client, the less she'd think back on the past, and that was what he wanted.

He wanted even more, though. Try as he might, he couldn't forget the time he'd kissed her. It had been an impulsive moment, but it had stuck in his mind, popping up to taunt him when he least expected it.

Jessica was, he decided during one of those times, the rosebud that hadn't quite bloomed. Having been married, she'd certainly been touched, but Carter would put money on the fact that her husband hadn't lit any fires in her. Her mouth was virginal. So was her body, the way she held it, not frightened so much as unsure, almost naive.

Carter had never been a despoiler of virgins. Even in his wildest days, he'd preferred women who knew the score. Tears over blood-stained sheets or unwanted pregnancies or imagined promises weren't his style. So he'd gone with an increasingly savvy woman—exactly the kind who now left him cold.

Kissing Jessica, albeit briefly, hadn't left him cold. He'd felt warm all over, then later, when he'd had time to remember the details of that kiss, tight all over. It amazed him still, it really did. That Jessica Crosslyn, snotty little prude that she'd been, should turn him on was mind-boggling.

But she did turn him on. Even now, with his attention on driving and the gearshift and a console between them, he was deeply aware of her— of the demure way she crossed her legs and the way that caused her slacks to outline shapely thighs, of the neat way her hands lay in her lap, fingers slender and feminine, of the loose way her sweater fell, leaving an alarmingly seductive hint of her breasts beneath. Even her hair, knotted with such polish, seemed a parody of restraint. So many things about her spoke of a promise beneath the facade. And she seemed totally unaware of it.

Maybe it was his imagination. Maybe the sexy things he was seeing were simply things that had changed in her, and it was his lecherous mind that was defining them as sexy. He saw women often, but it had been a while since he'd slept with one. Maybe he was just horny.

If that was true, of course, he could have remedied the situation through tried and true outlets. But he wasn't interested in those outlets. He wasn't running for any outlet at all. There was a sweetness to the arousal Jessica caused; there was something different and special about the tightness in his groin. He wasn't exactly sure where it would take him, but he wasn't willing it away just yet.

"You got a vote of confidence from a friend of mine," Jessica told him as they safely sped north. "She said she'd seen a project you did in Portsmouth."

"Harborside? I was thinking we'd hit that last, on the way home."

"She was impressed with it."

He shrugged. "It's okay, but it's not my favorite."

"What is?"

"Cadillac Cove. I hate the name, but the complex is special."

"Who decides on the name?"

"The developer. I just do the designs."

Jessica had been wondering about that. "Just the designs? Is your job done when the blueprints are complete?"

"Sometimes yes, sometimes no. It depends on the client. Some pay for the blueprints and do everything else on their own. Others pay me to serve as an advisor, in which case I'm involved during the actual building. I like it that way—" he speared her with a cautioning look "—and it has nothing to do with money. Moneywise, my time's better spent working at a drafting table. But there's satisfaction in being at the site. There's satisfaction seeing a concept take form. And there's peace of mind knowing that I'm available if something goes wrong."

"Do things go wrong often? I've heard some nightmarish stories. Are they true?"

"Sometimes." He curved his long fingers more comfortably around the wheel. "Y'see, there's a basic problem with architectural degrees. They fail to require internships in construction. Most architects and would-be architects see themselves as a step above. They're the brains behind the construction job, so they think, but they're wrong. They may be the inspiration, and the brains behind the overall plan, but the workmen themselves, the guys with the hammers and nails, are the ones with the know-how. The average architect doesn't have any idea how to build a house. So, sometimes the average architect draws things into a blueprint that can't possibly be built. Forget things that don't look good. I'm talking about sheer physical impossibilities."

A bell was ringing in Jessica's mind. "Didn't Gordon say you had hands-on building experience?"

"I spent my summers during college working on construction."

"You knew all along you wanted to be an architect?"

"No." He smirked. "I knew I needed money to live on, and construction jobs paid well." The smirk faded. "But that was how I first became interested in architecture. Blueprints intrigued me. The overall designs intrigued me. The guys who stood there in their spiffy suits, wearing hardhats, intrigued me." He chuckled. "So did the luxury cars they drove. And they all drive them. Porsches, Mercedes sportsters, BMWs—this Supra is modest compared to my colleagues' cars."

"So why don't you have a Porsche?"

"I was asking myself that same question the other day when my partner showed me his new one."

"What's the answer?"

"Money. They're damned expensive."

"You're doing as well as your partner."

He shrugged. "Maybe I don't trust myself not to scratch it up. Or it could be stolen. I don't have a secured garage space. I park in a narrow alley behind my building." He pursed his lips and thought for a minute before finally saying in a quieter voice, "I think I'm afraid that if I buy a Porsche, I'll believe that I've made it, and that's not true. I still have a ways to go."

Jessica was reminded of Nina, who defined happiness as a healthy bank account. Instinctively she knew that wasn't the case with Carter. He wasn't talking about making it economically, but professionally.

Maybe even personally. But that was a guess. She didn't know anything of his hopes and dreams.

On that thought, she lapsed into silence. Though she was curious, she didn't have the courage to suddenly start asking him about hopes and dreams, so she gave herself up to the smooth motion of the car and the blur of the passing landscape. The silence was comfortable, and surprising in that Jessica had always associated silence with solitude. Usually when she was with a man in a nonacademic setting, she felt impelled to talk, and since she wasn't the best conversationalist in the world, she wound up feeling awkward and inadequate.

She didn't feel that way now. The miles that passed beneath the wheels of the car seemed purpose enough. Moreover, if Carter wanted to talk, she knew he would. He wasn't the shy type—which was really funny, the more she thought of it. She'd always gravitated toward the shy type, because with the shy type she felt less shy herself. But in some ways it was easier being with Carter, because at any given time she knew where she stood.

At that moment in time, she knew that he was as comfortable with the silence as she was. His large hands were relaxed on the wheel, his legs sprawled as much as the car would allow. His jaw—square, she noted, like his chin—was set easily, as were his shoulders. He made no effort to speak, other than to point out something about a sign or a building they passed that had a story behind it, but when the tale was told, he was content to grow quiet again.

They drove straight for nearly four hours—with Carter's occasional apology for the lengthy drive, and a single rest stop—to arrive shortly before noon at Bar Harbor.

The drive was worth it. "I'm impressed," Jessica said sincerely when Carter had finished showing her around Cadillac Cove. Contrary to Crosslyn Rise, the housing was all oceanfront condominiums, grouped in comfortable clusters that simultaneously managed to hug the shore and echo the grace of nearby Cadillac Mountain. "Is it fully sold?"

He nodded. "Not all of the units are occupied year-round. This far north, they wouldn't necessarily be. A lot of them are owned on a time-sharing plan, and I think one or two are up for resale, but it's been a profitable venture for the developer."

"And for you."

"I was paid for my services as an architect, and I've cashed in on the praise that the complex has received, but I didn't have a financial stake in the project the way I might with Crosslyn Rise."

"Has Gordon talked with you more about that?"

"No. How about you?"

She shook her head. "I think he's starting to put feelers out, but he doesn't want to line up investors until we give him something concrete to work with."

Carter liked the "we" sound. "Does he work with a list of regular investors?"

"I don't really know." Something on his face made her say, "Why?"

"Because I know of a fellow who may be interested. His name's Gideon Lowe. I worked with him two years ago on a project in the Berkshires, and we've kept in touch. He's an honest guy, one of the best builders around, and whether or not he serves as the contractor for Crosslyn Rise, he may want to invest in it. He's been looking for something sound. Crosslyn Rise is sound."

"So you say."

"So I *know*. Hey, I wouldn't be investing my own money in it if it weren't." Without skipping a beat, he said, "I'm starved. Want to get something to eat?"

It was a minute before she made the transition from business to pleasure, and it was just as lucky she didn't have time to think about it. The less she thought, the less nervous she was. "Uh...sure."

He took her hand. "Come on. There's a place not far from here that has the best chowder on the coast."

Chowder sounded fine to Jessica, who couldn't deny the slight chill of the ocean air. Her jacket helped, as did his hand. It encircled hers in a grip that was firm and wonderfully warm.

The chowder was as good as he'd boasted it would be, though Jessica knew that some of its appeal, at least, came from the pier-front setting and the company. Along with the chowder, they polished off spinach salads and a small loaf of homemade wheat bread. Then they headed back to the car and made for the next stop on Carter's list.

Five stops—three for business, two for pleasure—and four hours later, they reached Harborside. As he'd done at each of the other projects they'd seen, Carter showed her around, giving her a brief history of the setting and how it had come to be developed, plus mention of his feelings about the experience. And as he'd done at each of the other projects, he stopped at the end to await her judgment.

"It's interesting," she said this time. "The concept—converting a mill into condominiums—limits things a little, but you've stretched those limits with the atrium. I love the atrium."

Carter felt as though he were coming to know her through her facial expressions alone, and her facial expression now, serious and somewhat analytical, told him that while she might admire the atrium, she certainly didn't love it. "It's okay, Jessica," he teased. He felt confident enough, based on her earlier reactions, to say, "You can be blunt."

She kept her eyes on the building, which was across the street from where they were standing. "I am being blunt. Given what you had to start with, this is really quite remarkable."

"Remarkable as in wildly exciting and dramatic?"

"Uh, not dramatic. Impressive."

"But you wouldn't want to live here."

"I didn't say that."

"Would you?"

Looking up, she caught the mischievous sparkle in his eye. It sparkled right through her in a way that something mischievous shouldn't have sparkled, but she didn't look away. She didn't want him to know how wonderfully warm he was making her feel by standing so close. "I think," she conceded a bit wryly, "that I'd rather live at Cadillac Cove."

"Or Riverside," he added, starting to grin in his own pleasure at the delightfully feminine flush on her cheeks. "Or the Sands."

"Or Walker Place," she tacked on, finishing the list of the places they'd visited. "Okay, this is my least favorite. But it's still good."

"Does that mean I have the job?"

Her brows flexed in an indulgent frown that came and went. "Of course, you have the job. Why do you ask?"

"Wasn't that the point of this trip—to see if you like my work?"

In truth, Jessica had forgotten that point, which surprised her, and in the midst of that surprise, she realized two things. First, she had already come to think of Carter as the architect of record. And second, she was enjoying herself and had been doing so from the time she'd first sat back in his car and decided to trust his driving. Somewhere, there, she'd forgotten to remember what a hell-raiser he'd been once. She was thinking of him in terms of the present, and liking him. Did she like his work? "I like your work just fine."

His handsome mouth twitched in gentle amusement. "You could say it with a little enthusiasm."

Bewitched by that mouth and its small, subtle movements, she did as he asked. "I like your work just fine!"

"Really?"

"Really!"

The twitch at the corner of his mouth became a tentative grin. "Do you think I could do something good for Crosslyn Rise?"

"I think you could do something great for Crosslyn Rise!"

"You're not just saying that for old times' sake?"

Gazing up at him, she let out a laugh that was as easy as it was spontaneous. "If it were a matter of old times' sake, I'd have fired you long ago."

Behind the look in her eye, the sound of her laugh and the softness of her voice, Carter could have sworn he detected something akin to affection. Deeply touched by that thought, he took her chin in his hand. His fingers lightly caressed her skin, while his eyes searched hers for further sign of emotion. And he saw it. It was there. Yes, she liked him, and that made him feel even more victorious than when she'd said she liked his work. Unable to help himself, he moved his thumb over her mouth. When her lips parted, he ducked his head and replaced his thumb with his mouth.

His kiss was whisper light, one touch, then another, and Jessica couldn't have possibly stopped it. It felt too good, too real and far sweeter even than those heady kisses she'd dreamed about. But her body began to tremble—she didn't know whether in memory of the dream or in response to his kiss—and she was frightened.

"No," she whispered against his mouth. Her hands came up to grasp his jacket. "Please, Carter, no."

Lifting his head, Carter saw her fear. His body was telling him to kiss her again and deeper; his mind told him that he could do it and she'd capitulate. But his heart wasn't ready to push.

"I won't hurt you," he said softly.

"I know." Though her hands clutched his jacket, her eyes avoided his. "But I...don't want this."

I could make you want it, Carter thought, but he didn't say it, because it was typical of something the old Carter would say, and the last thing he wanted to do was to remind her of that. "Okay," he said softly, and took a step back, but only after he'd brushed his thumb over her cheek. Half turning from her, he took a deep breath, dug his fists into the pockets of his jacket and pursed his lips toward the mill that he'd redesigned. After a minute, when he'd regained control over his baser instincts, he sent her a sidelong glance.

"You like my work, and I like that. So a celebration's in order. What say we head back and have dinner at the Pagoda. Do you like Chinese food?"

Not trusting her voice, Jessica nodded.

"Want to try it?" he asked.

She nodded again.

Not daring to touch her, he chucked his chin in the direction of the car. "Shall we?"

To nod again would have seemed foolish even to her. So, tucking her hands into her pockets, she turned and headed for the car. By rights, she told herself, she ought to have pleaded the need to work and asked Carter to drive her home. She didn't for three reasons.

First, work could wait.

Second, she was hungry.

And third, she wasn't ready to have the day end.

6

There was a fourth reason why Jessica agreed to have dinner with Carter. She wanted to show him that she could recover from his kiss, or was it herself that she wanted to show? It didn't matter, she supposed, because the end result was the same. She couldn't figure out why Carter had kissed her again, unless he'd seen in her eyes that she'd wanted him to, which she had. Since it wasn't wise for her to reinforce that impression, she had to carry on as though the kiss didn't matter.

It was easier said than done. Not only did the Pagoda have superb Chinese food, but it was elegantly served in a setting where the chairs were high backed and romantic, the drinks were fruity and potent, and the lights were low. None of that was conducive to remembering that she was there on business, that Carter's kisses most surely stemmed from either professional elation or personal arrogance, and that she didn't want or need anything from him but spectacular designs for Crosslyn Rise.

The atmosphere had *date* written all over it, and nothing Carter did dispelled that notion. He was a relaxed conversationalist, willing to talk about anything, from work to a television documentary they'd both seen, to the upcoming gubernatorial election. He drew her out in ways that she hadn't expected, got her thinking and talking about things she'd normally have felt beyond her ken. If she had stopped to remember where he'd come from, she'd have been amazed at the breadth and depth of his knowledge. But she didn't stop, because the man that he was obliterated images of the past. The man that he was held dominance over most everything, including, increasingly, her wariness of him as a man.

So her defenses were down by the time they returned to Crosslyn Rise. Darkness had fallen, lending an unreality to the scene, and while the drink had made her mellow, Carter had her intoxicated. That, added to her enjoyment of the evening, of the entire day, was why she gave no resistance when he slipped an arm around her as he walked her to the door. There, under the glow of the antique lamps, he took her chin again and tipped up her face.

"It's been a nice day," he told her in a voice that was low and male.

"I'm glad you agreed to come with me, and not only to see the real estate. I've enjoyed the company."

She wanted to believe him enough to indulge in the fantasy for a few last minutes. "It has been nice," she agreed with a shy smile, feeling as though she could easily drown in the depths of his charcoal-brown eyes and be happy.

"The real estate? Or the company?"

"Both," was her soft answer.

He lowered his head and kissed her, touching her lips, caressing them for an instant before lifting his head again. "Was that as nice?"

It was a minute before she opened her eyes. "Mmm."

"I'd like to do it again."

"You thought it was nice, too?"

"If I didn't, I wouldn't want to do it again," he said with the kind of logic that no mind could resist, particularly one that was floating as lightly as Jessica's. "Okay?"

She nodded, and when he lowered his head this time, her lips were softer, more pliant than before. He explored their curves, opening them by small degrees until he could run his tongue along the inside. When she gasped, he drew back.

"It's all right," he whispered. He slid his arms around her, fitting her body to his. "I won't hurt you," he said when he felt the fine tremors that shook her. "Flow with it, Jessica. Let me try again."

That was just what he did, caressing innocently at first, deepening the kiss by stages until his tongue was playing at will along the inside of her mouth. She tasted fruity sweet, reminiscent of the drinks they'd had, and twice as heady. When his arms contracted to draw her even closer, he wasn't thinking as much about her trembling body as his own. He needed to feel the pressure of her breasts, of her belly and thighs, needed to feel all those feminine things against his hard, male body.

Jessica clung to his shoulders, overwhelmed by the fire he'd started within her. It was like her dream, but so much more real, with heat rushing through her veins, licking at nerve ends, settling in ultrasensitive spots. When Carter crushed her closer, then moved her body against his, she didn't protest, because she needed the friction, too. His hardness was a foil for her softness, a salve for the ache inside her.

But the salve was only good for a minute, and when the ache increased, she remembered her dream again. She'd had a similar ache in the dream—until her mind had sparked what was necessary to bring her release.

For a horrid split second, she feared that would happen again. Then the split second passed, and she struggled to regain control of herself.

"Carter," she protested, dragging her mouth from his. Her palms went flat against his shoulders and pushed.

"It's okay," he said unevenly. "I won't hurt you."

"We have to stop."

It was another minute before his dark eyes focused. "Why? I don't understand."

Freeing herself completely, Jessica moved to the front door. She grasped the doorknob and leaned against the wood, taking the support from Crosslyn Rise that she'd taken from Carter moments before. "I'm not like that."

"Like what?"

"Easy."

Carter was having trouble thinking clearly. Either the throbbing of his body was interfering with his brain, or she was talking nonsense. "No one said you were easy. I was just kissing you."

"But it's not the first time. And you wanted more."

"Didn't you?" he blurted out before he could stop himself. And then he wasn't sorry, because the ache in his groin persisted, making him want to lash out at its cause.

Her eyes shot to his. "No. I don't sleep around."

"You wanted more. You were trembling for it. Be honest, Jessica. It won't kill you to admit it."

"It's not true."

"In a pig's eye," he muttered, and took a step back. Tipping his head the slightest bit, he studied her through narrowed lids. "What is it about me that you find so frightening? The fact that I'm the guy who made fun of you when we were kids, or the fact that I'm a guy, period."

"You don't frighten me."

"I can see it. I can see it in your eyes."

"Then you see wrong. I just don't want to go to bed with you. That's all."

"Why not?"

"Because."

"Because why? Come on, Jessica. You owe me an explanation. You've been leading me a merry chase all day, being just that little bit distant but closer than ever before. You've spent the better part of the day being a consummate tease—"

"I have not! I've just been me! I thought we were having a nice time. If I'd known there was a price to pay for that—" she fumbled in her purse for her keys "—I'd have been careful not to have enjoyed myself as much. Is sex part of your professional fee?"

Carter ran a hand through his hair, then dropped it to the tight muscles at the back of his neck. With the fading of desire came greater control, and with greater control, clearer thought. They were on the old, familiar road to name-calling, he knew, and that wouldn't accomplish a thing.

He held up a hand to signal a truce, then set about explaining it. In a very quiet voice, he said, "Let's get one thing straight. I want you because you turn me on."

"That's—"

"Shh. Let me finish." When she remained silent, he said even more slowly, "You turn me on. No strings attached. No price I expect you to pay for lunch or dinner. You…just…turn me on. I didn't expect it, and I don't want it, because you *are* a client and I don't get involved with clients. It's not the way I work. Sex has nothing to do with payments of any kind. It has to do with two people liking each other, then respecting each other, then being attracted to each other. It has to do with two people being close, but needing to be even closer. It has to do with two people wanting to know each other in ways that other people don't." He paused to take a breath. "That was what I wanted just now. It was what I've been wanting all day."

Jessica didn't know what to answer. If she'd been madly in love with a man, she couldn't have hoped for a sweeter explanation. But she wasn't madly in love with Carter, which had to be why she was having trouble believing in the sincerity of his desire.

"As for sleeping around," Carter went on in that same quiet voice, "it means having indiscriminate sex with lots of different people. I'm not involved with anyone else right now. I haven't been intimately involved with anyone for a while. And I feel like I know you better than I've known any woman in years. So if I took you to bed, I wouldn't be sleeping around. And neither would you, unless you've been with others—"

She shook her head so vigorously that he dropped that particular line of inquiry. He'd known it wasn't true anyway. "Have you been with anyone since your husband?"

She shook her head more slowly this time.

"Before him?"

She shook her head a third time.

"Was it unpleasant with him?" Carter asked, but he knew that he'd made a mistake the minute the words were out. Jessica bowed her head and concentrated on fitting the key to the lock. "Don't go," he said quickly, but she opened the door and stepped inside.

"I can't talk about this," she murmured.

He took a step forward. "Then we'll talk about something else."

"No. I have to go."

"Talk of sex doesn't have to make you uncomfortable."

"It does. It's not something two strangers discuss."

"We're not strangers."

She looked up at him. "We are in some ways. You're more experienced than me. You won't be able to understand what I feel."

"Try me, and we'll see."

She shook her head, said softly, "I have to go," and slowly closed the door.

For a second before the latch clicked in place, Carter was tempted to resist. But the second passed, and the opportunity was gone. Short of banging the knocker or ringing the bell, he was cut off from her.

It was just as well. She needed time to get used to the idea of wanting him. He could give her that, he supposed.

He gave her nearly an hour, which was how long it took him to drive back to Boston, change clothes and make a pot of coffee. Then he picked up the phone and called her.

Her voice sounded calm and professional. "Hello?"

"Hi, Jessica. It's me. I just wanted to make sure you're okay."

She was silent for a minute. Then she said in the same composed voice, "I'm fine."

"You're not angry, are you?"

"No."

"Good." He paused. "I didn't mean any harm by asking what I did." He tapped a finger on the lip of his coffee cup. "I'm just curious." He looked up at the ceiling. "You're afraid of me. I keep trying to figure out why."

"I'm not afraid of you," came her quiet voice, sounding less confident than before.

"Then why won't you let yourself go when I kiss you?"

"Because I'm not the letting-go type."

"I think you could be. I think you want to be."

"I want to be exactly what I am right now. I'm not unhappy with my life, Carter. I'm doing what I like with people I like. If that wasn't so, I'd have changed things. But I like my life. I really like my life. You seem to think that I'm yearning for something else, but I'm not. I'm perfectly content."

Carter thought she was being a little too emphatic and a little too repetitive. He had the distinct feeling she was making the point to herself as much as to him, which meant that she wasn't as sure of her needs as she claimed, and that suited him just fine.

"You're not content about Crosslyn Rise," he reminded her, then hurried on, "which is another reason I'm calling. I'm going to start making some preliminary sketches, but I'll probably want to come to walk around again. I'd like to take some pictures—of the house, the land, possible building sites, the oceanfront. They're all outside pictures, so you don't have to be there, but I didn't want to go wandering around without your permission."

"You have my permission."

"Great. Why don't I give you a call when I have something to show you?"

"That sounds good." She paused. "Carter?"

He held his breath. "Yes?"

After a brief hesitation, her voice came. This time it sounded neither professional nor insecure, but sincere. "Thanks again for today. It really was nice."

He let out the breath and smiled. "My pleasure. Talk with you soon."

"Uh-huh."

What time Jessica spent at home that week, she spent looking out the window. Or it seemed that way. She made excuses for herself—she was restless reading term papers, she needed exercise, she could use the time to think—but she managed to wander from room to room, window to window, glancing nonchalantly out each one. Her eyes were anything but nonchalant, searching the landscape for Carter on the chance that either she'd missed his car on the driveway or he'd parked out of sight.

She saw no sign of him, which mean that either he'd come while she was in Cambridge or he hadn't come at all.

Nor did he call. She imagined that he might have tried her once or twice while she was out, and for the first time in her life she actually considered buying an answering machine. But that was in a moment of weakness. She didn't like answering machines. And besides, it would be worse to have an answering machine and not receive a message, than to not have one and wonder. Where one could wonder, one had hope.

And that thought confused her, because she wasn't sure why she wanted hope. Carter Malloy was...Carter Malloy. They were involved with each other on a professional basis, but that was all. Yes, she'd enjoyed spending Sunday with him. She'd begun to realize just how far he'd come as a person in the years she'd known him. And she did hope, she supposed, that there might be another Sunday or two like that.

But nothing sexual was ever going to happen between them. He wasn't her type—a perfect example being his failure to call. In Jessica's book, when a man was romantically interested in a woman, he didn't leave her alone for days. He called her, stopped in to see her, left messages at the office. Carter certainly could have done that, but there had been no message from him among the pink slips the department secretary had handed her that week.

He was showing his true colors, she decided. Despite all his sweet talk—sex talk—he wasn't really interested in her, which didn't surprise her in the least. He was a compelling man. Sex appeal oozed from him. She, on the other hand, had no sex appeal at all. Her genes had been generous in certain fields, but sex appeal wasn't one.

So what did Carter want with her? She didn't understand the motive behind his kisses, and the more she tried to, the more frustrated she became. The only thing she could think was that he was having a kind of perverse fun with her, and that hurt. It hurt, because one part of her liked him, respected him personally and professionally and found him sexy as all get out. It would be far easier, she realized, to admire him from a distance, than to let him come close and show her just how unsatisfying she was to a man.

Knowing that the more she brooded, the worse it would be, Jessica kept herself as busy as possible. Rather than wander from window to window at home, by midweek she was spending as much time as possible at school. Work, like Poppycock, had a soothing effect on her, and there was work aplenty to do. When she wasn't grading exams, she was reading term papers or working with one of the two students for whom she was a dissertation advisor. And the work was uplifting—which didn't explain why, when she returned to Crosslyn Rise Friday evening, she felt distinctly let down. She'd never had that experience before. Work had always been a bellwether for her mood. She decided that she was simply tired.

So she slept late on Saturday morning, staying in bed until nine, dallying over breakfast, taking a leisurely shower, though she had nothing but laundry and local errands and more grading to do. She didn't pay any heed to the windows, knowing that Carter wouldn't come on a Saturday. Work was work. He'd be there during the week, preferably when she wasn't around. Which was just as well, as far as she was concerned.

It was therefore purely by accident that, with her arms loaded high with sheets to be laundered, she came down the back steps and caught a glimpse of something shiny and blue out the landing window. Heart thundering, she came to an abrupt halt, stared out at the driveway and swallowed hard.

He'd come. On a Saturday. When she was wearing jeans and a sweatshirt pushed up to the elbows, looking like one of her students playing laundress. But someone had to do the laundry, she thought a bit frantically; the days of having Annie Malloy to help with it were long gone.

Ah, the irony of it, she mused. Then the back bell rang, and she ceased all musings. Panicked, she glanced at her sweatshirt, then at the linens in her arms, then down the stairs toward the door. If she didn't answer it, he'd think she wasn't home.

That would be the best thing.

But she couldn't do it. Tucking the sheets into a haphazard ball, she ran down the stairs, crossed through the back vestibule and opened the door to Carter.

His appearance did nothing to ease her breathlessness. Wearing jeans and a plaid flannel shirt, he looked large and masculine. His clothes were comfortably worn—a far cry from the last time she'd seen him in jeans, when they'd been dirty and torn—and fit his leanly muscled legs like a glove. The shirt was rolled to the elbow, much as her sweatshirt was, only his forearms were sinewy, spattered with dark hair, striped on the inside with the occasional vein. His collar was open, showing off the strength of his neck and shoulders, and from one of those shoulders hung a camera.

"Hi," she said. In an attempt to curb her breathlessness, she put a hand to her chest. "How are you?"

He was just fine, now that he was here. All week he'd debated about when to stop by; he couldn't remember when he'd given as much thought to anything. Except her. She'd been on his mind a lot. Now he knew why. Looking at her, taking in the casual way she was dressed, the oversized pink sweatshirt and the faded blue jeans that clung to slender legs, he felt relieved. Her features, too, did that to him. She was perfectly unadorned—long hair shiny clean and drawn into a high ponytail, skin free of makeup and healthy looking, smile small but bright, glasses sliding down the bridge of her nose—but she looked wonderful. She was a breath of fresh air, he decided, finally putting his finger on one of the things he most liked about her. She was different from the women he'd known. She was natural and unpretentious. She was refreshing.

"I'm real fine," he drawled with a lazy smile. "Just stoppin' in to disturb your Saturday morning." His gaze touched on the bundle she held.

Wrapping both arms around the linens, she hugged them to her. "I, uh, always use Saturdays for this. Usually I'm up earlier. I should have had two washes done by now. I slept late."

"You must have been tired." He searched for shadows under her eyes, but either her glasses hid them, or they just weren't there. Her skin was clear, unmottled by fatigue, a smooth blend of ivory and pink. "It's been a busy week?"

"Very," she said with a sigh and a smile.

"Will you be able to relax this weekend?"

"A little. I still have more work to do, but then there are things like this—" she nodded toward the linens "—and the market and the drugstore, none of which are heavily intellectual tasks. I relax when I do those."

"No time to sit back, put your feet up and vegetate?"

She shook her head. "I'm not good at vegetating."

"I used to be good at it, back in the days when I was raising hell." His mouth took on a self-effacing twist. "Used to drive my mother wild. Whenever the police showed up at the door, she knew she'd find me sprawled out in the back room watching TV." The twist gentled. "I don't have much time for vegetating now, either—" he jabbed his chin toward the camera "—which is why I'm here. I thought I'd do that exploring. I have nothing to think about but Crosslyn Rise, and it's a gorgeous day." He made a quick decision, based on the open look on her face. "Want to come?"

Nothing seemed to be helping Jessica's breathlessness or the incessant fluttering of her insides. Suddenly she didn't seem to be able to make a decision, either. "I don't know...there's this laundry to do...and vacuuming." She could feel the warm air coming in past him, and it beckoned. "I ought to dust...and you'll probably be able to think more creatively if I'm not around."

"I'd like the company. And I won't talk if the creative mode hits. Come on. Just for a little while. It's too special a day to miss."

His eyes weren't as much charcoal brown today, she decided, as milk chocolatey, and their lashes seemed absurdly thick. Had she never noticed that before?

"Uh, I have so much to do," she argued, but meekly.

"Tell you what," Carter said. "I'll start out and follow the same route we took last time. You take care of what you have to, then join me."

That sounded like a fair compromise to Jessica. If he was willing to be flexible, she couldn't exactly remain rigid. Besides, Saturday or not, he was working on her project. Maybe he wanted to bounce ideas off her. "I may be a little while," she cautioned.

"No sweat. I'll be here longer than that. Take your time." With a wink, he set off.

The wink set her back a good ten minutes. Several of those were spent with her back against the wall by the door, trying to catch up with her racing pulse. Several more were spent wandering through the kitchen into the den, before she realized that she was supposed to be headed for the laundry, which was in the basement. The rest were spent getting the washer settings right, normally a simple task, now complicated by a sorely distracted mind.

Never in her life had she done the vacuuming as quickly as she did then. It was nervous energy, she told herself, and that reasoning held on through a dusting job that probably stirred more than it gathered. Fortunately, the rooms in question were only those few she used on a regular basis, which meant that she was done in no time. The bed linens were in the dryer and her personal things in the wash when she laced on a pair of sneakers, grabbed a half-filled bag of bread and slipped out the door.

Carter was sitting cross-legged on the warm grass by the duck pond. Though for all intents and purposes he was concentrating on the antics of the ducks, he'd kept a lookout for her arrival. The sight of her brought the warm feeling it always did, plus something akin to excitement— which was amusing, since in the old days he'd have labeled her the least exciting person in the world. But that was in the old days, at a time in his life when he'd appreciated precious little, certainly nothing subtle and mature, which were the ways in which he found Jessica exciting. He could never have appreciated her intellect, the way she thought through issues, the natural curiosity that had her listening to things he said and asking questions. She was a thoroughly stimulating companion, even in silence—unless she felt threatened. When that happened, she was as dogmatic and closed minded as he'd once thought her to be.

The key, of course, was to keep her from feeling threatened. Most of the time, that was easy, particularly since he felt increasingly protective of her. The times when it was difficult almost always had to do with sex, which was when he was at his least controlled both physically and emotionally.

But he'd try. He'd try, because the prize was worth it.

"Watch out for the muck!" he called, and watched her give wide berth to a spot of ground that hadn't quite dried out from the spring thaw. His eyes followed her as she approached, one hand tucked into the pocket of her jeans, her ponytail swaying gently with her step. "That was fast."

"Don't you know it," she said in a way that stunned him, then pleased him in the next breath. She'd drawled the words. Yes, there was self-mockery in them, but there was playfulness, too. Opening the bag of bread, she began breaking off chunks and tossing them toward the

ducks, who quacked their appreciation. "I hate cleaning. I do it duti-
fully. But I hate it."

"You should hire someone—and don't tell me you can't afford it.
That kind of help is cheap."

But she nixed the idea with the scrunch of her nose, which served
the double purpose of hitching her glasses up. "There's really not
enough to do." She tossed out another handful of bread and watched
the ducks try to outwaddle each other to where it landed. "I hire a crew
twice a year to do the parts of the house that I don't use, but there's no
good reason why I can't do the rest myself." She turned to stare at him
hard, but her voice was too gentle to be accusing. "Unless someone
stands at my door tempting me with the best spring weather that's come
along so far." She looked around, took a deep breath, didn't pause to
wonder whether the exhilaration she felt was from the air or not. She
was tired of wondering about things like that. She was too analytical.
For once, she wanted to—what was it he'd said—go with the flow.
"So," she said, reaching for more bread, "are you being inspired?"

"Here? Always. It's a beautiful spot." Tossing several feathers out
of the way, he patted the grass by his side.

She sat down and shot a look at the camera that lay in his lap. It
wasn't one of the instant models, but the real thing. "Have you used
it?"

He nodded. "I've taken pictures of the house, the front lawn and the
beach. Not here, yet. I'm just sitting."

She aimed a handful of bread crumbs toward the ducks. "Are you a
good photographer?"

"I'm competent. I get the shots I need, but they're practical, rather
than artistic." He took the camera up, made several shifts in the settings,
raised it to his eye and aimed it at her.

She held up a hand to block the shot and turned her head away. "I
hate having my picture taken even more than I hate cleaning!"

"Why?"

"I don't like being focused on." She dared a glance at him, relaxing
once she saw that he'd put the camera back down.

"Focused on" could be interpreted both broadly and narrowly. Carter
had the feeling that both applied in Jessica's case. "Why not?" he
asked, bemused.

"Because it's embarrassing. I'm not photogenic."

"I don't believe that."

"It's true. The camera exaggerates every flaw. I have plenty without
the exaggeration."

Looking at her, with the sun glancing off her hair and a blush of self-consciousness on her cheeks, Carter could only think of how pretty she was. "What flaws do you have?"

"Come on, Carter—"

"Tell me." The quacking of the ducks seemed to second his command.

Sure that he was ridiculing her, she studied his eyes. She saw no teasing there, though, only challenge, and where Carter challenged her, she was conditioned to respond. "I'm plain. Totally and utterly plain. My face is too thin, my nose is too small, and my eyes are boring."

He stared at her. "Boring? Are you kidding? And there's nothing wrong with the shape of your face or your nose. Do you have any idea what a pleasure it is for me to look at you after having to look at other women all week?" At her blank look, he said, "You've grown up well, Jessica. You may have felt plain as a child, but you're not a child anymore, and what you think of as plainness is straightforward, refreshing good looks."

Her blankness had yielded to incredulity. "Why do you say things like that?"

"Because they're true!"

"I don't believe it for a minute," she said. It seemed the only way to cope with the awkwardness she felt. Rising to her feet, she tossed the last of the bread from the bag and set off. "You're just trying to butter me up so I'll like your designs." Wadding up the bag, she stuffed it into a pocket.

Carter was after her in a minute, gently catching her ponytail to draw her up short as he overtook her. His body was a solid wall before her, his hand in her hair a smaller but no less impenetrable wall behind. Against her temple, his breath was a warm sough of emotion. "If I wanted to butter you up, I'd just do my work and mind my own business about the rest. But I can't do it—any more than I can sit back and listen to you denigrate yourself. I'm highly attracted to you. Why can't you believe that?"

Struck as always by his closeness, Jessica's breathing had quickened. Her eyes were lowered, focusing on his shirt, and though there was nothing particularly sensual about the plaid, there was something decidedly so about the faintly musky scent of his skin.

"I'm not the kind of women men find highly attractive," she explained in a small voice.

"Is that another gem of wisdom from your ex-husband?"

"No. It's something I've deduced after thirty-three years of observation. I don't turn heads. I never have and never will."

"The women who turn heads—the sharp lookers, the fashion plates—

aren't the women men want. Call it macho, but they want softer women. You're a softer woman. And I want you.''

"But you have your choice of the best women in the city.''

"And I choose you. Doesn't that tell you anything?''

"It tells me that you're going through a phase. Let's call it—'' she raised her eyes to his to make her point ''—the give-the-little-lady-a-thrill-for-old-times'-sake phase.''

Dangerously close to anger, Carter drew her closer until she was flush against him. "That's insulting, Jessica.'' His dark eyes blazed into hers. "Can't you give me a little credit for honesty? Have I ever lied to you?'' When she didn't answer, he did it for her. "No. I may have said cruel things, or downright wrong things, but they were the things I was honestly feeling at the time. We've already established that I was a bastard. But at least give me credit for honesty.''

His blood was pulsing more thickly as her curves imprinted themselves on his body. "I've been honest with words. And I've been honest with this.'' He captured her mouth before she could open hers to protest, and he kissed her with an ardor that could have been from hunger or anger.

Jessica didn't know which. All she knew was that her defenses fell in less time than ever before, that she couldn't have kept her mouth stiff if she'd tried, that she should have been shocked when his tongue surged into her mouth, but the only source of shock was her own enjoyment.

That thought, though, came a moment too soon, because she was in for another small shock. Well before she was ready, he ended the kiss. She hadn't even begun to gather her wits when he took her hand from its stranglehold of his shirt and lowered it to the straining fly of his jeans.

"No way,'' he said hoarsely, "no way could I fake that.'' Keeping his hand over hers, he molded her fingers to his shape, pressing her palm flat, manipulating it in a rubbing motion. A low sound slipped from his throat as he pressed his lips to her neck.

Jessica was stunned by the extent of his arousal, then stunned again when the heat of it seemed to increase. Her breathing was short and scattered, but Carter's was worse, and a fine quaking simmered in the muscles of his arms and legs.

No, he couldn't fake what she felt, and the knowledge was heady. It made her feel soft and feminine and eager to know more of the strength beneath her hand. Without conscious thought, she began to stroke him. Her eyes closed. Her head tipped to give his mouth access to her throat. Her free arm stole to the bunched muscles of his back. And when she became aware of a restlessness between her legs, she arched toward him.

Carter made a low, guttural sound. Wrenching her hand from him, he wrapped her in his arms and crushed her close, then closer still. "Don't move," he warned in a voice that was more sand than substance. "Don't move. Give me a minute. A minute."

The trembling went on as he held her tight, but Jessica wasn't sure how much of it was her own. Weak-kneed and shaky, she was grateful that his convulsive hold was keeping her upright. Without it, she'd surely have slid down to the grass and begged him to take her there, which was precisely what the tight knot at the pit of her stomach demanded.

That was probably the biggest shock of all. The dream she could reason away. She could attribute it to any number of vague things. But when she was being held in Carter's arms, when she felt every hard line of his body and not only took pleasure in the hardness but hungered to have it deeper inside her, she couldn't lie to herself any longer.

The issue, of course, was what to make of the intense desire she felt for him. The moment would pass now, she knew. Once Carter regained control of his libido, he would set her back, perhaps take her hand and lead her on through the woods. He might talk, ask her what she feared, try to get her to admit to his desire and to her own, but he wouldn't force her into anything she didn't want.

It wasn't that she didn't want sex with Carter, rather that she wasn't ready for it. She'd never been a creature of impulse. It was one thing to "go with the flow" and spurn housekeeping chores in favor of a walk on the woods, quite another to "go with the flow" and expose herself, body and soul, to a man. She'd done that once and been hurt, and though she'd never made vows of chastity, the memory of that hurt kept her shy of sex.

If she was ever to make love with Carter, she had to understand exactly what she was doing and why. She also had to decide whether the risk was worth it.

7

Carter didn't leave right away. Nor did he allow Jessica to leave. He insisted she stay while he took the pictures he needed at the duck pond, then walked her back to the house. She had feared he'd want to talk about what had happened, but either he was as surprised by its power as she, or he sensed she wasn't ready. He said nothing about the kiss, about the way she'd touched him, or about the fact that he'd nearly lost it there and then in front of the ducks.

Instead, he sent her inside to finish her chores while he completed his own outside. Then he drove her to the supermarket and walked up and down the aisles with her, tossing the occasional unusual item into her cart. When they returned to Crosslyn Rise, he made his special tuna salad, replete with diced water chestnuts and red pepper relish.

After lunch, he left.

He called on Monday evening to say that the photos he'd taken had come out well and that he was getting down to some serious sketching.

He called on Thursday evening to say that he was pleased with the progress he was making and would she be free on Sunday afternoon to take a look at what he'd drawn.

She was free, of course. The semester's work was over, exams and papers graded, grades duly recorded—which was wonderful in the sense of freeing her up, lousy in the sense of giving her more time to think. The thinker in her decided that she definitely wanted to see what he'd drawn, but she didn't trust him—or herself—to have a show-and-tell meeting at Crosslyn Rise.

So they arranged to meet at Carter's office, which satisfied Jessica's need on several scores. First, she was curious to see more of him in his professional milieu. Second, even if he kissed her, and even if she responded, the setting was such that nothing could come of it.

She guessed she was curious to see him, period. It had been a long week since the Saturday before, a long week of replaying what had happened, of feeling the excitement again, of imagining an even deeper involvement. Though it still boggled her mind, she had to accept that he did want her. The evidence had been conclusive. She still didn't know *why* he wanted her, and the possibilities were diverse, running from the wildly exciting to the devastating. But that was another reason why the setting suited her purpose. It was safe. She could see him, get to know him better, but she wouldn't have to take a stand on the physical side of the issue.

And then, there was Crosslyn Rise. The part of her that had acclimated itself to the conversion of the Rise was anxious to see what he'd drawn. That part wanted to get going, to decide on an architectural plan, have it formally drawn up and give it to Gordon so that he could enlist his investors. That part of Jessica wanted to act before its counterpart backed out.

Jessica wasn't sure what she'd expected when she took a first look at Carter's drawings, but it certainly wasn't the multicolored spread before her. Yes, there were pencil sketches on various odd pieces of paper, but he'd taken the best of those ideas and converted them into something that could well have been a polished promotion for the place.

"Who drew these?" she asked, slightly awed.

"I did." There were times when he left such drawings to project managers, but he'd wanted to do this himself. When it came to Crosslyn Rise, he was the project manager, and he didn't give a damn whether his partner accused him of ill-using the resources at hand. Crosslyn Rise was his baby from start to finish, even if it meant late nights such as the ones he'd put in this week. They were worth it. Concentrating on his work was better than concentrating on his need.

"But this is art. I never pictured anything like this."

"It's called a presentation," he said dryly. "The idea is to snow the client right off the bat."

"Well, I'm snowed."

"By the presentation, maybe, but do you like what's in it?"

At first glance, she did. At his caveat, she took a closer look, moving one large sheet aside to look at the next.

"I've drawn the main house in cross sections, as I envision it looking once all the work is done," he explained, "and a head-on view of the condo cluster at the duck pond. Since the clusters will all be based on the same concept, a variation on the Georgian theme, I wanted to try out one cluster on you first."

Her eyes were glued to the drawing. "It's incredible."

"Is it what you imagined?"

"No. It looks more Cape-ish than Georgian. But it's real. More modern. Interesting."

He wasn't sure if "interesting" was good or bad, but when he asked, she held up a hand and studied the drawing in silence for several minutes. "Interesting," she repeated, but there was a warmth in the word. Then she smiled. "Nice."

Carter basked in her smile, which was some consolation for the fact that he wanted to hug her but didn't dare. Not only did he sense that she wasn't ready for more hugs, but he feared that if he touched her, office or no, he wouldn't be able to stop this time. As it was, her smile, which was so rare, did dangerous things to him.

He cleared his throat. "Obviously this is rough. But I wanted to convey the general idea." He touched a lean finger to one area, then another. "The roof angle here is what reminds you of a Cape. It can be modified, but it allows for skylights. Today's market loves skylights." His finger shifted. "I've deliberately scaled down the pillars and balconies so that they don't compete with the main house. The main house should set the tone for stateliness. The clusters can echo it, but they ought to be more subtle. I want them to nestle into their surroundings. In some ways the focus of the clusters *is* those surroundings."

Jessica cast a sideways glance at him. He had a long arm propped straight on the drafting table and was close enough to touch, close enough to smell, close enough to want. Ignoring the last and the buzzing that played havoc with her insides, she said, "I think you're hung up on those surroundings."

"Me?" His dark eyes shone with indulgence one moment, vehemence the next. "No way. At least, not enough that it would color my better judgment. And my better judgment tells me that people will buy at Crosslyn Rise for the setting, nearly as much as for the nuts and bolts of what they're getting. Which isn't to say that we can skimp on those nuts and bolts." Again he referred to the drawing, tracing sweeping lines with his finger. "I've angled each of the units differently, partly for interest, partly for privacy. Either you and Gordon—or if you want to wait, the consortium—will have to decide on the size of the units. Personally, I'd hate to do anything less than a three bedroom setup. People usually want more space rather than less."

Jessica hadn't thought that far. "The person to speak with about that might be Nina Stone. She's a broker. She'd have a feel for what people in this area want."

"Do I know Nina Stone?" Carter asked, trying to place the name.

"She knew you," Jessica replied, wondering whether the two of them would hit it off and not sure she liked that idea. "Or rather, she knew *of* you. Your reputation precedes you."

Once he'd left New York, Carter had worked long and hard to establish himself and his name. "That's gratifying."

"Uh-huh. She already has you pegged as a ruggedly masculine individual."

Which wasn't the most professional of assessments, he mused. "You discussed me with her?"

"I mentioned we were working together."

He nodded his understanding, but, to Jessica's selfish delight, had no particular interest in knowing more about Nina. His finger was back on the drawing, this time tapping his rendition of the duck pond. "We may run into a problem with water. The land in this area is wetter than in the others. When we reach the point of having the backers lined up, I'll have a geological specialist take a look."

"Could the problem be serious?"

"Nah. It shouldn't be more than a matter of shifting the clusters to the right or the left, and I want them set back anyway so the ducks won't be disturbed. The main house draws water from its own wells. I'm assuming the condos would do the same, but an expert could tell us more on that, too."

Up to that point, Jessica had been aware of only two problems— coming to terms with the sale of Crosslyn Rise, and dealing with Carter Malloy. Now, mention of a possible water problem brought another to mind. "What if we can't get enough backers?"

Surprised by the question, he shot her a look. Her eyes were wide with concern. "To invest in the project? We'll get enough."

"Will we? You've had more experience in this kind of thing than I have. Is there a chance we'll come up with plans that no one will support?"

"It's not probable."

"But is it possible?"

"Anything's possible. It's possible that the economy will crash at ten past ten tomorrow morning, but it's no more probable that it will happen than that Gordon won't be able to find the backers we need." He paused, sliding his gaze over her face. "You're really worried?"

"I haven't been. I haven't thought about it much at all, but suddenly here you are with exciting drawings, and the project seems very real. I'd hate to go through all this and then have the whole thing fizzle."

Throwing caution to the winds, he did put his arm around her then. "It won't. Trust me. It won't."

The confidence in his voice, even more so than the words, was what did it. That, and the support his body offered. For the first time, she truly felt as though Carter shared the responsibility of Crosslyn Rise with her, and while a week or two before, that thought would have driven her wild, she was comfortable with it now. She'd come a long way.

"I have theater tickets for Thursday night," came Carter's low voice. "Come with me."

Taken totally off guard, she didn't know what to say.

His breath was warm on her hair. "Do you have other plans?"

"No."

"They're for *Cat on a Hot Tin Roof.*"

Tipping her head, she looked up at him. "You got tickets," she breathed in awe, because she'd been trying to get them for weeks without success. But going to the theater with Carter was a *date*.

"Will you come?"

"I don't know," she said a bit helplessly. Everything physical about him lured her, as did, increasingly, everything else about him. He was so good to be with. The problem, as always, lay with her.

"If you won't, I'm giving the tickets back. There's no one else I want to take, and I don't want to go alone."

"That's blackmail," she argued.

"Not blackmail. Just a chance to see the hottest revival of the decade."

"I know, I know," she murmured, weakening. It was easy to do that when someone as strong as Carter was offering support.

"The semester's over. What better way to celebrate?"

"I have to be at school all day Thursday planning for the summer term."

"But the pressure's off. So before it's on again, have a little fun. You deserve it."

She wasn't as concerned with what she deserved as with what going on a date with Carter would mean. It would mean a shift in their relationship, a broadening of it. Going on a date with Carter would mean being with him at night in a crowded theater, perhaps alone before or after. All kinds of things could happen. She wasn't sure she was ready.

Then again, she wasn't sure she could resist.

"Come on, Jessica. I really want to go."

So do I, Jessica thought. Her eyes fell to his mouth. She liked looking at his mouth. "I'd have to meet you there."

"Why can't I pick you up?" he asked, and the corners of that mouth turned down.

"Because I don't know exactly where I'll be."

"You could call me at the office and let me know. It's only a ten-minute drive to Cambridge."

Her eyes met his. "More in traffic. And it's silly for you to go back and forth like that."

"I want to go back and forth." If he was taking her out for the evening, he wanted to do it right. Besides, he didn't like the idea of her traveling alone.

Jessica, though, was used to traveling alone. More than that, she was determined to keep things light and casual. It was the only way she could handle the thought of a date with Carter. "Tell me where to meet you and when. I'll be there."

"Why are you being so stubborn?" he asked. In the next breath, he relented. "Sorry. Six-thirty at the Sweetwater Café."

"I thought *Cat on a Hot Tin Roof* was at the Colonial." She knew very well it was—and what he was trying to do.

His naughty eyes didn't deny it. "The Sweetwater Café is close by. We can get something to eat there before the show." When she looked momentarily skeptical, he said, "You have to eat, Jessica." When still she hesitated, he added, "Indulge me. I'm letting you meet me there, which I don't like. So at least let me feed you first."

Looking up into his dark eyes, she came to an abrupt realization. It was no longer a matter of not being sure. She *couldn't* resist—not when he had an arm draped so protectively across her shoulders, not when he was looking at her so intently, not when she wanted both to go on forever and ever. He made her feel special. Cared for. Feminine. She doubted, at that minute, that she'd have been able to refuse him a thing.

So she agreed. Naturally she had second thoughts, but after a day of suffering through those, she lost patience with herself. Since she'd agreed to go out with Carter, she told herself, she was going, and since she was going, she intended to make the most of it. She had her share of pride, and that pride dictated that she do everything in her power to make sure Carter didn't regret having asked her out.

He didn't regret it so far, at least; he called her each night just to say hello. But talking on the phone or having a business meeting or even driving north on a Sunday was different from going out at night to something that had nothing to do with work. She wanted to look good.

To that end, she arranged to finish up with work by two on Thursday. The first stop she made then was to the boutique where she'd bought the sweater she'd worn to Maine; if stylish had worked once, she figured it would work again. But stylish in that shop was funky, which wasn't her style at all. She was about to give up hope when the owner brought a dress from the back that was perfect. A lime-green sheath of silk that was self-sashed and fell to just above the knee, it was sleeveless and had a high turtleneck that draped her neck in the same graceful way that the rest of the fabric draped her body. The dress was feminine without being frilly. She felt special enough in it not to look at the price tag, and by the time she had to write out a check, she was committed enough to it not to mind the higher-than-normal cost.

Her second stop was at a shoe store, where she picked up a pair of black patent leather heels and a small bag to match.

Her third stop was at Mario's. Mario had been doing her hair—a blunt cut to keep the ends under control—bimonthly for several years, and for the first time she allowed him more freedom. Enhancing her own natural wave with rollers and a heat lamp, he gave her a look that was softer and more stylish than anything she'd ever worn. As the icing on the cake, he caught one side high over her ear with a pearl clip. The look pleased Jessica so much that she left the salon, went to the jewelry store next door and splurged on a pair of pearl earrings to match the clip. Then she returned to her office, where she'd left cosmetics and stockings.

The day had been warm and humid, as late spring days often were, and when Jessica left Harvard, retrieved her car and set off for Boston, dull gray clouds were dotting the sky. She barely noticed. Her thoughts were on the way she looked and the comments she'd drawn from the few of her colleagues she'd happened to pass as she left. They had done double takes, which either said she looked really good, or so different from how she usually looked that they couldn't believe it was her.

She couldn't quite believe it was her. For one thing, the fact that she liked the way she looked was a first. For another, the fact that she was heading for a date with a man like Carter Malloy was incredible. Unable to reconcile either, given that her nerves were jangling with excitement, she half decided that it wasn't her in the car at all, but another woman. That thought brought a silly grin to her face.

The grin faded, but the excitement didn't. It was overshadowing her nervousness by the time she parked in the garage under the Boston Common, and by the time she emerged onto the Common itself and realized that she was at the corner farthest from where she as going, she was feeling too high to mind. Her step was quick, in no way slowed by the unfamiliarity of the new heels.

What gave her pause, though, were the drops of rain that, one by one, in slow succession, began to hit her. They were large and warm. She looked worriedly at the sky, not at all reassured by the ominous cloud overhead or the blue that surrounded it in too distant a way. Furious at herself for not having brought an umbrella, she walked faster. She could beat the rain, she decided, but she wished she'd parked closer.

To her dismay, the drops grew larger, came harder and more often. She broke into a half run, holding her handbag over her head, looking around for shelter. But there was none. Trees were scattered on either side of the paved walks, but they were of the variety whose branches were too high to provide any shelter at all.

For a split second she stopped and looked frantically back at the entrance to the parking garage, but it seemed suddenly distant, separated from her by a million thick raindrops. If she returned there, she'd be farther than ever from the Sweetwater Café—and drenched anyway.

So she ran faster, but within minutes, the rain reached downpour proportions. She was engulfed as much by it as by disbelief. Other people rushed along, trying to protect themselves as she was, but she paid them no heed. All she could think of was the beautiful green silk dress that was growing wetter by the minute, the painstakingly styled hair that was growing wilder by the minute, the shiny black shoes that were growing more speckled by the minute.

Panicked, she drew up under a large-trunked tree in the hope that something, *anything* would be better than nothing. But as though to mock her, the rain began to come sideways. When she shifted around the tree, it shifted, too. Horrified at what was happening but helpless to stop it, she looked from side to side for help but there was none. She was caught in the worst kind of nightmare.

Unable to contain it, she cried out in frustration, then cried out again when the first one didn't help. The second didn't, either, and she felt nearly as much a fool for making it as for standing there in the rain. So she started off again, running as fast as she could given that her glasses were streaked with rain, her shoes were soaked and her heart felt like lead.

It was still pouring when she finally turned down the alley that led to the Sweetwater Café. As the brick walkway widened into a courtyard, she slowed her step. Rushing was pointless. There was nothing the rain could do to her that it already hadn't. She couldn't possibly go to the theater with Carter. The evening was ruined. All that was left was to tell him, return to her car and drive home.

Shortly before she reached the café's entrance, her legs betrayed her. Stumbling to the nearby brick wall, she leaned her shoulder against it, covered her face with her hands and began to cry.

That was how Carter found her, as he came from the opposite end of the courtyard. He wasn't sure it was her at first; he hadn't expected such a deep green dress, such a wild array of hair or nearly so much leg. But as he slowed his own step, he sensed the familiar in the defeated way she stood. His insides went from hot to cold in the few seconds it took him to reach her side.

"Jessica?" he asked, his heart pounding in dread. He reached out, touched the back of her hand. "Are you all right?"

With a mournful moan, she shrank into herself.

Heedless of the rain that continued to fall, he put a hand to the wall and used his body to shield her from the curious eyes of those who passed. "Jessica?" He speared his fingers into her hair to lift it away from her face. "What happened?" When she continued to cry, he grasped her wrist. "Are you all right? Tell me what happened. Are you hurt?"

"I'm wet!" she cried from behind her hands.

He could see that, but there was still an icy cold image of something violent hovering in his mind. "Is that all? You weren't mugged or...anything?"

"I'm just wet! I got caught in the downpour, and there wasn't anywhere to go, and I wanted to look so nice. *I'm a mess,* Carter."

Carter was so relieved that she hadn't been bodily harmed in some other, darker, narrower alley, that he gave her a tight hug. "You're not a mess—"

"I'll get you wet," she protested, struggling to free herself from his hold.

He ignored her struggles. "You're looking goddamned sexy with that dress clinging to every blessed curve." When she gave a soft wail and went limp, he said, "Come on. Let's get you dry."

The next few minutes were a blur in Jessica's mind, principally because she didn't raise her eyes once. For the first time in her life, she was grateful that her hair was wild, because it fell by her cheeks like a veil. She didn't want Carter to see her, didn't want *anyone* to see her. She felt like a drowned rat, all the more pathetic in her own mind by contrast to the way she looked when she left Cambridge.

With a strong arm around her shoulder, Carter guided her out of the alley and into a cab. He didn't let her go even then, but spoke soft words to her during the short ride to his apartment. Wallowing in misery, she heard precious few of them. She kept her head down and her shoulders hunched. If she'd been able to slide under the seat, she'd have done just that.

He lived on Commonwealth Avenue, on the third floor of a time-honored six-story building. Naturally the rain had stopped by the time they reached it. He knew not to point that out to Jessica, and ushered her into the lobby before she could figure it out for herself. Though she'd stopped crying, she was distraught. The tension in her body wasn't to be believed.

"Here we go," he said as he quickly unlocked the door to his place. He led her directly into the bathroom, pulled a huge gray bath sheet from a shelf and began to wipe her arms. When he'd done what he could, he draped it around her, took a smaller towel, removed her glasses and dried them, too. "Better?"

Jessica refused to look at him. "I'm hopeless," she whispered.

"You're only wet," he said, setting the glasses by the sink. "When I saw you crying, leaning against the wall that way in the alley, I thought you'd been attacked. I honestly thought you'd been mugged. But you're only wet."

She was beyond being grateful for small favors. Turning her face away from him, she said in a woefully small voice, "I tried so hard. I wanted to look nice for you. I can't remember the last time anything meant so much to me, and I almost did it. I was looking good, and I was looking forward to tonight, and then it started to rain. I didn't know whether to go back or go on, and the rain came down harder, and then it didn't matter either way because I was soaked." Her eyes were filled with tears when they met Carter's. "It wasn't meant to be. I'm a disaster when it comes to nice things like dinner and the theater. There was a message in what happened."

"Like hell," Carter said, blotting her face with the smaller towel. "It rained. I would have been caught in it, too, if I'd walked, but I was running late, so I took a cab." He began to gently dry her hair. "Sudden storms come on like that. If it had come fifteen minutes earlier or later, you'd have been fine."

"But it didn't, and I'm not. And now everything is ruined. My dress, my shoes, my hair—"

"Your hair is gorgeous," he said, and it was. Moving the towel through it was like trying to tame a living thing. Waving naturally, it was wild and exotic. "You should wear it down like this more often. Then again, maybe you shouldn't. It's an incredible turn-on. Let everyone else see it tied up. Wear it down for me."

"There was a clip in it. It looked so pretty."

Carter found the clip buried in the maple-hued mass. "Here. Put it back in."

"I can't. I don't know how to do it. Mario did it."

"Mario?"

"My hairdresser."

She'd gone to the hairdresser. For a dinner and theater date with him. That fact, more than anything else she'd said, touched him deeply. He doubted she went to the hairdresser often, certainly not to have something as frivolous as a clip put in. But she'd wanted to look nice for him.

"Ah, Jessica." Towels and all, he took her in his arms. "I'm sorry you got rained on. You must have looked beautiful."

"Not beautiful. But nice."

"Beautiful."

"But I'm a mess. I can't go anywhere like this, not to dinner, not to the theater. Call someone else, Carter. Get someone else to go with you."

He held her back and stared down onto her face. "Are you kidding?"

"No. Call someone."

He was about to argue with her when he caught himself. "You're right," he said. "Stay put." He left the bathroom.

Sinking down onto the lip of the tub, Jessica hugged the towel around her. But it was no substitute for his arms. It had neither living warmth nor strength—either of which might have helped soothe the soul-deep ache of disappointment she felt.

She knew it shouldn't matter so much. What was one date? Or one dress? Or one hairdo? But she'd so wanted things to be right. She hadn't realized how *much* she'd wanted that. But it was all ruined. The dress, the hairdo, her evening with Carter.

"All set," he said, returning to the bathroom. He'd taken off his jacket and tie and was rolling up his sleeves.

"What are you doing?" she asked, staring at the finely corded forearms that were emerging.

"Getting you dry."

"But I thought you phoned—"

"The ticket agent. I did. He's calling the tickets in to the box office. They'll be resold in a minute. We've got new ones for next week. Friday night this time. Okay?"

"But I thought—"

Hunkering down before her, he said softly, "You thought I was calling someone else to go with me, when I've been telling you all along that I don't want to go with anyone else." Leaning forward, he gave her a light kiss. "You don't listen to me, Jessica."

"But I've ruined your evening."

"Not my evening. Our evening. And it's not ruined. Just changed."

"What can we possibly do?" she cried. Absurdly her eyes were tearing again. He was being so kind and good and understanding, and she hadn't been able to come through at all on her end. "I'm a mess!"

Carter grinned. It was a dangerously attractive grin. "Any more of a mess and I'd lay you right down on the floor and take you here. You really don't know how sexy you are, do you?''

"I'm not."

"You are." His grin faded as his eyes roamed her face. "You are, and I want you."

"Carter—"

"But that's not what we're going to do," he vowed as he rose to his full height. "We're going to dry you off and then go out for dinner."

She wanted that more than anything. "But I can't go anywhere! My dress is ruined!"

"Then we'll order in dinner and wait for your dress to dry. First, you'll have to take it off."

Her cheeks went pink. "I can't. I haven't anything to put on."

Raising a promising finger, he left her alone for as long as it took him to fetch a clean shirt from his closet. Back in the bathroom, he dropped it over the towel bar, stood her up, turned her and unwound the towel enough so that he could get at the back fastening of her dress.

"I can do that," she murmured, embarrassed.

"Indulge me." Gathering her hair to one side, he carefully released the hooks holding the turtleneck together. Her hair had protected that part of her dress from the rain, so the lime color there was more vivid. Carter wished he'd seen her before the storm, wished it with all his heart. He knew how sensitive Jessica was about her looks, but she'd felt good about herself then. He would have given anything to be able to share that good feeling with her.

Not that he didn't think she looked good now. He meant it when he said she looked sexy. He was aroused, and being so close to her, gently lowering her zipper, working it more slowly as the silk grew wetter wasn't doing anything to diminish that arousal. Nor was watching as each successive inch of ivory skin was exposed. He told himself to leave the bathroom, but the heat in his body was making his limbs lethargic. He knew he'd die if he couldn't touch that smooth soft skin just once.

His fingertips were light, tentative on her spine between the spot where her zipper ended and her bra began. He heard her catch her breath, but the sound was as feminine as the rest of her and couldn't possibly have stopped him. Leaving his thumb on her spine, he flattened his fingers, moved them back and forth over butter-softness, spread them until they disappeared under the drape of her dress.

"Carter?" she whispered.

He answered by bending forward and putting his mouth where his fingers had been. Eyes closed, he reveled in the sweet smell of her skin and the velvet smoothness beneath his lips. He kissed her at one spot, slid to the next and kissed her again.

Each kiss sent a charge of sexual energy flowing through her. She clutched the towel to her front, but it was a mindless kind of thing, a need to hold tight to something. Carter's touch sent her soaring. Her embarrassment at his helping her undress was taking a back seat to the pleasure of his caress, which went on and on. His mouth moved over her skin with slow allure, his breath warming what his tongue moistened, his hand following to soothe it all.

Her knees began to feel weak, but she wasn't the only one with the problem. Carter lowered himself to the edge of the laundry hamper. Drawing her between his thighs, he slid both hands inside her dress. His fingers spanned her waist, caressing her while his mouth moved higher. His hands followed, skipping over the slim band of her bra to her shoulders, gently nudging the silk folds of her dress forward.

Jessica tried again, though she was unable to produce more than a whisper. "Maybe this isn't such a good idea."

His breath came against the back of her neck, his voice as gritty as hers was soft. "It's the best one I've had. Tell me it doesn't feel good."

The days when she might have told him that, in pride and self-defense, were gone. "It feels good."

"Then let me do it. Just a little longer."

A small sigh slipped from her lips as she tipped her head to the side to make room for his mouth below her ear. What he was doing did feel good. His thighs flanked hers, offering support, and the whispering kisses he was pressing to her skin were seeping deep, soothing away the horror of the rain. The warmth of his hands, his mouth, his breath made her feel soft and cherished. Eyes closed, she savored the feeling as, minute by minute, she floated higher.

With the slightest pressure, Carter turned her to face him. Her eyes opened slowly to focus on his. She didn't need her glasses to see the heat that simmered amid the darkness there.

He touched her cheek with the side of his thumb, then slid his fingers to the back of her neck and brought her head forward. His mouth was waiting for hers, hot and hungry, and it wasn't alone in that. Jessica's met it with an eagerness that might have shocked her once, but seemed the most natural thing now. Because something had happened to her. She would never know whether it was the words of praise and reassurance he'd spoken, or the gentle, adoring way he touched and kissed her. But she was tired of fighting. She was tired of doubting, of taking everything he said and trying to analyze his motives. If she was being shortsighted, she didn't care. She wanted to feel and enjoy, and if there would be hell to pay in humiliation later, so be it. The risk was worth it. She wanted the pleasure now.

So she followed his lead, opening her mouth wider when he did, varying its pressure from heavy to feather light. There were times when their lips barely touched, when a kiss was little more than the exchange of breath or the touch of tongues, other times when the exchange was a more avid mating. She found one as exciting as the next, as stimulating in a breath-stopping, knee-shaking kind of way. When the knee-shaking worsened, she braced her forearms on his shoulders and anchored her fingers in his hair. She held him closer that way, wanted him closer still. And while the old Jessica was too much with her to say the words, the new Jessica spoke with the inviting arch of her body.

Carter heard her. His hands, which had been playing havoc over the gentle curves of her hips, came forward to frame her face. After giving her a final fierce kiss, he held her back.

For a time, he said nothing, just let himself drown with pleasure in the desire he saw in her eyes. If there'd ever been a different Jessica, he couldn't remember her. The only reality for him was the exquisitely sensual creature he now held between his legs.

Something else was between his legs, though, and it wasn't putting up with prolonged silence. Its heat and hardness were sending messages through the rest of his body that couldn't be ignored. His need to possess Jessica was greater than any need he'd ever known before.

His hands dropped from her face to her shoulders, then lower, to her breasts. He touched them gently, shaping his hand to their curve, brushing their hardened tips. Jessica gave a tiny sound of need and closed her eyes for a minute. When she opened them, Carter was smiling at her. "You're so beautiful," he murmured, and rewarded her for that with another kiss. This one was slower and more gentle, and by the time their lips parted, her breathing had quickened even more.

With her forearms on his shoulders and her forehead against his, she whispered, "I didn't know a kiss could do that."

"It's more than the kiss," Carter said in a low, slightly uneven voice. "It's my looking at you and touching you. And it's everything else that we haven't dared do. We've been thinking about it. At least, I have. I want to make love to you so badly, Jessica. Do you want that?"

It was a minute before she whispered, "Yes."

"Will you let me?"

"I'm frightened."

"You weren't frightened when I kissed you or when I touched your breasts."

"I was carried away."

His eyes met hers. "I'll carry you even further, if you let me. I want to do that. Will you let me?"

"I'm not good at lovemaking."

"Could've fooled me just now. I've never been kissed like that."

"You haven't?"

"You're a bombshell of innocence and raw desire. Do you have any idea how that combination turns a man on?"

She didn't, because she wasn't a man. But she knew that she was turned on herself. She could feel the pulsing deep inside her. "Will you tell me when I do things wrong?"

"You won't—"

"Will you tell me? I don't think I could bear it if we go through the whole thing and I think it's great, and then you tell me it wasn't so hot after all."

She'd spoken with neither accusation nor sarcasm, which was why Carter was so struck by what she said. After a moment of intense self-reproach, he murmured, "I wouldn't do that to you. I know you still don't trust me, but I swear, I wouldn't do that."

"Just tell me. If it's no good, we can stop."

He put a finger to her mouth. "I'll tell you. I promise. But that goes two ways. If I'm doing something you don't like, or something that hurts, I want you to tell me, too. Will you?" His finger brushed her lips, moving lightly, back and forth. "Will you?" he whispered.

She gave a small nod.

"Then come give me a kiss. One more kiss before we hang this dress up to dry."

8

Jessica kissed him with every bit of the love that had been building inside her for days. She hadn't put the correct name to it then, nor did she **now**, but that didn't matter. Under desire's banner, she gave her mouth to him in an offering that was as selfless as the deepest form of love. And when his kiss took her places she'd never been, she gave in to the luxury of it. And the newness. She'd never known such pleasure in a man's arms. She'd dreamed it, but to live the fantasy was something else.

Her headiness was such at the end of the kiss that she didn't demur when he drew her dress down. Leaving the damp silk gathered around her waist, he put his mouth to the soft skin that swelled above the cup of her bra. She held tight to his neck as he shifted his attention from one breast to the other, and what his mouth abandoned, his hand discovered. In no time, he had released the catch of her bra and was feasting on her bare flesh.

Jessica tried to swallow the small sounds of satisfaction that surged from inside.

"Say it," Carter urged against her heated flesh. "How does it feel?"

"Good," she gasped. She bent her head over his. "So good."

"I'm not doing it too hard?"

"Oh, no. Not too hard."

"Do you want it harder?"

"A little."

Her nipple disappeared into his mouth, drawn in by the force of his sucking, and she couldn't have swallowed her satisfaction this time if she'd tried. She choked out his name and buried her face in his hair. He was a beautiful man, making her feel beautiful. She was on top of the world.

The feeling stayed with her for a time. Gently, between long, deep kisses that set her heart to reeling, Carter eased the dress over her hips and legs. Then, keeping her mouth occupied without a break, he lifted her in his arms and carried her into the bedroom. His body followed hers down to the spread, hands gliding over her, learning the shape of her belly, her hips, her thighs. He couldn't quite believe she was **there**, couldn't seem to touch enough of her at once. And everywhere he touched, she responded with a sigh or a cry or the arch of her body, which excited him all the more. His breathing was ragged when he finally pulled away and began to tug at the buttons of his shirt.

Jessica missed the warmth of his touch at once. Opening her eyes to see where he'd gone, she watched him toss the shirt aside and undo his belt. Her insides were at fever pitch, needing him back with her, but her mind, in the short minute that he was gone, started to clear. She couldn't tear her eyes from him. With his hair ruffled and falling over his forehead, his chest bare and massive, and his clothes following one another to the carpet, he was more man than she had ever seen in her life.

She couldn't help but be frightened. She was too inexperienced, for one thing, to take watching him in stride. For another, she'd lived too long thinking of herself as a sexless creature to completely escape self-doubt. Inching up against the headboard, she drew in her legs and folded her arms over her breasts.

"Oh, no, you don't," Carter said, lunging after her. "No, you don't." The mattress bounced beneath his weight, but his fierceness gave way to a gentle grin as he took her wrists and flattened them on the pillow. "Please don't get cold feet on me now, honey. Not when we're so close, when I want you so badly."

"I—"

"No." His mouth covered hers, kissing her hungrily, but if he meant to drug her, he was the one who got high. His kiss gentled, grew lazier, and, in that, more seductive. With a low groan, he pulled her away from the headboard, up to her knees and against his body. She cried out when her breasts first touched his chest, but he held her there, stroking her back in such a way that not only her breasts, but her belly moved against him.

He groaned again. "That feels...so...nice."

She thought so, too. The hair on his chest was an abrasive against her sensitive breasts, chafing them in the most stimulating of ways. His stomach was lean, firm against her, and his arousal was marked, a little frightening but very exciting. Coiling her arms around his neck, she held on for dear life as the force of desire spiraled inside her.

"You were made for me," he whispered brokenly. "I swear you were made for me, Jessica. We fit together so well."

The words were nearly as pleasurable as the feel of his hard body against hers. His approval meant so much to her. She desperately wanted to please him.

"I'm not too thin?"

He ran a large hand over her bottom and hips. "Oh, no. You've got curves in all the right places."

"You didn't think so once."

"I was a jackass then. Besides, I didn't see you like this then." He dipped his fingers under the waistband of her panty hose, then withdrew them in the next breath and gently lay her back on the bed. His eyes were dark and avid as they studied her breasts, his hand worshiping as it cupped a rounded curve. Then he met her gaze. "I'm going to take off the rest. I want to see all of you."

She didn't speak over the thudding of her heart, but she gave a short nod. Though she'd never have believed it possible, she wanted him to see her. She wanted him to touch her. She wanted him to make love to her. She was living the fantasy, and in the fantasy, she was a beautiful, desirable woman. Her insides were a dark, aching vacuum needing to be filled in the way that only he could.

She lifted her hips to help him. Her panties slipped down her legs along with the nylons, and all the while she watched his eyes. They followed the stockings off, then retraced the route over her calves and thighs to the dark triangle at the notch of her thighs. There they lingered, growing darker and more smoky.

Lifting his gaze to hers, he whispered in awe, "You are so very, very lovely."

At that moment, she believed him, because that was part of the fantasy. She was trembling. Her bare breasts rose and fell with each shallow breath she took, and the knot of desire grew tighter between her legs. She wanted him to touch her, to ease the ache, but she couldn't get herself to say the words.

Carter didn't need them. He had never seen such raw desire in a woman's eyes, had never known how potent such a look could be. It was pushing him higher by the minute, making him shake beneath its force. His body clamored for release. He wasn't sure how much longer he could hold back. But he wanted it to be good, so good for her.

"So very lovely," he repeated in a throaty whisper. Tearing his eyes from hers, he lowered his gaze to her body. With an exquisitely light touch, he brushed the dark curls at the base of her belly. When she made a small sound, he looked back up in time to catch her closing her eyes, rolling her head to the side, pressing a fist to her mouth. He touched her again, more daringly this time. She made another small sound and, twisting her body in a subtly seductive way, arched up off the bed.

It was his turn to moan. He was stunned by the untutored sensuality he saw, couldn't quite believe that a woman with Jessica's potential for loving had lived such a chaste life. But she had. He had no doubts about it, particularly when she opened her eyes and seemed as stunned as he.

"How do you feel?" he whispered. He stroked her gently, delved more deeply into her folds with each stroke.

Raising her hands to the pillow, she curled them into fists and swallowed hard. "I need you," she whispered frantically. "Please."

Between the look in her eyes, the sound of her whisper and the intense arousal to which her straining body attested, Carter was pushed to the wall. His blood was rushing hotly through his veins. He knew he couldn't wait much longer to take the possession his throbbing body demanded.

He paused only to shuck his briefs, before coming over her. "Jessica?" Unfurling her fists, he wove his fingers through hers.

She tightened the grip. Her body rose to meet his. "Please, Carter."

Rational thought was becoming harder by the second. He fought to preserve those last threads. "Are you protected, honey? Are you using something?" When she gave a frustrated cry and lifted her head to open her mouth against his jaw, he whispered, "Help me. Tell me. Should I use something?"

"No," she cried, a tight, high-pitched wail. "I want a baby."

Swearing softly—and not trusting himself to stay where he was a minute longer, because the idea of her having his baby sent a shock wave of pleasure through him—he rolled off her and crossed the room to the dresser.

"Carter," she wailed.

"It's okay, honey. Hold on a second."

"I need you."

"I know. I'll be right there." A minute later, he was back, sitting on the edge of the bed to apply a condom. A minute after that, he was back over her, his hands covering hers, his mouth capturing hers. While he took her lips with a rabid hunger, he found his place between her thighs. Slowly and gently in contrast to his ravishment of her mouth, he entered her.

Her name was a low, growling sound surging from his throat, a sound of pleasure and relief when her tightness surrounded him. He squeezed his eyes shut in a battle against coming right then, but she wasn't helping his cause. She lifted her thighs higher around his in an instinctive move to deepen his penetration.

He looked down at her. Her face was flushed, lips moist and parted, eyes half-lidded and languorous. Her hair was wild, the dark waves fanning out over the slate-gray spread.

In an attempt to slow things down, he anchored her hips to the bed with the weight of his own and held himself still inside her. "Am I hurting you?" he whispered.

"Oh, no," she whispered back. "Does it feel okay?"

"More okay than it's ever felt," he answered. His words were hoarse, his breathing ragged. "You're so small and tight. Soft. Feminine. You have an incredible body. Incredible body. Are you sure I'm not hurting you?"

She managed a nod, then closed her eyes because even without his moving, the pressure inside her was building. "Please," she breathed.

"Please what?"

"Do something. I want...I need..."

He withdrew nearly all the way, returned to bury himself to the hilt. In reward for the movement, she cried out, then caught in the same breath and strained upward. "Carter!"

"That's it honey," he said, and began to move in earnest. "Do you feel me?"

"Yes."

"That what I want." Catching her mouth, he kissed her while the motion of his hips quickened. He pulled out and thrust in, filling her more and more, seeming to defy the laws of space. A fine sheen of sweat covered his body, blending with hers where their skin touched.

He had never known such pleasure, had never dreamed that such a physical act could touch his heart so deeply. But that was what was happening, and the heart touching was an aphrodisiac he couldn't fight. Long before he was ready to have the pleasure end, his body betrayed him by erupting into a long, powerful climax. Only when he was on the downside of that did he feel the spasms that were quaking inside Jessica.

Forcing his eyes open, he watched her face while the last of her orgasm shook her. With her head thrown back on the pillow, her eyes closed, her lips lightly parted, she was the most erotic being he'd ever seen in his life.

Her breathing was barely beginning to calm when his arms gave out. Collapsing over her, he lay with his head by hers for several minutes before rolling to the side and gathering her close. Then he watched her until she opened her eyes and looked up at him.

He smiled. "Hi."

"Hi," she said, shyly and still a bit breathlessly.

"You okay?"

She nodded, but when he expected her to look away, she didn't. Her eyes were increasingly large, expectant, trepidant.

"Having second thoughts?"

"One or two."

"Don't. Do you have any idea how good that was?" When she hesitated, then gave a short shake of her head against his arm, he brushed her eyebrow with a fingertip. "It was spectacular."

Still she hesitated. "Was it?"

"Yes." His smile faded. "You don't believe me."

She didn't say a thing for a minute, then spoke in a small voice, "I want to."

"But?"

She didn't answer at all this time, simply closed her eyes and lay her cheek on his chest. Carter would have prodded if he wasn't so enjoying lying quietly with her. But her body was warm, delicate, kittenish by his. Gently he drew her closer.

Her voice was flat, sudden in the silence. "Tom used to say things after it was over. He'd tell me how lacking I was."

Carter felt a chill, part anger, part disbelief, in the pit of his stomach. "Didn't he come?"

"Yes, but that didn't matter. He told me I wasn't much better than a sack of potatoes. I suppose I wasn't. I used to just lie there. I didn't want to touch him."

Carter remembered the way her hands had tightened around his, the way she'd arched to touch him with her body when he had restrained her hands, the way she brought her knees up to deepen his surge. She had been electric.

"That was Tom's fault," he said in a harsh voice. "It was his fault that he couldn't turn you on."

"I always felt inadequate."

"You shouldn't have. You're exquisite." Cupping her face in his hand, he kissed her lightly. "I have no complaints about what we did, except that I wanted it to last longer. But that was my fault. I couldn't hold back. I've been wanting you for days. I've been imagining incredible things, and to find out that the imagining wasn't half as incredible as the real thing—" He kissed her again, more deeply this time. His tongue lingered inside her mouth, withdrawing more slowly, reluctantly leaving her lips. "Jessica," he said in a shaky whisper and clutched her convulsively. But the feel of her body did nothing to dampen his reawakening desire.

Moaning, he released her and lay back on the bed.

Jessica came up on an elbow to eye him cautiously. "What's wrong?" she whispered.

He covered his eyes with his arm. "I want you again."

She looked at that arm, looked at the silky tufts of dark hair beneath it, looked at his chest, which was hairy in thatches, then his lean middle. By the time her eyes had lowered over his belly to the root of his passion, she was feeling tingly enough herself not to be as shocked by his erection as she might have been.

Without forethought, she touched his chest. He jumped, but when she started to snatch her hand away, he caught it, placed it back on his chest and laughed. "It's like lightning when you touch me. I wasn't prepared. That's all." Her hand was lying flat. "Go on. Touch. I like it."

Very slowly she inched her hand over the broad expanse of hair-spattered flesh and muscle. She felt those muscles tighten, felt his heart-beat accelerate, knew that her own was doing the same, but she wasn't about to stop. "I never dreamed..." Her fingertips lightly skimmed the dark, flat nipples that were already pebble hard.

"Never dreamed what?" he asked in a strained voice.

"That I'd...that we'd...you know."

"That we'd make love?"

"Mmm." Her thumb made a slow turn around his belly button.

Clapping a hand over hers, he pinned it to his stomach. When she looked up at him in surprise, his dark eyes smoldered. "Once before you touched me. Remember? By the duck pond?" She nodded. "I was wearing jeans then, and more than anything I wanted to unzip them and put your hand inside." He swallowed, then released her hand. "Touch me, Jessica?"

She looked from his eyes to his hardness and back.

"Touch me," he repeated in a beseechful whisper. The same beseechfulness was reflected in his eyes. More than anything else, that was what gave her courage.

Slowly her hand crept the short distance down a narrow line of hair to its flaring, finally to the part of him that stood, waiting straight and tall. She touched a tentative finger to him, surprised by the heat and the silkiness she found. Gradually her other fingers followed suit.

Taking in a ragged breath, Carter pushed himself into her hand. He wanted to watch her, wanted to see the expression on her face while she stroked him, but the agony of her touch was too much. She seemed to know just what to do and how fast. Closing his eyes, he savored her ministrations as long as he could before reaching down and tugging her back up. Then, when his mouth seized hers, his hands went to work.

He touched her everywhere, taking the time to explore that which he hadn't been able to do before. Where his hands left, his mouth took over. It wasn't long before Jessica was out of her mind with need, before he was, too.

Incredibly they soared higher this time. When it was done, their bodies were slick with sweat, their hearts were hammering mercilessly, their limbs were drained of energy.

They dozed off, awakening a short time later to find the sun down and the room dark. Carter left her side only long enough to light a low lamp on the dresser and draw the bedspread back. Then he took her with him between the sheets, settled her against him and faced the fact that he wanted her there forever.

"I love you," he whispered against her forehead.

Her eyes shot to his, held them for a minute before lowering. "No." She couldn't take the fantasy that far. "You're not thinking straight."

"I am. I've never said those words to a woman. I've never felt this way, felt this need to hold and protect and be with all the time. I've never wanted to wake up next to a woman, but I want it now. I don't like the idea of your going back home."

"I have to. It's where I belong"

His arm tightened. "You belong with me." When she remained silent, he said, "Do you believe in fate?"

"Predestination?"

"Mmm."

She didn't have to think about it long. "No. I believe that we get what we do. God helps those who help themselves."

But Carter disagreed. "If that were true, I'd never have returned home from Vietnam."

His words hovered in the air while Jessica's heart skipped a beat. Sliding her head back on his arm, she looked up at him. He was regarding her warily. "What do you mean?"

"I deserved to die. I hadn't done a decent thing in my life. I deserved to die."

"No one deserves to die in war."

"But someone always does." He looked away. "Good men died there. I saw them, Jessica. I saw them take hits. Some died fast, some slow, and with each one who went, I felt more like a snake."

"But you were fighting right alongside them," she argued.

"Yes, but they were good men. They were intelligent guys, guys with degrees and families and futures. A lot of them were rich—maybe not rich, but comfortable, and here I was walking around with a chip on my shoulder because I didn't have what they did. So they died, and I lived." He made a harsh sound, half laugh, half grunt. "Which says something, I guess, about the important things in life."

Jessica was beginning to understand. "That was what turned you around."

"Yes." His eyes held the fire of vehemence when they met hers.

"Someone was watching over me there. Someone didn't let me die. Someone was telling me that I had things to do in life. I knew other guys who survived, but me, I never got the smallest scratch. That was fate. So was your asking me to work on Crosslyn Rise."

"Not fate. Gordon."

"But the setting was ripe for it." He turned on his side to look her in the eye. "Don't you see? You weren't married. You had been, but you were divorced. I never married. Never even had the inclination until I met you. Never wanted to think of having babies until I met you." Hearing the catch of her breath, he lowered his voice. "You do want them."

Her cheeks went red at the memory of what she'd cried out in the heat of passion.

He stroked that flush with his thumb. "I'll give you babies, Jessica. I couldn't take the chance before, because I wasn't sure you meant it. But you do, don't you?"

Silently she nodded.

"And until now the chances of it seemed remote, so you pushed it to the back of your mind. Then I said something about having children to leave the Rise to—"

"I won't be able to do that anyway. The Rise as I knew it will be gone."

"As you knew it. But all that's good about the Rise—its beauty and dignity, strength and stability—is inside you. You'll give that to your children. You'll make a wonderful mother."

Tears came to her eyes. What he was saying was too good to be true. *He* was too good to be true.

It was the aftermath of lovemaking, she decided. She didn't believe for a minute that he'd really want to marry her. Give him a day or two and he'd realize how foolish his talk was.

"I love you," he whispered, and she didn't argue. He kissed her once, then a second time, but the stirring he felt wasn't so much in his groin as in the region of his heart. He wanted to take care of her, to give her things, to do for her. She was a gentle woman, a woman to be loved and protected. He would do that if she let him.

Rubbing her love-swollen lips with the tip of his finger, he said, "You must be hungry."

"A little."

"If I order up pizza, will you have some?"

"Sure."

He kissed her a final time, then rolled away from her and out of bed. She watched him cross the room to the closet. His hips were narrow, his buttocks tight, the backs of his thighs lean and muscled, and if she'd thought that his walk was seductive when he was dressed, naked it was something else. When he put on a short terry-cloth robe, the memory of his nudity remained. When he returned to her, carrying the shirt from the bathroom, she felt shy.

"Uh-uh," he chided when she averted her eyes. "None of that." He helped her on with the shirt. "I've seen everything. I *love* everything."

"I'm not used to this, I guess," she murmured, fumbling with the buttons.

He could buy that, and in truth, he liked her shyness. It made the emergence of her innate sensuality that much more of a gift. "I'll give you time," he said softly, and led her out of the bedroom.

He was going to have to give her plenty of that, she mused a short time later. They sat on stools at the kitchen counter, eating the pizza that had just been delivered. Though it was a mundane act, she'd never done anything so cataclysmic. She couldn't believe that she was sitting there with Carter Malloy, that she was wearing nothing under his shirt, that she'd worn even less not long before.

Carter Malloy. It boggled her mind. *Carter Malloy.*

"What is it?" he asked with a perplexed half smile.

She blushed. "Nothing."

"Tell me."

Tipping her head to the side, she studied a piece of pizza crust. "I'm very...surprised that I'm here."

"You shouldn't be. We've been building toward this for a while."

He was right, but she wasn't thinking of the recent past. "I'm thinking farther back. I really hated you when I was little." She dared him a look and was struck at once by his handsomeness. "You're so different. You look so different. You *act* so different. It's hard to believe that a person can change so much."

"We all have to grow up."

"Some people don't. Some people just get bigger. You've really changed." Studying him, she was lured on by the openness of his features. "What about before Vietnam? I can understand how your experience there could shape your future, but what about your past? Why were you the way you were? It couldn't have been the money factor alone. What was it all about?"

Thoughtfully pursing his lips, Carter looked down at his hands. His mouth relaxed, but he didn't look up. "The money thing was a scapegoat. It was a convenient one, maybe even a valid one on some levels. Since my parents worked at Crosslyn Rise, we lived in town, and that town happens to be one of the wealthiest in the state. So I went to school with kids who had ten times more than me. From the very start, I was different. They all knew each other from kindergarten. I was a social outcast from the beginning, and it was a self-perpetuating thing. I was never easy to get along with.''

"But why? If you were still that way, I'd say that it was a genetic thing that you couldn't control. But you're easy enough to get along with now, and you don't seem to be suffering doing it. So if it wasn't genetic, it had to come from outside you. Some of it may have come from antagonism in school, but if you were that way when you first enrolled, it had to come from your family. That's what I don't understand. Annie and Michael were always wonderful, easygoing people.''

"You weren't their son," Carter said with a sharpness reminiscent of a similar comment he'd made once before.

Not for a minute did Jessica feel that the sharpness was directed at her. He was thinking back to his childhood. She could see the discomfort in his eyes. "What was it like?" she asked, needing to understand him as intimately as possible.

"Stifling.''

"With Annie and Michael?" she asked in disbelief.

"They loved me to bits," he explained. "I was their pride and joy, their hope for the future. I was going to be everything they weren't, and from the earliest they told me so. I'm not sure that I understood what it all meant at the time, but when I was slow doing things, they pushed me. I didn't like being pushed—I still don't, so maybe that's a biological trait after all. I stayed in the terrible-two stage for lots of years, and by that time, a pattern had been set. My parents were always on top of me, so I did whatever I could to thwart them. I think I was hoping that at some point they'd just give up on me.''

"But they never did.''

"No," he said quietly. "They never did. They were always loyal and supportive." He looked at her then. "Do you know how much pressure that can put on a person?''

Jessica was beginning to see it. "They kept hoping for the best and you kept disappointing them.''

"By the time I was a teenager, I had a reputation of being tough. That hurt my parents, too. People would look at them with pity, wondering how they ever managed to have a son like me.''

She remembered thinking the same thing herself, and not too long before. "They are such quiet, gentle people.''

Again Carter looked away, pursing his lips. He felt guilty criticizing his parents, yet he wanted Jessica to know the truth, at least as he saw it. "Too quiet and gentle. Especially my dad.''

"You would have liked him to be stronger with you?"

"With me, with *anyone*. He wasn't strong, period."

It occurred to Jessica that she'd never thought one way or another about Michael Malloy's strength. "In what sense?"

"As a man. My mother ran the house. She did everything. I can't remember a time when Dad doted on her, when he stood up for her, when he bought her a gift. The only thing he ever did was the gardening."

"Do you think she resented that?"

"Not really. I think it suited her purposes. She liked being the one in control." He took a minute to consider what he'd said. "So maybe when I use the word 'stifling' I should be using the word 'controlling.' In her own quiet way, my mother was the most controlling woman I've ever met. That was what I spent my childhood rebelling against—that, and the fact that my father never once opened his mouth to complain when, in her own gentle way, she ran roughshod over him."

He grew quiet, then looked down. "Lousy of me to be bad-mouthing them, when I treated them so poorly, huh?"

"You're not bad-mouthing them. You're just explaining what you felt when you were growing up."

He met her gaze. "Does it make any sense?"

"I think so. I always thought of Annie as, yes, gentle and quiet, but also efficient. Very efficient. She definitely took control of things in our house. I can understand how 'taking control' could become 'controlling' in her own house. And Michael was always gentle and quiet... just...gentle and quiet. That was what I liked about him. He was always pleasant, always smiled. For me, that was a treat."

"It used to drive me wild. I'd do anything just to rile him."

"Did you manage?"

Carter smirked. "Not often. And he's still like that. Still quiet and gentle. I doubt he'll ever change."

Jessica was relieved to hear the fondness in his voice. "You've accepted him, then?"

"Of course. He's my father."

"And you're close to him now?"

"Close? I don't know, close. We talk regularly on the phone, but for every five minutes Dad's on, Mom's on for ten. I suppose it's just as well. They like to hear what I'm doing, but I'm not sure they appreciate the details." He gave an ironic smile. "I've finally made it, just like they wanted me to, but that means my world is very different from theirs."

"Are they happy?"

"In Florida? Yes."

"For you?"

"Very." His smile was sheepish this time. "Of course, they don't know why I have a partner, since I can do so much better by myself. And they don't know why I'm not married."

Jessica knew they'd be pleased if Carter ever told them he loved her, but she prayed he wouldn't do that. To tie their hopes to something that would never go anywhere was a waste. Even if Carter did believe that he loved her, he'd see the truth once he got back to his normal, everyday life. The fewer people who knew of the night he'd spent playing at being in love, the better.

Jessica returned to Crosslyn Rise on Friday, soon after Carter left for work. She wanted to immerse herself in her own world, to push the events of Thursday night to the back of her mind.

That was easier said than done, because after dinner, they'd gone back to bed. Time and again during the night, they'd made love, and while Jessica never once initiated the passion, she took an increasingly aggressive part in it. That gave her more to think about than ever.

She seemed to bloom in Carter's arms. Looking back on some of the things she'd done, she shocked herself. She, who had never hungered for another man, had lusted for his body, and she couldn't even say that he taught her what to do. Impulses had just...come. She had wanted to touch him, so she had. She had wanted to taste him, so she had.

And he hadn't complained. Every so often, when she'd caught herself doing something daring, she'd paused, but in each case he had urged her on. In each case his pleasure had been obvious, which made her feel all the freer.

Freer. Free. Yes, she had felt that, and it was the strangest thing of all. Making love to Carter, even well after that first pent-up desire had been slaked, was a relief. With each successive peak she reached, she felt more relaxed. It was almost as if she'd done just what he had once accused her of doing—spent years and years denying her instincts, so that now she felt the sheer joy of letting them out.

She fought the idea of that. Once discovered, the passion in her wouldn't be as easily tucked away again—which was just fine, as long as Carter stayed with her. But she couldn't count on that happening. In the broad light of a Crosslyn Rise day, she had too many strikes against her.

She was plain. She was boring. She was broke.

Carter was just the opposite. He was on his way up in the world, and he would make it. She knew that now. She also knew that he didn't need someone like her weighing him down.

That was one of the reasons why, when he called at four to say that he was leaving the office and would be at Crosslyn Rise within the hour, she told him not to come.

9

"Why not?" Carter asked, concerned. "Is something wrong?"

"I just think that I ought to get some work done."

"You've had all day to do that."

"Well, I slept for some of the day, and I didn't concentrate well for the rest."

He didn't have to ask why on either score. "So give it up for today. You won't get much done anyway."

"I'd like to try."

"Try tomorrow. We agreed on dinner tonight."

"I know, but I'm not very hungry."

"Not now. But it'll be an hour before I get there, another hour before we get to a restaurant and get served." He paused, then scolded, "You're avoiding the issue. Come on, Jessica. Spit it out."

"There's nothing to spit out. I'd just rather stay home tonight."

"Okay. We'll stay home."

He was being difficult, she knew, and that frustrated her. "I'd rather be alone."

"You would not. You're just scared because everything that happened last night was sudden and strong."

"I'm not scared," she protested. "But I need time, Carter."

"Like hell you do," he replied, and slammed down the phone.

Forty minutes later, he careened up the driveway and slammed on his brakes. He was out of the car in a flash, taking the steps two at a time, and he might well have pounded the door down had not Jessica been right there to haul it open after his first fierce knock.

"You have no right to race out here this way," she cried, taking the offensive before he could. She was wearing a shirt and jeans, looking as plain as she could, and as angry. "This is my house, my life. If I say that I want to spend my evening alone, that's what I want to do!"

Hands cocked low on his hips, Carter held his ground. "Why? Give me one good reason why you want to be alone."

"I don't have to give you a reason. All I have to say is yes or no."

"This morning you said yes. What happened between now and then to make you change your mind?"

"Nothing."

"What happened, Jessica?"

"Nothing!"

His brown eyes narrowed. "You started thinking, didn't you? You started thinking about all the reasons why I can't possibly feel the way I say I do about you. You came back to this place, and suddenly last night was an aberration. A fluke. A lie. Well, it wasn't, Jessica. It isn't. I loved you then, and I love you now, and you can say whatever stupid things you want, but you can't change my mind."

"Then you're the fool, because I don't want to get involved."

"Baloney." His eyes bore into hers, alive with a fire that was only barely tempered in his voice. "You want a husband, and you want kids. You can pretend that you don't, and maybe it used to work, but it won't work now. Because, whether you like it or not, you *are* involved. You can't forget what happened last night."

"What an arrogant thing to say!"

"Not arrogant. Realistic, and mutual. I can't forget it, either. I want to do it again."

"You're a sex fiend."

His voice grew tighter, reflecting the strain on his patience. "Sex had nothing to do with what we did. That was lovemaking, Jessica. We *made* love, because we *are* in love. If you don't want to admit it, fine. I can wait. But I'm going to say it whenever I want. I love you."

"You do not," she scoffed, and pushed up her glasses.

"I love you."

"You may think you do, but give yourself a little time, and you'll come to your senses. You don't love me. You can't possibly love me."

"Why not?" He took a step toward her, and his voice was as ominous as his look. "Because you're not pretty? Because you lie like a sack of potatoes in my bed? Because you're a bookworm?"

"It's Crosslyn Rise that you love."

He eyed her as though she were crazy. "Crosslyn Rise is some land and a house. It's not warm flesh and blood like me."

"But you love it, you associate me with it, hence you think you love me."

"Brilliant deduction, Professor, but wrong. You're losing Crosslyn Rise. There's no reason why I would align myself with you if the Rise is what I want."

She took a different tack. "Then it's the money. If this project goes through, you'll be making some money. So you're confusing the issues. You feel good about the money, so you feel good about me.''

"I don't want the money that bad," he said with a curt laugh. "If you were a loser, no amount of money would lure me into your bed.''

"What a crass thing to say!''

"It's the truth. And it should say something about my feelings for you. We did it last night more times than I've ever done it in a single night before. My muscles are killing me. Still I want more. Every time I think of you I get hard.''

She pressed her hands to her ears, because his words alone could excite her. Only when his mouth remained still did she lower her hands and say very slowly, "Revenge is a potent aphrodisiac.''

"*Revenge.* What in the hell are you talking about?''

She tipped up her chin. "This is the ultimate revenge, isn't it? For all those years when I had everything you wanted?''

"Are you kidding?" he asked, and for the first time there was an element of pain in his voice. "Didn't you hear a word I said last night? Didn't any of it sink in—any of the stuff about Vietnam or my parents? I've never told anyone else about those things. Was it wasted on you?''

"Of course not.''

"But I didn't get through. You wanted to know what caused me to change over the years, and I told you, but I didn't get through.'' He paused, and the pain was replaced by a sudden dawning. "Or was that what frightened you most, because for the first time you could believe that the change was for real?'' He took a step closer. "Is that it? For the first time you had to admit that I might, just might be the kind of guy you'd want to spend the rest of your life with, and that scares you.'' He took another step forward. Jessica matched it with one back. "Huh?" he goaded. "Is that it?''

"No. I don't want to spend the rest of my life with *any* man.''

"Because of your ex-husband? Because of what he did?''

She took another step back as he advanced. "Tom and I are divorced. What he did is over and done.''

"It still haunts you.''

"Not enough to shape my future.'' She kept moving back.

"But you don't trust me. That's the crux of the problem. You don't trust that I'm on the level and that I won't hurt you the way that selfish bastard did. Damn it, Jessica, how can I prove to you that I mean what I say if you won't see me?''

"I don't want you to prove anything," she said, but her heels had reached the first riser of the stairs. When he kept coming, she sat down on the steps.

"Okay." He put one hand flat on the tread by her hip. "I'll admit things have happened quickly. If you want time, I'll give you time. I won't rush you into anything, especially something as important as marriage." He put his other hand by her other hip. His voice lowered. His eyes dropped to her mouth. "But I won't stand off in the distance or out of sight, either. I can't do that. I need to see you. I need to be with you."

Jessica wanted to argue, but she was having trouble thinking with him so close. She could see the details of the five-o'clock shadow that he hadn't had time to shave, could feel the heat of his large body, could smell the musky scent that was his alone. He looked sincere. He sounded sincere. She wanted to believe him...so...badly.

His mouth touched hers, and she was lost. Memory of the night before returned in a storm of sensation so strong that she was swept up in it and whirled around. She had to wrap her arms around his waist to keep herself anchored to something real, and then it wasn't memory that entranced her, but the sensual devouring of his mouth.

Over and over he kissed her, dueling with her lips for supremacy in much the same way they'd argued, though neither seemed to care who won, and, in fact, both did. When her glasses fogged up, he took them off and set them aside. Pressing her back on the stairs, he touched her breasts, then slid his fingers between the buttons of her shirt to reach bareness. When that failed to satisfy his craving, he unbuttoned the shirt and unhooked her bra, but no sooner had he exposed her flesh than she brushed the back of her hand over the rigid display on the front of his slacks.

"Oh, baby," he said, "come here." Slipping a large hand under her bottom, he lowered himself and pressed her close. In the next breath, he was kissing her again, and in the next, tugging at the fastening of her jeans.

"Carter," she whispered, breathless. "What—"

"I need you," he gasped, pushing at her zipper.

"Now?"

"Oh, yeah."

"Here?"

"Anywhere. Help me, Jess." He'd turned his attention to his belt, which was giving him trouble. Jessica did what she could, but her hands were shaky and kept tangling with his, and when it came to his zipper, his erection made things even more difficult. After a futile pass or two, the most important thing seemed to be freeing her own legs from their bonds.

She didn't quite make it. Her jeans were barely below her knees when

Carter pressed her back to the steps. With a single strong stroke, he was inside her, welcomed there hotly and moistly. Then the movement of his hips drove her wild, and she didn't care that they were in the front hall, that they were half-dressed, that the ghosts of Crosslyn Rise were watching, turning pink through their pallor. All she cared about was sharing a precious oneness with Carter.

That weekend was the happiest Jessica had ever spent, because Carter didn't leave her for long. He made love to her freely, wherever and whenever the mood hit. And wherever or whenever that was, she was ready. Hard as it was to believe, the more they made love, the more she wanted him.

As long as he was with her, she was fine. As long as he was with her, she believed his words of love, believed that his ardor could be sustained over the years and years he claimed, believed that his head would never be turned by another woman.

When he left her on Monday morning to go to work, though, she thought of him at the office, in restaurants, with clients, and she worried. She went to work, herself, and she was the quiet, studious woman she'd always been.

Maybe if people had looked at her strangely she would have felt somehow different. But she received the same smiles and nods from colleagues she passed. No one looked twice, as had happened when she'd dressed up the Thursday before. No one seemed remotely aware of the kind of weekend she'd spent.

She didn't know what she expected. Aside from a bundle of tender muscles, she was no different physically than she'd always been. But no one knew about the muscles. No one knew about Carter Malloy. No one knew about the library sofa, the parlor rug or the attic cot.

So she saw herself as the others saw her, and everything that was risky and frightening about her affair with Carter was magnified.

Until she saw him that night. Then the doubts seemed to waft into the background and pop like nothing more weighty than a soap bubble, and she came to life in his arms.

The pattern repeated itself over the next few weeks. Her days were filled with doubts, her nights with delight. Graduation came and went, and the summer session began, but for the first time in her life, there was a finite end to a day's work. That end came when Carter arrived. He teased her about it, even urged her to do some reading or class preparation on those occasions when he had brought work of his own with him to do, but she couldn't concentrate when he was with her. She would sit with a book while he worked, but her eyes barely touched the page, and her mind took in nothing at all but how he looked, what he was doing, what they'd done together minutes, hours or days before.

She was in love. She admitted it, though not to him. Somehow, saying the words was the most intense form of self-exposure, and though one part of her wished she had the courage because she knew how much he wanted to hear it, she wasn't that brave. She felt as though she were driving on a narrow mountain path where one moment's inattention could tip her over the edge. She wanted to be prepared when Carter's interest waned. She wanted to have a remnant of pride left to salvage.

His interest waned neither in her nor in Crosslyn Rise. Sketch after sketch he made, some differing from the others in only the most minor of features, but he wanted them to be right. He and Jessica had dinner one night with Nina Stone to get her opinion on the needs of the local real estate market; as a result of that meeting, they decided to offer six different floor plans, two each in two-bedroom, three-bedroom and four-bedroom configurations.

Also as a result of that meeting, Jessica learned that Carter wasn't interested in Nina Stone. Nina was interested in him; her eyes rarely left his handsome face, and when she accompanied Jessica to the ladies' room, she made her feelings clear.

"He's quite a piece of man. If things cool between you two, will you tell me?"

Jessica was surprised that Nina had guessed there was something beyond a working relationship between her and Carter. "How did you know?" she asked, not quite daring to look Nina in the eye.

"The vibes between you. They're hot. Besides, I've been sending him every come-hither look I know, and he hasn't caught a one. Honey, he's smitten."

"Nah," Jessica said, pleased in spite of herself. "We're just getting to know each other again." Far better, she knew, to minimize things, so that it wouldn't be as humiliating if the relationship ended.

Still there was no sign of that happening. On the few occasions that Carter mentioned Nina after their meeting, it was with regard to the project and with no more than a professional interest.

"Didn't you think she was pretty?" Jessica finally asked.

"Nina?" He shrugged. "She's pretty. Not soft and gentle like you, though, or half as interesting."

As though to prove his point, he spent hours talking with her. They discussed the economy, the politics in Jessica's department, the merits of a book that he'd read and had her read. He was genuinely curious about what she was thinking, was often relieved to find that she wasn't lost on some esoteric wavelength where he couldn't possibly join her.

When it came to Crosslyn Rise, he took few steps without having her by his side, considered few ideas without trying them out on her first. Though her feedback wasn't professional from an architectural standpoint, it was down-to-earth. When she didn't like something, she usually had good reason. He listened to her, and while he didn't always agree, he yielded as many times as not. Their personal, vested interests balanced each other out; when he was too involved in the design to think of practicality, she reminded him of it, and when she was too involved in the spirit of Crosslyn Rise to see the necessity of a particular architectural feature, he pointed it out.

By the middle of July, there was a set of plans to show Gordon. As enthusiastic about them as Carter was, Jessica set up the meeting. Then the two of them stood side by side, closely watching for Gordon's reaction as he looked over the drawings.

He liked them, though after he'd said, "You two make a good team," for the third time in ten minutes, Jessica was wondering what particular message he was trying to get across. She had tried not to look at Carter, and when he caught her hand behind her skirt and drew it to the small of his back, she was sure Gordon couldn't see.

Possibly he had sensed the same vibes Nina had, though she hadn't thought Gordon the type to sense vibes, at least not of that kind. She finally decided that it was the little things that gave them away—the light lingering of Carter's hand on her back when they first arrived, the way he attributed her ideas to her rather than taking credit for them himself, the mere fact that they weren't fighting.

The last made the most sense of all. Jessica remembered her reaction when Gordon had first mentioned Carter's name. She thought back to that day, to her horror and the hurt in those memories. At some point along the way, the hurt had faded, she realized. She had superimposed fondness and understanding on the Carter Malloy who had been so angry with the world and himself, and doing that took the sting off the things he'd once said. Not that she dwelt on those memories. He had given her new ones, ones that were lovely from start to finish.

"Jess?" Carter's low, gentle voice came through her reverie. She looked up in surprise, smiled a little shamefacedly when she realized her distraction. He motioned to the nearby chair. Blushing, she sank into it.

"Everything all right, Jessica?" Gordon asked.

"Fine. Just fine."

"You know these highbrow types," Carter teased, smiling indulgently. "Always dreaming about one thing or another."

Her cheeks went even redder, but she latched onto the excuse as a convenient out. "Did I miss anything?"

"Only Gordon's approval. I have to polish up the drawings some, but he agrees that we're ready to move ahead."

Jessica's eyes flew to Gordon. "Getting the investors together?"

Gordon nodded and opened a folder that had been lying on the corner of his desk. He removed two stapled parcels, handed one to each of them, then took up his own. "I've jumped the gun, I guess, but I figured that I'd be doing this work anyway, so it wouldn't matter. These are the names and profiles of possible investors, along with a list of their general assets and the approximate contribution they might be counted on to make. You can skip through page one—that's you, Jessica—and page two—that's you, Carter. The next three are William Nolan, Benjamin Heavey and Zachary Gould. You know Ben, don't you, Carter?"

"Sure do. I worked with him two years ago on a development in North Andover." To Jessica, he said, "He's been involved in real estate development for fifteen years. A conservative guy, but straight. He's selective with his investments, but once he's in, he's in." He looked at Gordon. "Is he interested?"

"When I mentioned your name, he was. I didn't want to tell him much else until the plans were finalized, but he just cashed in on a small shopping mall in Lynn, so he has funds available. Same with Nolan and Gould."

Jessica was trying to read as quickly as possible, but she'd barely made it halfway down the first sheet on Benjamin Heavey when Gordon mentioned the others. "Nolan and Gould?" She had to flip back a page to reach Nolan, ahead two to reach Gould.

"Are you familiar with either name?" Gordon asked.

"Not particularly." Guardedly she looked up. "Should I be?"

Carter shot her a dry grin. "Only if you're into reading the business section of the paper," which he knew, for a fact, she was not, since they'd joked about it just the Sunday before, when she'd foisted that particular section on him in exchange for the editorials.

"Bill Nolan is from the Nolan Paper Mill family," Gordon explained. "He started in northern Maine, but has been working his way steadily southward. Even with the mills up north, he has a genuine respect for the land. A project like this would be right up his alley."

Carter agreed. "From what I hear, he's not out for a killing, which is good, since he won't get one here. What he'll get is a solid return on his investment. He'll be happy." Turning several pages in his lap, he said to Gordon, "Tell me about Gould. The name rings a bell, but I can't place it."

"Zach Gould is a competitor of mine."

"A banker?" Jessica asked.

"Retired, actually, though he's not yet sixty. He was the founder and president of Pilgrim Trust and its subsidiaries. Two years ago he had a heart attack, and since he was financially set, he took his doctor's advice and removed himself from the fray. So he dabbles in this and that. He's the type who would drop in at the site every morning to keep tabs on the progress. Nice guy. Lonely. His wife left him a few years back, and his children are grown. He'd like something like this."

Jessica nodded. Determined to read the fine print when she had time alone later, she turned to the next page. "John Sawyer?"

Gordon cleared his throat. "Now we start on what I like to call the adventurers. There are three of them. None can contribute as much money as any of these other three men, or you or Carter, but each has good reason not only to want to be involved but to be sure that the project is a success." He paused for only as long as it took Carter to flip to the right page. "John Sawyer lives here in town. He owns the small bookstore on Shore Drive. I'm sure you've been there, Jessica. It's called The Leaf Turner?"

She smiled. "Uh-huh. It's a charming place, small but quaint." Her smile wavered. "I don't remember seeing a man there, though. Whenever I've been in, Minna Larken has helped me."

Gordon nodded. "You've probably been in during the morning or early afternoon hours. That's when John is home taking care of his son. By the time two-thirty rolls around, he has high school girls come in to play with the boy while he goes to work."

"How old is the kid?" Carter asked.

"Three. He'll be entering school next year. Hopefully."

At the cautious way he'd added the last, Jessica grew cautious herself. "Something's wrong with him?"

"He has problems with his hearing and his eyesight. John had tried him in a preschool program, but he needs special attention. He'll have a tough time in the public kindergarten class. There is a school that would be perfect for him, but it's very expensive."

"So he could use a good money-making venture," Carter concluded. "But does he have funds for an initial investment?"

Gordon nodded. "His wife died soon after the boy was born. There was some money in life insurance. John was planning to leave it in the bank for the child's college education, but from the looks of things he won't get to college unless he gets special help sooner."

"How awful," Jessica whispered, looking helplessly from Gordon to Carter and back. "She must have been very young. How did she die?"

"I don't know. John doesn't talk about it. They were living in the Midwest when it happened. He moved here soon after. He's a quiet fellow, very bright but private. In many respects, the stakes are higher for John than for some of these others. But he's been asking me about investments, and this is the most promising to come along in months."

"But will the money come through in time for him?" Carter asked. "If all goes well, we could break ground this fall and do a fair amount of framing before winter sets in. We may be lucky enough to make some preconstruction sales, but most of the units won't be ready for aggressive marketing until next spring or summer, and then the bank loans will have to be paid off first. I can't imagine that any of us will see any raw cash for eighteen months to two years. So if he's going to need the money sooner—"

"I think he's covered for the first year or two. But when he realized that the child's education was going to be a long-time drain, he knew he had to do something else."

"By all means," Jessica said, "ask him to join us." She focused her attention on the next sheet. "Gideon Lowe." She glanced at Carter. "Didn't you mention him to me once?"

"To you and to Gordon. You did call him then?" he asked the banker.

"By way of a general inquiry, yes. I named you as the contact. He thinks you're a very talented fellow."

"I think he's even more so. He takes pride in his work, which is more than I can say for some builders I know. Now that they're getting ridiculous fees for the simplest jobs, they've become arrogant. And lazy. Cold weather? Forget it—they can't work in cold weather. Rain? Same thing. And if the sun is out, they want to quit at twelve to play golf."

"I take it Gideon Lowe doesn't play golf?" Jessica asked.

"Not quite," Carter confirmed with a knowing grin. "Gideon would die strolling around a golf course. He's an energetic man. He needs something fast."

"Like squash?" she asked, because squash was Carter's game, precisely for its speed, as he'd pointed out to her in no uncertain terms.

"Like basketball. He was All-American in high school and would have gone to college on a basketball scholarship if he hadn't had to work to support his family."

Jessica's eyes widened. "Wife and kids?"

"Mother and sisters. His mother is gone now, and his sisters are pretty well-set, but he's too old to play college basketball. So he plays on a weekend league. Summers, he plays evenings." Recalling the few games he'd watched, Carter gave a slow head shake. "He's got incredible moves, for a big guy."

"And incredible enthusiasm," Gordon interjected. "He made me promise to call him as soon as I had something more to say about Crosslyn Rise."

"Then you should call him tomorrow," Jessica said, because Carter's recommendation was enough for her. She turned to the final page on her lap and her eyes widened. "Nina Stone?" She looked questioning at Gordon.

"Miss Stone called me," Gordon explained with a slight emphasis on the me. "She knows something of what you're doing since you've talked with her. She knows that I'm putting a group together. She wants to be included in that group and she has the money to do it."

Jessica sent him an apologetic look. "She was insistent?"

"You could say that."

"It's her way, Gordon. Some people see it as confidence, and it sells lots of houses. I can imagine, though, that it would be a little off-putting with someone like you, particularly on the phone. Wait until you meet her, though. She's a bundle of energy." As she said it, she had an idea. Turning to Carter, she said, "I'll bet she and Gideon would get along. You didn't say if he was married."

"He's not, but forget it. They are two very forceful personalities. They'd be at each other's throats in no time. Besides," he added, and a naughty gleam came into his eye, "they're all wrong physically. She's too little and he's too big. They'd have trouble making...it, uh, you know what I mean."

She knew exactly what he meant, but she wasn't about to elaborate in front of Gordon any more than he was. The only solace for her flaming cheeks was the rush of color to Carter's.

Fortunately, that color didn't hinder his thinking process. Recovering smoothly, he said, "If Nina has the money, I see no reason why she shouldn't invest." More serious, he turned to Jessica. "What's her motive?"

"She wants to go into business for herself. She wants the security of knowing she's her own boss. How about Gideon?"

"He wants the world to know he's his own boss. Respect is what he's after."

"Doesn't he have it now?"

"As a builder, yes. As a man who works with his hands, yes. As a man with brains as well as brawn, no. He's definitely got the brains— that's what makes him so successful as a builder. But people don't always see it that way. So he wants to be involved with the tie-and-jacket crowd this time.''

Jessica could understand how Carter might understand Gideon better than some. He'd seen both sides. "If Gideon wants to invest, would that rule out his doing the building?"

"I hope not," Carter said, and looked questioningly at Gordon.

"I don't see why it would," Gordon answered. "The body of investors will be bound together by a legal agreement. If Gideon should decide to bid on the job and then lose out to another builder, his position in the consortium will remain exactly the same."

"There wouldn't be a conflict of interest?"

"Not at all. This is a private enterprise." He arched a brow toward Jessica. "Theoretically, you could pick your builder now, and make it part of the package."

"I wouldn't know who to pick," she said on impulse, then realized that she was supposed to be in charge. Recomposing herself, she said to Gordon, "You pointed out that I have to be willing to listen to people, especially when they know more about things than I do. I think that Carter will help me decide on the builder. Do you have any problem with that?"

"Me? None. None at all."

Something about the way he said it gave Jessica pause. "Are you sure?"

Gordon frowned at the papers before him for a minute before meeting her gaze. "I may be out of line saying this—'' his gaze broke off from hers for a minute to touch on Carter before returning "—but I didn't expect that you two would be so close."

"We're very close," Carter said, straightening slightly in his seat. "With a little luck we'll be married before long."

"Carter!" Jessica cried, then turned to Gordon, "Forget he said that. He gets carried away sometimes. You know how it is with men in the spring."

"It's summer," Carter reminded her, "and the only thing that's relevant about that is that you'll have a few weeks off between semesters at the end of August when we could take a honeymoon."

"Carter!" She was embarrassed. "Please, Gordon. Ignore this man."

To her chagrin, Gordon looked to be enjoying the banter. "I may be able to, but the reason I raise the issue is that other people won't." He grew more sober. "It was clear from the minute you two walked in here that something was going on. I think you ought to know just what that something is before you face the rest of this group. The last thing you want them to feel is that they're at the end of a rope, swinging forward and back as your relationship does.''

"They won't," Jessica said firmly.

"Are you sure?"

"Very. This is a business matter. Whatever my relationship is or isn't with Carter, I'll be very professional. After all, the crux of the matter is Crosslyn Rise." She shot Carter a warning look. "And Crosslyn Rise is mine.''

10

"You're being unreasonable," Carter suggested, lengthening his stride to keep up with her brisk pace as they walked along the street after leaving the bank. Jessica hadn't said more than two words to him since the exchange with Gordon. "What was so terrible about my saying I want to marry you?"

"Whether we marry is between you and me. It's none of Gordon's business."

"He had a point, though. People see us together, and they wonder. Some things you can't hide. We are close. And there was nothing wrong with your deferring to me on the matter of a builder. As your husband, I'd want you to do that."

"You're my architect," she argued crossly. "You're more experienced than I am on things like choosing a builder. My deferring to you was a business move."

"Maybe in hindsight. At the time, it was pure instinct. You deferred to me because you trust me, and it's not the first time that's happened. You've done it a lot lately. Crosslyn Rise may be yours, but you're glad to have someone to share the responsibility for it." He half turned to her as they walked. "That's what I want to do, Jess. I want to help you, and it's got nothing to do with Crosslyn Rise and everything to do with loving you. Giving and sharing are things I haven't done much of in my life, but I want to do them now."

She had trouble sustaining crossness when he said things like that. "You do. You are."

"So marriage is the next step. Why are you so dead set against it?"

"I'm not dead set against it. I'm just not ready for it."

"Do you love me?"

She swung around the corner with him a half step behind. "I've been married," she said without answering his question. "Things change once the vows are made. It's as if there's no more need to put on a show."

That stopped Carter short, but only for a minute. He trotted a pace to catch up. "You actually think I've been putting on a show? That's absurd! No man—especially not one who spent years feeling second-rate, being ashamed of who he was—is going to keep after a woman the way I have after you if he doesn't love her for sure. In case you haven't realized it, I do have my pride.''

She shot him a glance and said more quietly, ''I know that.''

''But I'll keep asking you to marry me, because it's what I want more than anything else in my life.''

''It's what you *think* you want.''

''It's what I *want*.'' Grasping her arm, he drew her to a stop. ''Why won't you believe that I love you?''

She looked up at him, swallowed hard and admitted, ''I do believe it. But I don't think it will last. Maybe we should just live together. That way it won't be so painful if it ends.''

''It won't end. And we're practically living together now, but that's not what I want. I want you driving my car, living under my roof, using my charge cards. And my name. I want you using my name.''

She eyed him warily. ''That's not a very modern wish.''

''I don't give a damn. It's what I want. I want to take care of you. I want to be strong for you. I resented my father because he rode through life on my mother's coattails. I refuse to do that.''

Jessica was astonished. ''You couldn't do that with me. I don't *have* any coattails. My life is totally unassuming. You're more dynamic than I could ever be. You're more active, more aggressive, more successful—''

He put a finger to her lips to stem the flow of words. ''Not successful enough, if I can't convince you to marry me.''

With a soft moan, she kissed the tip of his finger, then took it in her hand and wagged it, in an attempt at lightness. ''Oh, Carter. The problem is with me. Not you. Me. I want to satisfy you, but I don't know if I can.''

''You do.''

''For now. But for how much longer? A few weeks? A month? A year?''

''Forever, if you'll give yourself the chance. Can't you try, Jessica?''

She could, she supposed, and each time she thought of marrying Carter, her heart took wing. Still, in the back of her mind, there was always an inkling of doubt. More so than either dating or living together, marriage made a public statement about a man and a woman. If that marriage fell apart, the statement was no less public and far more humiliating—especially when the male partner was Carter Malloy. Because Carter Malloy was liked and respected by most everyone he met. That fact became clear to Jessica over the next few weeks as they met with Gordon, with lawyers, with various investors. Despite Jessica's role as the owner of Crosslyn Rise, Carter emerged as the project's leader. He didn't ask for the position, in fact he sat back quietly during many of the discussions, but he had a straight head on his shoulders and seemed to be the one, more than any other, who had a pulse on the various elements involved—architectural plans, building prospects, environmental and marketing considerations, and Jessica.

Especially Jessica. She found that she was leaning on him more and more, relying on him for the cool, calm confidence that she too often lacked. Gone were the days when her life maintained a steady emotional keel. She seemed to be living with highs and lows. Some had to do with Crosslyn Rise—highs when she was confident it would become something worthy of its past, and lows when the commercial aspects of the project stood out. Some had to do with Carter—highs when she was in his arms and there was no doubt whatsoever about the strength of his love, and lows when she was apart from him, when she eyed him objectively, saw a vibrant and dynamic man and wondered what he ever saw in her.

As the weeks passed, she felt as though she were heading toward a pair of deadlines. One had to do with Crosslyn Rise, with the progress of the project, with the approach of the trucks and bulldozers and the knowledge that once they broke ground, there was no going back.

The other had to do with Carter. He would only wait so long. He'd been so good about not mentioning marriage, but she knew he was frustrated. When August came and it was apparent there would be no honeymoon, he planned a vacation anyway, spiriting her away for a week in the Florida Keys.

"See?" he teased when they returned. "We made it through a whole week in each other's company nonstop, and I still love you."

By late September, he was pointing out that they'd made it for five months and were going strong. Jessica didn't need that pointed out. Her life revolved around Carter. He was her first thought in the morning and her last thought at night, and though there were times when she scolded herself for being so close to him, so dependent on him, she couldn't do differently—particularly with the ground-breaking at Crosslyn Rise approaching fast. It was an emotional time for her, and Carter was her rock.

Even the most solid of rocks had its weak spot, though, and Jessica was Carter's. He adored her, couldn't imagine a life without her, but the fact that she wouldn't marry him, that she didn't even say that she loved him was eroding his self-confidence and hence, his patience. When he was with her, he was fine; he loved her, she loved him, he wasn't about to ruin their time together. Alone though, he brooded. He felt thwarted. He was tired of waiting. Enough was enough.

Such were the thoughts that he was trying unsuccessfully to bury when, late in the afternoon on the last Wednesday in September, he drove to Crosslyn Rise. Before Jessica had left him in Boston that morning, she had promised to cook him dinner. He hadn't spoken with her during the day, which annoyed him, since he wanted *her* to call *him* once in a while, rather than the other way around. He needed the reassurance. She wouldn't say she loved him, so he needed her to show she cared in other ways. A phone call would have been nice.

But there'd been no call. And when he opened the back door and came into the kitchen, there didn't look to be anything by way of pots and pans on the stove. Nothing smelled as though it were cooking. Jessica was nowhere in sight.

"Jessica?" he called, then did it again more loudly. *"Jessica?"*

He was through the kitchen and into the hall when he heard her call, "I'll be right there." He guessed she was upstairs in the bedroom—the master bedroom with its king-size bed, which she'd started using when he'd begun to sleep over regularly—and that thought did bring a small smile to his face. He was early. She always freshened up, changed clothes, combed out her hair when she knew he was coming. So she wasn't quite done. That was okay. He'd help her. He'd even help her with dinner.

Which went to show how lovesick he was. The thought of being with her, of maybe getting in a little hanky-panky before dinner was enough to wipe all the frustrating thoughts from his mind. And it wasn't just that the lovemaking could do it, but when they made love, he knew that she loved him. She came alive in his arms, showed him a side of her that the rest of the world never saw. No woman could respond to him— or give—in that way if she wasn't in love.

He took the stairs two at a time, but he hadn't reached the top when she came down the hall. One look at her face and he knew there would be no hanky-panky. Indeed, she looked as though she'd newly brushed her hair and changed her clothes, even put on a little makeup, but the dab of blusher didn't hide her pallor.

"What's wrong?" he asked, coming to an abrupt halt where he was, then taking the rest of the stairs more cautiously.

"We have a problem," she said in a tight voice.

"What kind of problem?"

"With Crosslyn Rise. With the construction."

He let out a relieved breath. "A problem with the project I can handle. A problem with us I can't." He reached for her. "Come here, baby. I need a hug.'' Enveloping her in his arms, he held her tightly for a minute, then relaxed his hold and kissed her lightly. She was the one who clung then, her face pressed to his neck, her arms trembling. There was something almost desperate about it, which made him a little nervous. ''He-ey.'' He laughed softly and held her back. ''It can't be all that bad.''

''It is,'' she said. ''The town zoning commission won't give us a permit. They say our plans don't conform with their regulations.''

Putting both hands on her shoulders, Carter ducked his head and stared at her. ''What?''

''No permit.''

''But why? There's nothing unusual about what we're doing. We're following all the standard rules, and we did go through the town for the subdivision allowances. So what are they picking on?''

''The number of units. The spacing of the units.'' She tossed up a hand, and her voice was a little wild. ''I don't know. I couldn't follow it. When I got the call, all I could think of was that here we are, ready to break ground, and now the whole thing's in danger.''

''No.'' Slipping an arm around her shoulder, he brought her down beside him on the top step. ''Not in danger. It only means a little more work. Who did you speak with?''

Jessica looked at her hands, which were knotted in her lap. ''Elizabeth Abbott. She's the chairman of the zoning commission.''

''I know Elizabeth Abbott. She's a reasonable woman.''

''She wasn't particularly reasonable with me. She informed me that the decision was made this morning at a meeting, and that we could apply for a waiver, but she suggested I call back the trucks. She didn't see how we could break ground until next spring or summer at the earliest.'' Jessica raised agonized eyes to Carter's. ''Do you know what a delay will mean? Carter, I can't afford a delay. I barely have the money to keep Crosslyn Rise going through another winter. I'm already up to my ears in loans to the bank. The longer we're held up, the longer it will be until we see money on the other end. That may be just fine for men like Nolan and Heavey and Gould, and it may be okay for you, but for me and the rest of us—it's too late!''

''Shh, honey. It's not too late.'' But he was frowning. ''We'll work something out.''

''She was vehement.''

Releasing her, Carter propped his elbows on his thighs and let his hands hang between his knees. ''Small towns aren't usually this rigid with one of their leading citizens.''

''I'm no leading citizen.''

"Crosslyn Rise is. It's the leading parcel of land here."

"That's probably why they're being so picky. They want to know exactly who's coming in and when."

Carter shook his head. "Even the snobbiest of towns don't do things like this. Something stinks."

Jessica held her breath for a minute. She looked at Carter, but his frown gave away nothing of his deeper thoughts. Finally, unable to wait any longer, she said, "It's Elizabeth Abbott. I could tell from her voice. She's the force behind this."

He eyed her cautiously. "How well do you know her?"

"Only enough to say hello on the street. We never had anything in common. I'm not saying that she's deliberately sabotaging our progress, but she's clearly against what we're doing. She seemed pleased to be making the call, and she wasn't at all willing to even *consider* accommodating us." Jessica's composure began to slip. "They could hold a special meeting, Carter. How difficult would it be for three people to meet for an hour? When I asked, she said that wasn't done. She said that they'd be more than happy to consider our waiver at their next scheduled meeting in February." Her voice went higher. "But we can't wait that long, Carter. We can't wait that long."

Carter continued to frown, but the curve of his mouth suggested disgust.

"Talk to her," Jessica said softly. "She'll listen to you."

His eyes shot to hers. "What makes you say that?"

"Because you had something going with her once. She told me."

His expression grew grim. "Did she tell you that it happened seven years ago, when I was still living in New York, and that it lasted for one night?"

"Go to her. You could soften her up."

"One night, Jessica, and do you want to know why?" His eyes held hers relentlessly. "Because she was something I had to do, something I had to get out of my system. That's all. Nothing more. We were classmates here in town way back when. She was a witness to some of my most stupid stunts. Far more than you in some ways, she was synonymous in my mind with the establishment around here. So when she came up to me that night—it was at a reception in one of the big hotels, I don't even remember which—I had this sudden need to prove to myself that I'd really made it. So I took her to bed. And it was the most unsatisfying thing I've ever done. I didn't see her again in New York, and I haven't seen her since I moved back here."

Jessica's heart was alternately clenching tightly and pounding against her ribs. She believed every word Carter said—and the truth was echoed in his eyes—still she pushed on. "But she'd like to see you again. I could tell. Maybe if you gave her a call—"

"I'll call one of the other members of the commission."

"She's the chairman. She's the one who can make things happen, but only if she wants. Talk to her, Carter. Make her want to help us."

Carter was beginning to feel uneasy. Sitting back against the banister to put a little more space between them, he asked cautiously, "How would you suggest I do that?"

Jessica had been tossing possibilities around for the better part of the afternoon, which was why she hadn't called him earlier to tell him about the problem. The solution she'd found was as abhorrent as it was necessary, but she was feeling desperate on several counts. "Smile a little. Sweet-talk her. Maybe even take her to dinner."

"I don't want to take her to dinner."

"You take prospective clients to dinner."

"Prospective clients take *me* to dinner."

"Then make an exception this time. Take her to dinner. Wine and dine her. She'll listen to you, Carter."

"Okay. You and I will take her to dinner."

"You're missing the point!" Jessica cried.

"No," Carter said slowly. His eyes were chilly, reflecting the cold he felt inside. "I don't think I am. I think that the point—correct me if I'm wrong—is that I should do whatever needs to be done to get a waiver from the commission, and if that means screwing Elizabeth Abbott, so be it." While he didn't miss the way Jessica flinched at his choice of words, he was too wrapped up in his own emotions to care. The coldness inside him was fast turning to anger. "Am I right?"

The harsh look in his eyes held Jessica silent for a minute.

"Am I right?" he repeated more loudly.

"Yes," she whispered.

"I don't believe it," he murmured, and though his voice was lower, the look in his eyes didn't soften. "I don't believe it. How can you ask me to do something like that?"

"It may be the only way we can go ahead with this thing."

"Is that all that matters to you? This *thing*? Crosslyn Rise?"

"Of course not."

"Could've fooled me. But then, it's no wonder. You won't say you love me, you won't say you'll marry me, and now you come up with this idiotic scheme."

"It's not idiotic. It would work. Elizabeth Abbott has a reputation for things like this."

"Well, I don't. I wouldn't demean myself by doing something like this. I'm no goddamned gigolo!'' Rising from the stairs, he stormed down three steps before turning to glare at her. "I love you, Jessica. If I've told you once, I've told you dozens of times, and I'm not just blowing off hot air. I love you. That means *you're* the woman I want. Not Elizabeth Abbott.''

Jessica swallowed hard. "But you were with her once—''

"And it was a mistake. I knew it at the time, and I know it even more now. I won't go so far as to say that she's holding up things for Crosslyn Rise because of me, because even when she used to call me and I wouldn't see her, she was gracious. I never thought of her as being vindictive, and I'm not about to now, but I won't sleep with her.'' Agitated, he thrust a hand through his hair. "How can you ask me to do that?'' he demanded, and through the anger came an incredible hurt. "Don't I mean anything to you?''

Jessica was so stunned by the emotions ranging over his face that it was a minute before she could whisper, "You know you do.''

But he was shaking his head. "Maybe I was fooling myself. Part of love is respect, and if you respected me for who and what I am, you wouldn't be asking this of me.'' Again he thrust a hand into his hair; this time it stopped midway, as though he were so embroiled in his thoughts that he couldn't keep track of his gestures. "Did you honestly think I'd go along? Did you think I'd seduce her? Did you think I'd really be able to get it *up*?'' He swore softly, and his hand fell to his side. "I blew it somewhere, Jessica. I blew it.''

In all the time she'd known him, Jessica had never seen him look defeated, but he did now. It was there in the bow of his shoulders and the laxness of his features, either of which put him a galaxy apart from the angry and vengeful boy he'd been so long ago. She knew he'd changed, but the extent of the change only then hit her. She was still reeling from it when she caught the sheen of moisture in his eyes. Her knuckles came hard to her mouth.

"I'd do most anything for you, Jessica,'' he said in a gut-wrenching tone. "So help me, if you asked me to lie spread-eagle on the railroad track until the train blew its whistle, I'd probably do it, but not this.'' Swallowing once, he tore his eyes from hers, turned and started down the stairs.

"Carter?'' she whispered against her knuckles. When he didn't stop, she took her hand away. "Carter?'' Still he didn't stop, but reached the bottom of the stairs and headed for the door. She rose to her feet and called him again, more loudly this time, then started down. When he opened the door and went through, she quickened her step, repeating his name softly now and with a frantic edge. By the time she reached the door, he was halfway to his car.

"Carter?" Her eyes were filled with tears. "Carter!" She was losing him. "Carter, wait!" But he was at the driver's side, reaching for the door. "Carter, stop!" He was the light of her life, leaving her. Panicked, she opened her mouth and screamed, *"Carter!"*

The heartrending sound, so unusual coming from her, stopped him. He raised his head wearing such a broken look that she couldn't move for another minute. But she had to keep him there, had to touch him, had to tell him all he meant to her. Forcing her legs into action, she ran toward the car.

Stopping directly before him, she raised a hand halfway to his face, wavered, mustered enough courage to graze his cheek with a finger before pulling back, then went with her own need and slipped her hand to the back of his neck. "I'm sorry," she tried to say, but the words were more mouthed than anything. "I'm sorry." She put her other hand flat on his chest, moved it up, finally slid it around his neck, went in close to him and managed a small sound against his throat. "I'm sorry, Carter, I'm sorry. I love you so much."

Carter stood very still for a long minute before slowly lifting his hands to her hips. "What?" he whispered hoarsely.

"I love you. Love you."

It was another long minute before he let out a breath, slid his arms around her and gathered her in.

Unable to help herself, Jessica began to cry. She could no more stop the tears than the words. "That was s-such a stupid thing for me to think of—and an insult t-to you. But something happened to me wh-when she said she'd known you before. Maybe I wanted to know what w-would happen—she's very attractive—but I l-love you so much—I don't know what I'd d-do if you ever left me."

He buried his face in her hair. Even muffled, his voice sounded rough. "You were pushing me away."

"I didn't know what else t-to do."

"You should have called me right away." He tightened his hold in a punishing way, and his voice remained gruff. "There's a solution, Jessica. There's always a solution. But you've got to keep your priorities straight. Top priority is us."

She knew that now. For as long as she lived, she'd never forget the sight of big, bad Carter Malloy with tears in his eyes. They had been tears of pain, and she'd put them there. They were humbling and hor-rifying. She never wanted to see them again.

Going up on tiptoe, she coiled her arms more tightly around his neck.

"I love you," she whispered over and over again until finally he took her face in his hands and held her back.

"What do you want?" he whispered. His face was inches from hers, his thumbs brushing tears from under her glasses while his palms held her still. "Tell me."

"You. Just you."

"But what do you want?"

She knew that he needed to hear the words, and though they represented the ultimate exposure, she was ready for that, too. "I want to marry you. I want to take your name and use your credit cards and drive your car. I want to have your babies."

Carter didn't react, simply looked at her as though he weren't quite sure whether to believe her. So, clutching his wrists, she added, "I mean it. All of it. I think it's what I've wanted since the first time we made love, but I've been so afraid. You're so much more than me—"

"I'm not."

"You are. You've done so much more, come so much further in life, and that makes you so much more interesting. I want to marry you. I do, Carter. But if we got married and then you wanted out, I think I'd *die*, I love you so much."

"I won't want out," he said.

"But I didn't know that for sure until just now."

"I've been telling it to you for weeks."

"But I didn't know." She closed her eyes and whispered, "Oh, Carter, I don't ever want to lose you. Not ever."

"Then marry me. That's the first way to tie a man down."

Her eyes came open. "I'll marry you."

"And give me kids. That's the second way to tie a man down."

"Okay."

"And keep on teaching, because I'm so *proud* of what you do."

"You are?" she asked with a hesitant half smile.

"Damn it, yes," he said and crushed her to him. "I've always been proud of you. I'll always *be* proud of you—whether you're a scholar, mother of my kids, my wife or my woman."

Jessica smiled against his neck, feeling lighter and happier than she'd ever felt before. "I do love you," she whispered.

"Then trust me, too," he said. Taking her by the shoulders, he put her back a step and eyed her sternly. "Trust that I mean what I say when I tell you I love you. I don't want other women. I never *have* wanted other women the way I want you. I've never asked another woman to marry me, but I've asked you a dozen times. I *choose* you. I don't *have* to marry you. I *choose* you. I *want* to marry you."

"I get the point," she murmured, feeling a little shamefaced but delighted in spite of it.

"Do you also get the point about priorities?" he went on, and though a sternness remained in his voice, there was also an exciting vibrancy. "Crosslyn Rise is beautiful. It is venerable and stately and historic. I've got a whole lot of time invested in it, and money now, too, but if I had to choose between the Rise and you, there'd be no contest. I'd turn my back on the time, the money and the Rise just to have you. And I'd do it without a single regret." His eyes grew softer. "So I don't want you worrying about the zoning commission. We'll call Gordon and Gideon and the others. We'll work something out. But all that is secondary. Do you understand?"

"I do," she whispered, and it was true. In those few horrible minutes when she had seen his tears, when he had walked away from her and she'd had the briefest glimpse of the emptiness of life without him, Crosslyn Rise had been the last thing on her mind. Yes, the Rise was in trouble, but she could handle it. With Carter by her side, she could handle anything.

THE DREAM UNFOLDS

1

They were three men with a mission late on a September afternoon. Purposefully they climbed from their cars, slammed their doors in quick succession and fell into broad stride on the brick walk leading to Elizabeth Abbott's front door. Gordon Hale rang the doorbell. It had been decided, back in his office at the bank, that he would be the primary speaker. He was the senior member of the group, the one who had organized the Crosslyn Rise consortium, the one who posed the least threat to Elizabeth Abbott.

Carter Malloy posed a threat because he was a brilliant architect, a rising star in his hometown, with a project in the works that stood to bring big bucks to the town. But there was more to his threat than that. He had known Elizabeth Abbott when they'd been kids, when he'd been the bad boy of the lot. The bad boy no longer, his biggest mistake in recent years had been bedding the vengeful Ms. Abbott. It had only happened once, he swore, and years before, despite Elizabeth's continued interest. Now, though, Carter was in love and on the verge of marrying Jessica Crosslyn, and Elizabeth had her tool for revenge. As chairman of the zoning commission, she was denying Crosslyn Rise the building permit it needed to break ground on its project.

Gideon Lowe was the builder for that project, and he had lots riding on its success. For one thing, the conversion of Crosslyn Rise from a single mansion on acres of land to an elegant condominium community promised to be the most challenging project he'd ever worked on. For another, it was the most visible. A job well-done there would be like a gold star on his résumé. But there was another reason why he wanted the project to be a success. He was an investor in it. For the first time, he had money at stake, *big* money. He knew he was taking a gamble, risking so much of his personal savings, but if things went well, he would have established himself as a businessman, a man of brain, as well as brawn. That was what he wanted, a change of image. And that was why he'd allowed himself to be talked into trading a beer with the guys after work for this mission.

A butler opened the door. "Yes?"

Gordon drew his stocky body to its full five-foot-ten-inch height.

"My name is Gordon Hale. These gentlemen are Carter Malloy and Gideon Lowe. We're here to see Miss Abbott. I believe she's expecting us."

"Yes, sir, she is," the butler answered, and stood back to gesture them into the house. "If you'll come this way," he said as soon as they were all in the spacious front hall with the door closed behind them.

Gideon followed the others through the hall, then the living room and into the parlor, all the while fighting the urge to either laugh or say something crude. He hated phoniness. He also hated formality. He was used to it, he supposed, just as he was used to wearing a shirt and tie when the occasion called for it, as this one did. Still he couldn't help but feel scorn for the woman who was now rising, like a queen receiving her court, from a chintz-covered wingback chair.

"Gordon," she said with a smile, and extended her hand, "how nice to see you."

Gordon took her hand in his. "The pleasure's mine, Elizabeth." He turned and said nonchalantly, "I believe you know Carter."

"Yes," she acknowledged, and Gideon had to hand it to her. For a woman who had once lain naked and hot under Carter, she was cool as a cucumber now. "How are you, Carter?"

Carter wasn't quite as cool. Losing himself to the opportunity, he said, "I'd have been better without this misunderstanding."

"Misunderstanding?" Elizabeth asked innocently. "Is there a misunderstanding here?" She looked at Gordon. "I thought we'd been quite clear."

Gordon cleared his throat. "About denying us the building permit, yes. About why you've denied it, no. That's why we requested this meeting. But before we start—" he gestured toward Gideon "—I don't believe you've met Gideon Lowe. He's both a member of the consortium and our general contractor."

Elizabeth turned the force of her impeccably made-up blue eyes on Gideon. She nodded, then seemed to look a second time and with interest, after which she extended her hand. "Gideon Lowe? Have I heard that name before?"

"I doubt it, ma'am," Gideon said. Her hand felt as cool as that cuke, and nearly as hard. He guessed she was made of steel and could understand why once had been enough for Carter. He knew then and there that he wasn't interested even in once, himself, but he had every intention of playing the game. "Most of my work has been out in the western counties. I'm new to these parts." If he sounded like a nice country boy, even a little Southern, that was fine for now. Women liked that. They found it sweet, even charming, particularly when the man was as tall as Gideon was, and—he only thought it because, after thirty-nine years of hearing people say it, he supposed he had the right—as handsome.

"Welcome, then," she said with a smile. "But how did you come to be associated with these two rogues?"

"That's a damn good question," he said, returning the smile, even putting a little extra shine in it. "Seems I might have been taken in by promises of smooth sailing. We builders are used to delays, but that doesn't mean we like them. I've got my trucks ready to roll and my men champing at the bit. You're one powerful lady to control a group of guys that way."

Elizabeth did something with her mouth that said she loved the thought of that, though she said a bit demurely, "I'm afraid I can't take all the credit. I'm only one of a committee."

"But you're its chairman," Gordon put in, picking up the ball. "May we sit, Elizabeth?"

Elizabeth turned to him with a look of mild indignance. "Be my guest, though it won't do you much good. We've made our decision. As a courtesy, I've agreed to see you, but the committee's next formal meeting won't be until February. I thought I explained all that to Jessica."

At mention of Jessica's name, Carter stiffened. "You explained just enough on the phone to upset her. Why don't you go over it once more, face-to-face, with us."

"What Carter means," Gordon rushed to explain, "is that we're a little confused. Until yesterday afternoon, we'd been under the impression that everything was approved. I've been in close touch with Donald Swett, who assured me that all was well."

"Donald shouldn't have said that. I suppose he can be excused, since he's new to the committee this year, but all is never 'well,' as you put it, until the last of the information has been studied. As it turns out, we have serious doubts about the benefit of your project to this community."

"Are you kidding?" Carter asked.

Gordon held up a hand to him. To Elizabeth, he said, "The proposal we submitted to your committee went through the issue of community impact, point by point. The town has lots to gain, not the least of which is new tax revenue."

Elizabeth tipped her head. "We have lots to lose, too."

"Like what?" Carter asked, though a bit more civilly.

"Like crowding on the waterfront."

Gordon shook his head. "The marina will be limited in size and exclusive, at that. The price of the slips, alone, will discourage crowds."

"That price will discourage the local residents, too," Elizabeth argued, "who, I might add, also pay taxes to this town."

"Oh, my God," Carter muttered, "you're worried about the common folk. Since when, Elizabeth? You never used to give a damn about anyone or anything—"

"Carter—" Gordon interrupted, only to be interrupted in turn by Elizabeth, who was glaring at Carter.

"I've moved up in the hierarchy of this town. It's become my responsibility to think of everyone here." When Carter snorted in disbelief, she deliberately looked back at Gordon. "There's also the matter of your shops and their effect on those we already have. The town owes something to the shopkeepers who've been loyal to us all these years. So you see, it's not just a matter of money."

"That's the most honest thing you've said so far," Carter fumed. "In fact, it doesn't have a damn *thing* to do with money. Or with crowding the waterfront or squeezing out shops. It has to do with you and me—"

Gordon interrupted. "I think we're losing it a little, here."

"Did you expect anything different?" Elizabeth said in a superior way. "Some people never change. Carter certainly hasn't. He was a troublemaker as a boy, and he's a troublemaker now. Maybe *that's* one of the reservations my committee has—"

Carter sliced a hand through the air. "Your 'committee' has no reservations. You're the only one who does. I'd venture to guess that your 'committee' was as surprised as we were by this sudden withholding of a permit. Face it, Lizzie. You're acting on a personal vendetta. I wonder what your 'committee' would say, or the townspeople, for that matter, if they were to learn that you and I—"

"Carter!" Gordon snapped at the very same time that Gideon decided things had gone far enough.

"Whoa," Gideon said in a firm but slow and slightly raspy voice. "Let's take it easy here." He knew Carter. When the man felt passionately about something, there was no stopping him. It had been that way with Jessica, whom he had wooed doggedly for months until finally, just the day before, she agreed to marry him. It was that way with Crosslyn Rise, where he had spent part of his childhood. Apparently it was that way, albeit negatively, with Elizabeth Abbott. But Gideon knew Elizabeth's type, too. Over the years, he had done enough work for people like her to know that the more she was pushed, the more she would dig in her heels. Reason had nothing to do with it; pride did.

But pride wouldn't get the consortium the building permit it needed, and the permit was all Gideon wanted. "I think," he went on in the same slow and raspy voice, "that we ought to cool it a second." He scratched his head. "Maybe we ought to cool it longer than that. It's late. I don't know about you guys, but I've been working all day. I'm tired. We're all tired." He looked beseechingly at Elizabeth. "Maybe this discussion would be better saved for tomorrow morning."

"I don't believe I can make it then," she said.

Gordon added, "Tomorrow morning's booked for me, too."

Carter scowled. "I have meetings in Springfield."

"Then dinner now," Gideon suggested. "I'm starved."

Again Gordon shook his head. "Mary's expecting me home. I'm already late."

Carter simply said, "Bad night."

Gideon slid a look at Elizabeth. "We could talk over dinner, you and I. I know as much about this project as these bozos. It'd be a hell of a lot more peaceful. And pleasant," he added more softly. "What do you say?"

Elizabeth was interested. He could see that. But she wasn't about to accept his invitation too quickly, lest she look eager. So she regarded him contemplatively for a minute, then looked at Gordon and at Carter, the latter in a dismissive way, before meeting Gideon's gaze again.

"I say that would be a refreshing change. You're right. It would be more peaceful. You seem like a reasonable man. We'll be able to talk." She glanced at the slender gold watch on her wrist. "But we ought to leave soon. I have an engagement at nine."

As announcements went, it was a bitchy one. But Gideon was glad she'd made it for several reasons. For one thing, he doubted it was true, which dented her credibility considerably, which made him feel less guilty for the sweet talking he was about to do. For another, it gave him an out. He was more than willing to wine and dine Elizabeth Abbott for the sake of the project, but he wasn't going beyond that. Hopefully, he'd have the concessions he wanted by the time dessert was done.

Actually he did even better than that. Around and between sexy smiles, the doling out of small tidbits of personal information and the withholding of enough else to make Elizabeth immensely curious, he got her to agree that though some of her reservations had merit, the pluses of the Crosslyn Rise conversion outweighed the minuses. In a golden twist of fate—not entirely bizarre, Gideon knew, since the restaurant they were at was the only place for fine evening dining in town—two other members of the zoning commission were eating there with their wives. Unable to resist showing Gideon how influential she was, Elizabeth insisted on threading her arm through his and leading him to their table, introducing him around, then announcing that she had decided not to veto the Crosslyn Rise conversion after all. The men from the commission seemed pleased. They vigorously shook hands with Gideon and welcomed him to their town, while their wives looked on with smiles. Gideon smiled as charmingly at the wives as he did at Elizabeth. He knew it would be hard for her to renege after she'd declared her intentions before so many witnesses.

Feeling proud of himself for handling things with such aplomb, he sent a wink to a waitress whose looks tickled his fancy, as he escorted Elizabeth from the restaurant. At her front door, he graciously thanked her for the pleasure of her company.

"Will we do it again?" she asked.

"By all means. Though I feel a little guilty."

"About what?"

"Seeing you, given our business dealings. There are some who would say we have a conflict of interest."

"They won't say it to me," Elizabeth claimed. "I do what I want."

"In this town, yes. But I work all over the state. I won't have you as my guardian angel other places."

Elizabeth frowned. "Are you saying that we shouldn't see each other until you're done with all of Crosslyn Rise? But that's ridiculous! The project could take years!"

In a soft, very gentle, slightly naughty voice, he said, "That's not what I'm saying at all. I'm just suggesting we wait until my work with the zoning commission is done."

Her frown vanished, replaced by a smug smile. "It's done. You'll have your permit by ten tomorrow morning." She tugged at his lapel. "Any more problems?"

He gave her his most lecherous grin and looked at her mouth. "None at all, ma'am. What say I call you later in the week. I'm busy this weekend, but I'm sure we'll be able to find another time when we're both free." He glanced at his watch. "Almost nine. Gotta run before I turn into a mouse." He winked. "See ya."

"So what was she like?" Johnny McCaffrey asked him the next afternoon after work.

They were at Sully's, where they went most days when Gideon was home in Worcester. Sully's was a diner when the sun shone and a bar at night, the watering spot for the local rednecks. Gideon's neck wasn't as red as some, but he'd grown up with these guys. They were his framers, his plasterers, his masons. They were his teammates—softball in the summer, basketball the rest of the year. They were also his friends.

Johnny was the closest of those and had been since they were eight and pinching apples from Drattles' orchard on the outskirts of town. Ugly as sin, Johnny had a heart of gold, which was probably why he had a terrific wife, Gideon mused. He was as loyal as loyal came, and every bit as trustworthy. That didn't mean he didn't live a little vicariously through Gideon.

"She was incredible," Gideon said now of Elizabeth, and it wasn't a compliment. "She has everything going for her—blond hair, blue eyes, nice bod, great legs—then she opens her mouth and the arrogance pours out. And dim-witted? Man, she's amazing. What woman in this day and age wouldn't have seen right through me? I mean, I wasn't subtle about wanting that permit—and wanting it before I touched her. Hell, I didn't even have to *kiss* her for it."

"Too bad."

"Nah. She didn't turn *me* on." He took a swig of his beer.

Johnny tipped his own mug and found it empty. "That type used to. You must be getting old, pal. Used to be you'd take most anything, and the more hoity-toity the better." He punctuated the statement with two raps of his mug on the bar.

Gideon drew himself straighter on his stool and said with a self-mocking grin, "That was before I got hoity-toity myself. I don't need other people's flash no more. I got my own."

"Watch out you don't start believing that," Johnny teased. "Give me another, Jinko," he told the bartender. To Gideon, he said, "I bumped into Sara Thayer today. She wanted to know how you've been. She'd love a call."

Gideon winced. "Come on, Johnny. She's a kid."

"She's twenty-one."

"I don't fool with kids."

"She doesn't look like a kid. She's got everything right where it's supposed to be. And she ain't gonna wait forever."

Sara Thayer was Johnny's wife's cousin. She'd developed a crush on Gideon at a Christmas party two years before, and Johnny, bless his soul, had been a would-be matchmaker ever since. Sara was a nice girl, Gideon thought. But she *was* far too young, and in ways beyond her age.

As though answering a call, the waitress chose that moment to come close and drape an arm around Gideon's shoulder. He slid his own around her waist and pulled her close. "Now this," he told Johnny, "is the kind of woman for me. Solid and mature. Dedicated. Appreciative." He turned to her. "What do you say, Cookie? Want to go for a ride, you and me?"

Cookie snapped her gum while she thought about it, then planted a kiss on his nose. "Not tonight, big guy. I gotta work till twelve, and you'll be sound asleep by then. Hear you landed a big new job."

"Yup."

"Hear it's on the coast."

"Yup."

"Now why'd you do that for, Gideon Lowe? Every time you sign up to build something off somewhere, we don't see you so much. How long is this one gonna take?"

"A while. But I'm commuting. I'll be around."

Cookie snorted. "You better be. If I've gotta look at this guy—" she hitched her chin toward Johnny "—sittin' here with the weight of all your other jobs on his shoulders for long, I'll go nuts."

"John can handle it," Gideon said with confidence. Johnny had been his foreman for years and had never once let him down. "You just be good to him, babe, and he'll smile. Right, John?"

"Right," Johnny said.

Cookie snapped her gum by way of punctuation, then said, "You guys hungry? I got some great hash out back. Whaddya say?"

"Not for me," Johnny said. "I'm headin' home in another five."

Gideon was heading home, too, but not to a woman waiting with dinner. He was heading toward a deskful of paperwork. The idea of putting that off for just a little longer was mighty appealing.

"Is it fresh, the hash?" he asked.

Cookie cuffed him on the head.

"I'll have some," he said. "Fast." He gave Cookie a pat on the rump and sent her off.

"So you're all set to get started up there now that the permit's through?" Johnny asked.

"Yup. We'll break ground on Monday, get the foundation poured the week after, then start framing. October can be a bitch of a month if we get rain, but I really want to get everything up and closed in before the snows come."

"Think you can?"

Gideon thought about that, thought about the complex designs of the condominium clusters and the fact that the crews he used would be commuting better than an hour each way, just like he would. He'd debated using local subs, but he really wanted his own men. He trusted his own men. They knew him, knew what he demanded, and, in turn, he knew they could produce. Of course, if the weather went bad, or they dug into ledge and had to blast, things would be delayed. But with the permit now in hand, they had a chance.

"We're sure as hell gonna try," he said.

They did just that. With Gideon supervising every move, dump trucks and trailers bearing bulldozers and backhoes moved as carefully as possible over the virgin soil of Crosslyn Rise toward the duck pond, which was the first of three areas on the property being developed. After a cluster of eight condominiums was built there, another eight would be built in the pine grove, then another eight in the meadow. The duck pond had the most charm, Gideon thought and was pleased it was being developed first. Done right, it would be a powerful selling tool. That fact was foremost in his mind as the large machines were unloaded and the work began.

Fortunately, he and Carter had paved the way by having things cited, measured and staked well before the heavy equipment arrived. Though they were both determined to remove the least number of trees, several did have to come down to make room for the housing. A separate specialty crew had already done the cutting and chipping, leaving only stumping for the bulldozers when they arrived.

Once the best of the topsoil had been scraped off the top of the land and piled to the side, the bulldozers began the actual digging. Carter came often to watch, sometimes with Jessica, though the marring of the land tore her apart. She had total faith in Carter's plans and even, thanks to Carter's conviction, in Gideon's ability to give those plans form. Still, she had lived on Crosslyn Rise all her life, as had her father before her. The duck pond was only one of the spots she found precious.

Gideon could understand her feelings for the Rise. From the first time he'd walked through the land, he'd been able to appreciate its rare beauty. Being intimately involved in the work process, though, he had enough on his mind to keep sentimentality in check.

Contrary to Jessica, the deeper the hole got, the more excited he was. There was some rock that could be removed without blasting, some that couldn't but that could be circumvented by moving the entire cluster over just a bit and making a small section of one basement a bit more shallow. But they hadn't hit water, and water was what Gideon had feared. The tests had said they wouldn't, but he'd done tests before and been wrong; a test done in one spot didn't always reveal what was in another. They'd lucked out, which meant that the foundation could be sunk as deeply as originally planned, which meant less grading later and a far more aesthetically pleasing result.

The cellar hole was completed and the forms for the foundation set up. Then, as though things were going too smoothly, just when the cement was to be poured, the rains came. They lasted only three days, but they came with such force—and on a Monday, Tuesday and Wednesday—that it wasn't until the following Monday that Gideon felt the hole had dried out enough to pour the foundation.

He mightn't have minded the layoff, since there were plenty of other things to be done on plenty of other projects that his crews were involved in, had it not been for Elizabeth Abbott's calls.

"She wants to see me," he told Gordon the following Saturday at Jessica and Carter's wedding reception. He'd cornered the banker at one end of the long living room of the mansion at Crosslyn Rise. They were sipping champagne, which Gideon rather enjoyed. He wasn't particularly enjoying his tuxedo, though. He felt slightly strangled in it, but Jessica had insisted. She wanted her wedding to be elegant, and Carter, lovesick fool that he was, had gone right along with her. When Gideon got married—*if* he ever did—he intended to wear jeans.

At the moment, though, that wasn't his primary concern; Elizabeth Abbott was. "I've already put her off two or three times, but she keeps calling. I'm telling you, the woman is either stubborn or desperate. She doesn't take a hint."

"Maybe you have to be more blunt," Gordon suggested. He was pursing his lips in a way that told Gideon he found some humor in the situation.

Gideon didn't find any humor in it at all. He felt a little guilty about what he'd done, leading Elizabeth on. Granted, he'd gotten his permit, which had made the entire eight-member consortium, plus numerous on-call construction workers very happy. None of the others, though, were getting suggestive phone calls.

"Oh, I can be more blunt," he said. "The question is whether there's anything else she can do to slow us down from here on. She's a dangerous woman. She's already shown us that. I wouldn't want to do or say anything to jeopardize this project."

Gordon seemed to take that part a bit more seriously. He thought about it for a minute while he watched Carter lead Jessica in a graceful waltz to the accompaniment of a string quartet. "There's not much she can do now," he said finally. "We have written permits for each of the different phases of this project. She could decide to rescind one or the other, but I don't think she'd dare. Not after she pulled back last time, then changed her mind. I don't think she'd want people knowing that it was Carter last time and you this time."

"It *isn't* me," Gideon said quickly. "I haven't slept with her. I haven't even gone *out* with her, other than that first dinner, and that was business."

"Apparently not completely," Gordon remarked dryly.

"It was business. The rest was all innuendo." His eyes were glued to the bride and groom, moving so smoothly with just the occasional dip and twirl. "Where in the hell did Carter learn to do that? He was born on the same side of the tracks as me. The son of a bitch must've taken lessons."

Gordon chuckled. "Must've."

Gideon followed them a bit longer. "They look happy."

"I'd agree with that."

"He's a lucky guy. She's a sweetie."

"You bet."

"She got any sisters?"

"Sorry."

Gideon sighed. "Then I guess I'll have to mosey over and see if I can't charm that redheaded cutie in the sparkly dress into swaying a little with me. I'm great at swaying." He took a long sip of his champagne. After it had gone down, he put a finger under his collar to give him a moment's free breath, set his empty glass on a passing tray, cleared his throat and was off.

The redheaded cutie in the sparkly dress turned out to be a colleague of Jessica's at Harvard. She swayed with Gideon a whole lot that night, then saw him two subsequent times. Gideon liked her. She had a spark he wouldn't have imagined a professor of Russian history to have. She also had a tendency to lecture, and when she did that, he felt as though he were seventeen again and hanging on by his bare teeth, just trying to make it through to graduation so that he could start doing, full-time, what he'd always wanted, which was to build houses.

So he let their relationship, what of it there had been, die a very natural death. Elizabeth Abbott, though, wasn't so easy to dispose of. The first time she called after the wedding, he said that he had a previously arranged date. The second time, he said he was seeing the same woman and that they were getting pretty involved. The third time, he said he just couldn't date other women until he knew what was happening with this first.

"I'm not saying we have to *date*," Elizabeth had the gall to say in a slithery purr. "You could just drop over here one evening and we could let nature take its course."

He mustered a laugh. "I don't know, Elizabeth. Nature hasn't been real kind to me lately. First we had rain, now an early frost. Maybe we shouldn't push our luck."

The purr was suddenly gone, yielding to impatience. "You know,

Gideon, this whole thing is beginning to smell. Have you been leading me on all this time?''

He figured she'd catch on at some point. Fortunately, he'd thought out his answer. "No. I really enjoyed the dinner we had. You're one pretty and sexy lady. It's just that I was madly in love with Marie for years before she up and married someone else. Now she's getting a divorce. I was sure there wouldn't be anything left between us, but I was wrong. So I could agree to go out with you, or drop in at your place some night, but that wouldn't be fair to you. You deserve more than a man with half a heart." *Half a heart.* Not bad, bucko.

Elizabeth wasn't at all impressed. "If she's married and divorced, she's a loser. Weak women make weak marriages. You're looking for trouble, Gideon."

"Maybe," he said, leaving allowance for that should the day come when Elizabeth found out there wasn't anyone special in his life after all, "but I have to see it through. If not, I'll be haunted forever. I have to know, once and for all, whether she and I have a chance."

She accepted his decision, though only temporarily. She continued to call every few nights to check on the status of his romance with Marie. Gideon wasn't naturally a liar and certainly didn't enjoy doing it over and over again, but Elizabeth pushed him into a corner. There were times when he thought he was taking the wrong tactic, when he half wanted to take her up on her invitation, show up at her house, then proceed to be the worst lover in the world. But he couldn't do it. He couldn't demean her—or himself—that way.

So she continued to call, and he continued to lie, all the while cursing himself for doing it, cursing Carter and Gordon for setting him up, cursing Elizabeth for being so goddamned persistent. He was fit to be tied, wondering where it would end, when suddenly, one day, at the very worst possible moment, she appeared at the site.

At least he thought it was her. The hair was blond, the clothes conservative, the figure shapely, the legs long. But it had rained the night before, and the air was heavy with mist, reducing most everything to blandly generic forms.

He was standing on the platform that would be the second floor of one of the houses in the cluster and had been hammering right along with his crew, getting an end piece ready to raise. The work was done. The men had positioned themselves. They were slowly hoisting the large, heavy piece when the creamy figure emerged from the mist.

"Jeez, what's that?" one of the men breathed, diverting the attention of a buddy. That diversion, fractional though it was, was enough to upset the alignment of the skeletal piece. It wobbled and swayed as they tried to right it.

"Easy," Gideon shouted, every muscle straining as he struggled to steady the wood. "Ea-sy." But the balance was lost, and, in the next instant, the piece toppled over the side of the house to the ground.

Gideon swore loudly, then did it again to be heard above the ducks on the pond. He made a quick check to assure himself that none of his men had gone over with the frame. He stalked to the edge of the platform and glared at the splintered piece. Then he raised his eyes and focused on the woman responsible.

2

She was dressed all in beige, but Gideon saw red. Whirling around, he stormed to the rough stairway, clattered down to the first floor, half walked, half ran out of the house and, amid fast-scattering ducks, around to where she stood. Elizabeth Abbott had been a pain in the butt for weeks, but she hadn't disturbed his work until now. He intended to make sure she didn't do it again.

The only thing was that when he came face-to-face with her, he saw that it wasn't Elizabeth. At first glance, though, it could have been her twin, the coloring was so similar. His anger was easily transferred. The fact was that *regardless* of who she was, she was standing where she didn't belong.

"What in the hell do you think you're doing, just popping up out of thin air like that?" he bellowed with his hands on his hips and fury in his voice. Disturbed by his tone, the ducks around the pond quacked louder. "In case you didn't see the sign out front, this is private property. That means that people don't just go wandering around—" he tossed an angry hand back toward the ruined framework "—and for good reason. Look what you've done. My men spent the better half of a day working on that piece, and it'll have to be done over now, which isn't real great, since we were racing to get it up before the rain started again this afternoon. And that's totally aside from the fact that someone could have been hurt in this little fiasco. I carry insurance, lady, but I don't count on people tempting fate. You could have been killed. *I* could have been killed. Any of my *men* could have been killed. A whole goddamned feast worth of *ducks* could have been killed. This is no place for tourists!"

It wasn't that he ran out of breath. He could have ranted on for a while, venting everything negative that he was feeling, only something stopped him, something to do with the woman herself and the way she looked.

Yes, her coloring was like Elizabeth's. She had fair skin, blue eyes, and blond hair that was pulled back into a neat knot. And to some extent, she was dressed as he imagined Elizabeth might have been, though he'd only seen her that one time, when she'd been wearing a dress. This woman was wearing a long pleated skirt of the same cream color as her scarf, which was knotted around the neck of a jacket that looked an awful lot like his old baseball jacket, but of a softer, finer fabric. The jacket was taupe, as were her boots. She wore large button earrings that could have been either ivory or plastic—he wasn't a good judge of things like that in the best of times, and this wasn't the best of times. He was still deeply shaken from what had happened. The look on her face, the way her eyes were wide and her hands were tucked tightly into her pockets, said that she was shaken, too.

"I'm not a tourist," she said quietly. "I know the owner of Crosslyn Rise."

"Well, if you were hoping to find her out here in the rain, you won't. She's working. If you were really a friend of hers, you'd know that."

"I know it. But I didn't come to see Jessica. I came to see what was happening here. She said I could. She was the one who suggested I do it."

If there was one thing Gideon hated, it was people who managed to hold it together when he was feeling strewn. This woman was doing just that, which didn't endear her to him in the least. "Well, she should have let me know first," he barked. "I'm the one in charge here, I ought to know what's going on. If we're having visitors to the site, I can alert my men. There's no reason why they should be shocked the way they were."

"You're right," she agreed. "What's wrong with them? Haven't they ever seen a woman before?"

She was totally innocent, totally direct and quite cutting with that last statement. Gideon shifted her closer in ilk to Elizabeth again. "Oh, they've seen women. They've seen lots of them, and in great and frequent intimacy, I'd wager. But what you just did was like a woman showing up in the men's john."

She had the gall to laugh, but it, too, had an innocent ring. "Cute analogy, though it's not quite appropriate. The sign out front says Private Way. It doesn't say No Women Allowed. Is it my fault if your men get so rattled by the sight of a woman that they become unglued? Face it. You should be yelling at them, not me."

She had a point, he supposed, but he wasn't about to admit it. She had a quiet confidence to her that didn't need stroking. "The fact is that your appearance here has messed us up."

"I'm sorry for that."

"Fine for you to be sorry, after the fact."

"It's better than nothing, which is what I'm getting from you. You could try an apology, too."

"For what?"

"Nearly killing me. If I'd been a little closer, or that piece had shattered and bounced, I'd be lying on the ground bleeding right now."

He gave her a once-over, then drawled, "That wouldn't do much for your outfit."

"It wouldn't do much for your future, unless you have a fondness for lawsuits."

"You don't have the basis for any lawsuit."

"I don't know about that. You and your men were clearly negligent in this case."

Gideon drew himself straighter, making the most of his six-foot-four-inch frame. "So you're judge and jury rolled into one?"

She drew herself straighter to match, though she didn't have more than five foot seven to work with. "Actually, I'm an interior designer. It may well be that I'll be working on this project."

"Not if I can help it," he said, because she was a little too sure of herself, he thought.

"Well, then," she turned to leave, "it's a good thing you're not anyone who counts. If I take this job, I'll be answerable to the Crosslyn Rise consortium, not to some job foreman who can't control his men." With a final direct look, she started off.

Gideon almost let her go. After all, they were far enough from the building that his men hadn't heard what she'd said, so he didn't have to think about saving face, at least, not before them. There was, of course, the matter of his own pride. For years he'd been fighting for respect, and he was doing it now, on several levels, with this project. The final barrier to fall would be with people like this one, who were educated and cultured and arrogant enough to choke a horse.

"**You** really think you're something, don't you?" he called.

She stopped but didn't turn. "No. Not really. I'm just stating the facts."

"You don't know the facts."

"I know that the consortium controls this project. It isn't some sort of workmen's cooperative."

"In some ways it is. Carter Malloy is in the consortium, and he's the architect of record. Nina Stone is in the consortium, and she'll be marketing us."

There was an expectancy to her quiet. "So?"

He savored the impending satisfaction. "So I'm not just 'some job foreman.' I'm the general contractor here. I also happen to be a member of that consortium."

For another minute, she didn't move. Then, very slowly she turned her head and looked at him, in a new light, he thought.

He touched a finger to the nonexistent visor of the wool cap perched on the top of his head. "Name's Gideon Lowe. See y'in the boardroom." With that, he turned back to his men, yelled, "Let's get this mess cleaned up," and set about doing just that with a definitive spring to his step.

Christine Gillette was appalled. She hadn't imagined that the man who'd blasted her so unfairly was a member of the consortium. Granted, he was better spoken than some of the laborers she'd met. But he'd been bullheaded and rough-hewn, not at all in keeping with the image she had of polished men sitting around a boardroom table with Jessica Crosslyn Malloy at its head.

Unsure as to what to say or do, she turned and left when he returned to his work. During the forty-minute drive back to her Belmont office, she replayed their conversation over and over in her mind and never failed to feel badly at its end. She wasn't normally the kind to cut down other people with words, though she did feel she'd had provocation. She also felt that she was right. She *had* apologized. What more could she do?

The fact remained, though, that in several weeks' time she'd be making a presentation to the Crosslyn Rise consortium. Gideon Lowe would be there, no doubt wearing a smug smile on his handsome face. She was sure he'd be the first to vote against her. Smug, handsome, physical men were like that, she knew. They defined the world in macho terms and were perfectly capable of acting on that principle alone. No way would he willingly allow her to work on his project.

She wished she could say that she didn't care, that Crosslyn Rise was just another project, that something else as good would come along. But Crosslyn Rise was special, not only in terms of the project itself but what it would mean to her. She'd been a designer for nearly ten years, working her way up from the most modest jobs—even freebies, at first—to jobs that were larger and more prestigious. This job, if she got it, would be the largest and most prestigious yet. From a designer's standpoint, given the possibilities between the condominium clusters and the mansion, it was exciting. In terms of her career, it was even more so.

Her mind was filled with these thoughts and others when she arrived at her office. Margie Dow, her secretary, greeted her with a wave, then an ominous, "Sybil Thompson's on the warpath. She's called three times in the last two hours. She says she *needs* to talk with you."

Chris rolled her eyes, took the other pink slips that Margie handed her and headed into her office. Knowing that waiting wouldn't make things any better, she dialed Sybil's number. "Hi, Sybil. It's Chris. I just this minute got back to the office. Margie tells me you have a problem."

"*I* have a problem?" Sybil asked, giving Chris a premonition of what was coming. "*You* have a problem. I just came from Stanley's. Your people put down the wrong rug."

Stanley was Sybil's husband and a lawyer, and the carpeting in question was for his new suite of offices. Chris had been hired as the decorator one short month before and had been quite blunt, when Stanley and his partners had said that they wanted the place looking great within the week, about saying that quality outfittings were hard to find off the rack. They'd agreed to the month, and she'd done her best, running back and forth with pictures and swatches and samples, placing rush orders on some items, calling around to locate others in less well-traveled outlets. Now Sybil was saying that one of those items wasn't right.

Propping a shoulder to the phone to hold it at her ear, Chris went around her desk to the file cabinet, opened it and thumbed through. "I was there yesterday afternoon when it was installed, Sybil. It's the one we ordered."

"But it's too dark. Every tiny little bit of lint shows. It'll look filthy all the time."

"No. It's elegant." She extracted a file. It held order forms, sales receipts and invoices relating to the Thompsons' account. "It goes perfectly with the rest of the decor." She began flipping through.

"It's too dark. It really is. I'm sure we chose something lighter. Check the order form and you'll see."

"That's what I'm doing right now. According to this," Chris studied the slip, "we ordered Bold Burgundy, and Bold Burgundy is the color we installed yesterday."

"It can't be."

"It is." She spoke gently, easily understanding Sybil's confusion. "Everything was done quickly. You looked at samples of carpeting, chose what you wanted, and I ordered it. When things move fast like that, with as much done at one time as you did, it's only natural to remember some things one way and some things another way. I'd do it myself, if I didn't write everything down." Of course, that wasn't the only reason she wrote everything down. The major reason was to protect herself from clients who ordered one thing, saw it installed, then decided that it wasn't what they wanted after all. She didn't know whether Sybil fell into that category or whether this was an innocent mix-up. But Chris did have the papers to back up her case.

"I suppose you're right," Sybil said. "Still, that carpet's going to look awful."

"It won't. The cleaning people come through to vacuum every night. Besides, you don't get half the lint in a lawyer's office as you get at home, especially when you're dealing with the upscale clientele that your husband is. Trust me. Bold Burgundy looks great."

Sybil was weakening. "You think so?"

"I know so. Just wait. Give it a few weeks and see what the clients say. They'll rave about it. I'm sure. That carpeting gives a rich look. They'll feel privileged to be there, without knowing why."

Sybil agreed to wait. Satisfied, Chris hung up the phone and returned the folder to the cabinet. Then she opened another drawer, removed a thick cardboard tube, slid out the blueprints for Crosslyn Rise and spread them on her desk.

Carter was brilliant. She had to hand it to him. What he'd done—taking the Georgian colonial theme from the mansion, modifying columns and balconies, elongating the roof and adding skylights to give just a hint of something more contemporary—was perfect. The housing clusters were subtle and elegant, nestling into the setting as though they'd been there forever.

She sighed. She wanted to work on this project in one regard that had nothing to do with either challenge, prestige or money. It had to do with Crosslyn Rise itself. She thought it was gorgeous, real dream material. If ever she pictured a place she would have liked to call home, it was the mansion on the rise. Doing the decorating for it was the next best thing to living there.

She wanted that job.

Picking up the phone, she dialed Jessica Malloy's Harvard office. Despite what she'd told Gideon, Jessica and she were less friends than acquaintances. They had a mutual friend, who was actually the one to suggest to Jessica that Chris do the work on the Rise. They had met after that and hit it off. Though Chris knew that other designers were being considered for the job, she was sure she could compete—unless Gideon Lowe blackballed her.

"Hi," she said to the secretary who answered, "this is Christine Gillette. I'm looking for Jessica. Has she come back from her honeymoon?"

"She certainly has," the woman said. "Hold on, please."

Less than a minute later, Jessica came on the phone. "Christine, how are you?"

"I'm fine, but, hey, congratulations on your marriage." Last time they'd talked, Jessica had been up to her ears in plans. Apparently the wedding had been something of a last-minute affair thanks to Carter, who had refused to wait once Jessica had finally agreed to marry him. "I take it everything went well?"

"Perfectly," Jessica said.

Chris could hear her smile and was envious. "And the trip to Paris?"

"Too short, but sweet."

And terribly romantic, Chris was sure. Paris was that way, or so she was told. She'd never been there herself. "I'm sure you'll get back some day. Maybe for your fiftieth anniversary?"

"Lord, we'll be doddering by then," Jessica said, laughing, and again Chris was envious. To have someone special, like Jessica had Carter, was precious. So was growing old with that someone special. She hoped Jessica knew how lucky she was.

"I wouldn't worry about doddering. You have years of happiness ahead. I wish you both all the best."

"Thanks, Chris. But enough about me. Tell me what's doing with you. You are getting a presentation ready for us, aren't you?"

"Definitely," Chris said and took a breath, "but I had a small problem this morning. I'm afraid I went out to the Rise to walk around, and I upset some of the men working there."

"You upset them? I'd have thought it'd be the other way around. What they're doing to my gorgeous land upsets me to no end."

"But the mess is only temporary. You know that."

"I know, and I'm really excited about Carter's plans and about what the Rise will be, and I know this was my only out, since I couldn't afford the upkeep, not to mention repairs and renovations—" She caught her breath. "Still, I have such sentimental feelings for the place that it's hard for me when even the smallest tree is felled."

"I can understand that," Chris said with a smile. She really liked Jessica, among other things for the fact that she wasn't a money grubber. In that sense, Chris identified with her. Yes, the conversion of Crosslyn Rise would be profitable, but it was a means to an end, the end being the preservation of the Rise, rather than the enhancement of Jessica's bank account. Likewise, Chris sought lucrative jobs like decorating Stanley Thompson's law firm, redecorating the Howard family compound on the Vineyard, and yes, doing Crosslyn Rise, for a greater cause than her own. Her personal needs were modest and had always been so.

"Tell me what happened to you, though," Jessica was saying, returning to the events of that morning.

Chris told her about appearing at the site and jinxing Gideon's crew.

"It was an innocent mistake, Jessica. Honestly. I never dreamed I'd disturb them, or I never would have gone. I thought I was being unobtrusive. I just stood there, watching without saying a word, but one of the guys saw me and two others looked and then the damage was done. I really am sorry. I tried to tell your contractor that, but I'm not sure I got through."

"To Gideon? I'm sure you did. He's a sensible guy."

"Maybe when he's cool, but he was pretty hot under the collar when that framework fell, and I don't blame him. Someone could have been hurt, and then there's the time lost in having to redo the piece, and the rain that he was trying to beat. I, uh, think we may have gotten off on the wrong foot, Gideon and I. He was annoyed and said some things that irked me, so I said some irksome things back, and I may have sounded arrogant. I'm not usually like that."

"And now you're worried that he'll stand in the way of your getting this job."

"That, and that if I do get the job, he and I will have trouble working together. He's a macho type. I don't do well with macho types. I kind of pull in and get intimidated, so I guess I put up a wall, and then I come off sounding snotty. I'm sure that's what he thinks."

"He'll change his mind when he meets you in a more controlled setting."

"When there are other people, *civilized* people around, sure. But if we work together, it won't always be in that kind of controlled setting. There won't always be other people around. We'll be spending a lot of time at the site. His subs and their crews may be around, but if today was any indication, they won't be much help."

The telephone line was quiet for a minute before Jessica asked, "Are you saying that you don't want to try for the job?"

"Oh, no!" Chris cried. "Not at all! I *want* the job. I want it a *lot!*"

Jessica sounded genuinely relieved. "That's good, because I really like what I've seen of your work. It has a sensitivity that I haven't found in some of the others' things. I don't want the Rise to look done up, or glossy. I don't want a 'decorated' look. I want something different and special, something with feeling. Your work has that. *You* have that, I think."

"I hope so, at least as far as my work goes," and she was deeply gratified to hear Jessica say it. But that wasn't why she'd called. "As far as this business with Gideon Lowe goes—"

"Don't think twice about it, Chris. You may not believe it, but Gideon is really a pretty easygoing kind of guy."

"You're right. I don't believe it."

Jessica laughed. "He is. Really. But he takes his work very seriously. He may have overreacted this morning, in which case he's probably feeling like a heel, but he'll get over it. This project means a lot to him. He has money invested in it. He'd be the first one to say that when we pick people to do the work, we have to pick the best."

"Is that why he picked himself as the builder?" Chris couldn't resist tossing out. She barely had to close her eyes to picture his smug smile or the broad set of his shoulders or the tight-hipped way he'd walked away from her.

"He's good. I've seen his things. Carter has worked with him before, and *he* says he's good. Gideon's reputation's at stake here, along with his money. He wants the best. And if the best turns out to be you, once we hear all the presentations, he'll go along with it."

"Graciously?" Somehow Chris couldn't see it.

"Graciously. He's a professional."

Chris thought a lot about that in the days following. She figured Jessica might be right. Gideon was a professional. But a professional what? A professional builder? A professional businessman? A professional bruiser? A professional lover? No doubt he had a wife stashed away somewhere, waiting with the television warmed and the beer chilled for the time when he got home from work and collapsed into his vinyl recliner. Chris could picture it. He looked like that type. Large, brawny, physical, he'd be the king of whatever castle he stormed.

Then again, he was a member of the consortium. Somehow that didn't jibe with the image. To be a member of a consortium, one needed money and brains. Chris knew there was good money in building, at least for the savvy builder, and the savvy builder had to be bright. But there were brains, and there were brains. Some were limited to one narrow field, while others were broader. She didn't picture Gideon Lowe being broad in any respect but his shoulders.

That was one of the reasons why she grew more nervous as the day of the presentation drew near. She burned the midnight oil doing drawings, then redoing them, trying to get them just right. She sat back and rethought her concept, then altered the drawings yet again to accommodate even the slightest shift. She knew that, given Gideon's predisposition, she'd have to impress the others in the group in a big way if she wanted the job.

The day of the meeting was a beautiful one, cool and clear as the best of November days were along the North Atlantic shore. Gideon felt good. The first roof section had gone up despite a last-minute glitch that had kept Carter and him sweating over the plans the weekend before. But things had finally fit, and if all went well, the second, third and fourth roof sections would be up by the end of the week. Once that was done, the snows could come and Gideon wouldn't give a hoot.

It had also been eight whole days since he'd last heard from Elizabeth Abbott.

So he was in a plucky mood when the eight members of the consortium held their weekly meeting at seven that evening in Gordon's office. It occurred to Gideon as he greeted the others and took his place at the table, that he was comfortable with the group. It hadn't been so at first. He had felt self-conscious, almost like an imposter, as though he didn't have any business being there and they all knew it. Over the weeks that they'd been meeting, though, he'd found himself accepted as a peer. More than that, his status as the general contractor actually gave him a boost in their eyes. He was the one member of the group most closely aligned with the reality of the project.

There were Carter and Jessica, sitting side by side, then the three men Gordon had brought in from other areas—Bill Nolan, from the Nolan Paper Mill family in Maine, Ben Heavey, a real estate developer well-known in the East, and Zach Gould, a retired banker with time and money on his hands, who visited the site often. Rounding out the group were John Sawyer, a local bookseller, and Nina Stone, the realtor who would one day market the project.

Being single, Gideon had taken notice of Nina at the start. They'd even gone out to dinner once, but neither had wanted a follow-up, certainly not as a prelude to something deeper. Nina was a tough cookie, an aggressive woman, almost driven. Petite and a little bizarre, she wasn't Gideon's type at all. By mutual agreement, they were simply friends.

After calling the meeting to order, Gordon, who always sat in as an advisor of sorts, gave them a rundown of the money situation, then handed the meeting over to Carter, who called in, one by one, the interior designers vying for the project.

The first was a woman who worked out of Boston and had done several of the more notable condo projects there in recent years. Gideon thought her plans were pretentious.

The second was a man who talked a blue streak about glass and marble and monotonic values. Gideon thought everything about him sounded sterile.

The third was Christine Gillette, and Gideon didn't take his eyes off her once. She was wearing beige again, a suit this time, with a tweedy blazer over a solid-colored blouse and skirt, and he had to admit that she looked elegant. She also looked slightly nervous, if the faint shimmer of her silk blouse was any indication of the thudding of her heart. But she was composed, and obviously well rehearsed. She made her presentation, exchanging one drawing for another with slender fingers as she talked about recreating the ambience that she believed made Crosslyn Rise special. Her voice was soft, but it held conviction. She clearly believed in what she was saying.

Quite against his wishes, Gideon was impressed. Her eyes had glanced across his from time to time, but if she was remembering their last encounter, she didn't let on. She was cool, but in a positive way. Not haughty, but self-assured. She didn't remind him at all of Elizabeth Abbott.

At the end of her presentation she left, sent home, as the others had been, with word that a decision would be made within the week. It was obvious, though, where the group's sentiment lay.

"Christine's plans were the warmest," John Sawyer said. "I like the feeling she captured."

Zach Gould agreed. "I liked her, too. She wasn't heavy-handed like the first, or slick like the second."

"Her estimates are high," Ben Heavey reminded them. He was the most conservative of the group.

"All three are high," Nina said, "but the fact is that if we want this done right, we'll have to shell out. I have a feeling that Christine, more than the others, will be able to get us the most for the least. She seems the most inventive, the least programmed."

"I want to know what Gideon thinks," Carter said, looking straight at him. "He'll be spending more time with the decorator than the rest of us. There are things like moldings, doors, flooring and deck work that I specified in my plans but that are fully changeable if something else fits better with the decor. So, Gideon, what are your thoughts?"

Gideon, who had been slouched with an elbow on the arm of his chair and his chin on his fist, wasn't sure *what* those thoughts were. Christine was the best of the three, without a doubt, but he wasn't sure he wanted to work with her. There was something about her that unsettled him, though he couldn't put his finger on what it was.

"She's the least experienced of the lot," he finally said, lowering the fist and sitting straighter. "What's the setup of her firm?"

Jessica answered. "She's something of a single practitioner. Her office is small. She has one full-time secretary and two part-time assistants, both with degrees in decorating, both with small children. They're job-sharing. It works out well for them, and from what she says, it works out well for Chris."

"Job-sharing," John mused with a grin. "I like that." They all knew that he was a single parent, and that though he owned his bookstore, he only manned the cash register during those hours when he had a sitter for his son. He had a woman who sold books for him the rest of the time, so he was basically job-sharing, himself.

Job-sharing didn't mean a whole lot to Gideon. Men did the work in his field, and even if their bosses allowed it, which they didn't, they weren't the types to leave at one in the afternoon to take a toddler to gym-and-swim.

He wondered what the story was on Christine Gillette. The résumé she'd handed out said nothing whatsoever about her personal life. He hadn't seen a wedding band, though that didn't mean anything in this day and age. He wondered whether she had a husband at home, and was vaguely annoyed at the thought.

"Does *she* have little kids who she'll have to miss work for each time they get a cold?" he asked, looking slightly miffed.

"Whoa," said John. "Be compassionate, my friend."

But Gideon wasn't a father, and as for compassion, there seemed to be plenty in the room for Christine Gillette without his. "Carter's right. If we decide to use this woman, I'm the one who'll be working most closely with her. Job-sharing may be well and good in certain areas, but construction isn't one. If I have to order bathroom fixtures, and she's off taking the kid to Disney World over school vacation so she can't meet with me, we'll be held back." He thought the argument was completely valid and he was justified to raise it. Christine might be able to charm the pants off this consortium, but if she couldn't come through when *he* needed her, he didn't want her at all! "I keep things moving. That's the way I work. I need people who'll be there."

"Chris will be there," Jessica assured him. "There are no little ones at home. From what I've been told—and from more than one source—she puts in fifty-hour weeks."

"Still," he cautioned, "if she's a single practitioner—"

"With a secretary and assistants," Jessica put in.

"Okay, with a secretary and assistants, but she's the main mover. Both of the other candidates for this position have partners, full partners, people who could take over if something happened."

"What could happen?" Jessica asked. "Chris is in good health. She has a reputation for finishing jobs on time, if not ahead. She's efficient and effective. And she needs this job." She held up a hand before he could comment on that. "I know, I know. You're going to ask me why she's so desperate, and she's not. Not desperate. But this job could give her career a boost, and she wants that. She deserves it."

Barbara Delinsky

Gideon didn't want to think that Christine, with her fair-haired freshness, her poise, and legs long enough to drive a man wild, deserved a thing. "Hey, this isn't a charity. We're not in the business of on-the-job training."

"Gideon," Jessica said with a mocking scowl, "I know that. More than *anyone* here, I know it. I've lived on Crosslyn Rise all my life. I'm the one who's being torn apart that I can't leave it the way it always was—" She stopped for a minute when Carter put a hand on her arm. She nodded, took a calming breath. "I want the Rise to be the best it can possibly be, and if Chris wasn't the best, I wouldn't be recommending her."

"She's a friend," Gideon accused, recalling what Chris had told him.

"She's a friend of a friend, but I have no personal interest in her getting this job. If anything, I was wary when my friend mentioned her to me, because I'm *not* in the business of doing favors. Then I looked at pictures of other jobs Chris has done. Now, looking at what she's come up with for us, I'm more convinced than ever that she's the right one." She stopped, had another thought, went on. "Besides, there's a definite advantage to working with someone with a smaller client list. It's the old issue of being a small fish in a big pond, or vice versa. Personally, I'd rather be the big fish in Chris's pond, than a small fish in someone else's, particularly since no one else's ideas for this project are anywhere near as good as hers."

Gideon might have said more, but didn't. Clearly the others agreed with Jessica, as the vote they took several minutes later proved. Christine was approved as the decorator for Crosslyn Rise by a unanimous vote. Or a nearly unanimous one. Gideon abstained.

"Why did you do that?" Carter asked quietly after the meeting had adjourned and most of the others had left.

Gideon didn't have a ready answer. "I don't know. Maybe because she didn't need my vote. She had the rest of you wowed."

"But you like her ideas."

"Yes, I like her ideas."

"Think you can work with her?"

Gideon jammed his fists into his pockets and rocked back on his heels. "Work with her? I suppose."

"So what bothers you?"

"I don't know."

Carter was beginning to have his suspicions, if the look on Gideon's face went for anything. "She's pretty, and she's single."

"Single?" Somehow that made Gideon feel worse.

"Single. Available. Is that a threat?"

"Only if she's on the make. Is she looking for it?"

"Not that I know of." Carter leaned closer. "Word has it she lives like a monk."

Gideon glowered. "Is that supposed to impress me?"

"If you're worried about being attacked, it should."

"Attacked? Me? By *her*? That's the last thing I'm worried about. Listen, man, I've got plenty of women to call when I get the urge. Snap my fingers, there they are."

"Christine isn't likely to do that."

"Don't you know it. She's the kind to snap *her* fingers. Well, I don't come running so fast, and I don't give a damn *how* pretty she is. Long legs are a dime a dozen. So are breasts, bottoms and big blue eyes, and as far as that blond hair of hers goes, it's probably right out of a bottle." He paused only for the quickest breath. "I can work with her. As long as she produces, I can work with her. But if she starts playing games, acting high and mighty and superior, and botching things up so *my* work starts looking shabby, we'll be in trouble. Big trouble."

Actually Gideon was in big trouble already, but it wasn't until three weeks had passed, during which time he couldn't get Christine Gillette out of his mind for more than a few hours at a stretch, that he realized it. The realization was driven home when she called to make an appointment to see him and he hung up the phone with a pounding heart and a racing pulse.

3

Christine was having a few small physical problems of her own as she left Belmont early that Thursday morning and headed north toward Crosslyn Rise. Her stomach was jumpy. Tea hadn't helped. Nor had a dish of oatmeal. Worse, the jitters seemed to echo through her body, leaving a fine tremor in her hands.

It was excitement, she told herself. She'd been flying high since receiving the call from Jessica that she'd landed the Crosslyn Rise job. She'd also been working her tail off since then to get ahead on other projects so that she'd have plenty of time to devote to the Rise. So maybe, she speculated as she turned onto Route 128, the trembling was from fatigue.

Then again, maybe it was nervousness. She didn't like to think so, because she'd never felt nervous this way about her work, but she'd never worked with anyone like Gideon Lowe before. She'd always managed to keep her cool, at least outwardly, with even the most intimidating of clients, but Gideon was something else. He was large, though she'd worked with larger men. He was quick-tempered, though she'd worked with some even more so. He was chauvinistic, though heaven knows she'd met worse. But he got to her as the others hadn't. He stuck in her mind. She wasn't quite sure why.

As the car cruised northward on the highway, she pondered that, just as she had been doing practically every free minute since her interview at the bank three weeks before.

She'd been slightly stunned to see him there—not to see him, per se, but to see how he looked. At the site, he'd been a craftsman. His work boots had been crusted with dirt, his jeans faded and worn. He'd been wearing a down vest, open over a plaid flannel shirt, which was open over a gray T-shirt dotted with sweat in spite of the cold. His dark hair had stuck out in a mess around the wool cap he wore. He needed a shower and a shave.

When she saw him at the bank, he'd had both. His hair was neatly combed, still longer than that of the other men in the room, though cut well. His jaw was smooth and tanned. His shoulders looked every bit as broad under a camel hair blazer as under a down vest. He knew how to knot a tie, even how to pick one, if indeed he'd picked out the paisley one he wore. And in the quick look she'd had, when the men had briefly stood as she entered then left the room, his gray slacks had fit his lean hips nearly as nicely as had a pair of jeans.

He was an extremely good-looking man, she had to admit, though she refused to believe that had anything to do with her nervousness. After all, she'd already decided that he was married, and anyway, she wasn't on the lookout for a man. She had one, a very nice one named Anthony Haskell, who was even-tempered and kind and took her to a show or a movie or to dinner whenever she had the time, which wasn't often. She didn't see him more than two or three times a month. But he was pleasant. He was an amiable escort. That was all she asked, all she wanted from a man—light companionship from time to time as a break from the rest of her life.

So, Gideon Lowe wasn't any sort of threat to her in that regard. Still he was so *physical*. A woman couldn't be within arm's reach of him and not feel his force. Hell, she'd been farther away than that in the boardroom at the bank, and she'd felt it. It started with his eyes and was powerful.

So he was slightly intimidating, she admitted with a sigh, and that was why she was feeling shaky. Of course, she couldn't let him know that. She'd taken the bull by the horns and called him for an appointment, making sure to sound fully composed, for that reason. Gideon looked to be the predatory type. If he sensed weakness, he'd zoom right in for the kill.

Fortifying herself with the determination to do the very best job for Crosslyn Rise that she possibly could, she turned off the highway and followed the shore road. Actually she would have preferred meeting Gideon at the bank or at Carter's office, either of which were safer places, given what had happened on that last misty morning. But Gideon had said that they should see what they were discussing, and she supposed he had a point.

The good news was that the day was sunny and bright, not at all like that other misty one. The bad news was that it was well below freezing, as was perfectly normal for December. There had already been snow, though barely enough to shovel. She couldn't help but wonder how Gideon's men kept from freezing as they worked.

As for her, she'd dressed for the occasion. She was wearing wool tights under wool slacks, a heavy cowl-neck sweater and a long wool coat. Beside her on the seat were a pair of mittens and some earmuffs. It had occurred to her that Gideon was testing her mettle, deliberately subjecting her to adverse conditions, but if so, she wasn't going to come up short. She could handle subfreezing weather. She'd done it many times before.

Of course, that didn't mean that she was thrilled to be riding in her car dressed as heavily as she was. If it hadn't been for the seat belt, she'd have shrugged out of her coat. She'd long since turned down the heat, and even then, by the time she arrived at Crosslyn Rise, she felt a trickle of perspiration between her breasts.

She drove directly to the duck pond over the trail that the trucks had made, but when she reached it, it looked deserted. There wasn't a car or truck in sight. She sat for a minute, then glanced at her watch. They'd agreed on eight-thirty, which it was on the nose. Gideon had told her, a bit arrogantly, she thought, that his men started work an hour before that. But she didn't see a soul working on this cold, crisp morning. She opened her door and stepped out. The only noise came from the ducks, their soft, random quacks a far cry from the sharp sounds of construction.

Slipping back into the car, she turned it around and retraced the trail to the point where the main driveway led to the mansion. She followed it, parked and went up the brick walk, under the ivy-draped portico, to the door. Putting her face to the sidelight, she peered inside.

The place was empty. Jessica and Carter had finally finished clearing things out, putting some in storage, selling others in a huge estate sale held several weekends before. The idea was for Gideon's men to spend the worst of the winter months inside, working on the renovations that would eventually make the mansion into a central clubhouse, health center and restaurant for the condominium complex. Whether Jessica and Carter would buy one of the condo units was still undecided. For the time being, they were living in Carter's place in Boston.

Reaching into her pocket, Chris took out the key Jessica had given her and let herself into the mansion. Seconds later, she was standing in the middle of the rotundalike foyer. Ahead of her was the broad sweeping staircase that she found so breathtaking, to the right the spacious living room lit by knee-to-ceiling windows bare of drapes, to the left the similarly bright dining room.

That was the direction in which she walked, her footsteps echoing through the silent house. As she stood under the open arch, looking from window to window, chandelier to wall sconce, spot to spot where paintings had so recently hung, she imagined the long, carved mahogany table dominating the room once more. The last time it had been used was for the wedding, and though she hadn't been there, she could easily picture its surface covered with fine linen, then silver tray after silver tray of elegantly presented food. Giving herself up to a moment of fancy, she felt the excitement, heard the sounds of happiness. Then she blinked, and those happy sounds were replaced by the loud and repeated honking of a horn.

She hurried back to the front door in time to see Gideon climb from his truck. He was wearing his work clothes with nothing more than the same down vest, which surprised her, given the weather. So he was hot-blooded. She should have guessed that.

"I thought we agreed to meet down there," he said by way of greeting. He looked annoyed. "I've been waiting for ten minutes."

She checked her watch. "Not ten minutes, because I was there five minutes ago. When you didn't show, I thought I'd take a look around here. Where is everyone? It's a gorgeous day. I thought for sure there'd be work going on one place or the other."

"There will be," Gideon said, holding her gaze as he approached. Stopping a few feet away, he hooked his hands on his hips. "The men are picking up supplies. They'll be along." He smirked. "This works out really well, don't you think? We can talk about whatever it is you want to talk about, then you can be long gone by the time they get here, so they can work undisturbed."

His reference to what had happened the last time was barely veiled. The look in his eye took it a step further with the implication that she'd been the one at fault. That bothered her. "You deliberately planned it this way, I take it."

He scratched his head, which was hatless, though from the looks of his hair, he'd just tumbled out of bed, stuck on his clothes and come. The thought made her feel warmer than she already was.

"Actually," he said, "the guys had to pick up the stuff either today or tomorrow anyway. After you and I arranged to meet, today sounded real good."

"It's a shame. I was hoping they'd be here. They'll have to get used to seeing me around. I will be, more and more, once things get going."

His smirk deteriorated. "Yeah. Well..."

"They won't bother *me* if that's got you worried," she went on, gaining strength from her own reassuring tone. "I'm with workmen all the time. It's part of my job. Plumbers, plasterers, painters—you name it, I've seen it. They may not love having me poking around, but at least if they know I'll be wandering in from time to time, they won't be alarmed when it happens."

"My men weren't alarmed," Gideon argued, "just distracted at a very critical time."

"Because they weren't expecting me. They had no idea who I was. Maybe it would help if I met them."

"It wouldn't help at all! You don't have any business with them. You have business with *me!*" He eyed her with sudden suspicion. "You want them around for protection, I think. You don't like being alone with me. Is that it? Is that what this is about? Because if it is—" he held both hands up "—I can assure you, you're safe. I don't fool with the hired help. And I don't fool with blondes."

"I'm relieved to hear *that*," she said, deliberately ignoring the business about "hired help" because it was a potential firecracker. The other was easier to handle. "What's wrong with blondes?"

"They're phony."

"Like rednecks are crude?"

Gideon glared at her for a minute, looking as though there were a dozen other derogatory things he wanted to say. Before he could get any out, though, she relented and said, "Look, I'm sorry. I'm not here to fight. I have a job to do, just like you. Name-calling won't help."

He continued to glare. "*Do* I make you nervous?"

"Of course not. Why would you think that?"

"You were nervous at the meeting at the bank."

And she thought she'd looked so calm. So much for show. "There were eight people—nine, counting the banker—at that meeting. I was auditioning for a job I really wanted. I had a right to be nervous." She wondered how he'd known, whether they'd all seen it or whether those dark gray eyes were just more keen than most.

"Were you surprised when you got the job?" he asked innocently enough.

"In a way. The others have bigger names than I do."

Again, innocently, he asked, "Did you think that I'd vote against you?"

"That thought did cross my mind."

"I didn't."

"Thank you."

"I abstained."

"Oh." She felt strangely hurt, then annoyed. "Well. I appreciate your telling me that. I'm glad to know you think so highly of my work."

He didn't blink. "I think your work is just fine, but I don't relish the idea of working with you. We rub each other the wrong way, you and me. I don't know why, but we do."

That about said it all. There wasn't much she could add. So she stood with her hands buried deep in the pockets of her coat, wondering what he'd say next. He seemed bent on throwing darts at her. She imagined that if she let him do it enough, let him get every little gripe off his chest, they might finally be able to work together.

Unfortunately, the darts stung.

He stared at her for a long, silent time, just stared. Holding her chin steady and her spine straight, she stared right back.

"Nothing to say?" he asked finally.

"No."

He arched a brow. "Nothing at all?"

She shook her head.

"Then why are we here?"

Chris felt a sudden rush of color to her face. "Uh, we're here to discuss business," she said, and hurried to gather her thoughts. Something had happened. Gideon's eyes must have momentarily numbed her mind. "I want to see where you're at with the condos. I thought maybe I could get a bead on things like roofing materials, stairway styles and so on." She stopped, took a deep breath, recomposed herself. "But I told you all that when I called. You were the one who said we should walk through what you've done." She gestured in the direction of the duck pond. "Can we?"

He shrugged. "Sure." He turned back toward his truck. "Climb in. I'll drive you down."

"Thanks, but I'll follow in my car."

He stopped and turned back. "Climb *in*. I'll drive you back here when we're done."

"That's not necessary," she said, but there was a challenge in his look. She wasn't sure whether it had to do with the idea of their being alone in the cab of a pickup or the idea of her climbing into a pickup, period, but in either case she had a point to make. "Okay. Let me get my purse." Crossing the driveway to her car, she took the large leather satchel in which she carried pen and paper, along with other necessities of life such as a wallet, tissues, lip gloss and appointment book. Hitching the bag to her shoulder, she grabbed her earmuffs and mittens. Then, putting on a show of confidence, she walked to the passenger's side of the truck, opened the door and climbed up.

"That was smooth," Gideon remarked.

She settled herself as comfortably as she could, given that she felt rattled. "My father is an electrician. I've been riding around in trucks all my life." And she knew how intimate they could be. A truck was like a man's office, filled with personal belongings, small doodads, tokens of that man's life. It also had his scent. Gideon's was clean, vaguely leathery, distantly coffee flavored, thanks to a half-filled cup on the console, and overwhelmingly male. She felt surrounded by it, so much so that it was a struggle to concentrate on what he was saying.

"Funny, you don't look like the type."

She swallowed. "What type?"

"To have an electrician for a father. I'd have thought your old man would be the CEO of some multinational corporation. Not an electrician."

Another dart hit home. She bristled. "There's nothing wrong with being an electrician. My father is honest and hardworking. He takes pride in what he does. *I'm* proud of what he does. And who are *you* to say something like that?"

"You asked. I answered." He shrugged. "I still don't peg you as the type to be around trucks."

"You think I'm lying?"

"No. But I think you could."

"What's *that* supposed to mean?"

"That I'd more easily believe you if you said you've had a silver spoon in your mouth for most of your life, got bored with doing nothing, so decided to dabble around as a decorator. Real estate and interior decorating—those are the two fields women go into when they want people to think they're aggressive little workers."

That dart hurt more than the others, no doubt because she was already bruised. "You don't know what you're talking about," she said.

"If the shoe fits, wear it."

His smug look did it. Turning to face him head-on, she said, "Well, it doesn't. And, quite frankly, I resent your even suggesting it. I work hard, probably harder than you do, and so do most of the women I know in *either* of the fields you mentioned. We have to work twice as hard to get half the respect, thanks to people like you." She took a fast breath. "And as for 'types,' I didn't have a silver spoon in my mouth at birth or at any *other* time in my life. My parents couldn't afford silver, or silk, or velvet, but they gave me lots and lots of love, which is clearly something you know nothing about. I feel badly for your wife, or your woman, whoever the hell it is you go home to at night." She reached for the door. "I'll take my own car, after all. Being cooped up in a truck with you is oppressive." In a second, she was out the door and looking back at him. "Better still, I think maybe we'd better do this another time. I'm feeling a little sick to my stomach."

Slamming the door, she stalked back to her car. She was trembling, and though she doubted he could see, she wouldn't have cared. She felt pervasive anger and incredible hurt, neither of which abated much as she sped back to Belmont. By the time she was back in her office, sitting at her desk with the door closed on the rest of the world, she was also feeling humiliated.

He'd won. He'd badgered her and she'd crumbled. She couldn't believe she'd done that. She prided herself on being strong. Lord knows, she'd had to overcome adversity to get where she was. She'd faced critics far more personal and cutting than Gideon Lowe and survived. With him, though, she'd fallen apart.

She was ashamed of herself.

She was also frightened. She wanted, *needed* to do Crosslyn Rise. By running, she may well have blown her credibility. If she'd thought working with Gideon was going to be hard before, it could well be impossible now. He'd seen her weakness. He could take advantage of it.

He could also spread word among the consortium members about what had happened, but she doubted he'd do that. He wasn't exactly an innocent party. He wouldn't want the others to know of his part. He had an image to protect, too.

Then again, he could lie. He could tell them that she made appointments, showed up, then took off minutes later. He could say that she wasted his time. He could suggest that she was mentally unbalanced.

If he spread that kind of word around, she'd be in a serious fix. Crosslyn Rise was supposed to make her career, not break it!

What to do, what to do. She sat at her desk with her feet flat on the floor, her knees pressed together, her elbows on the glass surface, her clasped hands pressed to her mouth, and wondered about that. She could call Jessica, she supposed. But she'd done that once regarding Gideon. To do it again would be tattling. Worse, it would smack of cowardice. Jessica might well begin to wonder what kind of woman she'd hired.

Nor could she call Carter. Gideon was his friend.

And she certainly couldn't call Gideon. They'd only get into another fight.

But she had to do something. She'd committed herself to Crosslyn Rise. Her reputation, her future was on the line.

The phone rang. She watched the flashing light turn solid when Margie picked it up. Distractedly she glanced at the handful of pink slips on the desk, all telephone messages waiting to be answered. She shuffled them around. Nothing interesting caught her eye.

The intercom buzzed. "Chris, you have a call from a Gideon Lowe. Do you want to take it, or should I take a message?"

Gideon Lowe. Chris's pulse skittered, then shot ahead. She didn't want to talk with him now. She was still stinging from his last shots. And embarrassed. And confused. And feeling less sure of herself than she had in years and years.

Did she want to take the phone? *No!* But that was foolish.

Bolstering herself with a deep breath, she said to Margie, "I'll take it." But she didn't pick up Gideon's call immediately. It took a few deep breaths, plus several seconds with her eyes shut tight before she felt composed enough. Even then, her finger shook when she punched in the button.

"Yes, Gideon." She wanted to sound all business. To her own ear though, she sounded frightened, just as she was feeling inside. She waited for him to blast her about driving off, leaving their meeting almost before it had begun. But he didn't say a thing. She looked at the telephone, thinking that maybe they'd been cut off. "Hello?"

"I'm sorry," he said in as quiet a tone as she'd heard from him yet. "That was not very nice of me. I shouldn't have said those things. Any of them."

"Then why did you?" she cried, only then realizing how personally she'd taken his barbs. She didn't understand *why* they bothered her so, since she and Gideon weren't anything more to each other than two people temporarily working together. But the fact was that they did, and she was upset enough to lose the cool she'd struggled to gain in the moments before she'd picked up the phone.

"Do you have something special against me?" she asked. "Have I ever done anything to you that warrants what you've been doing? I mean, I wandered innocently onto the site one day and was standing there, minding my own business, when your men saw me and botched the work they were doing. Forget that it wasn't my fault. I apologized, but it didn't make any difference. You've had it in for me ever since. Am I missing something here? Do I remind you of someone else, maybe someone unpleasant, someone who hurt you once, or who let you down? Why do you *hate* me?"

She ran out of breath. In the silence that ensued, she heard all that she'd blurted out and was appalled. She'd blown professionalism to bits, but then, that was something she seemed to do a lot in Gideon's company. She was debating hanging up the phone and burying her head in the trash can when he spoke again. His voice was still low. He actually sounded troubled.

"I don't hate you. I just look at you and...something happens. I can't explain it. Believe me, I've been trying. I've worked with lots of people over the years, lots of women, and I've never been this way before. People usually think I'm easygoing."

Chris recalled Jessica saying something to that extent. She hadn't believed it then, and she didn't believe it now. "Easygoing, like an angry bull," she murmured.

"I heard that. But it's okay. I deserve it."

In response to the confession, she softened a bit. "If you've never been this way before, then it's me. What is it I'm doing wrong? I'm trying. Really I am. I'm trying to be agreeable. I felt we should talk, because that's part of my job, and when you wanted to meet at the site, I agreed, even though it wasn't my first choice. I try to overlook some of the things you say, but they hurt, you know. I'm not a shallow person. I haven't gotten anything in life for free. I work hard at what I do, and I'm proud of that. So why do I annoy you so much?''

He was a minute in answering, and then he didn't get out more than a word when he was cut off by the operator. ''All right, all right,'' he muttered. ''Hold on Chris.''

She was puzzled. ''Where are you?''

She heard the clink of coins, then, ''At a pay phone in town. The phones have been taken out at the Rise, and none of the ones on the street take credit cards. Can you believe that? We're building a complex that's state-of-the-art as far as living goes, in the middle of a town that's old-fashioned as hell. I'm probably gonna have to get a car phone before this project is done.''

''Truck phone.''

''Hmm?''

She sat back in her chair. ''You drive a truck. Wouldn't you call it a truck phone?''

''I don't know. Do they? The guys who make them?''

''Beats me.''

''You don't have a phone in your car?''

''No. They're expensive. Besides, I like silence when I drive. It gives me a chance to think.''

''Aren't you worried about making the most of every minute?'' he asked.

''I am. Making the most, that is. Thinking is important.''

''Yeah, but all I hear from people is that I could be answering phone calls, communicating with clients, even getting new jobs if I had a phone in my car. Don't all those things apply to you?''

Chris had heard the arguments, too. ''If someone is so desperate for my work that they can't wait until I get back into my office to talk with me, I don't want the job. You can bet it would be a nightmare. Even the most simple jobs run into snags. But one where the client wants instant satisfaction? I'll pass those up, thanks. I'm no miracle worker.'' She tacked on a quiet, ''I wish I was.''

''If you were, what would you do?''

She took another deep breath, a calmer one this time. She'd settled down, she realized. When he wasn't yelling at her, Gideon's deep voice was strangely soothing. ''Wave my magic wand over you so that whatever it is that bugs you about me would disappear. I want to do a good job at Crosslyn Rise. I'm a perfectionist. But I'm also a pacifist. I can't work in an atmosphere of hostility.''

"I'm not feeling hostile now.''

She thought about the conversation they were having, thought about the civility that they'd somehow momentarily managed to achieve. Her heart started beating faster, in relief, she figured. "Neither am I.''

"That's 'cause we're talking on the phone. We're not face-to-face.''

"What is it about my *face* that bugs you, then?''

"Nothing. It's beautiful.''

The unexpected compliment left Chris speechless. Before she had a chance to start stammering simply to fill in the silence, Gideon said, "You guessed right, though. That first time, I thought you were someone else. She'd been such a royal pain in the butt that I guess I took my frustration out on you.'' Elizabeth had called the week before; he told her he was still seeing Marie. "After that, I couldn't confuse you with her. You're different.''

Chris didn't know whether that was a compliment or not. She was still basking in the first, though she felt foolish for that. What did it matter that Gideon thought she was beautiful? He was someone she'd be working with. By all rights, she should be furious that he was thinking of her in terms of looks rather than ability. He was as sexist as they came. And as deceitful, if indeed he was married.

"Uh, Chris?'' He sounded hesitant.

"Yes.''

"I think there's something we ought to get straight right about now. What you said before in the truck about me and a wife or a woman or whoever—''

Her heart was hammering again. "Yes?''

"There isn't any wife. I'm not married. I was once, for a real short time, years ago. But I liked having fun more than I liked being married. So it died.''

Chris felt a heat in the area of her breasts that had nothing to do with her heavy cowl-neck sweater. She almost resented his saying what he'd said, though deep down she'd known he wasn't married. But they had actually been getting along. Now, having his availability open and confirmed threw a glitch into the works. "Why are you telling me this?''

"Because I think it's part of the problem. For me, at least. I'm single, and you're single. Every time I look at you I get a little bothered.''

"Bothered?'' If he meant what she thought he meant, they were in trouble. Suddenly she didn't want to know. "Listen, if you're worried about me, don't be. I won't accost you. I'm not in this business to pick up men.''

"That's not what I meant—"

"In fact," she cut in, "I'm not looking for a man at all. There's someone I've been seeing for a while, and he's a really nice guy, but to tell you the truth, I don't even have much time for him. I spend all my free time working."

"What fun is *that*?" Gideon asked indignantly.

On the defensive again, she sat straighter. "It's plenty of fun. I enjoy my work—except for those times when I get cut to ribbons by builders who take pleasure in making other people miserable."

"I don't do it on purpose. That's what I'm trying to tell you."

"Well, try something else. Try changing. Don't assume things about me, or make value judgments. Just because I think or act differently from you, doesn't mean that I'm wrong. I don't tell you what to like. Don't tell *me* what to like."

"I'm not *doing* that," Gideon insisted. "I'm just expressing my opinion. So I express it in a way that you find offensive. Well, maybe you're too sensitive."

"Maybe I'm human! Maybe I like to get along with people. Maybe I like to please them. Maybe I like to have their respect every once in a while."

"How can you have my respect," he threw back, "if you don't hang around long enough for me to get to know you? You got upset by what I said, so instead of sticking around and fighting it out, you took off. That doesn't solve anything, Chris."

Her hand tightened on the phone. "Ah. I knew we'd get around to that sooner or later. Okay. Why don't you say what you think, just get it off your chest. I'm already feeling crushed. A little more won't hurt."

He didn't say a word.

"Go on, Gideon. Say something. I know you're dying to. Tell me that I'm a coward. Tell me that you were being overly optimistic when you abstained in that vote. Tell me that you seriously doubt whether I have the wherewithal to make it through the decorating of Crosslyn Rise." She paused, waiting. "Tell me I'm in the wrong field. Tell me I should be doing something like secretarial work. Or teaching. Or waitressing." She paused again. "Go ahead. Be my guest. I'm steeled for it." A third time, she paused. Then, cautiously she said, "Gideon?"

"Are you done?"

She was relieved that he hadn't hung up. "Yes."

"Want to meet me for lunch tomorrow?"

That wasn't what she'd expected to hear. She was taken totally off guard. "Uh, uh—"

"Maybe you were right. Maybe what we need is a neutral place to talk. So you choose it. Wherever you want to go, we'll go. I can drive down there, you can drive up here, we can meet somewhere in the middle. But we both have to eat lunch. We can even go dutch if you want. I'm perfectly willing to pay, but you women have a thing about a man treating you. Heaven forbid you might feel a little indebted to him.''

"That's not why we do it. We do it because it's the professional thing to do.''

"If that's so, why is it that when I go out for a business lunch with another guy, one of us usually pays, with the understanding that the other'll do it the next time? Sometimes it's easier just to charge it rather than split the bill in two. But modern women have to make things so hard.''

"Then why do you bother with us?''

"I don't, usually. On my own time, I steer as far away from you as I can get. Give me the secretary or the teacher or the waitress any day. They're not hung up on proving themselves. They like it when a man opens the door for them, or helps them with their coat, or holds their chair. They like to be treated like women.''

"So do I.''

"Could've fooled me.''

"You were the one who suggested we go dutch. If you want to pay for lunch, be my guest. You probably make a whole lot more money than I do, anyway.''

"What makes you think that?'' he asked.

"You've invested in Crosslyn Rise, haven't you?''

"Yeah. With every last cent I had to my name. As far as cash flow goes, I'm just about up the creek.''

"Was that a wise thing to do?''

"Ask me that two years from now and I may have an answer. I've got a whole lot riding on—'' The telephone clicked, cutting him off. He came back in ripe form. "Damn, I'm out of change. Look, Chris, will you meet me or not?''

"Uh, tomorrow?'' She looked at her calendar. "I wouldn't be able to make it until two. My morning's wild.''

The phone clicked again. "Two is fine,'' he said hurriedly. "Name the place.''

"Joe's Grille. It's in Burlington. Right off the Middlesex Turnpike.''

"Joe's Grille at two. See you then.''

She wasn't sure whether he hung up the phone or the operator cut him off, but after a minute of silence, she heard a dial tone. As the seconds passed, it seemed to grow louder and more blaring, almost like an alarm, and well it might have been. She'd arranged to see Gideon again. Granted, the conditions were more to her liking this time, but still she felt uneasy.

He was a very, very confusing man, annoying her most of the time, then, in the strangest ways and when she least expected it, showing charm. Not that she was susceptible to the charm. She'd made it clear that she wasn't available, and it was true. Still, she wished he was married. She'd have felt safer that way.

But he wasn't. And the fact was that they'd be working together. It helped some to know how much Crosslyn Rise meant to him. If he was telling the truth about his financial involvement, he couldn't afford to have anything go wrong, which ruled out his sabotaging her work. And he hadn't suggested that she pull out of the project. She'd given him the chance, had all but put the words into his mouth, but he hadn't used them.

That was the up side of the situation. The downside was the lunch that she'd stupidly agreed to. A meeting at the bank would have been better. Being in a restaurant, having lunch with Gideon seemed so... personal.

But she was a professional with a job to do. So she'd meet him, and she'd be in full control, and she'd show him that she was done being bullied. She could stand up to him. It was all a matter of determination.

4

Gideon was looking forward to lunch. He felt really good after their phone conversation, as though they'd finally connected, and that mattered to him. Despite everything that he found wrong with Chris, she intrigued him. She wasn't what he'd first assumed her to be. He suspected she wasn't what, even now, he assumed her to be. She was a mystery, and he was challenged.

He was also excited in a way that had nothing to do with making progress on Crosslyn Rise and everything to do with having a date with an attractive woman. Because it was a date. Chris could call it a professional lunch, and it was, a little, but in his mind it was first and foremost a date. His motives were far from professional. He wanted to get to know Chris, wanted to start to unravel the mystery that she was. "Start" was the operative word, of course, because he envisioned this as only the first of many dates. She had already proclaimed that she wasn't looking for a man, so clearly she wasn't going to be rushed. But there'd be fun in that. Gideon was anticipating the slow, increasingly pleasant evolution of their relationship.

This first date was very important in that it would be laying the groundwork for those to come. For that reason, he was determined to be on his best, most civil and urbane behavior. He would have liked to add sophisticated or cultured to that, only he wasn't either of those things. Pretending might have worked with Elizabeth, but it wouldn't work with Chris. She'd see through him in a minute. She was sharp that way—knew damn well that he hadn't been waiting at the duck pond for ten minutes and caught him on it, though he'd only exaggerated a little. But he didn't want to be caught again, not when he wanted to impress. So he'd be himself, or that part of himself that would be most apt to please her.

For starters, he dressed for the occasion. Though he was at Crosslyn Rise at seven-thirty with the rest of his men and put in a full morning of work, he left them on their own at midday and drove all the way home to clean up. After showering and shaving, he put on a pair of gray slacks, a pink shirt, a sweater that picked up variations of those shades, and loafers. It was his yuppie outfit, the one he'd bought in Cambridge on the day he had decided to invest in Crosslyn Rise. He figured that he owed himself a small extravagance before the big splurge, and that he could use the clothes. He hated shopping. But he had to look the part of the intelligent investor, and so he'd bought the outfit, plus a blazer, two ties and a blue shirt. But he liked the pink one, at least to wear for Chris. She'd appreciate the touch.

After all, rednecks didn't wear pink.

He also put on the leather jacket that his mother had sent him several birthdays ago. It was one of the few gifts she'd given him that he liked. Most of the others were too prissy, reminding him of all she wanted him to be that he wasn't. The leather jacket, though, was perfect. It was conservative in style and of the richest brown leather he'd ever seen. He wore it a lot.

Leaving his truck in the yard, he took the Bronco, allowing plenty of time for traffic, and headed for Burlington. The route was the same to Crosslyn Rise. There were times when he felt he could do it in his sleep, except that he liked driving. Chris used her road time to think; he used his to relax, which was why he resisted getting a car phone, himself. A phone would interfere with his music. With sophisticated stereo setups in both of his vehicles, his idea of heaven was cruising along the highway at the fastest speed the traffic would bear, listening to Hank Jr., Willie or Waylon.

He didn't listen to anyone now, though, because he was too busy thinking about Chris. She really was a knockout, pretty in a soft-as-woman kind of way, despite the air of professionalism she tried to maintain. She turned him on. Oh, yeah. There was no mistaking the heat she generated. He was old enough and experienced enough—and blunt enough—to call a spade a spade. Sure, he was a little nervous to see her. Sure, it was cold outside. Sure, he hadn't eaten since six that morning. But the tiny tremors he felt inside weren't from any of those things. They were from pure, unadulterated lust.

That was the last thing he wanted Chris to know. And since it got worse the longer he thought about her—and since she was probably sharp enough to see *that* first thing, if he didn't do something to cool off—he opened the windows, turned on the music and began to sing at the top of his lungs. By the time he turned off the Middlesex Turnpike into the parking lot of Joe's Grille, his cheeks were red from the cold, his voice faintly hoarse, and his hands, as they pushed a comb through his windblown hair, slightly unsteady. He pulled on his jacket, checked the rearview mirror one last time to make sure he looked all right, took a breath and stepped out.

He was early. They were supposed to meet at two, and it was ten before the hour. He went into the restaurant just to make sure she hadn't arrived, gave his name to the hostess, along with a five for a good table and a wink for good cheer, then entered the adjoining mall and, hands stashed in his pockets, started walking around. With less than three weeks to go before Christmas, the holiday season was in full bloom. One store window was more festive, more glittery, more creative than the next. Almost as an escape from tinsel overload, he found himself gravitating toward the center of the mall, where a huge tree stood, decorated not with the usual ornaments, but with live flowers.

He stood there for a while, looking at the tree, thinking how pretty it was and that he didn't think he'd ever seen one quite like it before.

"I'm sorry," someone gasped beside him. He looked quickly down to see Chris. Her cheeks were flushed, and she was trying to catch her breath, but there was the hint of a smile on her face, even as she pressed a hand to her chest. "I got here a few minutes early, so I thought I'd pick up a gift or two, only the salesperson messed things up at the register and didn't know how to correct it, so I had to stand around waiting while he got his supervisor. The store was at the other end of the mall. I had to race back." She barely paused. "Have you been here long?"

"Not long," he said. He wondered if she was babbling because she was nervous, and hoped it was a good sign. "I was just wandering around. Everything's so pretty." But Chris took the cake. She was wearing a navy sweater and slacks and a long beige coat with a wool scarf hanging down the lapels. She might have pulled off the business look if it hadn't been for her cheeks and her hair, a few wisps of which had escaped its knot and were curling around her face, and her mouth, which looked soft, and her eyes, which were blue as the sky on a clear summer's day.

It struck him that she was more beautiful than the tree, but he wasn't about to say it. She thought she was here on business, and business partners didn't drool over each other. So he looked back at the tree. "I've never seen one decorated this way. The flowers are pretty. How do they stay so fresh?"

He hadn't actually been expecting an answer, but Chris had one nonetheless. "The stem of each is in a little tube that holds enough water to keep the flowers alive. If they're cut at the right time, lilies last a while."

"Those are lilies?"

"Uh-huh. Stargazers. I use them a lot in silk arrangements for front foyers or buffets or dining room tables. They're elegant."

He eyed her guardedly. "You do silk arrangements?"

"No. Someone does them for me. She's the artist, but whenever I see an arrangement of fresh-cuts that I like, I make a note and tell her about it later.''

"I hate silk arrangements. They look fake.''

"Then you've never seen good ones. Good silks are hard to tell from the real thing.''

"I can tell. I can always tell.''

"You've seen that many?''

"Enough to know that it's a matter of moisture.'' His gaze fell to her mouth. "I don't care how good the silk is, it doesn't breathe the way a real flower does. It doesn't shine or sweat. A real flower is like human skin that way.'' He brushed her cheek with the pad of his thumb, feeling the smoothness, the warmth, the dewiness that her run down the mall had brought. He also felt his own body responding almost instantaneously, so he cleared his throat, stuck his hand back into his pocket and said, "Are you hungry?''

She nodded.

"Wanna get lunch?''

"Uh-huh.'' She sounded breathless still.

Gideon wasn't rushing to attribute that breathlessness to anything other than the most innocent of causes, but he hadn't missed the way her eyes had widened just a fraction when he'd touched her face or the fact that she seemed glued to the spot.

He hitched his chin toward the restaurant.

With an effort, it seemed, Chris nodded again, then looked down to make sure that she had her bundle safely tucked under her arm.

"Can I carry that for you?'' he asked.

"Uh, no. It's okay.''

They started off. "What did you buy, anyway? Or is it a secret, maybe something black and sexy for your mom?'' He faltered, suddenly wondering whether he'd put his foot in his mouth. "Uh, she's still around, isn't she?''

Chris smiled. The affection she so clearly felt for her mother brought added warmth to her eyes. "Quite. She's an energetic fifty-five. But she'd be embarrassed out of her mind to get something black and sexy. She doesn't define herself that way. No, this is for another relative. Something totally different. As a matter of fact, I don't know *what* to get my mother.''

"What does she do?'' Gideon asked, hoping to get hints about Chris through this mother she cared for.

"She reads, but books are so impersonal.''

"What else does she do?''

"Needlepoint, but she's already in the middle of three projects and doesn't need a fourth."

"What else?"

"She cleans and cooks—" this was offered facetiously "—but I don't think she'd appreciate either a bottle of window cleaner or a tin of garlic salt."

Gideon was picturing a delightful homebody, someone he'd feel comfortable with in a minute. "How about a clay pot?"

Chris drew in her chin. "Clay pot?"

He'd seen them advertised on the back of one of the dozens of unsolicited catalogues that came in the mail every week. Rolled tight, those catalogues were kindling for his fire. Once in a while, something registered while he was doing the rolling. "You know, the kind you cook a whole meal in, kind of like a Crockpot, but clay." They'd reached the restaurant. He held the door for her to go through first.

"How do you know about clay pots?" she asked, shooting him a curious glance as she passed.

He shrugged. With a light hand on her waist, he guided her toward the hostess, who promptly led them to the quietest table in the house. Unfortunately, that wasn't saying a whole lot. The restaurant was filled, even at two, with a cross of business types from nearby office buildings and shoppers with kids. The business types were no problem, but the kids and their mothers were loud. Noting that the table the hostess had given them—a table for four, at that—was set slightly apart from the others, Gideon felt his money had been well spent. Every little bit of privacy helped when a man was pursuing his cause.

"Would you like me to hang up your coat?" he asked just before Chris slid into her seat.

She glanced at the nearby hooks. "Uh, okay." Depositing her bag and purse on one of the free chairs, she started to slip the coat off. Gideon took it from her shoulders and hung it up, then put his own jacket beside it. When he returned to the table, she was already seated. He took the chair to the right of hers, which was where the hostess had set the second menu, but no sooner had he settled in than he wondered if he'd made a mistake. Chris was sitting back in the pine captain's chair with her hands folded in her lap, looking awkward.

"Is this where I'm supposed to sit for a business lunch?" he asked, making light of it. "Or should I be sitting across from you?"

"I think," she said, glancing out at the crowd, "that if you sit across from me, I won't be able to hear a word you say. I thought most of the kids would be gone by now, but I guess at Christmastime anything goes."

"I take it you've been here before."

"Uh-huh. My family comes a lot."

"Family," he prodded nonchalantly, "as in mother and father?"

"And the rest. I'm the oldest. The youngest is just fifteen. It's harder now than it used to be, but we still try to do things together whenever we can." She opened her menu, but rather than looking at it, she took a drink of water. "The club sandwiches are good here. So are the ribs. I usually go for one of the salads. There's a great Cobb salad, and a spinach one."

"I hate spinach."

The blunt statement brought her eyes finally to his. "Like you hate silk flowers?"

"Pretty much." He paused, held her gaze, watched her cheeks turn a little pink and her slender fingers tuck a wisp of hair behind her ear. Unable to help himself, he said, "I like your outfit. You look nice in navy." He paused again. "Or aren't I supposed to say that at a business lunch?"

She looked at him for another minute, then seemed to relax. "Technically, it is a sexist thing to say."

"It's a compliment."

"Would you give a compliment like that to one of your men?"

"Like that? Of course not. He'd think I was coming on to him."

She arched an eloquent brow.

"I'm not coming on to you," Gideon told her, and in one sense it was true. He'd complimented her because he really *did* like the way she looked, and he was used to saying what he thought. "I'm just telling you you look pretty. It's a fact. Besides, I do give my men compliments. Just not like that."

"Like what, then?"

"Like...hey, man, that's a wild shirt...or...cool hat, bucko."

"Ah," she said gravely. "Man talk." She lowered her eyes to his shirt, then his sweater, and the corner of her mouth twitched. "I'll bet they had choice words to say about what you're wearing now."

Feeling a stab of disappointment, he looked down at himself. "What's wrong with what I'm wearing?"

"Nothing. It's a gorgeous outfit. But it's way different from what I've seen you wearing at the Rise."

It's a gorgeous outfit. Did that ever make him feel good! "Thanks, but I wasn't working in this." He snickered. "You're right. The guys would have kidded me off the lot. No, I went home to change."

She was silent, almost deliberative, for a minute before asking, "Where's home?"

"Worcester."

Her eyes went wide. "Worcester? That's halfway across the state. You're not actually commuting from there to Crosslyn Rise every day, are you?"

He nodded. "I can do it in an hour and a quarter."

"Speeding."

He shrugged.

"And you drove all that way this morning, then drove home, then drove all the way back to meet me?"

"I couldn't very well meet you in my work clothes. You wouldn't have wanted to sit across from me, much less next to me. Besides, I didn't have to drive *all* the way back. Crosslyn Rise is still farther on up."

"But I would have picked some place even closer, if I'd known." Her voice grew softer. "I'm sorry."

"Hey," he said with a puzzled smile, "it's no big thing. I asked you to name the place, and you named it." He looked around. "This is a nice place."

"Hello," the waitress said, materializing between them as though on cue. "My name is Melissa, and I'll be serving you today. May I get you something from the bar?"

Gideon raised his brows toward Chris.

She shook her head. "Tea for me, please."

"And you, sir?"

He wanted a beer, but that wasn't part of the image. Then again, he couldn't see himself ordering wine. So he settled for a Coke. "And maybe something to munch on," he said, waving his fingers a little. "What do you have?"

Chris spoke before Melissa could. "We'll have an order of skins, please. Loaded."

The minute Melissa left, he asked, "How do you know I like skins?"

"Do you?"

"Sure."

"Loaded?"

"Sure."

There was satisfaction in her smile. "So do my father and brothers, and they're all big and physical like you."

Gideon was thinking that being like her father and brothers was a good thing, since she clearly liked them, when he had a different thought. "What about your boyfriend? Does he like them?"

"My boyfriend? Oh, you mean Anthony. Uh, actually, he doesn't."

"So what does he eat when he comes here?"

"He doesn't."

"Doesn't eat?"

"Doesn't come here. He lives in Boston. And he's really not my boyfriend. Just a friend. I don't have time for a boyfriend. I told you that. I'm not interested."

"A girlfriend then?" he asked before he could think to hold his tongue.

She scowled at him. "Why *are* you so offensive." It wasn't a question.

He held up a hand and said softly, "Hey, I'm sorry. It's just that I like to know what's going on. I mean, why is a woman as beautiful and talented as you are still single?"

She threw the ball right back at him. "You're still single. What's *your* excuse?"

"I told you. I blew marriage once."

"A long time ago, you said. But you haven't tried again."

"But I date. I date a whole lot. There's just no one I like well enough to want to wake up to in the morning." He let the suggestiveness of that sink in, along with all the sexy images it brought. He could picture Chris in his bed, could picture it easily, and wondered if she could picture it, too.

She didn't look to be panting. Nor did she speak right away. Finally, slowly she said, "Then you live alone?"

He fancied he detected interest and grabbed onto the thought. "That's right."

"In an apartment?"

"A house. That I built."

A small smile touched the edge of her mouth. "Mmm. I should have guessed." She paused, seemed deliberative again. He guessed that she wasn't sure how personal to get.

"Go on," he coaxed gently. "Ask. I'll answer."

Given permission, she didn't waste any time. "You live all alone in a big house?"

"It's not big. But it's nice. And it's all I need."

"And you take care of yourself—cook, clean, do laundry?"

"I cook. I have someone come in to do the rest." He didn't see anything wrong with that. She couldn't expect that he'd do everything for himself when he had important work to do every day.

"You really do cook?"

"Enough to stay alive." He wondered what she was getting at. "Why?"

"Because you know about clay pots," she mused, and seemed suddenly, seriously pleased. "That's not a bad idea. My mother doesn't have anything like it. It's really a *good* idea. Thank you."

Gideon grinned. "Glad to be of help." Then his eyes widened at the sight of the skins that suddenly appeared on the table. They looked incredible and he was famished.

"Are you ready to order the rest?" Melissa asked.

Chris looked inquiringly at Gideon, but he hadn't even opened his menu. "Some kind of sandwich," he said softly. "You choose. You know what's good."

She ordered a triple-decker turkey club for him and a Cobb salad for herself. Then she hesitated, seeming unsure for a minute.

"Sounds great," he assured her, and winked at Melissa, who blushed and left. When he looked back at Chris, she was reaching into her purse and pulling out a notebook. Tugging a pen from its spiral binding, she opened to a page marked by a clip.

"What are you doing?" Gideon asked. He was being the gentleman, waiting for her to help herself to a potato skin before he dug in.

"I have questions for you. I want to make notes."

"About me?"

"About Crosslyn Rise."

"Oh." He looked longingly at the skins. Taking the two large spoons resting beside them, he transferred one to Chris's plate.

She protested instantly. "Uh-uh. Those are for you."

"I can't eat them all."

"Then you'll have to take them home for supper. All I want is a salad."

"Aha," he breathed, "you're one of those women who's always on a diet." He shot a quick look at her hips. "I don't see any fat."

"It's there."

"Where?"

"There." She sat back in her chair and stared at him.

Fantasize all he might, but that stare told him she wasn't saying a word about her thighs or her bottom or her waist or her breasts, if those were the spots where she imagined there was fat. So he helped himself to a skin and said, "Okay, what are your questions?" He figured that while he was eating, they could take care of business, so that by the time he was done they could move on to more interesting topics.

He had to hand it to her. She was prepared. She knew exactly what she wanted to ask and went right to it. "Will you consider putting wood shingles on the roof?"

"No." He said. "Next question." He forked half a skin into his mouth.

"Why not?"

"Mmm. These are great."

"Why not wood shingles?" she repeated patiently.

"Because they're expensive and impractical."

"But they look so nice."

"Brick does, too, but it's expensive as hell."

She held his gaze without so much as a blink. "That was my next question. Couldn't we use brick in a few select areas?"

"That's not part of Carter's concept. He wants clapboard."

"What do you think?"

"I think you should talk with Carter."

"What do *you* think?"

"I think we can do very well without that expense, too. Next question." He took another skin, cut it in two, downed the half.

"Windows. What about some half-rounds?"

"What about them?"

"They'd look spectacular over the French doors in the back."

Gideon had to agree with her there, but he was a realist. "It's still a matter of cost," he said when he'd finished what was in his mouth. "I based my bid on the plans Carter gave me. Half-rounds are expensive. If I go over budget, it's money out of my pocket any way you see it."

"Maybe you won't have to go over budget," she said hopefully, "not if you get a good deal from a supplier."

"You know a supplier who'll give us that kind of deal?"

Her hope seemed to fade. "I thought you might."

He looked down at his plate as he cut another skin, arching little more than a brow in her direction. "You're the one with connections in the business. Me, I'm on my own." He popped the skin into his mouth.

"You don't have any relatives in construction?"

After a minute of chewing, he said, "None living. My dad was a housepainter. But he's been gone for ten years now."

She sobered. "Ten years. He must have been very young."

"Not so young overall, but too young to die. There was an accident on the job. He never recovered." Gideon sent her a pointed look. "That's one of the reasons I go berserk when I see carelessness at my sites."

After a minute's quiet, she said, "I can understand that." She'd put down the notebook, had her elbows on the arms of the chair and was making no attempt to look anywhere but at him. "Were you working with him at the time?"

"No. I worked with him when I was a kid, but I was already into construction when the accident happened. He did a lot of work for me in those last years, but when he fell, it was on another job. The scaffolding collapsed.''

''I'm sorry,'' she said, and sounded it. ''Were you two close?''

''Growing up, he was all I had.''

''Your mother?''

''Left when I was three.''

''Just left?'' Chris asked, looking appalled.

''She met someone else, someone with more promise. So she divorced my dad, married the other guy and moved to California.'' He put down his fork. ''She did well. I have to give her that. She's become a very nice society lady—with silk arrangements all over her house.''

''Ah, but not *good* silks, if you thought they looked fake.'' She smiled for a second, then sobered again. ''Do you see her often?''

''Once, maybe twice a year. She keeps in touch. She even wanted me to come live with her at one point, but I wasn't about to betray my dad that way. Then, after he died, I wasn't about to move. My roots are here. My business is here.'' He smirked. ''She isn't wild about what I do. Thinks it's a little pedestrian. But that's okay. California doesn't tempt me, anyway. I'm not the beach boy type.''

Chris mirrored his smirk. ''Not into surfing?''

''Not quite. Softball and basketball. That's it.''

''That's enough,'' she said with feeling.

''Your father and brothers, too?'' he guessed.

''Brothers,'' she answered. ''They're basketball fanatics.''

''How about you? Are you into exercise?''

''Uh-huh. I do ballet.''

Ballet. He might have known. He had about as much appreciation for ballet as he did for Godiva chocolates. He was a Hershey man all the way. ''Do you dance in shows?''

''Oh, no. Even if I were good enough, which I'm not, and even if I were young enough, which I'm not, I wouldn't have the time. I go to class twice a week, for the fun and the exercise of it. In a slow and controlled kind of way, it's a rigorous workout.'' She took a fast breath. ''So why did you move from painting to construction?''

He wanted to know more about her, but she kept turning the questions back at him, which bothered him, on the one hand, because he wasn't used to talking about himself so much, at least not on really personal matters. For instance, he didn't usually tell people about his mother. Then again, Chris seemed genuinely interested, which made it easy to talk. She wasn't critical. Just curious. As though he were a puzzle she wanted to figure out.

So he'd be her puzzle. Maybe she'd be as intrigued with him as he was with her.

"Painting to construction?" He thought back to the time he'd made the switch, which had been hard, given his father's preference. "Money was part of it. The construction business was booming, while painting just went along on the same even keel. I also had a thing for independence. I didn't want to be just my dad's son. But I guess most of it had to do with challenge." He narrowed an eye. "Ever spend day after day after day painting a house? When I first started, I thought it was great. I could stand up there on a ladder, goin' back and forth with a brush, listening to my music from morning to night. Then the monotony set in. I used to feel like I was dryin' up inside. I mean, I didn't have to *think*."

"You certainly have to do that now."

"Thank you."

"I mean it."

"I know. Believe me, I *know* how much I have to think every day. There are times when it's a major pain in the butt, but I wouldn't trade what I do for any other job."

Chris looked puzzled at that. "But you've invested in Crosslyn Rise. You're a member of the consortium. Isn't that like stepping over the line?"

"I'm kind of straddling it right now."

"Then it's not a permanent move into development?"

Gideon thought about it for a minute. A month before, he'd have had a ready answer, but he didn't have one now. "I invested in the Rise because I've never invested in a project before. It was a step up the ladder, something I wanted to try, something I *had* to try." He frowned down at his plate, nudging it back and forth by tiny degrees. "So I'm trying it, and I'm finding that I really want it to work, I mean, *really* want it to work, and there's pressure that goes with that." His eyes sought hers. "Do you know what I mean?"

She nodded, but he wasn't done. "The pressure isn't all fun. And then there's the thing about working in an office, versus working at a site. I like the meetings at the bank. I like being involved at that level. But when the meetings adjourn and we all shake hands, there isn't the feeling of accomplishment that I get at the end of a day when I stand back and see the progress that's been made on a house. Or the feeling," he said, coming alive just at the thought, "of standing back and seeing the finished product, seeing people move in, seeing them live in a place I've built and loving it. I could never give up building. I could never give up that kind of satisfaction."

He said back quietly in his chair, thinking about what he'd said, feeling sheepish. "Funny, I hadn't quite put all those thoughts into words before. You're a positive influence."

"No," she said softly. "You'd have said those things, or recognized that you felt them, sooner or later. I just happened to ask the question that triggered it, that's all."

"I'll bet you do that a lot for people. It takes a good listener to ask a good question. You're a good listener."

She shrugged, then looked quickly up and removed a hand from the table when Melissa delivered their lunches. When they were alone again, she said, "Listening is important in my line of work. If I don't hear what a client is saying, I can't deliver." She dunked her tea bag into the minicarafe of hot water. "Speaking of which, I have more questions about Crosslyn Rise."

"If they involve spending money—"

"Of course they involve spending money," she teased, her blue eyes simultaneously dead serious and mischievous.

"Then you might as well save your breath," he warned, but gently. "We're locked into our budget, says Ben Heavey. He's one of the men you met at the bank that night, and a tightwad? He gives new meaning to the word."

"But what if I can save money here—" she held out her right hand, then her left "—and use it there?"

He pointed his fork at her plate. "Eat your salad."

"Take the flooring. Carter's blueprints call for oak flooring throughout the place, but the fact is that in practically every home I've decorated, the people want carpeting in the bedrooms. If we were to do that, substituting underlayment for oak in the bedrooms, even just the upstairs bedrooms, with the money we'd save, we could pickle the oak downstairs. *That* would look *spectacular*."

"Pickled oak is a bitch to keep clean."

"Only if you have little kids—"

"*I'd* have trouble with it—"

"Or big kids who don't know how to wipe their feet, but how many of those will we attract at Crosslyn Rise? Think about it, Gideon. Or ask Nina Stone. She'll be the first one to tell you that we're aiming at a mature buyer. Not a retiree, exactly, but certainly not a young couple with a whole gang of kids."

"How many kids did you say were in your family?"

"I didn't. But there are six."

"Six kids." He grinned. "That's fun. From what to fifteen?"

She saw through the ruse at once and told him so with a look.

"Thirty-three. I'm thirty-three. Is that supposed to have something to do with Crosslyn Rise?"

"Would you move there?"

"If I wanted to live on the North Shore, which I don't, because my business is in Belmont."

"Where do you live now?" Of the information he wanted, that was one vital piece.

She hesitated for just a minute before saying, "Belmont."

"To be near your family?"

She nodded slowly. "You could say that."

"Because you're all so close," he said quickly, so that she wouldn't think he was interested, *personally* interested, in where she lived. "Do you know how lucky you are about that? I've never had any brothers or sisters. Thanksgiving was my dad and me. Christmas was my dad and me. Fourth of July was my dad and me."

"Didn't you have any friends?"

"Sure, lots of them, and we were invited places and *went* places all the time. But that's different from being home for the holidays." He grew still, picked up his sandwich and took a bite.

Chris speared a piece of lettuce. For a minute she seemed lost in her thoughts. Then, quietly she said, "My family means the world to me. I don't know what I'd do without them."

"Is that why you haven't married?"

She raised her head. "I told you why. Marriage just isn't high on my list of priorities."

"Because you're too busy. But you made time to have lunch with me."

"This is business."

"It's also fun. At least, I think so. It's the most fun I've had at lunch in a while." It was true, he realized. He'd had more bawdy lunches, certainly wilder ones, but never one that excited him more. Even aside from the sexual attraction, he liked Chris. She was intelligent. Interesting.

Concentrating on her salad, she began to eat, first a piece of lettuce, then a slice of olive, then some chicken and a crumble of blue cheese. Gideon, too, ate in silence, but he was watching her all the while.

"Well?" he said when he couldn't stand it any longer.

She looked up. "Well what?"

"Are you enjoying yourself?"

"Right now, no. I'm feeling very awkward."

"Because I'm watching you eat?"

"Because you're waiting for me to say something that I don't want to say.'' With care, she set down her fork. ''Gideon, I'm not looking for a relationship. I thought I made that clear.''

''Well, you said it, but do I have to take it for gospel?''

''Yes.''

''Come on, Chris. I like you.''

''I'm glad. That'll make it easier for us to work together.''

''What about after work? Can I see you?''

''No. I told you. I don't have the time or desire for something like that.''

Sitting back in his chair, he gave her a long, hard look. ''I think you're bluffing,'' he said, and to some extent he was himself. He wasn't a psychologist. He wasn't into analyzing people's motives. But he was trying to understand Chris, to understand why she wouldn't date him, when he had a gut feeling they'd be good together. ''I think you're protecting yourself, because maybe, just maybe you're afraid of involvement. You've got your family, and that's great, and I imagine it's time-consuming to give a big family a hunk of yourself. But I think that if the right thing came along, you'd have all the time in the world for it—'' he leaned close enough to breathe in the gentle floral scent that clung to her skin ''—and more desire than a man could begin to hope for.'' He stayed close for a minute, because he just couldn't leave her so soon. Unable to resist, he planted a soft kiss on her cheek. Then he straightened and sat back.

''I'm not giving up, Chris.'' His voice was thick, vibrating in response to all he felt inside. ''I'll wait as long as it takes. I've got all the time in the world, too—and more desire than you could ever want.''

5

Chris never knew how she made it through the rest of lunch. She felt warm all over, her insides were humming, and even after Gideon took pity on her and changed the subject, she was shockingly aware of him—shockingly, because the things she kept noticing she hadn't noticed in any man, *any* man since she'd been eighteen years old, and even then, it was different.

Brant had been eighteen, too. He'd been big and brawny, a football player, far from the best on the team but good enough to earn a college scholarship. She remembered the nights they'd spent before graduation, parked in the shadowy grove behind the reservoir in his secondhand Chevy. She'd worshiped him then, had thought him the most beautiful creature on earth. With his sable hair and eyes, his strong neck and shoulders, and hands that knew just what to do with her breasts, he excited her beyond belief. Wanting only to please him, she let him open her blouse and bra to touch her naked flesh, and when that wasn't enough, she let him slip a hand inside her jeans, and when even that wasn't enough, she wore a skirt, so that all he had to do was take off her panties, unzip his pants and push inside her. It had hurt the first time, and she bled, but after that it was better, then better still.

Looking back, trying to remember how she could have been so taken in, she wondered if she wasn't half-turned-on by the illicitness of what they were doing. She hadn't ever been a rebel, but she was a senior in high school and feeling very grown-up in a houseful of far younger siblings. And then, yes, there was Brant. Looking back, she saw that he was a shallow cad, but at the time he was every cheerleader's dream with his thick hair, his flexing muscles, his tiny backside and his large, strong thighs.

Gideon Lowe put her memory of Brant Conway to shame. Gideon was mature, richly so, a freewheeling individual with a wealth of character, all of which was reflected in his physicality. The things she noticed about him—that stuck in her mind long after she left Joe's Grille—were the dark shadow of a mustache over his clean-shaven upper lip, the neat, narrow lobe of his ear and the way his hair swept vibrantly behind it, the length of his fingers and their strength, their newly scrubbed look, the scar on the smallest of them. She noticed the tan—albeit fading with the season—on his neck and his face, the crinkles radiating outward from the corners of his eyes, the small indentation on his cheek that should have been a dimple but wasn't. She remembered his size—not only his largeness, but the way he leaned close, making her feel enveloped and protected. And his scent, she remembered that with every breath she took. It was clean, very male and very enticing.

The problem, of course, was resisting the enticement, which she was determined to do above all else. She meant what she told him. She didn't have time for a serious man in her life. Her career was moving, and when she wasn't working, her time was happily filled with family. Thanksgiving had been larger—now that Jason was married, Evan engaged, and Mark and Steven bringing friends home from college—and more fun than ever. Christmas promised to be the same. She wanted to enjoy the holiday bustle. And then, there was work, which felt the Christmas crunch, too. Clients wanted everything delivered and looking great for the holidays. That meant extra phone calls on Chris's part, extra appointments, extra deliveries, extra installations. She *really* didn't have time for Gideon Lowe.

Of course, trying to explain that to Gideon was like beating her head against a brick wall. He called an hour after she returned to the office, on the day they met for lunch, to make sure she'd gotten back safely. He called two days later to say that, though he couldn't promise anything, he was getting estimates on half-round windows. He called three days after that to ask her to dinner.

Just hearing his voice sparked the heat in her veins. She couldn't possibly go to dinner with him. Couldn't *possibly*. "I'm sorry, Gideon, but I can't."

"Can't, or won't?"

"Can't. I have other plans." Fortunately, she did.

"Break them."

"I can't do that." The Christmas concert was being held at the high school that night. She wouldn't miss it for the world.

"Then tomorrow night. We could take in a movie or something."

She squeezed her eyes shut and said more softly, "No. I'm sorry."

He was silent for a minute. "You won't see me at all?"

"I don't think it would be a good idea. We work together. Let's leave it at that."

"But I'm lonely."

She cast a helpless glance at the ceiling. When he was blunt that way, there was something so endearing about the man that she wanted to strangle him. He was making things hard for her. "I thought you said you date. In fact, you said you date *a whole lot*." She remembered that quite clearly.

"I did, and I do, but those women are just friends. They're fine for fast fun, but they don't do anything for loneliness. They don't fill my senses the way you do."

"For *God's* sake, Gideon," she breathed. He was being corny as hell, but she liked it. It wasn't fair.

"Say you'll see me this weekend. Sometime. Anytime."

"I have a better idea," she said, trying to regain control of herself and the situation. "I'll talk with you on the phone again next week. There are questions that I didn't get around to asking you when we had lunch—" questions that she hadn't had the presence of mind to ask after he'd leaned close and kissed her "—and I've had other thoughts on the Rise since then. What do you say we talk a week from today?"

"A week!"

"This is an awful season for me. I'm up to my ears in promises and commitments. A week from today? Please?"

Mercifully her plea got through to him, because he did agree to call her the following Thursday. She was therefore unprepared when, on that Tuesday, between calls to a furniture factory in North Carolina, a ceramic tile importer in Delaware and an independent carpenter in Bangor, Maine, she heard an unmistakably familiar male voice coming from the outer office.

After listening to it for a minute, she knew just what was happening. She had told Margie that she needed an uninterrupted hour to make all her calls. So Margie was giving Gideon a hard time. But Gideon wasn't giving up.

Leaving her chair, Chris opened the office door, crossed her arms over her breasts and leaned against the jamb. "What are you doing here, Gideon?" she asked in as stern a voice as she could produce, given the way her heart was thudding at first sound, then sight of him. He was wearing jeans, a sweater and a hip-length parka. His hair was combed, but he hadn't shaved, which suggested that he'd come straight from work, with the benefit of only cursory repairs in the truck. The image of that unsettled her even more. But the worst was the way his eyes lit up when she appeared.

"Hey, Chris," he said, as though finding her here were a total surprise, "what's up?"

"What are you doing here?" she repeated, but she was having trouble keeping a straight face. For a big, burly, bullheaded guy, he looked adorably innocent.

Sticking his hands into the pockets of his jeans—knowingly or unknowingly pushing his parka in the process to reveal the faithful gloving of his lower limbs—he shrugged and said, "I was in the neighborhood and thought I'd drop in. How've you been?"

She steeled herself against his charm. "Just fine since we talked last week."

"Have a good weekend?"

"Uh-huh. And you?"

"Lonely. Very lonely. But I told you it would be." The look in his eye told her that if she didn't invite him into her office, he'd elaborate on that in front of Margie.

Chris didn't want even the slightest elaboration. She didn't trust where he'd stop, and it wasn't only Margie who'd hear, but Andrea, who was with a client in the second office and would no doubt be out before long. Then there would be comments and questions and suggestions the minute he left, and she couldn't bear that. No, the less attention drawn to Gideon, the better.

Dropping her arms, she nodded him into her office. The minute he was inside with the door closed, she sent him a baleful stare. "I told you I couldn't see you, and I mean it, Gideon. I have work to do. I'm *swamped.*" She shook a hand at her desk. "See that mess? That's what the Christmas rush is about. I don't have time to play." Her eyes widened. "What are you doing?"

"Taking off my jacket. It's warm in here."

Didn't she know it. Something about the two of them closed in the same room sent the temperature soaring. She felt the rise vividly, and it didn't help that he looked to be bare under his sweater, which fell over his pectorals with taunting grace.

"Put that jacket back on," she ordered, and would have helped him with it if she dared touch him, which she didn't. "You're not staying."

"I thought we could talk about the Rise."

"Baloney. You're not here about the Rise, and you know it," she scolded, but she seemed to have lost his attention. He was looking around her office, taking in the apricot, pale gray and chrome decor.

"Not bad," he decided. Crossing to the upholstered sofa, he pushed at one of the cushions with a testing hand, then turned and lowered his long frame onto the piece. He stretched out his arms, one across the back of the sofa, the other along its arm, and looked as though he'd be pleased to stay there a week.

Chris had her share of male clients, many of whom had been in her office, but none had ever looked as comfortable on that sofa as Gideon did. He was that kind of man, comfortable and unpretentious—neither of which helped her peace of mind any more than his sweater did, or his jeans. "I have to work, Gideon," she pleaded softly.

He gestured toward the desk. "Be my guest. I won't say a word."

"I can't work with you here."

"Why not?"

"You'll distract me."

"You don't have to look at me."

"I'll see you anyway."

"Ahh." He sighed. "A confession at last."

She blushed, then scowled in an attempt to hide it. "Gideon. Please."

Coming forward, he put his elbows on his spread thighs and linked his hands loosely between his knees. His voice went lower, his eyes more soulful. "It's been just over a week since I've seen you, but it feels like a month. You look so pretty."

Chris was wearing a burgundy jumper that she'd pulled from the closet, and a simple cream-colored blouse with a large pin at the throat. It was one of her oldest outfits. She didn't think she looked pretty at all and was embarrassed that he should say it. "Please, Gideon."

But he wasn't taking back the words. "I think about you a lot. I think about what you're doing and who you're with. I think about—wonder about—whether you're thinking of me."

She shut her eyes tight against the lure of his voice. "I told you. Things have been wild."

"But when you're home alone at night, do you think about me then?"

She pressed two fingers to her lips, where, just the night before, she'd dreamed he'd kissed her. From behind the fingers, she breathed a soft, "This isn't what I want."

"It's not what I want, either, but it's happening, and I can't ignore it. I feel an attraction to you the likes of which I haven't felt in years. I've tried to hold back, Chris. I tried not to come today because I know how you feel. But I'm not real good at waiting around. Call it impatient or domineering or macho, but I'm used to taking the lead. I want to see you again."

Anthony Haskell waited around, Chris realized. Anthony waited around all the time for her to beckon him on, but when she did, there was never any heat. There was heat now, with Gideon. She felt it running from her head to her toes, stalling and pooling at strategic spots in between.

Needing a buffer, she took refuge in the large chair behind the desk. "I thought we agreed to talk on Thursday," she said a little shakily.

"We did. And we can. But you're right. I didn't come to talk about the Rise. And I don't really want to talk about it on Thursday. There's nothing pressing there, certainly nothing that can't wait until the beginning of January, especially if you're as busy now as you say."

"I *am* busy."

"I believe you," he said genially. "But you have to take a break sometime. Why can't you take one with me?"

"I don't *want* to."

"Why not?"

She could think of dozens of answers, none of which she was ready to share.

Gideon didn't have that problem. "Don't you like me?"

She scowled. "Of course, I like you. If I didn't, I'd have already called the police to kick you out. You're interfering with my business."

"Do I still make you nervous?"

"Not nervous. Exasperated. Gideon," she begged, "I have to work."

"Do I excite you?"

"Yeah, to thoughts of mayhem." She glowered at him. "This isn't the time or place for a discussion like this."

"You're right. Let me take you to dinner tonight."

She shook her head.

"Tomorrow night, then. Come on, Chris, you have to eat."

"I do eat. With my family."

"Can't they spare you for one night?"

She shook her head.

"Then let me come eat with you." He seemed to warm to the idea once it was out. "I'd like that. I mean, I'd really like it. Big family dinners are something I always wanted but never had. I'll bring flowers for your mom. I'll bring cigars for your dad—"

"He doesn't smoke."

"Then beer."

"He doesn't drink."

"Then cashew nuts."

She shook her head. "Sorry. Doctor's orders."

Gideon looked appalled. "The poor guy. What does he *do* for the little joys in life?"

"He sneaks out to the kitchen when he thinks none of us is looking and steals kisses from my mom while she does the dishes."

That shut Gideon up. For a minute he just stared at her as though he couldn't grasp the image. Then his expression slid from soft to longing. "That's nice," he finally said, his voice a little thick. "I'm envious of you all."

Chris was beginning to feel like the worst kind of heel. If she was to believe Gideon's act, he was all alone in the world. But he dated, he dated *a lot*. And he had a mother in California. Maybe even a stepfamily. No doubt there would be numerous brightly wrapped gifts under his Christmas tree. So why did he look as though spending a little time with her family might be the best gift of all?

"Look," she said with a helpless sigh, "my parents have a Christmas open house every year." It would be packed. She could do her good deed, ease her conscience and be protected by sheer numbers. "It's this Sunday. If you want, you could come."

He brightened. "I'll come. Tell me where and when."

Taking a business card—deliberately, as a reminder of the nature of their relationship—she printed the address on the back. "It runs from three to seven, with the best of the food hitting the table at six."

"What should I wear?" he asked as he rose from the sofa to take the card.

"Something casual. Like what you wore to lunch last week."

He looked at the card, then stretched a little to slide it into the front pocket of his jeans. Chris was barely recovering from the way that stretch had lengthened his body when he turned, grabbed his coat and threw it on. For a split second his sweater rose high enough to uncover a sliver of skin just above his jeans. In the middle of that sliver, directly above the snap, was a belly button surrounded by whorls of dark hair.

She felt as though she'd been hit by a truck.

Oblivious to her turmoil, Gideon made for the door. Once there, he turned and gave her an ear-to-ear grin. "You've made my day. Made my *week*. Thanks, Chris. I'll see you Sunday." With a wink, he was gone.

Five days was far too soon to see him again, Chris decided on Sunday morning as she pulled on a sweatshirt and sweatpants and went to help her mother prepare for the party. He was still too fresh in her mind— or rather, the effect he had on her was too fresh. Every time she thought of him, her palms itched. Itched to touch. Itched to touch hair-spattered male flesh. And every time she thought of doing it, she burned.

She didn't know what was wrong with her. For fifteen years, she hadn't felt the least attraction to a man, and it hadn't been deliberate. She was with men when she worked. Her dad had men over. So did her brothers. But none had ever turned her on, it was as simple, as blunt as that.

What she felt for Gideon Lowe made up for all those chaste years, so much so that she was frightened. She sensed she'd need far more than crowds to lessen the impact he had on her. She only prayed he'd arrive late to coincide with the food. The less time he stayed, the better.

* * *

Gideon would have arrived at three on the nose if it hadn't been for his truck, which coughed and choked and balked at having to go out in the cold. He called it every name in the book as he worked under its hood, finally even threatened to trade it in for a sports car. That must have hit home, because the next time he tried it, the engine turned smoothly over and hummed nicely along while he went back into the house to scrub his hands clean.

It was three-thirty when he pulled into the closest spot he could find to the address Chris had written down. The street was pretty and tree lined, though the trees were bare, in a neighborhood that was old and well loved. Wood-frame houses stood, one after another, on scant quarter-acre lots. Their closeness gave a cozy feeling that was reinforced by wreaths decorating each and every door and Christmas lights shining from nearly every window. None of the houses was large, including Chris's parents', but that added to the coziness.

From the looks of things, the party was in full swing. The front door was open, there were people preceding him up the walk, and the side stoop was occupied by a group of college-age kids who seemed oblivious to the cold.

Leaving his truck, he followed the walk to the door, dodging two young girls who darted out of the house to join their friends. Once on the threshold, he felt a little unsure for the first time since he'd bulldozed the invitation from Chris. He'd gone to parties at the homes of people far more wealthy and influential, but none mattered more to him than this one.

He assumed that he was looking a little lost, because he barely had time to take more than two steps into the house when he was greeted by a tall gray-haired man. "Welcome," the man said in a voice loud enough to be heard above the din. "Come on in."

Gideon extended his hand. "Mr. Gillette?"

"That I am," the man said, giving him a hearty shake, "but probably not the one you want. I'm Peter. If you're looking for my brother Frank, he's mixing the eggnog, which is real serious business, so I'd advise you to leave him be. If he messes up, we all lose out, if you get my drift."

"Actually," Gideon said, searching for a blond head among those crowded into the living room, "I'm looking for Christine. I'm a friend of hers, Gideon Lowe."

"Even better," Peter said with a broad grin. "Tell you what. Why don't you hang your coat up in the closet while I go find her."

Gideon was already working his way out of the leather jacket.

"That's okay. I'll go." Spotting a hook at the end of the closet, he freed himself of the jacket. "Which direction?"

Peter looked first toward the dining room on the left, then the living room on the right, then back toward the dining room. "The kitchen, I guess. If she's not helping Frank, she'll be helping Mellie." He pointed through the dining room. "That way."

With a nod, Gideon started off. The dining room was filled with people helping themselves to drinks and the small holiday cookies and cakes that covered plate after plate on the table. At one end was a huge punch bowl, into which a man Gideon assumed to be Frank was alternately pouring eggnog and brandy. He was a good-looking man, Gideon thought, tall and stocky, with salt-and-pepper hair and a ruddy complexion. Despite the good-natured coaxing and wheedling of several onlookers, he was concentrating solely on his work.

Gideon inched between two people here, three others there, until he'd made his way to the far end of the dining room and slipped through the door into a small pantry that led to the kitchen. There he saw Chris. She was standing at the counter by the sink with her back to him. Beside her was the woman who had to be her mother, if the similarity of height, build and coloring were any indication. They were slicing hot kielbasa, putting toothpicks in each slice, arranging the slices on a platter.

Coming up close behind Chris, he bent and put a gentle kiss beneath her ear.

She cried out and jumped a mile, then whirled on him in a fury. "Gideon! Don't *ever* do that again! My God—" she pressed her hand to her heart "—you've aged me fifteen years."

He gestured toward her mother, who was eyeing him curiously. "If this lovely lady is any indication of what you'll look like fifteen years from now, you've got it made." He extended his hand toward Mellie. "Mrs. Gillette?" There was no mistaking it. The eyes were the same, the hair, the mouth. Chris was slimmer and, wearing loose pants with a tunic top, more stylishly dressed, but they were very definitely mother and daughter.

"Gideon...?"

"Gideon Lowe, Mom. He's the builder for Crosslyn Rise and may well be the death of me before I even get to the project." She scolded him with her eyes, then her voice. "I thought you were coming later."

"You suggested six if I was starved. I figured I'd give myself a while to build up to that." He shook Mellie's hand warmly.

"It's nice to meet you, Mr. Lowe."

"Gideon. Nice to meet you, too, ma'am." He let her take her hand back and return to her work. "This is quite some party." He looked down at the platter. "Can I help?"

"No," both women said at the same time.

Chris elaborated. "Men don't cook in my mother's kitchen. My father does the eggnog, but not in here. Men are good for cleaning up. That's all."

"And a few other things," Mellie added softly, almost under her breath. Then she looked straight at Gideon and spoke up, "But I don't want you in here. You're a guest. Christine, leave these now. I'll finish up. Take Gideon out and introduce him around."

Gideon thought Chris was going to argue, but even he could see that Mellie wasn't taking no for an answer. So she washed and dried her hands, then led him through another door into a hallway that led back to the front. This hallway, too, was crammed with people, giving Gideon ample excuse to stay close to Chris.

"You look fantastic," he murmured into her ear as they inched their way along.

"Thanks," she murmured back.

"You taste even better."

"Oh, please," she whispered, but before he had a chance to come back with anything wickedly witty, she half turned, took his elbow and drew him alongside her. "Gideon, this is my brother Steven. He's a junior at U. of Mass. Steven, meet Gideon Lowe, a builder I work with."

Gideon shook hands with a blond-haired young man who also had the family features. "You must be one of the basketball fanatics," he said, noting that Steven stood nearly as tall as he did.

Steven grinned. "You got it. You, too?"

"You bet. If not for this gorgeous sister of yours, I'd be at the game right now." Leaning close, he asked out of the corner of his mouth, "Any fix on the score?"

In every bit as low a tone, Steven answered, "Last time I checked, the Celts were up by eight. Game's on upstairs, if you want."

Gideon slapped his shoulder and straightened. "Thanks for the word. Maybe later."

"Don't you dare go up and watch that game," Chris warned, leading him on by the hand. "That would be very rude."

"Keep holding my hand," he whispered, "and I'll stay right by your side." He raised his voice. "Ah, here comes another brother."

Chris shot him an amused grin. "This is Jason. He works with Dad. His wife's over there—" She stood on tiptoe, looking around, "Jase, where's Cheryl?"

Jason shook hands with Gideon. "Upstairs nursing the baby."

"Gideon Lowe," Gideon said. "What baby?"

"A little boy," Chris explained. "He's their first."

"Hey, congratulations."

"Thanks," Jason said, but he had something else on his mind. "Chrissie, you seen Mark? He parked that rattletrap of his in the driveway in back of the Davissons and they have to leave."

"Try the front steps. Last I knew he was holding court out there." Jason promptly made for the door, but before Chris and Gideon could make any progress, a loud cheer came from the dining room. Seconds later, a grinning Frank Gillette emerged through a gauntlet of backslapping friends. When he caught sight of Chris, his eyes lit up even more.

"Go on in and try it, honey. They say it's better than ever."

"I will," Chris said. Her hand tightened on Gideon's. "Dad, I'd like you to meet Gideon Lowe. He and I work together."

"Nice to meet you," Frank said, "and glad you could come."

"It's kind of you all to welcome me."

"Any friend of Chrissie's, as they say. Hey, Evan," he called, "get over here." Seconds later, he was joined by another fair-haired son. "Evan, say hello to Gideon Lowe. Gideon, this is my second oldest son, and his fiancée, Tina."

Gideon smiled and nodded to them. Waving, they continued on into the living room. Gideon was beginning to wonder how Chris kept her brothers apart when yet another stole by. This one was younger and faster. He would have made it out the front door if Frank hadn't reached out and grabbed his arm. "Where you off to so fast?"

"I want to see Mark's friends. Steve says there're a couple'a cool girls out there."

Chris grinned up at Gideon. "That's Alex, the baby."

Alex looked instantly grieved. "Come on, Chris. That's not fair. I'm fifteen. Besides, I'm not the baby. Jill is."

"Jill?" Gideon asked. Chris had said there were six kids in the family. He was sure he'd already met ten. "There's another one?"

"Yeah," Alex said, "and there she is." He pointed to the girl coming down the stairs. While everyone looked that way, he escaped out the door.

"Come over here, girl," Frank said, but it was to Chris's side that the girl came.

Accordingly Chris was the one to make the introduction. "Say hi to Gideon," she told Jill. "He's the builder for Crosslyn Rise, but be careful what you say. He's also on the consortium."

Jill grinned. "Ah, he's the one?"

"He's the one."

Gideon couldn't take his eyes off Jill. With her long brown hair and her large brown eyes, she was different from every other Gillette he'd met. A beauty, she looked to be at least seventeen, yet Alex had called her the baby, and he was fifteen. Gideon wondered if they were twins, with Jill the younger of the two by mere minutes. She couldn't possibly be *fourteen.*

He stuck out his free hand. "Hi, Jill."

For a split second she seemed a little shy, and in that second he almost imagined she could be younger. Then she composed herself and gave him her hand, along with Chris's smile. "Nice to meet you."

"The pleasure's mine. It's not often that I get to hang around with *two* gorgeous women."

Chris arched a brow at Jill. "Didn't I tell you?"

Grinning back, Jill nodded.

"What?" Gideon asked.

"You know how to throw it around," Jill said.

Gideon looked at Frank. "Was that bull? Are these two women gorgeous, or are they gorgeous?"

"They're gorgeous," Frank confirmed, "but who'm I to judge. I got a vested interest in them."

Gideon considered that interest as he looked from Chris's face to Jill's and back. "All those blondes and one brunette," he said to no one in particular. To Jill he said, "How old are you?"

"Fifteen."

To Chris, he said, "I thought Alex was fifteen."

"He is."

"Then they're twins?"

"Not exactly."

"Irish twins?"

Chris slid an amused glance at Jill before saying, "No. Jill is five months younger."

"Five months?" He frowned. "No, that can't be—" He stopped when Chris and Jill burst out laughing, then looked questioningly at Frank, who was scowling at Chris.

"That's not real nice, Chris. I told you not to do it. It isn't fair to put people on the spot like that."

"Thank you," Gideon told him, and directed his gaze at Chris. It was Jill, though, who offered the explanation he sought.

"I'm not his," she said, tossing her dark head toward Frank. "I'm *hers.*" Her head bobbed toward Chris.

Hers? For a long minute, Gideon didn't make the connection. When he did, he ruled it out as quickly as it had come.

Chris squeezed his hand, which she hadn't let go of once. She was looking up at him, her eyes surprisingly serious. "Say something."

Gideon said the first thing that came to mind. "You're too young, and she's too old."

"I was eighteen when she was born."

"You look like sisters."

"If she were my sister, she'd be blond."

"But she has the Gillette smile."

"That's my smile. She's my daughter."

Daughter. Somehow, the word did it—that, and the fact that with two witnesses, one of whom had originally made the claim and the other of whom wasn't opening his mouth to rebut it, Gideon figured it had to be true. "Wow," he breathed. "A daughter."

"Does that shock you?"

"Yeah," he said, then felt it worth repeating. "Yeah."

"Kind of throws things into a new light?" Chris asked, but before he could answer, she released his hand, said a soft, "Excuse me, I want to check on Mom," and escaped into the crowd.

"Chris—"

Frank put a tempering hand on his arm. "Let her go. She'll be back."

But Gideon's eyes continued to follow her blond head as it moved farther away. "She'll misinterpret what I just said. I know she will. She'll think I don't want any part of her because she has a child, but that's not what I'm feeling at all. I'm feeling that, my God, she's done this wonderful thing in life, and I haven't ever done anything that even comes *close* in importance to it."

"This is getting heavy," Jill drawled.

Gideon's eyes flew to hers. He'd forgotten she was there, and was appalled. "Hey, I'm sorry. I didn't mean to offend you, too. I really like...your mom. If you're her daughter, I like you, too. Hell, I like the whole damned family. I don't have *any* family."

Jill's eyes widened. "None?"

But before he could answer, there was an uproar at the door. Frank turned around, then, wearing a broad grin, turned back and leaned close to Gideon. "See that bald-headed son of a bitch who just walked in? I haven't seen him in twenty years." To Jill, he said, "Take Gideon around, honey. If you run out of things to say, point him toward the game. He's a fan."

"Chris said I couldn't," Gideon told him.

Frank made a face. "Mellie says I can't, but do I listen?" Slapping his shoulder, he went off to greet his friend.

"You don't have *any* family?" Jill repeated, picking up right where she'd left off.

He shook his head. His hand felt empty without Chris's, so he slipped it into his pocket.

"No family."

"That's awful. Do you live all alone?"

"All alone."

"Wow, I don't think I could do that. I'd miss having people around and things happening."

Gideon was trying to think back to what Chris had said about herself. There wasn't a whole lot. She had evaded some questions and turned others right back to him. He didn't think she had ever lied to him, per se, but she'd obviously chosen every word with care.

When it came to where she lived, he had the distinct impression that she had her own place close to her family's. He suddenly wondered whether, there too, she'd stretched the words. "You don't live *here*, do you?"

"Oh, no. We're next-door. But we're here all the time."

"Next-door?" He was trying to remember what that house had looked like. "To the right or the left?"

"Behind. We're in the garage."

"The *garage*."

She nodded. "Uh-huh."

"You're stuck in the *garage*?"

She shot him a mischievous grin. "Want to see?"

"Yeah, I want to see." It occurred to him that Chris's daughter was a treasure trove of information on Chris, and that he wasn't adverse to getting what he could.

Jill led him around the crowd at the door, out and across the frozen lawn to the driveway. "My friends love my place," she said when he'd come up alongside her. "They keep bugging their parents to do something like it for them."

From what Gideon could see, the garage was like any other. Detached from the house, it was set far back at the end of a long driveway, with a single large door that would raise and lower to allow two cars inside. His builder's mind went to work imagining all the possibilities, but when Jill opened a side door and beckoned him inside, he wasn't prepared for what he found.

The garage had been elongated at the rear and converted into a small house, with an open living-room-kitchen-dining area, then a balcony above, off which two doors led, he assumed, to bedrooms. To compensate for a dearth of windows, there were indirect lights aplenty, as befitted the home of the daughter and granddaughter of an electrician. But what impressed Gideon even more than that was the decor. Nearly everything was white, and what wasn't white was a soft shade of blue. There was a light, bright, clean feel to the place. He couldn't believe he was in a garage.

"This is fantastic," he said.

Jill beamed. "Mom designed it, and Gramp's friends did it. I was just a baby and Mom was still in school, so it meant she could leave me with Gramma and Alex during the day, then have me to herself here at night."

Gideon was still looking around, taking in the small, sweet touches— like pictures of Jill at every imaginable age, in frames that were unique, one from the other—but he heard what she said. "So you grew up right alongside Alex?"

"Uh-huh. He's not bad for an uncle."

Gideon looked at her to find a very dry, very mature grin on her face. Narrowing an eye, he said, "You get a kick out of that, don't you?"

"Kinda." She dropped onto the arm of a nearby sofa with her legs planted straight to the floor. "People don't know what to think when they meet Alex and me. I mean, we're in the same grade and we have the same last name but we look so different. They don't believe it when we tell them the truth. They get the funniest looks on their faces—like you did before."

He wondered what explanation she gave for where her own father was. He wanted to ask about that himself, but figured it was something better asked of Chris. "Do you mind your mom working?"

Jill shrugged. "She has to earn a living."

"But you must miss her."

"Yes and no. I have Gramma. She's always around. And I have a house full of uncles. And then Mom comes home at night and tells me about everything she did at work that day."

"Everything?"

Jill nodded. "We're very close."

He had the odd feeling that it was a warning. Cautiously he asked, "What did she say about me?"

Without any hesitancy—as though she'd been wanting the question and he'd done nothing more than follow her lead—she said, "That you were a builder, that you were on the committee that interviewed her, and that you were a real jerk." When Gideon's face fell, she burst out laughing. "Just kidding. She didn't say that. She did say that you were very good-looking and very confident and that she wasn't sure how easy it'd be working with you.'' Jill paused, then added, "She likes you, I think.''

"I know she likes me—"

"I mean, *likes* you.''

Gideon studied her hesitantly. "Think so?'' When she nodded, he said, "How do you know?''

"The way she ran off after we told you about me. She was nervous about what you'd think. She wouldn't have been if she didn't care. And then there was the thing with the hands.''

"What thing?''

"She was holding yours. Or letting you hold hers. She doesn't usually do that with men. She's very prim.''

"But you noticed the hands.''

"I sure did.''

Gideon ran a finger inside the collar of his shirt. "How old did you say you were?''

"It was only hands," she said in a long-suffering way. "And I *ought* to notice things like that. She's my mother. I care about what she does with her life.''

He could see that she did, and had the oddest sense of talking with Chris's parent rather than her child. "Would it bother you if I dated her?''

"No. She ought to have more fun. She works too hard.''

"What about Anthony?''

"Anthony is a total dweeb.''

"Oh.'' That about said it. "Okay. Then he isn't competition?''

"Are you kidding?'' she said with a look of such absurdity on her face that he would have laughed if they'd been talking about anything else. But his future with Chris was no laughing matter.

"So we rule out Anthony. Are there any others I should know about?''

"Did she say there were?''

"No.''

Jill tipped her head. "There's your answer.''

"And you wouldn't mind it if I took her out sometimes?''

The head straightened and there was a return hint of absurdity in her expression. "Why would I mind?''

"If I took her out, it would be taking her away from time spent with you.''

Jill didn't have to consider that for long. "There are times when I want to do things with friends, but I feel so guilty going out and leaving Mom alone here. She can go over to the house and be with everyone there, but it's not the same. I mean, I love her and all, but my friends go shopping or to the movies on the weekends, and it's fun to do that. And then there's college. I want to go away. I've never *been* away. But how can I do that if it means leaving her alone?''

Gideon scratched his head. ''Y'know, if I didn't know better, I'd wonder whether you're trying to marry her off.''

''I'm not,'' Jill protested, and came off the sofa. ''I wouldn't be saying this to just anyone, but you like her, and she likes you, and what I'm saying is that you can't use me as an excuse for not taking her out. I'm a good kid. I don't drink or do drugs or smoke. I'll be gone in three years. I won't be in the way.''

Gideon hadn't had much experience with fifteen-year-old girls, but he knew without doubt that this one had a soft and sensitive side. She might be totally adjusted to the fact of her parentage; she might be far more mature than her years. But only in some respects. In others, she was still a girl wanting to please the adults in her life.

The fact that she considered him one of those adults touched him to the core. Crossing to where she stood, he tipped her chin up and said, ''You could never be in the way, Jill. I don't know what'll happen between your mother and me. Our relationship has barely gotten off the ground. But believe me when I say that your existence is a plus. A big, big plus. I've been alone most of my life. I *like* the idea of being with someone who has family.''

''Family can get in the way sometimes.''

''You wouldn't say that if you've been without the way I have.''

''Are you gonna tell Mom that?''

''As soon as I can get her alone long enough to talk.''

''What's going on here?'' Chris asked from the door.

Jill slipped away from his hand. ''Whoops. Looks like you'll have that chance sooner'n you thought.'' She grinned. ''Hi, Mom. I think I'll go back to the house and get something to drink. I'm parched.'' She was halfway past Chris when she said, ''Invite him for Christmas dinner. He's nice.'' Before Chris could begin to scold, she was gone.

6

―――――――

"Whose idea was it to come back here?" Chris asked. She wasn't quite angry, wasn't quite pleased. In fact, she wasn't quite sure *what* she was feeling, and hadn't been since she'd shocked Gideon with the fact of Jill.

"Uh, I'm not sure. I think it was kind of mutual."

"Uh-huh." Chris understood. "It was Jill's idea. You're protecting her."

Gideon held up a cautioning hand. "Look, she may have suggested it, but only after I started pestering her about where you two lived." Dropping the hand to his pocket, he looked around. "It's a super place, Chris. I like it a lot."

"So do I, but it's only a place. Jill's a person. She means more to me than anything else on earth. I don't want her hurt."

Gideon straightened. "You think I could *hurt* her?"

That was exactly what Chris thought. "You could get real close, then lose interest. When I said that she throws a new light on things, I meant it."

"Hold on a minute. I'm not romancing Jill. It's you—"

"But she's part of the package," Chris interrupted, feeling the urgency of the message. "That's what I'm trying to tell you. You say you want to date me. You hoodwinked me into inviting you here today. Well, okay, you're here, and I'll date you, but you have to know where my priorities lie. I'm not like some women who flit around wherever the mood takes them. I'm not an independent agent. I'm not a free spirit."

"I never thought you were," Gideon said soberly. "From the start, you've been serious and down-to-earth. You made it clear how much your family means to you."

"Jill is more than family. She's someone I created—"

"Not alone."

"Someone I *chose* to bring into this world. I have a responsibility to her."

"And you think you're unique?" Gideon challenged impulsively. "Doesn't every mother feel that responsibility? Doesn't every single mother feel it even more strongly, just like you do? For God's sake, Chris, I'm not trying to come between you and your daughter. Maybe I'm trying to add something to both of your lives. Ever thought of it that way? I sure as hell know I'm trying to add something to mine." He swore again, this time under his breath. "*Trying* is the operative word here. You get so goddamned prickly that I'm not making a helluva lot of headway." He stopped, then started right back up in the next breath. "And as far as Jill's existence throwing a new light on things, let me tell you that I find the fact that you have a daughter to be incredibly wonderful—which you would have known sooner if you hadn't run off so fast. You do that a lot, Chris. It's a bad habit. You run off before things can be settled."

"There's nothing to be settled here," Chris informed him, staunchly sticking to her guns, "since nothing's open for discussion. Jill is my daughter. For the past fifteen years, she's been the first thought on my mind when I wake up in the morning and the last thought before I fall asleep at night."

"Is that healthy?" Gideon asked innocently, but the words set her off.

"Healthy or not, that's the way it is," she snapped. "A woman with a child isn't the same as one without. You ought to think really hard about that before you do any more sweet-talking around here." She turned and made for the door, but Gideon was across the floor with lightning speed, catching her arm, drawing her back into the living room and shoving the door shut.

"Not so fast. Not this time. This time we talk."

"I can't talk now," she cried. "I have a house full of Christmas guests to entertain."

But Gideon was shaking his head. "Those guests entertain themselves, and besides, there are a dozen other hosts in that house." His voice softened, as did his hand on her arm, though he didn't release her. "Just for a minute, Chris. I won't keep you long, but I want to make something very clear."

She glanced up at him, and her heart lurched. The look in his eyes was gentle, almost exquisitely so.

"I like you," he said. "God only knows why, because you give me a hard time, but I like you a lot. You could've had *five* kids, with half of them in diapers, and I wouldn't care. Knowing about Jill now, I respect you even more for what you've done with your business, and you've obviously done something right with her, or she wouldn't be as nice a kid as she seems to be." He paused. "When I said I was shocked back there, it was because you never let on—I didn't expect it. You just didn't strike me as the type to—''

"Get knocked up?"

"Have a baby so young. Okay, yeah, maybe be with a guy so young." A tiny crease appeared between his brows. Quietly he asked, "Who was he?"

"It doesn't matter," Chris said, and tried to turn back toward the door only to have Gideon lock a grip on her other arm, too.

"Did you love him?" he asked, still quietly, even unsurely.

Chris had been prepared for criticism, which was what she'd gotten most often when she'd first become pregnant. *Didn't you know what you were doing? Didn't you use anything? Didn't you stop to consider the consequences?* Rarely had she been asked what Gideon just asked her. Looking up into his deep charcoal eyes, she almost imagined he was worried.

"I thought I did," she told him in a voice as quiet as his. "We were both seniors. He was handsome and popular, full of charm and fun. I was totally snowed. We didn't have anywhere to go, so we used to park up behind the reservoir. That's where Jill was conceived."

She thought Gideon started to wince, but he caught himself. "What happened after?"

"He didn't want me or the baby," she said bluntly. She'd long since passed the time when she blamed herself for that. She might have loved Brant at the time, or thought she did, but the only person Brant had loved was himself. "He denied it was his."

This time Gideon's wince was for real. "What kind of selfish bastard was he?"

Chris shrugged. "He was going to college on a scholarship and didn't want anyone or anything to slow him down."

"So he left you in the lurch. You must have been furious."

"Furious, hurt, frightened."

"I'd be angry still."

"Why? I got the better part of the deal. I got Jill."

Gideon seemed momentarily stunned, as though that idea had never occurred to him. Finally, in a hoarse whisper, he said, "That's what I think I like about you so much. You feel things. You love."

Chris too was stunned, nearly as much by his whispered awe as by the reverence in his eyes. Then she didn't have time to think of either, because he lowered his head to kiss her. At least, that was what she thought he was going to do. She felt the approach of his mouth, the warmth of his breath—then he pulled back and looked at her again, and in the look, something gave inside her.

"Do it," she whispered, suddenly wanting his kiss more than anything else.

His lips were smooth and firm. They touched hers lightly, rubbed them open in a back and forth caress, then, just as his hands left her arms and framed her face, came in more surely.

Chris was overwhelmed by the warmth of the kiss, its wetness, and by Gideon's fresh male scent that seemed to fill her and overflow. Needs that had lain dormant for better than fifteen years suddenly came to life, touching off an explosion of awareness inside her. Her limbs tingled, her heart pounded, her blood rushed hot through her veins. Feeling dizzy and hungry at the same time, she clasped fistfuls of sweater at his waist, gave a tiny moan and opened her mouth to his silent demand.

The demand went on and on, sometimes pressing, sometimes hovering, sometimes sucking so strongly that she was sure she'd never emerge whole again. When, with several last, lingering touches, the kiss ended, she felt bereft.

It was a minute before she realized exactly what had happened, and by that time, Gideon had his mouth pressed to her temple and his arms wrapped tightly around her. With her slow return to reality came the awareness of a fine tremor snaking through his large frame.

"Gideon?" she whispered, shaky herself.

"Shh," he whispered back. "Give me a minute."

She knew all too well why he needed the time. She could feel the reason pressing insistently against her thigh, and while the strength of it shocked her, it also excited her beyond belief. She wanted another kiss. She wanted some touching. She wanted something even harder, something to relieve the deep ache she was feeling.

"I knew it'd be like that," he whispered again.

"I didn't know it *could* be."

He made a low, longing sound and crushed her even closer.

"That's not helping," she whispered, but neither was breathing against his neck the way she was doing. His skin was firm and hot and smelled wonderfully of man.

"I know, but I need it. I can't let you go just yet."

"You'll have to soon. Someone's apt to come looking."

Raising his head, he caught her eyes. His voice remained little more than a ragged train of breath. "Know what I'd do if I had my way?" When she shook her head, he said, "I'd back you right up to that door and make love to you here and now."

She felt a searing heat deep in her belly and had to swallow before she could get a word out. "You can't."

"Yes, I can. I'm hard. Can't you feel?" Slipping his hands to her bottom, he manipulated her hips against his. His arousal was electrifying.

She had to close her eyes against its force. "Don't, Gideon," she cried, her breath coming in shallow gusts. She lowered her forehead to his throat.

His mouth touched her ear. "Right against that door. Then, after that, on your bed. You've never done it on a bed, have you?"

"No." She tugged at his sweater, which she was still clutching for dear life. "Don't talk."

"Why not?"

"Because you're making things harder."

"I'll say," he muttered with the nudge of his hips.

Moaning against the fire that small movement sparked, she slipped her arms around his neck, drawing herself up on tiptoe, and hung on tight. Her body felt foreign but wonderful. It knew what it wanted. Her mind wasn't so sure. "I have to get back to the house."

"You don't want to."

"I have to." But she moved against him, needing the friction to ease the knot between her legs.

"You want to stay here and make love with me."

"Oh, Gideon!" she cried.

"You do. I'd make it so good, baby, so good. I wouldn't rush you, wouldn't hurt you, and it'd be so incredibly good." He slipped a hand from her bottom to her thigh, then moved upward and inward.

"Don't," she begged, but the plea was empty. Between his words and his closeness, she was floating, then soaring, burning up from the inside out. When he touched her where she was most sensitive, she cried out, and when he began to caress her, she held on tighter to his neck.

"You're so hot here," he whispered.

"Gideon," she moaned. "Oh, no." She was arching into his hand, coming apart with no way to stop it.

His stroking grew bolder. "That's it, baby. That's it. Feel it. Let it come."

She was lost. In a moment of blinding bliss, she convulsed into an orgasm that left her gasping for air. She couldn't speak, could only make small, throaty sounds. Gradually they eased. The next sound she made was a humiliated sob. Twisting away from Gideon with such suddenness that he was taken off guard, she stumbled around the sofa and collapsed into its corner, pressing her knees together and huddling low over them.

"It's okay, sweetheart," Gideon said, reaching out to stroke her hair. She felt his hand and would have pulled away if there was anywhere to pull to. "That shouldn't have happened," she cried. "I'm so embarrassed."

Barely removing his hand, Gideon came around the end of the sofa and squatted close before her. "Don't be," he said. "I'm not. I feel so *good*."

"You can't feel good. You didn't...get anything."

"Wrong. Way wrong. I got a whole lot." His strong hands were framing her neck, and his voice, though hoarse, was astonishingly tender. He leaned forward so that his breath brushed her cheek. "Was that the first time since—"

She gave a sharp, quick nod against her knees.

"The first time since Jill's father?"

She repeated the same sharp nod.

"You've never done it yourself?"

She kicked his leg.

"Chris?" When she didn't answer, he said again, "Chris?"

Her voice was small. "What?"

"I think I'm falling in love with you."

"Don't *say* that."

"But it's true."

She pressed her hands to her ears and shook her head.

Forcibly removing her hands, he raised her head until she was sitting up, looking at him. "I won't say it again, if it makes you uncomfortable. It shakes me a little, too. We don't know each other much, do we?"

Unable to take her eyes from his, she gave a feeble shake of her head.

"But there's a remedy for that," he went on. "You can stop cooking up cockamamy excuses for why you can't see me."

Chris pulled back as much as his hands would allow. "They're not cockamamy excuses. This is the busiest time of the year for me. Between work and all the things I want to do with Jill—"

"Invite me along. We don't have to be alone all the time."

She made a disbelieving face. "What kind of man wants to put up with that?"

His voice went low and husky again. "The kind of man who knows his woman is made of fire. As long as I know it's coming, I can wait."

Chris felt her cheeks go red. "I won't ever live that down, will I?"

"Not if I can help it. It was the most beautiful, most sensual, most natural and spontaneous response I've ever experienced with a woman."

She had to look away. His eyes were too intense. Very softly she said, "You've been with lots of women, haven't you?"

"Over the years? Enough." He paused. "But if it's the health thing that's got you worried, don't be. I've always used a rubber. Always. For birth control, as much as anything. I'm clean, Chris.''

Focusing on a cable twist in his sweater, she murmured. "I wasn't worried about that.'' She was actually worried about the issue of experience, because, other than with Brant, she was very much without.

"I don't want to use anything with you.''

Her eyes shot to his. "You have to. I don't have—I'm not taking—''

His mouth cut off the words, kissing her gently, then less gently, before he regained control and drew up his head. "If you got pregnant by me, I wouldn't run away. I'd want you and the baby and Jill and your family. I'd marry you in a minute.''

Chris was having trouble breathing again. "This conversation is very premature.''

"Just so you know how I feel.''

"How can you feel that way so soon?''

"Beats me, but I do.''

"I think you're getting carried away on some kind of fantasy.''

"No fantasy. Just you.''

How was she supposed to answer *that*? She swallowed. "I have to get back to the house.''

Gideon sat on his heels. "I'm staying till the party's over. Can we talk more then?''

"Maybe we shouldn't. Maybe we should let things cool off a little.''

"It won't help. The fire's there, whether we're together or not. It's there even when I sleep. I had a wet dream last night—''

"Gideon, for goodness' sakes!''

"I did.''

"But don't *tell* me.''

"Why not?'' he asked reasonably. "I know damned well you're going to think back on what happened here and be embarrassed, and I just want you to know that you're not the only one who loses control sometimes. You had far more reason to than I did, what with the way I was touching you—''

She pressed a hand to his mouth. "Please,'' she begged in a whisper, "don't say another word.'' She waited. He was silent. She moved her fingers very lightly over his lips. "I'm going to get up now and go back to the house. If you'd like, you can come, too. You can talk with people—Jessica and Carter may be here by now—or even watch the game if it isn't over.''

"The Lakers come on next,'' he murmured against her fingers.

"Okay. The Lakers. My brothers will be watching. You can get something to eat and stay as long as you want, but I can't go out with you afterward. I want to help my mother clean up. Then I want to spend some time with Jill. Then I want to go to bed. Tomorrow's as busy as Mondays get.'' Her hand slid from his mouth to the shirt collar that rose above the crew neck of his sweater.

"What's on for tomorrow night?"

"I have deliveries to supervise until eight."

"So Jill will be here with your folks?"

"She has Driver Ed on Monday nights. I'll pick her up on my way home."

"What about supper?"

"I'll grab something when I get home."

"Why don't I pick up Chinese and stop by your office?"

"Because I won't be at my office."

"So I'll go where you are."

"You can't. Not with food. My clients would die."

"Okay. What about Tuesday night? No, forget Tuesday night. I have a game." His eyes lit up. "Come see me play."

For an instant, he was so eager that she actually wished she could. But the logistics wouldn't work. "In Worcester?"

"Too far, hmm?"

"And I have ballet."

"Okay. What's on for Wednesday night?"

"Jill's piano recital."

"I'll come."

"You will not. She's nervous enough at recitals without having to worry about her mother's new boyfriend showing up."

Gideon grinned. "New boyfriend. I like that. It's better than the builder." His grin vanished. "But I won't make her nervous. She likes me."

"She likes you here, now, today. That's because you're one of lots of people coming to party. She's apt to be threatened when she realizes something's going on between us."

"She already does. And she won't be threatened. She *likes* me. Besides, she wants you to date. She told me so."

"She told you?"

"Yes."

Chris felt just the slightest bit betrayed. "What else did she tell you?"

"Not much. You came along before she had a chance. But, damn it, Chris, we haven't settled anything here. When can I see you again? We're up to Thursday."

"Thursday's no good. I have ballet again, and then we're going shopping."

"I'll go with you."

But she shook her head. Last-minute Christmas shopping was something that had become almost traditional with Jill and her. Chris wasn't ready to let someone else intrude.

"Okay," Gideon said, "that brings us to the weekend, and to Christmas Eve. So are you inviting me over, or what?"

Chris didn't know what to do. Christmas Eve, then Christmas Day were every bit as personal and special and traditional for the whole family as last-minute shopping was for Jill and her alone.

"Jill said you should," he reminded her.

"Jill was out of line."

"What are all your plans?"

"Dinner, caroling, then Midnight Mass on Christmas Eve, and a huge meal on Christmas Day."

"Is it all just family?"

"No," Chris answered truthfully. "Friends come, too." She sighed and sent him a beseeching look. "But this is happening too fast, Gideon. Can't we slow it down?"

"Some things won't be slowed down—like what happened a little while ago."

She squeezed her eyes shut.

"What are you afraid of, Chris? What's holding you back?"

She had asked herself the same question more than once in recent weeks. Slowly she opened her eyes and met his. "Being hurt. I'm afraid of that. Jill may be the highlight of my life, but what Brant did hurt. I got over it. I came back and built a life, and I think I've been a great mother. Things are going smoothly. I don't want that to change."

"Not even for the better?"

"I don't *need* things to be better."

The look on Gideon's face contradicted her even before he spoke. "I think you do. There's a closeness only a man can give that I think you crave. It's like the way you held my hand back at the house, and the way you came apart before, even the way you're touching me right now."

"I'm not—"

"You are. Look at your hand."

Chris did. Her hand was folded over his collar, her fingers against the warm skin on the inside. Very carefully she removed them and put her hand into her lap. "I didn't know I was doing that," she said meekly.

"Like I didn't know what was happening until I woke up panting this morning. There's something to be said for the subconscious. It's more honest than we are sometimes.''

He had a point, she supposed. She could deny that she wanted him, deny that she wanted any kind of relationship, but it wouldn't be the truth. Still, despite his arguments, she meant what she'd said about slowing things down.

"New Year's Eve," she said, focusing on her lap. "You probably already have plans—"

"I don't, and I accept. What would you like to do? We can work around Jill's plans or your family's plans. Just tell me. I'm open."

Hesitantly she raised her eyes. "Jill is going to a party at a friend's house. I have to drop her there, then pick her up. She's bringing two other friends home for a sleep-over."

"A sleep-over? Wow, that'd be fun!"

"Gideon, you're not invited to the sleep-over."

"So what *do* I get?"

"Four hours, while she's at the party. We could go somewhere to eat, maybe dance. Or we could go to First Night."

"First Night is loud and cold and crowded. I vote for the other."

"We may have trouble getting reservations this late."

"I don't want reservations. I want to eat here."

She didn't know whether to laugh or cry. "I didn't *invite* you to eat here."

"But it makes sense, doesn't it?" he argued. "Go to a restaurant on New Year's Eve, and it's crowded and overpriced and slow. You'll be nervous about getting back in time, so you won't be able to relax. On the other hand, if we eat here, we can talk all we want. We really need to do that, Chris, just talk. Besides, if we go somewhere fancy, I'll have to go shopping. You've already seen the sum total of my fancy wardrobe, and I hate shopping. Don't make me do it, not until after Christmas at least."

"If you hate shopping, why did you offer to go with Jill and me?"

"Because that would be fun. It's shopping for *me* that I hate."

She was bemused. "Why?"

"Because it's so damned hard to get things that fit. I'm broad up here, and long down there, so things have to be tailored, which means having some salesclerk feel me up."

She sputtered out a laugh. "That's terrific."

"No, it's sickening. Anybody feels me up, I want it to be you. So what do you say? Dinner here on New Year's Eve? Nice and quiet and relaxed? I'll bring some food if you want. Better still, give me a list and I'll pick up groceries so we can make dinner together. Now *that's* a good idea.''

Chris had to admit that it was. She wasn't a big one for public New Year's Eves and had always spent hers quietly. The idea of being with Gideon for those few hours while Jill was at her party was appealing.

"Okay," she said.

He broke out into a smile. Standing, he tugged her to her feet and wrapped an arm around her waist as he started for the door. "What time should I come? Four? Five?"

"Try eight-thirty." Jill's party began at eight. That would give Chris time to come home, change, get things ready.

"No way am I waiting around until eight-thirty, when everything closes at midafternoon. Five-thirty. I'll come at five-thirty. Then I can talk with Jill before she leaves."

"Jill will be totally preoccupied with her hair."

"So I'll be here to tell her how great it looks."

"Come at seven-thirty. You can go with me when I drive her to the party."

"Six. We can have appetizers early."

"Seven, and that's the earliest, the absolute earliest you can come."

"Can I bring champagne?"

"Wine. I like it better. And wear your fancy outfit. Is that the one you were wearing that day at the bank?" She wanted to see it again. Even through her nervousness his handsomeness that day had registered.

"Yeah," he protested, "but that defeats the purpose of staying in."

She shook her head and said softly, "It's New Year's Eve. If we're having a nice dinner with wine, we have to dress the part. And don't say I've already seen it, because I don't work that way. You don't have to wear something different every time you see me. I'm not that shallow."

"I didn't say you were. But it's me. My pride."

"Your pride is misplaced if you're hung up on clothes. Wear the blazer and slacks."

"The blazer and slacks?"

"Yes."

He sighed, gave her a squeeze and opened the door. "Okay. The blazer and slacks it is." He inhaled a hearty breathful of the fast-falling winter's night. "Wow, do I feel good."

Chris was surprised to realize that she did, too.

The feeling persisted. On the one hand, she could say it was the Christmas spirit. Her family always made the holiday a happy time.

Deep down, though, she knew there were other reasons this year. Jill was happy. The business was going well. And Gideon had come on the scene.

He didn't let her forget that last fact. He called her every night, usually around ten, when he knew she'd be home, and though he never kept her on the phone for long—just wanted to see how her day had been or tell her something about his—the calls were sweet.

Jill was aware of them. She was the one who sat by the phone doing her homework when the ring pierced the quiet night, or talking with a friend when the call-waiting clicked. Sometimes Chris took the call in the same room, sometimes in another room. Each time, Jill acknowledged it afterward.

Not that Chris would have tried to hide anything. She knew that if she wanted Jill to be open and communicative with her, she had to be the same way right back. Their relationship had always been honest that way. And besides, there wasn't anything to hide. Gideon liked her. So he was calling her.

Of course, Jill wanted to know more. "Do you like him?" she asked, wandering down to the kitchen after one of the calls.

In a burst of late-night energy, Chris was making wreath cookies, which required a minimum of brain and a modicum of brawn. She was vigorously stirring the butter and marshmallows that she'd unceremoniously dumped into a pot.

"He's nice," she answered. "I didn't expect him to be after what happened at the Rise that first day." She'd told Jill about that when it happened, albeit more philosophically than she'd felt at the moment of confrontation. "So I'm surprised. But I still don't know him very well."

"It sounds like he wants to change that."

"Uh-huh." Chris felt the same shimmer of excitement she always felt when she anticipated seeing Gideon again.

"Why isn't he coming for Christmas?"

Chris kept stirring. "Because I didn't invite him."

"Why not?"

"Because he's too new. Christmas is for people we're really close to. Our family is special. If you're not one of us, you have to *earn* a place at our table." She'd been trying for a little dry wit. It went right past Jill.

"But he's alone. He'll be sitting there in a lonely apartment all by himself. He probably doesn't even have a tree."

Chris felt a moment's unease, wondering just how thickly Gideon had poured it on. If there was one thing she wouldn't abide, it was his using Jill to get to her. "Did he mention a lonely apartment?"

"No, but he said he had no family."

"Okay, that's true. But he doesn't live in an apartment, to begin with. He lives in a house that he built himself—"

"So he's sitting in a lonely house."

"He is not. Jill, he has lots of friends. I'm sure he's doing something with them." She hadn't asked, exactly, but she assumed that was the case. He was a really friendly guy, and he said he dated, he dated *a lot*. Chris didn't believe that he'd left all of his holiday time free.

Of course, he would have come for Christmas if she'd invited him, and he jumped at her first mention of New Year's Eve, so apparently whatever plans he had weren't etched in stone. She didn't want to think a woman was involved, didn't want to think he would break a date and disappoint someone. Better, she decided, to imagine that if he wasn't with her, he'd be with a large group of friends.

Maybe some of his workmen.

Maybe his basketball teammates.

She wondered what he wore on the court and how he looked.

"Do you think you could like him?"

Brought back from a small distance, Chris stirred the melting marshmallows with greater force. The roughness of the wooden spoon against the bottom of the pot told her that there was some sticking, apt punishment for a wandering mind. "I do like him. I told you that."

"Love him?"

Though she couldn't help but remember what Gideon had said about falling in love with her, Chris shook her head. "Too soon. Way too soon. Ask me that in another year or two."

"That's not how love happens. It happens quickly."

"Says the authority. Sweetheart, I forgot to take out the food coloring. Can you get it for me? Green?"

Jill took the small vial from the baking supply shelf and removed its lid. "How many drops?" She held it poised.

"Start with four."

Jill squeezed. Chris stirred. Gradually the thick white stuff turned a faintly minty shade.

"A little more, I think."

Jill squeezed, she stirred, but if she had hoped Jill would let the matter of love go, she was mistaken.

"You loved my father when I was conceived."

"Uh-huh." They had discussed that at length several years before, when Chris had sat down with Jill and explained what getting a period was about. Given the slightest encouragement, Jill had asked questions about making babies and making love. She knew who her father was, that he had left Massachusetts before her birth, that he was selling real estate in Arizona. At that time, she had wanted to know about Chris's relationship with him.

Chris had been forthright in telling her about feeling love and the specialness of the moment. She never wanted Jill to feel unwanted, though in essence Brant had made it clear that she was. His whole family had moved away—conveniently, a job transfer had come through for his father—and, to Chris's knowledge, none of them had been back. Outside of family, few people knew who Jill's father was.

"But you'd only been dating him for two months."

"I was young. When you're young, you're more quickly taken with things like love. Another drop, maybe?"

Jill added it, while Chris kept stirring.

"Don't you think it's more romantic when it's fast? I mean, I think what happened to you was *really* romantic. You saw each other in English, started doing homework together, fell in love and did it. Do you think he's married now?"

"Probably."

"Do you think he ever wonders about me?"

Chris sent her an affectionate smile. "He must. You're that strong a being."

"Think he ever wants to see me?"

"I think he doesn't dare." She tried to keep it light. "Seeing you, he'll realize all he's missed. He'll hate himself."

Jill frowned. "But what kind of parent isn't curious about his own child?"

Chris had asked herself that question dozens of times, and in many of those times she'd thought the lowliest things about Brant. But she'd vowed many years ago not to bad-mouth him in front of Jill. "The kind who may not be able to forgive himself for leaving you behind. He knows you exist. I imagine—" it was a wild guess, giving Brant a big benefit of the doubt "—that knowledge has been with him a lot."

Jill thought about that, standing back while Chris dumped the pre-measured cups of corn flakes into the pot with the melted marshmallows that were now a comfortable Christmas green. Finally Jill said, "Do you ever imagine that you might open the front door one day and find him there?"

"No." That was the last thing Chris wanted. She had no desire to see Brant, no desire to have Brant see Jill. Jill was *hers*. She felt vehemently about that. For Jill's sake alone, she tempered her feelings. "He's probably very involved with his own life. His family only lived here for three years. They were midwesterners to begin with. They have no ties here.''

"That didn't mean he couldn't have married you if he loved you.''

Chris had to work hard stirring the mess in the pot, but she appreciated the physical demand. It was a good outlet. "He had plans. He was going to college. He had a scholarship.''

But Jill was insistent. "If he loved you, he could have married you.''

Her petulance, far more than the words themselves, stopped Chris. Leaving the wooden spoon sticking straight up, she turned and took Jill's face in her hands. "Then I guess he didn't love me,'' she said softly, "at least, not as much as I thought. And in that sense, it's a good thing we didn't get married. The marriage wouldn't have been good. We'd have been unhappy together. And you would have suffered.'' She paused. "Do you miss having a father so much?''

"No. Not so much. You know that.'' They'd talked about it before. "There are times when I wonder, that's all. There are times when I think it would be nice to go places, just the three of us.''

"So what would Gramma and Gramps do?'' she teased. "And Alex? And the others?''

Jill thought about that for a minute, gave a small smile of concession and shrugged, at which point Chris planted a kiss in the middle of her forehead. She was about to turn back to the pot when Jill said, "I still think you should have invited Gideon for Christmas dinner.''

"Uh-oh. We're on this again?''

"It was just a thought.''

"Well, here's another one. I think that sticky stuff in the pot may have hardened. You gonna clean up the mess?''

In a blink, Jill was the picture of innocence. "Me? I still have homework to do.'' She slipped smoothly away and was up the stairs before Chris could think to scold. Not that she would have. All too soon, Jill would be slipping smoothly away to college, then beyond. Chris wasn't about to scold away their time together, not when it was so dear.

7

Come New Year's Eve, Chris wasn't thinking of spending time with Jill, but spending time without her. Christmas with the family had been wonderfully fun and absorbing—her mother had *loved* the clay pot—but in the week that followed, in all the little in-between moments when her mind might have been on something else but wasn't, Chris thought of Gideon. Each time, she felt a warm suffusion of desire.

He continued to call every night, "just to make sure you don't forget me," he teased, which was a laugh. She couldn't have forgotten him if she'd tried. He was like a string tied around her finger, a tightness around her insides, cinching deeply and pleasantly.

Had anyone read her mind during that week, she would have been mortified, so carnal were her thoughts. Rather than picturing Gideon in his blazer and slacks, she pictured him in every state of undress imaginable. It didn't help that she was haunted by glimpses of a sliver of skin, a whorl of dark hair and a belly button. When he called at night, she pictured him lying in bed wearing briefs, or nothing. She pictured his body, pictured the dark hair that would mat it, clustering more thickly at some places than others. She pictured him coming to her on New Year's Eve, unbuttoning his shirt, removing it, opening his pants, removing them, baring himself to her, a man at the height of his virility and proud of it.

At times, she wondered if there was something wrong with her, if she was so sex starved that anyone would do. But the courier, who stopped by the office several times that week and was very attractive, didn't turn her on. Nor did her hairdresser, who was surprisingly straight. Nor did Anthony Haskell, who called several times wanting to see her and whom she turned down as gently as she could.

She didn't remember ever feeling quite so alive in quite as feminine a way as she did with the approach of New Year's Eve. Like an alarm that kept going off every few minutes, the buzz of arousal in the pit of her stomach had her counting the minutes until Gideon arrived.

Seven, she had told him. Fortunately, she was ready early, because when the bell rang at six-forty-five, she had no doubt who it was. Pulling the door open, she sent him a chiding look.

He shrugged. "I left extra time in case there was traffic, but there wasn't."

How could she get angry when the mere sight of him took her breath away? He was wearing a topcoat with the collar up against the cold, and between the lapels she caught sight of his blazer and slacks, but he looked far more handsome than he had that day at the bank. No doubt, she decided, it had to do with the ruddy hue on his cheeks.

That hue bemused her. "You look like you've been out in the cold." But he'd been in a heated car.

"Had the windows open," he said, not taking his eyes from her. She looked bright, almost glowing, sophisticated, but young and fresh. He decided that the young part had to do with her hair. Rather than pinning it in its usual knot, she'd left it down. It was shiny and smooth, swept from a side part, its blunt-cut ends dancing on her shoulders. "It was the only way I could keep my mind on the road."

She didn't have to ask where his mind would have been otherwise. The hunger in his eyes answered that quite well. It made her glad that she'd splurged on a new dress, though the splurging hadn't been painful. Contrary to Gideon, she loved to shop. She kept herself on a budget, but she'd been due for a treat. His appreciation made the effort more than worth it.

"May I come in?" he asked.

She blushed. "Of course. I'm sorry. Here, let me take that." She reached for the grocery bag he held in one arm. They had agreed that he would bring fresh French bread and some kind of dessert, since there was a bakery not far from his house. But he held tight to the bag and, instead, handed her the two bottles of wine that he was grasping by the neck with the fingers of one hand. She peered suspiciously at the bag, which seemed filled and heavy. "What's in there?"

"I got carried away," he confessed, thinking about sweets for the sweet and other trite expressions, but loath to voice them lest she think him a jerk. Elbowing the door shut behind him, he headed for the kitchen. He set the bag on the counter, relieved her of the wine and stood it beside the bag, then gave her a slow up and down.

"You look great," he said in an understatement that he hoped his appreciative tone would correct.

Her temperature was up ten degrees, making her words breathy and warm. "Thanks. You, too." Feeling a dire urge to touch him, she laced her fingers together in the area of her lap. "Please, take your coat off." When he'd done so, she hung it in the closet, then turned to find him directly behind her.

"Where's Jill?" he whispered.

"Upstairs," she whispered back.

"Does she know I'm here?"

"She must have heard the bell."

"Do we have time for a kiss?"

"If it's a quick one."

"I don't know if I can make it quick. I've been dreaming about it for more than ten days." His whisper was growing progressively rough. He felt desperately in need. "What I had in mind was something slow and deep and wet—"

"Hey, you guys," came Jill's full voice from halfway down the stairs. She trotted down the rest, her steps muted by the carpet. "What're you whispering about?"

Chris felt she'd been caught in the act of doing something naughty. It was a minute before she could compose herself enough to realize that she hadn't—and that even if she had, she was the mother and had that right. "Gideon was saying things that *definitely* shouldn't be heard by tender ears such as yours," she drawled, and made for the kitchen. "Do me a favor, sweetie? Keep him company while I get these hors d'oeuvres?"

Gideon put his hands into the pockets of his blazer and angled them forward to hide his arousal from Jill. "Can I help?" he called after Chris. To Jill, he said, "You may think I'm one of those helpless males, but believe me, I'm not. I'm a very handy man to have around the house. I know how to crack eggs, whip cream and brew coffee."

"We could've used you around here earlier," Jill said. "Mom ruined two batches of stuffed mushrooms before she finally got one that was edible. They're supposed to be her specialty. So she thought she knew the ingredients by heart, only she blew it. That was the first time. The second time she burned the meat."

"Distracted, huh?" Gideon asked, pleased by the thought.

"You could say that." She took a step back. "How do I look?"

He checked her over. "Spectacular. Great jeans skirt. Great sweater. Great legs. Is this a boy-girl party you're going to?"

She tossed a glance at the ceiling. "Of course! I am old enough for that, y'know."

He knew all too well. Where he'd grown up, fifteen-year-old girls did far more than go to parties. Instinct told him, though, that Jill wasn't that way. Common sense told him that Chris wouldn't have stood for it. "You're gonna knock 'em dead," he told her, feeling a pride he had no right to feel. "And your hair looks great, too."

"I'm not done with my hair."

"But it looks perfect."

"It looks blah," she maintained, drawing up a thick side swath with two fingers. "I think I need a clasp or something. And some earrings. Mom—" she called, only to be interrupted when Chris approached.

"No need to yell. I'm right here." To Gideon she said apologetically, "They weren't hot enough. They'll be ready in a minute."

"I need something large and silver, Mom."

"For her hair and ears," Gideon prompted in a soft voice to Chris, who was looking a bit helplessly at Jill.

"The last time I lent you something silver," she said, thinking of a bangle bracelet that she hadn't seen in months, "I didn't get it back. You can borrow something *only* if it's returned in the morning."

"She's so fussy," Jill said to Gideon. Then she turned and went back up the stairs, leaving Gideon and Chris momentarily alone.

Gideon started whispering again. "How long do you think she'll stay up there?"

"Five seconds," Chris whispered back.

Jill yelled down, "Can I wear the enamel hair clip you bought at the Vineyard last summer?"

"I thought you wanted something silver," Chris called back.

"But the enamel one has earrings to match."

"It also," Chris murmured for Gideon's benefit, "cost an arm and a leg. She's been wanting to wear that set since I bought it. I think she's taking advantage of the company and the night."

"You can always tell her no," Gideon suggested.

Chris snorted softly, then called to Jill, "If you're very, very, *very* careful." She caught Gideon's eye. "Don't look at me that way."

"Are you always such a pushover?"

"No. But we're talking a hair clip and some earrings here. If she asked for a quart of gin, I'd say no. Same for cigarettes or dope, if I had either around the house, which I don't. The way I see it, you have to pick and chose your battles."

Gideon considered that, then nodded. "Sounds right." He shot a glance over her shoulder toward the stove. "Think your mushrooms are hot yet?"

"It's only been a minute since I last checked."

"Check again," he said, and ushered her to the farthest reaches of the kitchen. Once there, he backed her to the counter, lowered his head and captured her lips in what would have been a deep, devouring kiss had not Jill's call intruded.

"Mom?"

With a low groan, he wrenched his mouth away and stepped back.

Chris felt she was spinning around, twisting at the end of a long, spiraling line. She was hot, dizzy and frustrated. It was a minute before she could steady herself to answer. "Yes?"

"Where *is* the set?"

Chris made a small sound and closed her eyes for a minute. Then, shaking her head, she sent Gideon an apologetic look and pushed off from the counter. Jill was at the top of the stairs.

"Just tell me where it is," she called down.

But Chris didn't remember exactly where it was. "I'm coming," she said lightly. Once upstairs, it took several minutes of searching through drawers before she finally located the clip and earrings. She handed them over with a repeat of the warning, "You'll be very, very, *very* careful."

"I will. See?" She held the earrings in her hand. "They're perfect with what I'm wearing."

Chris knew that just about anything would go with a blue denim skirt. But Jill had a point. The swirls of blue-and-green enamel picked up the color of her sweater beautifully.

Rubbing her hands together, she took a deep breath. "Okay. Are you all set now? Anything else you need?"

"Nope. Thanks, Mom."

"If you're using my perfume—" which happened often "—remember, a little goes a long way. You don't want to hit the party smelling like a whorehouse."

"Okay."

"I'll be downstairs. Come on down when you're ready and have some hors d'oeuvres."

"If there are any left. Gideon looks hungry."

You should only know, Chris thought, then was grateful Jill didn't. Too soon, she'd be into serious dating. Too soon, she would know about hunger, about the urges that drove men and women together at times that weren't always the wisest. What Chris had done with Brant sixteen years before hadn't been smart at all, though she'd never had cause to regret having Jill. She meant what she'd told Gideon, that she was happy with her life.

Would she be happier with a man in the picture? She didn't know. She did know that she was drawn to Gideon in an elemental way that refused to be ignored. She was older and wiser. Still, she was drawn. Even now, returning to the kitchen to find that he'd opened the wine and was filling two glasses, she felt a flare of excitement. For a split second, she was at the end of that truncated kiss again, spinning on a spiral of desire, feeling the frustration.

"Is Jill all set?" he asked, handing her one of the glasses.

"Uh-huh."

"To us, then," he said, raising the other.

Chris touched her glass to his, then took a sip. "Mmm. This is nice." Focusing on the amber liquid, she whispered, "Sorry about before. The timing was unfortunate."

"Did I complain?" he whispered back, coming in close to her side. "It just lengthens the foreplay, that's all."

Chris felt a soft shuddering inside. "Uh, maybe we ought to sit down."

"Maybe we ought to have something to eat."

"Right." Setting her wine on the counter, she put on mitts and removed the tray of mushrooms from the oven. She arranged half of them on a dish that also held a wedge of cheese and some crackers, then put the rest back. "So they'll stay warm."

Gideon carried the dish to the low glass table in front of the living room sofa. When Chris joined him there, he popped a mushroom into his mouth. "Whoa," he drawled when it was gone, "that was worth two wasted batches."

Chris went red. "I wasn't paying attention to what I was doing."

"Like my men weren't that day at Crosslyn Rise?" he teased, because he couldn't resist, and leaned close. "Was I the cause of your distraction?"

She focused on his tie, which was silk and striped diagonally in blue, yellow and purple. "Of course not. I was thinking about work."

"I'm work, aren't I?"

"Not actively. Not yet."

"I got some half-rounds."

Her eyes flew to his, wide and pleased. "You did?"

He nodded. "Above the French doors, like you wanted. Put them in last week."

"All those phone calls, and you didn't tell me?"

"I wanted to surprise you." His gaze fell to her mouth and stuck there. "Thought if I saved it for a special time, it might win me a kiss." His voice was rough. "How about it?"

Without a moment's hesitancy, Chris reached up and put a soft kiss on his mouth. Then, because it had been so sweet and too short, she followed it with a second.

"You smell good," he whispered against her lips. "I'll bet you smell like this all over." When she caught in a small gasp, he sealed it in with the full pressure of his mouth, giving her the kind of hard, hungry kiss he craved.

Chris wanted the hardness and more. She opened to the sweep of his tongue, but he was barely done when he ended the kiss. She felt she was hanging in midair. "What's wrong?"

"Too fast," he whispered, breathing heavily. "Too hot." He shot a glance toward the stairs. "Too public." Pulling away from her, he bent over, propping his elbows on his knees. The low sounds that escaped his throat as he tried to steady his breathing told her of his discomfort.

Chris felt dismayed. In the moment when he'd kissed her, she'd forgotten that Jill was still upstairs. "I should have realized," she whispered.

"Not your fault alone. It takes two to tango."

It was a figure of speech, but she latched on to it as a diversion from desire. "Do you tango?"

"Nope. Can't dance much at all. But I make love real good."

She moaned, picturing that with far too great an ease. In desperation, she reached for the dish of mushrooms. "Here. Have another. And tell me what else is happening at the Rise."

With a slightly shaky but nonetheless deep breath, Gideon straightened. He ate another mushroom, then a third. "These are really good." He glanced back toward the kitchen. "And something else smells good." He frowned, trying to identify it.

"Rock Cornish Hens," she said. "It's the orange sauce that you smell." But she wasn't feeling at all hungry for that. "Tell me about the Rise," she repeated. She needed to think of something settling.

Gideon understood and agreed. He really hadn't intended to start things off hot and heavy. It had just happened. For both of them. But the civil thing was to talk and visit and eat first.

Casually crossing an ankle over his knee as he would have done if he'd been with the guys, he began to talk. He told Chris about the progress his crew had made, the few problems they'd run into, the solutions they'd found, that they'd moved inside. The diversion worked. When Jill joined them some fifteen minutes later, they were involved in a discussion of staircase options.

"You look great, honey," Chris told her with a smile.

"Better than great," Gideon added. "Those poor guys won't be able to keep their hands off you."

Chris shot him a dirty look. "They'd better." To Jill, she said, "One swift kick you know where."

Jill seemed embarrassed. She glanced at Gideon before sitting close to Chris and saying quietly, "My hair looks awful."

"Your hair looks great."

"I should have had it cut."

"If you had, you'd be tugging at the ends to make it longer."

"It never curls the way I want. I've been fiddling with it for an hour, and it's still twisting the wrong way."

"You're the only one who knows that. To everyone else, me included, it looks great."

"You're just saying that because you're my mother."

"I'm not your mother," Gideon said, "and I say it, too."

Jill eyed him warily. "You'd say anything to please Mom."

"No way," he argued. "If you'd been down sooner, you'd have heard me telling her that she could grovel all night if she wanted, but I was not putting in winding staircases at Crosslyn Rise."

"This man," Chris told Jill, "is a cheapskate. There's a huge winding staircase in the mansion. It would be *perfect* to have smaller versions in the condos. Don't you think so?"

Jill crinkled her nose. "Winding staircases are good for long, sweeping dresses, but modern people don't wear them."

"That's right," Gideon chimed in. "They spend their money on skylights and Jacuzzis and Sub-Zero refrigerators instead. Face it, Chris, you're outvoted."

But Chris shook her head. "I still think they'd be great, and I'm the decorator."

"Well, I'm the builder, and I say they're too expensive. We can't fit them into the budget. That's all there is to it."

"You won't even *try*?"

"We're talking *ten grand* per staircase! I just can't do it."

Chris sensed that she could argue until she was blue in the face and she wouldn't get anywhere. She arched a brow Jill's way. "So much for trying to please me."

Jill's gaze bounced from Chris to Gideon and back. "Did I cause that fight?"

"Of course not—"

"It wasn't a fight—"

"You both look pretty ticked off."

"I'm not ticked off—"

"I never get ticked off—"

"Maybe you shouldn't be talking work on New Year's Eve."

"I don't know—"

"Yeah, well—"

Jill looked at her watch. "Hey, can we leave now?"

"Have something to eat first," Chris told her, escaping into the role of mother with ease.

"They'll have food at the party."

"Uh-huh. Pizza, but not for a few hours, I'd wager."

"They'll have munchies," Jill argued, and rose to get her coat. "We're picking up Jenny and Laura on the way, so they can put their stuff right in the car." She grew hesitant, again looking back and forth. "Uh, whose car?"

"My Bronco," Gideon said, "if that's okay with you. And it's fine about the stuff. We'll bring it in when we get back here."

Chris hadn't known they were picking up the two other girls and sensed that it had been a last-minute deal. She wondered if it had anything to do with Gideon being there, or more specifically, with the fact that Chris was seeing him. None of Jill's friends had ever seen Chris with a man. Maybe Jill wanted her friends to know that her mother was human.

Oh, she was human, all right, human and female. Once in the truck, sitting in the front seat with Gideon, she was as keenly aware of him as she'd been back in the house. Each move he made seemed to register. Fortunately, he kept up a steady conversation with Jill, asking about the party, who was going, who of those going she was closest to. That led into a fast discussion about school, what she was taking, what she liked best and worst. By the time they reached Jenny's house, Chris had picked up several tidbits even she hadn't known.

Jill and Jenny talked softly in back from there. They were soon joined by Laura, who directed Gideon the short distance from her house to the one where the party was being held. When they arrived, and Jenny and Laura climbed out, Jill hung back for a minute.

"So, you guys are going back home for dinner?"

"Uh-huh," Chris said.

"You're not going out to a movie or anything later?"

Chris gave her cheek a reassuring touch. "We'll be home. If there's any problem, just call and we'll be right here. Otherwise, we'll be back to pick you up at twelve-thirty." She kissed her. "Have a super time, honey."

"You, too, Mom," Jill said softly, then raised her voice. "You, too, Gideon."

"Thanks, Jill. Have fun. We'll be back."

With the slam of the door, she was gone. She glanced back once on the way to join her friends, then disappeared with them into the house.

"Was that nervousness?" Gideon asked as he shifted into gear and started off.

"I'm not sure. I think so. She's so grown-up in some ways, then in others..."

He knew just what she meant. Jill was physically mature. She was personable and poised. But the look in her eye from time to time told the truth. "She's only fifteen. That's pretty young."

"Sometimes I forget. We're such good friends."

"She's a really nice girl." He reached for Chris's hand, needing her warmth. "Even if she did interrupt what was promising to be one of the best kisses of my life."

Chris closed her fingers around his, but she didn't say a word. Left hanging, of course, was the fact that they could resume that kiss the minute they got home without worry of interruption.

"What are your parents doing tonight?" he asked a drop too casually. He was thinking of interruptions, too, but it seemed crass to let on. Hadn't he decided that they should talk and eat first?

"They're having dinner with friends. There's a local group that's been spending their New Year's Eves together for years. It used to be Mom and Dad would make a point to be home before midnight to be with us—Jill and me and anyone else who was home—but everyone's out this year."

"Except you," he said softly.

"Except me." She held more tightly to his hand. When he gave a tug, she slid closer to him.

"Are *you* nervous?" he asked. He supposed it was a form of talk, though it was getting right to the point.

She studied his face. Muted in the dark, his expression was strangely dear. "A little."

He drove quietly for a time before saying, "Does it help to know I am, too?"

"You? Buy why?"

"Because you're special. I want to make things good for you."

A light tremor shimmered through her insides. Swallowing, she said, "I think you could do that with your eyes closed."

"I don't want them closed. There's too much to see."

Like frames of a movie, the images that had haunted her flicked one after another through her mind. "Uh, Gideon?" she whispered. "I think there's something you should know."

"Don't tell me you're a virgin."

"I'm not, but—"

"You've had a baby, Chris."

"I know that," she said quickly, quietly, putting her cheek against his arm, "but the sum total of my experience with a man took place in the back seat of a '72 Chevy."

He was amused by that. "The back seat, eh?"

"It was dark. I didn't see much."

"I never did it in a car." Most everywhere else when he'd been younger, but never in a car. He'd gotten too big too fast. "What was it like?"

"That's not the point."

"But I want to know." He flattened her hand on his thigh and held it there. "Wouldn't I have to be kind of crunched up?"

"Gideon—"

"I'm too tall for a car."

She sighed. "No, you're not. You could do it. It'd just take a little ingenuity."

He began moving her hand around. "Like with positions?"

She nodded, still against his arm. She was picturing the wildest things. "You'd have to be kind of half on, half off the seat."

"I'd be on top?"

That was the only position Chris had ever known, but she'd read of others. "Or under," she murmured.

"Would we be undressed?"

"Just...vaguely."

"Could I touch your breasts?"

She sucked in a breath. "If you wanted to."

"Bare? Could I open your bra?"

"It might be cold."

His low voice, angled into her hair, was like liquid fire, which was precisely what was searing his gut. "I'd want to do it anyway. I want to see what you look like all over, then I'd warm you up."

She pressed her face into his arm. "Gideon—"

He slid her hand upward, urging it back and forth at the very top of his thigh. "Heating up?"

"Oh, yes."

"It doesn't take much with us."

"I know. I don't understand it. All these years, and I haven't been attracted to any other man." But she could feel the heat in him searing her palm and curling right through her. Later, thinking back on it, she wouldn't know which of them moved first, but suddenly she was covering his sex, shaping her fingers to his arousal, cupping the heaviness beneath.

"Chris." He made a deep, choking sound. She started to take her hand away, but he held it fast. "It's okay, okay." He made another sound when he swallowed. "How much longer till we're home?"

Chris looked out the window. It was a minute before she could focus, a minute more before she could identify the street they were on. "Two more blocks." She glanced up at his face, where the tension was marked. A surge of feeling welled up from inside, propelling her mouth to his jaw. She kissed it once, moved an inch, kissed it again. Her voice was like down against his rough skin. "Can you make it?"

"Oh, yeah," he gritted, and released her hand. "Loosen my tie, Chris? I'm being strangled."

She loosened it and unbuttoned the top button. "Better?"

"Yes...listen, Chris, if you think there's even the slightest chance that you may get cold feet on me and want to call this off, better tell me now so I can run around the block a couple of times before we go inside." He didn't think they were going to get in much talking or visiting or eating. They'd already passed that point.

"I won't get cold feet," she said, and knew she wouldn't, couldn't. She was too hot.

"What about the food?"

"It'll hold." She took a shallow breath. "Gideon, what I said the other night about birth control? I still don't have anything. I was thinking I should see my doctor, then I didn't know whether we'd really, uh, get together, and I felt funny. Do you have something?"

Turning into her street, he nodded. In a gritty whisper, he said, "Will you help me put it on?"

Her insides grew swollen at the thought. "I don't know how."

"I'll show you."

"So we'll be sharing the responsibility?"

"I wasn't thinking of it that way."

"What were you thinking of?"

"The turn-on. Having you touch me—having you look at me—" He was torturing himself, unable to stop.

"Gideon, what I was trying to tell you before—"

"Jeez, I've never talked about making love this way. Does it sound calculated?" He turned onto the driveway.

"It sounds hot."

"I *feel* hot." He pulled as close to the garage as he could.

"Gideon, there's something I want to *tell* you." She rushed the words out, fearful of being cut off again. "I may have had a baby, but I'm pretty new at this. I haven't even—"

"Shh," he whispered, pressing his fingers to her mouth. Opening the door, he slid out, drawing her along in nearly the same motion. A supportive arm circled her shoulders and hugged her to him as he guided her quickly toward the door. Once inside, with the cold air and all of humanity locked out, he pressed her to the wall, ran his mouth from her forehead, down her nose to her lips. She smelled sweet, almost innocent, and was soft to match. That softness burned into him, from the spot, waist high, where their bodies met to the one at the knee where they parted. She was giving, yielding. Her chin tipped up under the light urging of his thumbs. Her mouth opened to his, welcoming him inside. Every move she made was untutored, purely instinctive, intensely feminine. Each one called to the man in him that craved her possession.

"The nice thing," he breathed against her forehead as he pushed away the shoulders of her coat, "would have been to wait on this until later, but I can't, Chris." The coat slipped to the floor. "If that makes me a not-nice man, I guess that's what I am, but I need you too much now." His fingers met at her throat, touched the collar of her dress and the top buttons, then separated and slid over silk to her breasts. It was the first time he'd touched her there. She was full and firm. Even through her dress and a bra, he could feel the tightness of her nipples.

The sensation of being touched and held was so charged, Chris thought she'd die—just explode. With a small sound, she covered his hands.

He was instantly concerned. As aroused as he was, he had promised to make it good for her, and if it killed him, he intended to do just that. "Hurt?"

"Not enough." She felt impatient and greedy. Transferring her hands from her chest to his, she ran her open palms over him while he worked at the buttons of her dress. When it was open to the waist, she felt him part the fabric, then release the center clasp of her bra. She was holding him at the hips by that time, needing an anchor, feeling momentarily shy when he peeled back the lace and cool air hit her breasts.

Gideon sensed her shyness, and it fueled his fire. In the past, he'd had the most experienced of women, but none sparked him as Chris did. Angling his upper body away, he took pleasure in what he'd unclothed. Her breasts were pale, strawberry at their crests, quivering with each shallow breath she took.

He was smitten. Never in his life had he seen anything as beautiful as Chris against that door with her fingers clutching his hips, her eyes lowered to his belt, her dress open and her breasts bare and waiting. Unable to resist, he ducked his head and put his mouth to one. He drew it in. His tongue raked its turgid tip.

She cried out, a frantic whisper of his name.

"I want you so badly," he moaned. Dragging himself from her breast, he straightened and tore off his blazer. Holding her gaze, which had risen with him, he tugged off his tie, unbuttoned his shirt and unfastened his pants. Then he slid his fingers into her hair, held her head still and took her mouth in a strong, sucking kiss.

Chris wanted more than that. "Upstairs," she gasped when he finally allowed her a breath. "I want you in my bed." She took his hand, but no leading was necessary. He was right beside her, half-running up the stairs, stopping midway for another deep kiss before continuing to the top.

Her room was shadowed, lit only from the hall, though neither of them seemed aware. They were kissing again within seconds, but this time their hands were at work, fumbling with buttons, zippers and sleeves. Their fingers tangled. They alternately laughed, moaned and gasped. She was sitting on the edge of the bed pulling the stockings from her feet when he came down beside her.

"Help me," he said, fiddling with a small foil pack.

For a minute, she couldn't breathe. He was stark naked and fully aroused. She'd known he would be, of course, still her startled eyes were drawn to the thickly thatched spot from which his arousal jutted so tall and straight.

At her utter stillness, Gideon raised his head. He didn't have to follow her gaze to know what she was looking at. The thought that she might be afraid gave him the control he wouldn't otherwise have had. "It won't hurt," he whispered, drawing her close. "You know that. You've done this before."

"But I've never seen it before," she whispered back. "That was what I've been trying to tell you. I have lots of brothers, but by the time they reached puberty, I was out of the house. And with Brant it was always so dark." Tremulously she touched his stomach. "I'm not afraid. You're very beautiful." From his navel, she brushed the back of her fingers down the thin, dark line to where the hair grew more dense, then on to his velvety strength. Satin on steel, it seemed to her. She explored it lightly, felt it flex and grow.

Gideon croaked out her name.

She looked up. "Too much?"

"Too little." He reached again for the foil pack, but no sooner had he removed the condom than she took it from him.

"Tell me how," she whispered.

He told her. With surprising ease, given her trembling and his hardness, she had the condom on. Then, feeling proud and excited and filled with something else that was nearly overwhelming, she slipped her arms around his neck and put her mouth to his. "Love me?"

"I do," he muttered, near the end of his tether. With an arm around her slender waist, he fell over onto the bed, sweeping her beneath him as he drew them both up toward the pillows.

That was when Chris felt the full force of his nakedness. He was man through and through, from the luxury of his weight to the friction of his limbs. His hands seemed everywhere, touching her in large sweeps from her breasts to her hips, then the hot spot between her legs. Suddenly without patience, she opened for him.

"Hurry!"

Taut and trembling, Gideon lifted himself, positioned himself and slowly, slowly sank into the tightest sheath that had ever encased him. "There. Ah. Chris, you're so small."

She felt it. Small, feminine and cherished. And she loved it.

"Am I hurting you?" he asked.

"Oh, no. You feel so new. So special. So big."

Gideon nearly came. He went very still for a minute, shut his eyes tight, gritted his teeth until he'd regained control. "What you do to me."

Chris was thinking the same thing about him, because the small pinching she'd first felt at his entry was gone, leaving only a yearning to be stroked. Grasping his hair, she looked up at him and said, "Make love to me now, Gideon. Do it."

He didn't need any more urging than that. Withdrawing nearly all the way, he surged back with a cry of triumph, then repeated the pattern in a rhythm that seemed to anticipate, then mirror her need. Chris surrendered to that need, letting it take her higher and higher until, closing her eyes and arching her back, she tumbled head-on into a mindless riot of sensation.

Somewhere at the tail end of the riot, a low light came on, but awareness was slow to return. When her breathing had finally slowed and she opened her eyes, she found Gideon propped above her, looking down with a smile. He'd managed to light the lamp beside the bed without leaving her; he was as rigid as ever inside her. But that didn't seem to be bothering him. Though the muscles of his upper arms were taut beneath her hands and his breathing was heavy, something pleased him immensely.

"What?" she whispered with a shy smile.

"You wouldn't ask that if you could see what I do," he replied. His voice was low and husky, as tight as his body, but he wasn't rushing toward his own release. There was too much pleasure to be gained just in looking at Chris, with her blond hair mussed, her cheeks pink, her skin aglow with a light sheen of sweat, her lips rosy and full. There was too much pleasure to be gained just in holding himself inside her, knowing that for a short time she was all his. He felt more loved than he ever had in his life. "Was it good?"

She nodded. "You touch me, and...poof!"

His grin broadened. "That's good. I want it like that."

"But you haven't come."

"I will." He took a deep, shuddering breath. "I do love you, y'know."

She felt a burst of heat in the area of her heart. "How can you tell?"

"Because of what I feel, like I could stay this way forever and be perfectly happy. Before, when we were downstairs and then in the car, I thought I'd die if I didn't get into you fast, and maybe I would have. But now that I'm here, there's no rush. What you looked like when you came—what that look did to me—was more satisfying than any climax I've ever had."

Chris felt tears pool in the outside corners of her eyes. "That's beautiful," she whispered. She touched his chest, running a finger by his small, dark nipple. "You're beautiful." Giving more freedom to her hands, she let them familiarize themselves with the wedge of fine hair beneath his collarbone, the muscular ridges of his shoulders, the tapering strength of his back. She was entranced by his perfection, his mix of hard and soft, ragged and smooth, flat and curved. "You *are* beautiful," she whispered again. Curving her hands to his backside, she arched her back and rose off the bed to put her mouth to his throat.

Gideon lost it then. In her slow, gentle way, she was driving him to distraction. Unable to wait any longer, he began to make love to her again. He tempered himself only at the end, when he felt her coming so close, and when her senses erupted for a second time, he gave in to his own powerful release.

Later, much later that night, after the New Year had been welcomed in with toasts and kisses, after Jill and her friends had been fetched and settled, after Gideon had left for the ride back to Worcester and Chris was in bed, she thought about all that had happened.

Gideon had been incredible. He'd made love to her yet another time in her bed, then once in the shower before they dressed. It wasn't the fact of his physical prowess that impressed her as much as the soft things he'd said, the adoring look in his eye and the cherished way he'd made her feel.

Brant had never done that.

More than once, as she lay in bed that night, then on subsequent nights after talking with Gideon on the phone, she wondered if she loved him. The thought was a sobering one. She didn't have faith in herself when it came to love. She'd misjudged once before, and had spent fifteen years trying to make up for it to Jill. If she loved Gideon now, if she became more deeply involved with him than she already was, Jill was bound to be affected. Worse, if the involvement deepened and Jill came to love him, too, and then something happened, Chris would never forgive herself.

The dilemma was whether to take the chance or leave things the way they were. The answer eluded her.

8

Of all the months of the year, Chris liked January the least. It was the coldest and most bleak, physically and emotionally, a necessary evil to be suffered through to reach February, which had a vacation, at least. And then March came with its lengthening days, and April with its promise of rebirth, and by then she had it made.

This year, January was fun. For one thing, she got down to serious work on Crosslyn Rise, poring over Carter's plans, visiting the site at least once a week to check on the progress, wading through swatches of wallpaper and carpeting, studying furniture and cabinetry designs, pondering electrical and bathroom fixtures, and kitchen appliances.

Though she would be working with buyers as they came along later that summer, the plan was to completely outfit a model apartment in one of the units for potential clients to see. Moreover, she would be decorating the entire mansion, once it was subdivided into a restaurant, a health club and a meeting place. For that, she would be calling in experts to help, but she was the coordinator.

There was lots to think about, but she loved it. She also loved spending time with Gideon, which was probably why she went to the Rise so often, given the season and the relatively slow rate of the work. They argued often, but within reason. Though she'd yielded on the issue of winding stairways, she wanted marble tiles in the bathrooms, Corian in the kitchens, and full walls of brick where the fireplaces would go. Invariably Gideon rebelled at the cost, just as inevitably he went out of his way to try to accommodate her. Sometimes he made it, sometimes he didn't. But he tried. She couldn't ask for more.

January was also bright because she saw him after work. She kept it to once a week, on the weekend when Jill might have other plans, but the anticipation of that one night, along with his regular phone calls, kept her feeling alive in ways she hadn't known she'd been missing.

Come February, he asked to stay the weekend at her place, but she was uncomfortable with that. "Jill will be in and out. I just can't."

They were lying face-to-face on a bed in a small motel off the highway not far from Crosslyn Rise. It was three o'clock on a Thursday afternoon. Working together at the Rise shortly before, they'd suffered a sharp desire attack. The motel had been Gideon's suggestion. Chris hadn't protested.

Now, in the afterglow of what had been more hot and exciting than ever, Gideon only knew that he needed more of her. "Jill knows what's going on."

"She doesn't know that we sleep together." They'd been careful about that, choosing their time together with care.

"She knows," he insisted. "She's a perceptive kid. She sees the way we look at each other, the way we touch. She was the one who noticed the hand-holding that first day. You think she doesn't suspect that there's more than hands involved now?"

"I don't know what she suspects," Chris replied, feeling unsettled because it was true. And it was her own fault. She didn't have the courage to ask. "But I think it would be awkward for her if you slept over. It's too soon."

Nothing could be too soon for Gideon, whose love for Chris kept growing. Although he sensed she wasn't really ready, he wanted to ask her to marry him, which was a *really* big step. He'd been footloose and fancy-free for a good long time. But he was willing to give it all up for Chris. He *had* given it all up. Since meeting her, he hadn't dated another woman. Footloose and fancy-free had lost its lure.

He did agree, though, that Jill was a concern. "Does she ask you questions about what we do?"

"Surface ones, like where we ate and what we had for dinner."

"Do you think she accepts me?" He knew that Jill liked him, and remembered all too clearly the permission she'd given him to date Chris. But that had been before he'd started doing it. Faced with the reality of having someone to compete with for her mother's time, she might have had second thoughts.

Chris moved her hand through the hair on his chest. "She accepts you as someone I have a good time with on the weekends."

"But not as my lover?"

"She doesn't know you are."

"You think."

After a minute, she admitted, "I think."

"Maybe you should tell her. You're young. You're healthy. You're an adult. You have every right to want to be with a man."

"I'm supposed to set an example for her."

The sound of that gave Gideon a chill. He drew her closer to ward it off. "You're not doing anything illegal or immoral. You're making love with a man you care deeply about." His voice lowered. "You do care that way, don't you?"

Her eyes were soft, as was her voice. "You know I do." For a minute, secure in his arms, enveloped by his scent and lost in his gaze, she was engulfed by a longing for forever. Then the minute passed and reality returned. "But you have to understand, Gideon. You're the first man I've dated, really dated, in Jill's memory, and we haven't been doing it for long. If I suddenly have you staying the night, she's apt to think that it's okay to do that after a couple of dates."

"It is. Sometimes."

"She's only fifteen!"

"And you're thirty-three. She's bright enough to see the difference. It's okay for you to be doing what we're doing, Chris. It's *right* for you to be doing it, given what you feel. You're a passionate woman." How well he knew. Each time they made love, she was more hungry, more aggressive. "How you kept it locked away for so long is beyond me."

"It wasn't any big thing. I never wanted another man the way I do you."

"Not even Brant?" he couldn't resist asking.

"Not even Brant," she said, and knew it was true. What she felt for Gideon, what she did with him, had nothing to do with growing up, experimenting, feeling her oats or rebelling. It had to do with mature desires and deep inner feelings. "We were young. Too young. I don't want Jill doing what we did."

"You can't put a chastity belt on her."

"No, but I can teach her the importance of waiting."

"Would you have her be a virgin at her wedding?"

"I wouldn't mind it."

"That's unrealistic, Chris."

"I know. But it's not unrealistic to encourage her to wait until someone important to her comes along. I've tried to teach her that lovemaking is special."

"It is. So why can't you tell her that we do it?"

"I can't. She'll jump to conclusions."

"So talk to her. Explain."

But Chris wasn't ready for that. "She's always come first in my life. She may get nervous."

"So you'll talk to her more. You'll explain more. You two are close. You talk about everything else. Why not this?"

She wished she could make him understand. "Because it's so *basic*."

"You're right about that," Gideon drawled, then grew intense. "Lord, Chris, do you know how much I want to sleep with you? Not make love. *Sleep*. Roll over with you tucked up against me. Wake up that way, too."

"And then what would happen?" she asked knowingly.

"We'd make love."

"Right. With Jill in the next room, listening to the headboard bang rhythmically against the wall."

"So we'll pull the bed out."

"The *frame* squeaks."

"I'm a handyman. I'll fix it."

"You're missing the *point*."

"So we won't make love. I'll just go through the rest of the day suffering silently—"

"Gideon," she pleaded softly, "I need time. That's all. I need time to get Jill accustomed to a man in my life. I owe it to her, don't you see?"

As he saw it, she owed things to herself, too. But, then, he'd never been a parent. He'd never felt the kind of responsibility for another human being that Chris felt so keenly for Jill. Loving Chris as he did, he had to respect her feelings.

"Okay," he said in surrender, "then we go to plan B."

"Plan B?"

"We go away together."

Chris was dumbfounded. "Did you hear *anything* I said?"

"All three of us. Jill has school vacation coming up in two weeks. So we'll make reservations and go somewhere together. That way, she'll be able to get used to the idea of our being together."

"But that'll be no different than having you over at the house! The same problem exists."

"Not if we book separate rooms." When Chris seemed to listen at that, he went on. "You and Jill room together. I'll have my own. We could either go north to ski or south to sun and swim."

Chris wanted to tell him he was crazy, except that idea wasn't bad. In fact, the more she thought of it, the more she liked it. "Do you ski?" she asked.

"Sure, I ski," he answered. "I mean, I may not do my turns as neatly as I do my lay-ups, but neither do I make a fool out of myself." He could see she was tempted. "Ever been to Stowe?"

She shook her head against his shoulder. "Only to Woodstock, and not for skiing. Stowe is farther north. I never wanted to drive that long."

"Would you want to with me?"

"I wouldn't mind it."

"What about Jill?"

"She'd be game. She's dying to go skiing."

"Does she know how?"

"Barely."

"No sweat. The instructors are good. Would you prefer a condo or an inn?"

"An inn."

"Separate rooms?"

She nodded.

"Would you visit me in mine?"

She grinned. "Maybe."

With a grin of his own, he slid an arm around her hips, which was where, by a stretch of the imagination, there was a touch of fullness. "Maybe?"

"If it isn't too hard."

"It'll definitely be hard."

"Is that a warning," she asked softly, "or a promise?"

Eyes smoldering, he rolled to his back and drew her on top. His large hands cupped her head, directing her down for his kiss. It was the only answer he gave.

When Chris told Jill that they were going skiing, her eyes lit up. When she told her that Gideon would be coming, the light faded a little. "I didn't know he skied," she said with reluctant interest.

"I didn't, either. But he does. And he's been to Stowe before, so he knows the good places to eat."

"Will we rent a condo?"

"I thought we'd go to an inn." She paused. "I thought you'd be more comfortable that way."

"Will I have my own room?"

"We'll share, you and me."

Jill seemed surprised by that, and relieved. "You're not rooming with Gideon?"

Chris shook her head. "I'm rooming with you."

"Won't he mind?"

"He knows that's the way it has to be."

Jill considered that. "Do you wish it was different?"

"In what sense?"

"That you two were going away alone?"

"Of course not. You're my best friend."

"And what's he?"

"He's a man I'm seeing, who I like a lot."

"Do you love him?"

"You've asked me that before. What did I tell you then?"

"That it was too soon to ask you, but you've seen him a lot since then. You must have some idea what you feel. Or what you think you can feel. If we're going skiing with him—"

"We're doing it because it sounds like fun."

"We could drive up there, you and me, just ourselves."

"But it was Gideon's idea." She gave Jill a funny look. "Weren't you the one who felt so badly that he had to spend Christmas all by himself in a lonely house?"

"Yeah, but this is different. This is purely voluntary. It's my vacation time. Not his."

Chris felt a stab of concern. "Would you rather he not go?"

"No. He can go."

"Such enthusiasm," she teased, trying to hide her unease. "I thought you liked him."

"I *do*. And I'm *glad* we're going skiing with him. I just want to know if you love him."

Chris thought about it for a minute before finally, truthfully, saying, "I don't know. There are times when I think I do, but then there are so many considerations—"

"Like what?"

"Like whether he's prepared to play second fiddle to you. You come first, Jill. You always have and always will."

"But that's not fair to you. Maybe you want to be with Gideon. Maybe you *should* be with him."

"How would you feel if I were?"

Jill was awhile in answering. The words were cautious when they came. "Happy for you. Happy for Gideon."

"And for you?"

"Happy, too, I guess."

"You don't sound convinced."

She looked at her hands. "I don't know. It just takes some getting used to. I mean, I'd really like it because then you'd have things to do, yourself, and I wouldn't feel badly leaving you home all alone."

Chris hadn't realized. "Do you do that?"

"Sometimes. But then I like knowing you're here. I like knowing you're waiting for me. Selfish, huh?"

Brushing a wisp of dark hair from Jill's cheek, Chris said, "Not selfish at all. Just a little worried. You've been used to one thing, and now you see the possibility of things changing. Don't you think the idea of change frightens me, too? Don't you think it comes into play when you ask if I love Gideon?"

"Does it?"

"Sure, it does. I'm used to my life, our life. I like it. I'm not sure I want anything to disturb it."

"But if you love Gideon—"

"I don't know for sure that I do, which is one of the reasons why I really want the three of us to go on this trip. If I'm going to love any man, you'll have to feel comfortable with him—and vice versa—because no matter what else happens, I'm your mother. Always. I'll be here for you even if I love *ten* guys."

Jill smirked. "Ten guys? Fat chance. You're such a prude."

"What is that supposed to mean?" Chris asked with an indignance that was only half-feigned.

"You haven't even gone to bed with Gideon! I mean, look at him. He's gorgeous. Jenny and Laura are *still* drooling over him. Why aren't you?"

"Why aren't I drooling?"

"Why aren't you sleeping with him?"

Chris swallowed. As openings went, it was perfect. Remembering the conversation she'd had such a short time before with Gideon, she knew he was right. She and Jill were close. She'd always prided herself on forthrightness. She could explain her feelings. They could talk. It was time.

"How do you know I'm not?" she asked gently.

While Jill didn't jump immediately at the suggestion, she grew more alert. "When do you have time?"

"You make time for what you want."

"I mean, when have you had the *chance*?"

"You find chances, if you want them."

Jill was quiet. After a minute, she blurted out, "So have you—or haven't you?"

"Is it important to you to know?"

She backed down. "Not if you don't want to tell me."

"I do. I want to tell you. I want to, because some of the things Gideon and I have shared have been very, very beautiful. I've always told you that. With the right person, making love is precious."

Jill seemed suddenly shy, as though this Chris was a new and different person from the one she'd known moments before. "So you have," she whispered.

Chris nodded. "He is...very special."

"Does he love you?"

"Yes."

"Do you think you'll marry him?"

Chris had taught her that lovemaking should be with someone special, that marriage should be with someone special. So Jill had made the connection, as the mother in Chris wanted her to. Now Chris was caught in the middle.

"I don't know, honey. If what I feel for him proves to be love, I might. But that would be a long way off."

"Why?"

"Because I wouldn't do anything until you went to college."

"Will a man like Gideon wait around that long?"

"If he loves me enough. Maybe that's the test."

"What if you get pregnant before that?"

"Pregnant. Jill, I've taught *you* about using birth control. Don't you think I practice it myself?" She'd seen her doctor right after New Year's.

"What do you use?"

"*Jill.*"

"I'm not supposed to ask that?"

Chris closed her eyes for a second, then reached for her daughter's hand. "Of course you can. This is new for me. That's all."

"Birth control is?"

"Telling you about *my* using it is."

"Wouldn't you want to know what I used?"

"Jill, you're not—"

"No! But if I were, wouldn't you want me to discuss it with you?"

"Definitely."

"So?"

Chris sighed. "I got a diaphragm."

"Do you like it?"

"Uh, well, uh, it's okay, I mean, it's safe and effective, and if you, uh, if you have to use something—"

Jill started to laugh.

"What's so funny?"

"You. You're all red."

"This is *embarrassing.*"

"Why? You've told me so many other things without getting embarrassed."

"This is different." She searched for the words. "It's like you're my mother, but I've never had this kind of discussion with my mother."

"That's why I came along."

"And the very best thing you were. I've never, *never* regretted having you, though there are times when I wished my timing had been better. There are times when I wish I could have given you a family of your own, maybe brothers and sisters."

"You could have more babies."

"Hey, I just said I was using birth control."

"But you could stop. Any time you wanted to. You're young enough to have lots more kids. Does Gideon want them?"

"I don't know. We haven't gotten that far."

"Do you?"

"I don't know. You'd be a pretty hard act to follow."

"Naturally," Jill said with a grin.

Chris grinned right back. "Naturally." She took a breath. "So. What do you say? Want to go skiing?"

The inn was small and quaint, with six guest rooms on the second floor and two baths. If she'd wanted to be secretive, Chris would have stolen into Gideon's room, which was down the hall from hers and Jill's, when she was supposedly using the bathroom. But Jill would have known. Besides, she wanted more time.

So she and Gideon returned to his room shortly after Jill had joined an afternoon ski class. Knowing that it would be three hours before she was done, they felt they had all the time in the world.

Chris never failed to marvel at Gideon's body, and this time was no exception. Wearing ski garb—navy stretch pants that clung to him like static and a lime-green turtleneck sweater that matched his navy-and-green parka—he presented the kind of figure that was regularly photographed for the pages of *W*. When that garb came off, though, slowly revealing broad shoulders, a lean stomach and long, long legs, he was Chris's own very personal fantasy come to life.

Dropping her panties onto the floor by the rest of her things, she approached him. Her hands found his shoulders, then moved down and around and back. "When we're out on the slopes," she said in a sultry whisper, "women do double takes when you pass. Your moves may not be studied, but you have a natural grace." She moved closer, bringing her breasts, her belly, her thighs into contact with his. "You do this way, too," she said. Opening her mouth on his neck, she dragged her lips over that corded column. "You are an incredible male." Her palms chafed his thighs, moving slowly in to frame his sex.

Gideon was sure he'd died and gone to heaven. "You make me this way," he said. "It's all for you." Lowering his head, he caught her lips at the same time that he lifted her legs to his hips. He slid into her with the comfort and ease of an old lover and the excitement of a new one.

Familiarity gave them the confidence to be inventive, and a boundless hunger gave them the fuel. Gideon loved her standing up, then sitting on the edge of the bed, then, with Chris astride, on the sheets. He paused midway to love her with his tongue until she was wild with need, then shot back into her with a speed and force that she welcomed. The quiet in the room was broken by gasps and cries. By the time those finally eased, they were both sated, their bodies slick with sweat, tangled but limp.

"Marry me, Chris."

She was half-asleep. "Hmm?"

"I want to marry you."

"I know," she mumbled.

"Will you?"

Eyes closed, she kissed the smooth, soft spot just before his armpit. "Ask me later. Can't think now."

Gideon gave her ten minutes. Then he nudged her partly awake, tipped up her face with a finger and kissed her the rest of the way.

She grinned. "Hi."

"Hi, yourself." He looked at her, then looked some more. Never in a million years would he tire of seeing her after they made love, when she was warm and wet and sensual. He had never before had the stamina to make love three or four times in a night, but he had it with Chris. She inspired him to great heights. "Are you up?"

Sleepily she nodded. "This is so nice. I'm *so* glad we came here."

"Me, too." He paused, figuring he'd take a different, less direct tack this time. "Hard to believe the week's almost done. I could take this on a regular basis for the next thirty or forty years."

Even in her half-dreamy state, Chris knew what he meant. "There's something about ski country. The air is so clear. So cold. So invigorating. It's so warm coming inside."

"When I grow up," Gideon said, "I'm going to buy a place, maybe not as far north as this, but closer, so I can use it on weekends." He ran the pad of his thumb over her eyebrows, first one, then the other. "What do you think? Make any sense?"

Chris thought the idea sounded divine. "What kind of place?" she asked, dreaming wide awake now.

"Something old. With charm."

"A Victorian on the edge of a town green, with the white spire of a church at one end and the stone chimney of the local library at the other."

"You got it. I'd do the place over inside myself, so that it had every modern convenience. I'd break down walls so everything was open, and redo the fireplace so you could see the fire front and back. I'd put in lofts and skylights and spiral stairways and—"

"A Jacuzzi."

"You'd like one?"

"Definitely."

"We've never made love in a Jacuzzi."

"I know." Chris let herself imagine it. "I'd like to."

He was getting hard just thinking of it. "So would I."

"You should have put one in when you built your house."

"But I hadn't met you then. Real men don't soak in tubs unless there's a woman with them, and you're the only woman I've ever entertained at my house."

"The only one?"

"Only one. I love you."

She smiled helplessly. "I know."

"How 'bout you?"

"I'm workin' on it," she teased.

But he was serious. "How far have you come?"

"I'm at the point," she said, "of being happier with you than I've ever been before in my life." There were times when she felt delirious inside, so pleased and excited that she didn't know what to do with her excess energy.

"How far is that from being in love?"

"Pretty close, I guess."

"How long will it take to make 'pretty close' *there*?"

"I don't know." That was where things got hairy, because she knew what was coming next.

"I need you, Chris," he said in the slow, rumbling voice that she'd come to associate with Gideon at his most intense. "I want to be with you morning and night for the rest of my life. I want us to get married."

She'd heard him ask her before, of course, but in the afterglow of loving, she'd pushed it from her mind. She couldn't do that now. She looked up at him to answer, then was momentarily stunned by the look in his eyes. They were so filled with love—and desperation—that she had to fight for a breath.

Coming up over him, she kissed him softly. Her forearms, resting on his chest, held her in position to meet his gaze. "I never thought I'd say this, I really didn't, because marriage wasn't something I ever spent much time considering, but I could almost see myself marrying you, Gideon. I could. I feel so much for you that it overwhelms me sometimes."

"That's love."

"Maybe. But I have to be sure. For me, and for you, and for Jill. I have to know it'll last."

"It'll last."

"So says every couple when they exchange wedding vows, but look at the statistics. I thought I was in love once, and I wasn't."

"You were too young to know what love was about. You're older now."

"We're both older. Look at you. You're almost forty. You were married once, and it didn't work, and now you've been single for years. Is what you feel for me different from what you felt for your first wife?"

"Totally," he said with conviction. "I never wanted to spend all my time with her, not even at the beginning. She had a limited time and place in my life. I had my friends, my business, my games, and I didn't want her to have any part of them. With you, I'm passing up all those other things just to be with you.''

''You shouldn't—''

''I *want* to. I'd much *rather* be with you than be with anyone else. I'd much rather be with you than be alone. My first marriage wasn't fun. Being with you is. Know what I want?'' The look in his eyes was precious in its enthusiasm.

''What?''

''I want us to work together all the time. We'd be partners. I build, you decorate. Would you like that?''

She would, a whole lot, but her throat was so tight that she could only nod her answer.

He ran his finger over her lips. ''I want to make you happy, Chris, and that's another thing that's different from the first time. I never thought about making Julie happy. I was almost defiant about going on with my life as though marriage didn't change it at all.'' He made a small sound. ''I'm not even married to you yet, and my life has changed. Everything I do is geared to when I'll be seeing you again, and I love it that way.'' He gave her a lopsided grin. ''Johnny thinks I'm sick. We were having a sandwich at the diner the other day and these two women came in. Ten, fifteen, twenty minutes went by and he started looking at me strangely.''

''Why?''

''Because he thought they were real lookers and I wasn't even interested. I guess they were pretty, but that's all. Hell, I don't even wink at Cookie anymore!''

''Poor Cookie.''

''Yeah, she was kinda hurt.''

''You have my permission to wink. There's no harm in that.''

''But winking is a kind of come-on. It's like me saying, 'I'm a man, and I think you're cute.' But I'm not thinking about anyone else being cute anymore. No one but you.''

''Oh, Gideon.''

''I've even thought about living arrangements. We could buy a piece of land halfway between Worcester and Belmont, something really pretty, big and wooded. There're lots of bedroom communities with good schools for Jill—''

''I can't change her.''

''Why not?''

''Because she's in high school. She's with friends she's grown up with, and they're just getting to the fun years. It'd be cruel to take her away from that.''

"Then we'll live in Belmont until she's done with high school, and in the meanwhile we can be building our dream house—"

She pressed a hand to his mouth. "Shh."

"What?"

"You're being too accommodating."

"That's the point. I love you, so I *want* to be accommodating."

"But I can't be accommodating back!" she cried. "Don't you see? You're right about love meaning that, but I'm not free to love that way. I have Jill. I want things to be so right for her in the next few years."

Gideon felt that they had circled around and were right back to the point where they'd been weeks before. It was frustrating, but he wasn't about to give up. "I want things right for her, too. My coming into your life doesn't have to change anything."

"But it will. It will. And then if something goes wrong—"

"What something?"

"With our relationship, and there'd be tension and upset. I don't want to subject Jill to that. She's been so good about not having a father."

"But that's *another* thing," he went on. "You could *give* her a father, if you wanted. Me."

"It's not the same."

Gideon let the words sink in, along with the look on Chris's face. The moment was enlightening. "You feel guilty about that, don't you?"

"Yes, I feel guilty."

Wrapping his arms around her, he hugged her. "After all you've given Jill, the last thing you should be feeling is guilty. My God, Chris, you've been a saint."

"Not quite," she murmured, though she liked hearing him say it.

"Jill has had more love than most kids with *two* parents get. She wouldn't be as well adjusted if that weren't so."

"I want her to stay well adjusted."

"So do I," he said, and let it go at that. He knew from experience that where Jill's welfare was concerned, Chris was unyielding. It was simply going to be up to him, over the next weeks and months, to show her that he'd be good for Jill, too.

9

Gideon had the best of intentions. When he took Chris to a movie, he suggested Jill bring a friend along. When a foot of snow fell and school was canceled, he drove in from Worcester with a toboggan and took them all sliding. When Jill wanted to buy a gift for Chris's birthday, he took her to not one mall, not two, but *three* before she found what she wanted. And he was thrilled to do it. He genuinely enjoyed Jill. And he thought she enjoyed him.

Chris did, too. Jill looked forward to seeing him. At other times, though, she was more quiet than usual. More than once, when she was at the kitchen table doing homework at night and Chris was nearby, talking softly on the phone to Gideon, she sensed Jill looking at her, sensed a pensiveness that had nothing to do with schoolwork. At times, she thought that pensiveness was brooding, but when she asked, Jill shook her head in denial.

March came, then April, and Chris began to worry in earnest. Jill just wasn't herself. She was doing fine in school, and her social life was as active as ever, but at home she was definitely distracted. She continued to deny there was a problem, and Chris could only push so far. She thought, though, that it might be wise for them to spend some time alone together. They hadn't done it much of late, what with Chris's work—she was up to her ears with orders both for the model condo at Crosslyn Rise and the mansion, itself—and Gideon's presence. So, over dinner at home one midweek night, she broached the topic.

"Any thoughts on vacation, Jill?" When Jill set down her fork, alert but silent, Chris said, "I was thinking that we could go down to New York for a few days."

"New York?"

"Uh-huh. Just the two of us. We could shop, eat out, maybe take in a show or two. Would you like that?"

Jill lifted her fork again and pushed a piece of chicken around the plate.

"Jill?"

The fork settled. Looking young and vulnerable, Jill met her gaze. "I was thinking I'd use that vacation for something else."

"What's that?"

"I want to meet my father."

Chris felt the blood leave her face. Of all the things she'd imagined Jill wanting to do, that wasn't one. "Your father?"

"He's out there. I want to meet him."

"Uh, uh, what—" she cleared her throat "—what brought this on?"

Jill shrugged. "I'm curious."

"Is this what's been getting you down lately?"

"Not getting me down. But I've been thinking about it a lot. I really want to know who he is. I want to see him."

Chris felt dizzy. She took a deep breath to steady herself. "Uh, honey, I don't know where he is."

"You said he was in Arizona," Jill shot back in an accusing tone.

Chris tried to be conciliatory. "He was, last time I heard, but that was second- or thirdhand, and years ago."

"Where in Arizona?"

"Phoenix."

"So I could start looking there."

"In *person*?"

"Of course not. I'd call Directory Assistance. How many Brant Conways can there be?"

"Lots."

"Okay. You said he sells real estate. There must be some state list of people who do that. If he was there even ten years ago, he must have worked with someone who's kept in touch with him. I could find all that out on the phone."

Chris realized that Jill had given the possibilities a certain amount of very adult thought. She wondered how far that adult thought had gone. "And then what?"

"Then I'll call him, then fly out to see him during vacation."

"What if he doesn't want that?"

"Then we'll arrange another time to meet."

"What if he doesn't want that, either?"

"Then we'll arrange something else. There has to be *some* way we can get together."

Chris studied the napkin she was clutching so tightly in her lap. "Has it occurred to you that he might not want to see you?"

Sounding defiant but subdued, Jill said, "Yes. And if he doesn't, I won't go."

"But you'll be hurt in the process. I don't want that, Jill. I've tried to protect you from hurt. You don't *need* Brant. Trust me. You have everything that's good for you here, without him."

"But he's my father."

"Biologically, yes. Beyond that, he's nothing to you."

"He may be a very nice man."

"He may be, but he has his own life and you have yours."

"I don't want to be *in* his life. I just want to *meet* him."

Chris had always recognized the possibility of that, but she had kept it a very distant thought. Suddenly it was real and near, and she wasn't prepared to handle it.

She felt betrayed. She knew it was wrong. But that was how she felt.

"Why now?" she asked, half to herself.

"I already told you that."

But she had a sudden, awful suspicion. "It has something to do with Gideon, doesn't it?"

"What could it have to do with him?"

"He's the first man I've been interested in. In the past few weeks, he's probably come as close as you've ever come to having a father around." She'd known it. Damn it, she'd *known* something would happen. "I'm right, aren't I?"

"I like Gideon. I like being with him."

"But he's made you think of your father."

"It's not *Gideon's* fault."

But Chris had known. She'd *known*. Bolting from the table, she started pacing the room. "I told him it was too much, too fast. I asked him to slow things down, but did he? No. *He* knew what was best."

"Mom—"

"Over and over, I asked him to be patient. I told him I didn't want anything upsetting you. I told you needed time."

"Mom—"

"The big expert, sticking his nose into other people's business."

"Mom." She was twisted around in her chair. When Chris looked at her, she said, "This is *not Gideon's fault*! I love Gideon. He loves you, and you love him."

"I don't—"

"You do! I see it every night. It's written all over your face when you talk him on the phone. And I think it's great. I *want* you to love him. I *want* you to marry him. I think it'd be fun to be a family. That's something I could never have with my father, and I accept that. I don't want anything with him. I like what I have. I just want to meet the man, so that I'll know who he is and who I am. Then I can be a stepdaughter to Gideon."

There had been certain times over the years when Chris had found motherhood to be overwhelmingly emotional. One had been when she'd first been presented her gooey, scrunched-up baby girl, another when Jill had gone off on the school bus for the very first time, another when

Jill had had the lead in the middle school's musical production of *Snow White and the Seven Dwarfs*. Intense pride always affected Chris.

Intense pride was what she felt at that moment, along with a bit of humility. Fighting back tears, she put her arm around Jill and gave her a tight hug. "You are incredible."

Jill hugged her back. "I do love you, Mom. I'll always love you. I don't think I could ever love *him*, but I want to know who he is."

Regaining a modicum of composure, Chris slid back into her chair. She wanted to think clearly, wanted Jill to do the same. "I don't really know much about him. If he has a slew of other children, how will you feel?"

"Okay."

"What if he's big and bald and fat?"

"Haven't you been the one to always tell me not to judge a book by its cover?"

"But this is your father. You may be fantasizing that he's some kind of god—"

"If he were that, he'd have come for me, not the other way around." She took a breath, seeming strong now that she'd aired what had clearly been weighing so heavily on her mind. "Mom, I'm not looking for someone to take your place, and I'm *not* looking for another place to live. I just want to meet my father. Once I've seen him, I'll know who he is and that he exists, and that he knows *I* exist. Then I can go on with my life."

The words were all correct. They were grown-up and sensible. Chris knew that, but the knowledge was small solace for the fear she felt. Jill had been her whole life, and vice versa, for so long, that the thought of Brant intruding in any way was upsetting. She sensed that, for the first time, there was a crack in her relationship with Jill—not a crack as in hostility, but one as in growing up and separating. That too was inevitable, but Chris wasn't ready for it.

Nor was she ready for Gideon when he called that night. "I'm really tired. Why don't we connect later in the week."

He was immediately concerned. "Aren't you feeling well?"

"I'm fine. Just tired."

When he called the next night, she didn't claim fatigue, but she was quiet, answering his questions as briefly as possible, not offering anything extra. "Is something wrong?" he finally asked after five minutes of trying to pull her usual enthusiasm from her.

"Of course not. What could be wrong?"

He didn't know. But he knew she wasn't herself, and he feared that what was upsetting her had to do with him. "You sound angry."

"Not angry. Just busy."

"At ten o'clock at night?"

"I'm trying to get some papers in order. I have a slew of deliveries coming for five different jobs, and if the invoices get messed up—"

"I thought Margie took care of paperwork like that."

"Margie isn't involved the way I am, and I want these things to be right. If there are screwups, I'll have to be cleaning them up at the same time that Crosslyn Rise is picking up—"

Gideon interrupted. "Chris, why are you working so hard?"

"Because I'm a professional. I have commitments."

"But you don't have to work *this* hard."

"I have bills to pay," she snapped. "In case you've forgotten, I have a teenage daughter to support."

"I haven't forgotten," Gideon said quietly. "I want to help you do that."

"You've done enough!"

A heavy silence stretched between them before he said, "What's that supposed to mean?"

"Nothing."

"*What*, Chris?"

She sighed and rubbed the back of her neck. "*Nothing.* Listen, I'm tired and short-tempered. You'd probably be best to avoid me for a little while."

He didn't like the sound of that at all. "A little while?"

"A few days."

"No way. We have a date for dinner tomorrow night."

"Look, maybe that's not such a good idea."

"I think it is." He paused. "You're angry. What have I done? Damn it, Chris, if you don't tell me, I won't know and I can't do a goddamned thing about remedying it. Come on. *Talk* to me."

"Not tonight," she said firmly. "I'll be back in the office sometime after three tomorrow. Call me then and we'll decide what to do about dinner."

Gideon didn't call. True to form, he was there, waiting in her office when she returned. She stopped at the door when she saw him, feeling an overwhelming rush of sensation. He could arouse that, whether she was annoyed with him or not, and it wasn't only physical. Her heart swelled at the sight of him, which was probably why she hadn't wanted to see him. Looking at him, feeling the warm embrace of his eyes and the love that was so clearly behind it, she was more confused than ever about the anger she felt.

"Hi, doll," he said with a gentle smile. He went to her and kissed her cheek, then leaned back. "Uh-oh. I'm still in the doghouse?"

She slipped past him to her desk, where she deposited her briefcase and the folders she carried.

"Chris." He drew her name out in a way that said he knew something was wrong and wanted to know what it was before he lost his patience.

Knowing that she wouldn't have a chance of keeping still with him right there—and realizing she didn't *want* to—she sat down at her desk, linked her hands tightly in her lap, and said, "Jill wants to contact her father."

Gideon hadn't been expecting that, but he wasn't surprised. "Ahh. And that upsets you."

To put it mildly. "Of course, it upsets me! She wants to go off and find a man who, for all intents and purposes, doesn't want her around."

"How do you know that?"

"Because she's fifteen, and he's never once made the slightest attempt to see her—" she held up both hands "—and that's okay by me, because she doesn't need him in her life, but she's suddenly decided that she wants to know who he is. She's going to be hurt. I know it." Her fingers knotted again. "*That's* what I don't want!"

Knowing Chris the way he did, knowing what she wanted in life for Jill, Gideon could understand why she was upset, though he didn't completely agree. "She doesn't have to be hurt. He may be cordial. He may even welcome her."

Chris felt deep, dark fears rush to the surface. "And if that happens, she may want to see him again and again, and that'll mess her up completely."

"Her, or you?"

"What?"

"Are you afraid for her," Gideon repeated patiently, "or for you?"

Chris was furious that he was so calm when she felt as if the bottom of her world were falling away. "For *me*?" Emotional stress brought her out of her chair. "You think I'm being selfish?"

"No, that's not—"

"How *dare* you suggest that!" she fumed. "I've spent the better half of my life doing and thinking and feeling for that child. I've sacrificed a whole lot, and I'd do the same thing again in a minute." Trembling, she steadied her fingertips on the chrome rim of her desk. "Selfish? Who in the *hell* are you to tell me I'm selfish? You've never sacrificed for a child. You've never sacrificed for anyone!"

Gideon was on the verge of coming to his own defense, when Chris raced on. She needed to air what she was feeling, he realized. He also realized that he wanted to know it all. He'd been a nervous wreck wondering what was wrong with her. So, much as it hurt him, he leaned back against the wall, arms folded on his chest, and listened.

"You've lived life for your own pleasure and enjoyment," she charged. "You wanted something, you took it, and that included me. But that wasn't enough, was it? It wasn't enough that we started dating, even though I didn't want to, or that we kept *on* dating, even though I didn't want to, or that we started sleeping together. That wasn't enough for you. You wanted marriage, and you wanted it fast. When I said I was worried about Jill, you said, 'No sweat, she loves me,' and maybe she does. But it's thinking about you and wondering about us and whether we're getting married that's now making her think about Brant!"

Gideon remained quiet, waiting. When she didn't say anything, simply glared at him—albeit with tears in her eyes now, and that tore through him—he said, "Are you done?"

"If it hadn't been for you, pushing your way into our lives, it wouldn't have *occurred* to her to think of him!"

Again Gideon was quiet, though it was harder to remain so with each word she said. In the old days, he wouldn't have put up with a woman throwing unjust claims at him. He'd either have thrown them right back or walked out the door. So maybe he was sacrificing for Chris now. If so, he was more than happy to do it.

"Can I speak?" he asked, but again his quiet words spurred her on.

"Everything was so good! We had our lives together, she was well adjusted and happy, not going for alcohol or drugs the way some of the kids at her school are, I was beginning to earn some real money. Then you came along—" she caught her breath, a single trickle of tears escaping from each eye "—then you came along and upset it all!"

It was the trickle of tears that did it. Unable to stand still any longer, he left the wall and went to her. "Honey, I think you're confusing the issues," he said softly, but when he reached for her, she batted his hands away.

"I'm not! I've done nothing but go over and over every single aspect of this for the past two days."

"You've lost perspective."

"I have *not!*"

"Maybe if you'd shared it sooner, you would have seen—"

"Seen what?" she cut in shakily. "That you're the answer to my problems? That all I have to do is marry you and let you take me away from here, so Jill can find herself with her father?"

"Of course not!" Gideon argued. "Jill is part of our lives. It's you, me and her. It has been right from the start."

"But it's *not* her," Chris cried, and her chin began to wobble. "She's going off to Arizona to see Brant.'' Her breathing grew choppy. ''Things won't ever be the same again!''

Gideon had had enough. He pulled her into his arms, then held her tighter when she struggled. Within seconds, she went limp against him, and within seconds of that, clutching his sweater, she began to cry softly.

''Oh, baby,'' he said, crushed by the sound of her sobs. He stroked her blond hair, rubbed her slender back, held her as close as he could until her weeping began to abate. Then he sat against the edge of the desk and propped her between his thighs. Her head was still down, her cheek against his chest. Quietly he began to speak.

''You're right, Chris. Things won't ever be the same again. We've found each other, Jill's growing up, Crosslyn Rise has been gutted. That's growth. It's progress. And you're afraid, because for the first time in a long time things are changing in your life, and that makes you nervous. It would make me nervous, too, I suppose, but that's just a guess, because you're right, I haven't been in your shoes. I haven't had a child. I haven't raised that child and poured every bit of myself into it. So I don't know what it's really like when suddenly something appears to threaten that relationship.''

''I'm so scared,'' Chris whimpered.

He tightened his arms around her. ''I know, baby, I know, but there are a couple of things you're not taking into consideration. First off, just because Jill wants to see Brant, that doesn't mean she'll have an ongoing relationship with him.''

''She will. I know she will.''

''How do you know?'' he challenged. When she didn't answer, he gentled his voice again. ''You don't know, because you don't know who Brant is now, and because you're underestimating Jill. She wouldn't do anything to hurt you.''

''She wants to see him!''

''She *needs* to see him. It's part of growing up. It's part of forming her identity. She's been wondering about him for a long time, now she needs to finally see who he is, so that she can put the wondering aside and go on living.''

The thoughts sounded strangely familiar. In a slow, suspicious voice, Chris asked, ''Did you discuss this with her?'' The idea that Jill would go to Gideon before she went to her own mother was cutting.

But Gideon was quick to deny it. ''Are you kidding? She wouldn't open to me that way. At least, not yet.''

''But she said nearly the same thing you just did.''

''That's because it's what she's feeling.''

Chris looked up. ''How would you know what she's feeling?''

He brushed at tear tracks with the pads of his thumbs. ''Because I felt those same things myself when I was a kid. I was younger than she is. I didn't understand it the way she probably does, but after the fact I could see it. My mother came to visit me when I was little, but it wasn't the same. I couldn't put her in any kind of context. I reached a point of wanting—no, *needing*—to go to her, to see where she lived and who she lived with." He arched a dark brow. "You think my dad was pleased? He was *furious*! Couldn't understand why I'd spend all that money to fly all the way across the country to see a woman who hadn't cared enough to hang around. He yelled and yelled and carried on for a good long time until it finally hit me that he was jealous."

"I'm not jealous," Chris claimed, but more quietly. Her mind had been so muddled since Jill had mentioned Brant that she hadn't realized—hadn't remembered—that Gideon had been in a situation not unlike the one Jill was in. "I'm just scared."

"Well, my dad was, too. He was scared that I'd take a look at her life and reject him the way she had. He was scared that I'd pick up and move out to California to live with her, and that he'd be left all alone. He didn't even have family, the way you do."

Needing the cushion, she returned her head to his chest. "That doesn't make it any easier."

"I know," he crooned against her hair, "I know. The loss of a child like that would be traumatic in any case. But the fact was that he didn't lose me. I saw where my mother lived, and sure, she had plenty of money and could have given me a hell of a lot if I'd gone out there to live with her, but the fact is that I wouldn't have traded my father's love for a penny of her money in a million years."

It was a minute before his words penetrated fully and sank deep into her soul. Moaning, she slipped her arms around his waist. He was so dear.

But he wasn't done talking. "Don't you think Jill knows what a good thing she has in you? Don't you think she knows how much she loves you?"

"Yes, but she doesn't know how much I love *her*. She doesn't know that I'd be destroyed if she ever decided to live with Brant. He was so horrible doing what he did to me—and to her. One part of me is absolutely infuriated that she even wants to *see* him."

His breath was warm against her forehead. "But you can't tell her that—or show her, because that's not the way you are—so you took your anger out on me. And that's okay, Chris. I'd rather you took it out on me than on her. But you owed me an explanation, at least. It's not fair to refuse to talk to me, like you've done for two nights on the phone. If you want to scream and yell at me, fine. That's what I'm here for. Screaming and yelling is sometimes the only way to get anger out of your system. Or fear. Or worry." His voice grew more fierce. "Just don't shut me out, damn it. Don't shut me out."

Slipping her arms higher on his back, Chris buried her face against his neck. "I'm sorry," she whispered. "I guess you were the only scapegoat around. I've just been so miserable since she brought it up. I keep thinking of all the possibilities—"

"Not all of them. Only the worst ones."

He was probably right, she knew. "I keep thinking that she'll find him and like him and want to stay, or that she'll hate him but he'll like her and want a part of her, even, God forbid, sue for visitation rights. I keep worrying that her going after Brant will open a whole can of worms. She's such a terrific kid. I don't want her messed up."

"She won't be messed up."

Chris raised her eyes to his. "Look at all the kids whose parents are divorced."

"What about them?"

"They're messed up."

"Not all of them. But your situation isn't the same."

"If there's suddenly a tug-of-war between Brant and me, it's the same."

"There won't be any tug-of-war. Jill won't want to live with him. She's happy here, with you and all the friends she's grown up with. You said that yourself when I suggested we build a house somewhere other than Belmont, and it made sense. She isn't about to want to pick up and relocate all of a sudden."

"What if Brant wants it?"

"He won't want it. Not at this late date."

"But what if he does?"

"You'll tell him no."

"What if he fights?"

"You mean, goes to court? He won't do that." He snorted. "Talk about cans of worms. If he goes to court, you can sue him for back child support. Think he'll pay up?"

"What if he does? What if he does, and then wants visitation rights?"

"He won't have much of a chance of getting them. He knew he had a child fifteen years ago. He chose to ignore her. He didn't give money, and he didn't give time. No court is going to feel terribly sympathetic toward him. Besides, Jill isn't a baby. She's old enough to express her feelings and to have them taken into account."

"In court. Oh, God. I don't want her dragged through anything like that."

"She *won't* be." He took her face in his hands and put conviction into his words. "The chances of anything like that happening are so remote that it's absurd to even be thinking of it now."

"It's not absurd to me. I'm her mother. I *care*."

"So do I, Chris," he stated fiercely, "but it won't do her any good if you're a basket case worrying about worst-case scenarios. Chances are she'll meet the man, and that'll be it."

For the first time, hearing his words and the confidence behind them, Chris let herself believe it might be true. "I'd give anything for that."

He kissed her nose. "She's a good, sensible young woman, her mother's daughter all the way. My guess is that if she ever knew how upset you've been, she'd cancel her plans."

"If she did that, she'd always wonder."

"Uh-huh."

Though she could have done without his agreement, she felt herself beginning to relax. The breath she took was only slightly shaky, a vague reminder of her recent crying jag. "You don't think I'll lose her?"

"No *way* could you lose her. She'll probably go see Brant and then come back and be her good old self." He frowned. "You say the guy's in Arizona?"

"He was in Phoenix last time I heard. I told Jill we'd make some calls this weekend."

"Then you'll help her."

"Of course. I wouldn't put her through this alone. I wouldn't trust *him* alone with her."

"And you'll go out there with her?"

Chris nodded.

"It'll be the first time you've seen him since—"

She nodded again.

"Think you'll feel anything?"

Even if she hadn't sensed his unsureness, she would have said the same thing. "I'll feel exactly what I felt when he told me he didn't know if the baby was his and walked away—anger, frustration and fear." She touched Gideon's lean cheek and said softly. "But you have nothing to worry about. He won't interest me in the least."

"Maybe I could come with you."

"That might put more pressure on Jill."

"Then maybe I can help you find him. I have a friend who lives out there—" He stopped when she shook her head. "Why not? It might speed things up."

"It might tell her you're trying to get rid of her."

Gideon couldn't believe his ears. "Are you kidding? She knows better than that!" But Chris was wearing a strange expression. "But maybe you don't.'' He swore against the anguish that shot through him. ''When will you accept the fact that I want her with us?''

''Some men wouldn't.''

''I'm not some men,'' he barked.

''You've been a bachelor for a long time. It's one thing to live with a woman, another to suddenly inherit her teenage daughter.''

He was hurt. ''Have I ever complained? Have I ever suggested, even in the slightest way, that I didn't want her around?''

''I remember a few very frustrating times—''

''Yeah, I remember them, too, and I'd have felt that frustration whether it was Jill we had to behave for or a child that you and I had ourselves, but that doesn't mean I don't want her. Or them. I want kids, Chris. We're using birth control because we're not married yet, and because we want you to have a choice this time, but I do want kids. I want them for us, and I want them for Jill. She'd love some brothers and sisters. She told me so.''

''She did?''

He nodded. ''When we were out shopping the other week. She said that you were a great mother, and that she hoped you'd have some children so you'd have someone to take care of when she went off to school.''

Chris's face fell. ''Off to school. College.''

''She is going.''

''I know. It's creeping up so fast.'' Closing her eyes, she made a small, helpless sound. ''Why do things have to change?'' It was the question she'd been asking herself over and over again.

Gideon had never pretended to be a philosopher. All he could do was to speak from the heart. ''Because we grow. We move on to things that are even better. Hey, listen, I know it's scary. Change always is. But just think—if Jill goes to see Brant and gets him out of her system, you won't have to worry about that anymore. Then, if you and I get married and have a few kids who adore Jill so much that they raise holy hell when she goes off to college, you'll have something else to think about besides an empty nest.''

''Empty nest—hah. From the sounds of it, you've got the nest so full, there may not be room for any of us to breathe!''

''Not to worry,'' was his smug response. ''I'm a builder. I'll enlarge the nest.'' He doubted it was the time or place, still he couldn't resist pressing his point. ''So, what do you think?''

''About what?''

''Having kids.''

''What about my career?''

''You'll cut back a few hours. So will I. Between the two of us, we'll handle things." He paused, wanting to believe but afraid to. "Are you considering it?"

"Not now. All I can do now is to get through this thing with Jill and Brant."

"You'll get through it," he said. Ducking his head, he kissed her on the lips. When she didn't resist, he did it again, more persuasively this time, more deeply. Just as he felt the beginning of her response, he tore his mouth away. "Do you still blame me for Jill wanting to go?"

Closing her eyes against his chin, Chris whispered, "How can I blame you for anything when you kiss me that way?"

"Are you gonna shut me out again?"

"You'll only barge your way back in."

"How about dinner tonight?"

"Goin' for broke, hmm?"

"Damn right."

She opened her eyes and slowly met his. "Okay, but I have to be home early. Jill will be back from her friend's at nine, and I want to be there."

Understanding why, Gideon nodded.

Chris studied his face, feature by handsome feature, for another minute before wrapping her arms around his neck. "Thank you, Gideon."

"For what?"

"Being my friend."

"My pleasure."

She was silent for a minute, thinking about how very much she did love him and how, surprisingly, she was coming to depend on him. She hadn't wanted that at all, but just then, she wasn't sorry. Having someone to lean on was a luxury. Sure, she had her parents and brothers, but it wasn't the same. Gideon was a man. Her man. Holding on to him, being held in return, was the nicest thing that had happened to her in two whole days.

10

Gideon would have liked to have been there when Chris made the call to Brant Conway. He knew the call was, in some respects, a pivotal point in her life, and he wanted to be part of it. But he also knew how worried she was about Jill. He could appreciate how sensitive a time it was for her. The last thing he wanted was to complicate things with his presence.

That didn't mean he couldn't keep in close contact by phone. He wanted to give Chris support, to show her that he could listen and comfort, even absorb her anger and frustration.

Actually, there was far less anger and frustration than he expected. When she finally contacted Brant, then called to tell him about it, she was more tired than anything else.

"It was so easy," she said in a quiet voice, talking in the privacy of her bedroom after Jill had finally gone to sleep. "One call to Directory Assistance did it. He's still living in Phoenix, still selling real estate."

Gideon wanted to know everything. "Who talked, you or Jill?"

"Me," Chris said emphatically. "Jill wanted to do it, but I put my foot down. Can you imagine what she'd have felt if he'd denied he was her father?"

"Did he?"

"I didn't give him a chance. He was slightly stunned when I told him my name. He never expected to hear from me. So I had an advantage to start with, and I pressed it. I told him Jill was fifteen, that she looked just like him, and that she wanted to see him. I told him we'd be flying out during April vacation."

"What'd he say?"

"He stammered a little. Then he said that he had a wife and two little boys, and that Jill's showing up out of nowhere would upset them."

"The bastard," Gideon muttered.

"Uh-huh."

"So what'd you say?"

"I wanted to tell him that he was the scum of the earth and the last person I wanted my daughter to see, but Jill was sitting right there beside me, hanging on my every word. So I just repeated what I'd said, that she wanted to see him. I made it sound as if we were coming whether he liked it or not. I suggested that we would stay in a hotel and that he could visit with her there.''

"Did he agree?"

"Reluctantly. He must have figured that he had no choice. We'd gotten his phone number. We could get his address. I doubt he wants us showing up at his house and surprising the wife and kids.''

Gideon heard bitterness at the last. "Does it bother you—the idea that he has a family?"

"I kind of figured he did," Chris said. She didn't have to think long about her feelings on that score. "I'm not personally bothered in the least. I wouldn't want the creep if he was presented to me on a silver platter. What does bother me is that he's given legitimacy to two other children, while denying it to Jill.''

"She's better off without him. You know that."

"I do." Chris sighed. "I just wish she did."

"She will. Give her time." His thoughts jumped ahead. "When will you go?"

"A week from Monday. We'll come back Wednesday. That leaves Tuesday to see Brant."

Gideon remembered the trips he'd made to see his mother, when he'd flown west, visited and flown home. Years later, he wished he'd taken greater advantage of the cross-country flight. "What about seeing the Southwest? I hear it's beautiful. Maybe you could kind of make it a treat for Jill. I mean, since you're going so far—"

"I thought of doing that, and one part of me would like to. The other part doesn't think it would be so good."

"Why not?"

"Two reasons." She really had thought it out. "First, I don't want her directly associating Brant with that part of the country. I'd rather she see it at a separate time."

"The second reason?"

"You," Chris said softly. "I'd rather not be away from here so long."

Gideon swore. "Damn it, Chris, how can you say something like that on the phone, when I can't hold you or kiss you or love you?" The mere thought of doing all that made his body tighten.

"You asked."

"Right." And since she was in an answering mode, he went for it all. "You do love me, don't you?"

She sighed. "Yes, Gideon, I do love you."

"Since when?"

"I don't know since when. I knew I was in trouble way back at the beginning when you bothered me so much. You kept zinging me with these little darts. I think they had some kind of potion on them.''

"Will you marry me?"

"Uh-huh."

"When?"

"Someday."

"'Someday'? What's *that* supposed to mean?"

"I have to get this business with Jill straightened out first."

Gideon's mind started working fast. "Okay. This is April. The trip's comin' right up. Can we plan on a wedding in May?"

"We can't plan on *anything*. We'll have to take it day by day."

"But you will marry me?" He was so desperate for it he'd even wear a tux if she asked. "Marry me, Chris?"

"Yes." And she knew she would. With his enthusiasm, his sense of humor, adventure and compassion, his gentleness and his fire, he had become a vital part of her life. "I do love you," she said, knowing he wanted to hear the words again, knowing he deserved them.

"Ahh." He let out his breath and grinned. "You've just made me a very happy man, Christine Gillette. Horny, but happy."

Both feelings persisted through the next day, which was Saturday. The first was remedied that night, in the coziness of Chris's bed, while Jill was at a movie with friends. The second just grew.

Sunday night, though, Chris phoned him in a state of restrained panic. Her sentences were short and fast, her voice higher than usual. "Brant called a little while ago. Jill answered the phone. I was in the bath. You won't believe what he did, Gideon! I still can't believe it myself! He is such a snake," she hissed, "such a snake!"

"Shh." His heart was pounding, but he said, "Take it slow, honey. Tell me."

"Instead of waiting until I could get to the phone, he talked directly to her. He said that his parents want her to stay with them. Her. Not me. Just her. He said that I shouldn't even bother coming out, that he would meet the plane himself and then deliver Jill to her grandparents." She nearly choked on the words. "Her grandparents. Well, at least he acknowledges that she's his, but to call those people her grandparents when they haven't given any more of a damn than he has all these years—"

"Chris, shh, Chris. Maybe they didn't know."

She was trembling, though whether from anger or fear she didn't know. "That's beside the point. They don't have any right to her. *He* doesn't have any right to her. She's mine. He should have made his plans through *me*." She caught in a livid breath. "Can you believe the *audacity* of the man to go over my head that way?"

"You'll tell him no."

"That's what I told Jill, and she got really upset. She said that he sounded nice, that she was old enough to travel alone, and that that was what she'd been planning to do in the first place." Her voice dropped to a desperate whisper. Though she had her door shut, she didn't want to take the chance that Jill might hear. "But how can I *let* her, Gideon? How can I let her fly all that way alone, then face a man who—for all I know—is strange or sadistic? It's been more than fifteen years since I've seen him. We were kids ourselves. I have no idea what kind of person he's become."

"Did you know his parents?"

"I met them once or twice, but that was all." She could barely picture what they looked like. "What should I do, Gideon? This is my *baby*."

Gideon was silent for a bit. She wanted his opinion, but he was still a fledgling, as parents went. Talk about trial by fire...

"Have you run this by your parents?"

"Not yet. I want to know what *you* think."

"I think," he said slowly, "that you need more information before you can make any kind of judgment."

"Sure, I do," she returned facetiously. "I need a complete dossier on the man, but there's no way I can get that without hiring an investigator, and I refuse to do that! I shouldn't have to pay the money, and we don't have the time."

"I have a friend in Phoenix," Gideon reminded her. "He's a builder there. If he hasn't run across Conway himself, he's bound to know people who have. Let me call him. He may be able to tell us something about what kind of person he is."

"What kind of person is your friend?"

"A trustworthy one."

Chris wasn't about to look a gift horse in the mouth. She agreed to let Gideon do it and was grateful for his offer. Late the next day, he called with the information his friend had provided.

"According to Paul, Brant Conway has made a good name for himself. He's successful in his field, has some dough, lives in a nice house in Scottsdale. He isn't exactly a fixture in high society but he's respected and liked. His parents live in Scottsdale, too. They all do well for themselves."

Chris had mixed feelings about that. She was pleased for Jill, not so pleased for herself. If the report had come back in any way negative, she might have been able to cancel the trip. It looked as though she didn't have any grounds for that.

"And your friend is reliable?" she asked.

"'Fraid so," Gideon answered.

She paused. "Do you think I should let her go?"

"I think that if you don't, Jill may resent it. The fact is that if she wants to go, she'll go anyway, whether it's now or later. It would be awful if your refusal put a wedge between you. I think you have to trust that you've raised her the right way, and that she'll be able to take care of herself and know to call if there's any problem."

That was pretty much what Chris's parents had said when she'd talked it over with them that morning. She had wanted to argue then, just as she wanted to argue now, but she knew that they were all right. Jill wasn't a small child. She would be met at the airport and cared for by her grandparents, who possibly felt far more for her than Brant. Most importantly, Jill had a sane head on her shoulders. If something went wrong, she would know to get herself to the nearest phone.

Heart in her mouth, Chris saw Jill off for Phoenix on the Monday of her school vacation. Brant had suggested that she stay until Friday—another suggestion that Chris resented but that she was helpless to deny.

She did deny Gideon the chance of going to the airport. "My folks want to drive us. Any more people and it'll be a major production." But he was on the phone with her as soon as she returned to the office, and when she got home that night, he was waiting with his overnight bag in the bedroom.

Deliberately that first night, he didn't make love to her. Sex wasn't the reason he'd come. He was there to be with her, to hold her, to talk through her unease and help her pass the time until she heard from Jill.

Jill called late Monday night to say that the flight was fine, that Brant's parents' house was pretty and that Brant had been nice. Chris would have been reassured if she felt that Jill had been making the call in private. She could tell from the conversation, though, that Jill wasn't alone.

"Do you think she's hiding something?" Chris asked Gideon fearfully the minute they'd hung up.

Gideon had no way of knowing that, but he felt he had a handle on Jill. "Your daughter is no wilting violet. If there's something she wanted to tell you but couldn't, she'll find another time to call."

"What if they won't let her?"

"She'll find a way." Taking her in his arms, he hugged her tightly. "Chris, don't expect the worst. You have no reason to believe that Brant's parents are anything but lovely people just discovering a very beautiful granddaughter. Jill sounded well. She's doing fine."

The call that came from Phoenix Tuesday night was like the first, sweet and correct. This one held news on the weather, which was warm, the desert, which was in bloom, and her grandparents' swimming pool, which was "radical."

"See?" Gideon said when they hung up the phone this time. "She's being treated very well." He said it as much for Chris's benefit as for his own. Living with Chris, being part of her daily life, anticipating what it would be like when they married, he was approaching things from a new angle. He missed Jill. In truth, though he kept telling himself there was no cause, he was worried, too. "If they took her on a Jeep tour of the desert, they're obviously making an effort to show her the sights."

"Brant's parents are," Chris conceded reluctantly. "She doesn't say much about Brant."

"Maybe that's just as well. If she's seen him, her curiosity is satisfied. If there's going to be any kind of continuing relationship, let it be with his parents."

Chris couldn't imagine going through the hell of that kind of visit several times a year, but she knew Gideon was right. Grandparents were often kinder than parents. She supposed, if she was looking to the positive, she should be grateful they were there.

Clinging to that thought, she calmed herself some, enough so that she didn't fall apart when Jill called on Wednesday night sounding like she wanted to cry.

"What's wrong, baby?" she said softly. She could recognize throat-tight talk when she heard it, particularly in the daughter she knew so well.

After an agonizing minute, Jill said, "I miss you."

Tears came to Chris's eyes. "Oh, sweetheart, sweetheart, I miss you, too." She clutched Gideon's hand, wishing Jill had one as strong to hold. "Aren't you having a good time?"

Jill's voice fell to a murmur. "It's okay. But they're strangers. I don't think they knew I existed at all until he told them, after you called. They don't know what to do with me." Her murmur caught. "I wish you were here. You were right. We should have both come. We could have stayed at a hotel. Then it wouldn't have been so awkward."

Chris swallowed her tears. "Day after tomorrow you'll be home."

"I wish I was now."

"Hang in there, sweetheart. We'll be at the airport Friday to pick you up."

"Gideon, too?"

"Yeah. He misses you."

"Mom?"

"What?"

The murmur dropped to a whisper. "I'm glad you didn't marry Brant. Gideon's so much better."

"Oh, honey." Pressing her hands to her lips, Chris looked at Gideon through a pool of tears.

"What?" he whispered. He'd about had it with sitting still, trying to catch the gist of the conversation from Chris's short words and now her tears. Clearly Jill was upset. He wanted to snatch the phone away and talk to her himself, only he didn't know how appropriate it was. Chris might think he was butting in where he didn't belong, and though *he* knew he belonged there, he didn't know if Chris saw that yet.

In place of an answer, Chris transferred her fingers from her lips to his. To Jill, she said a soft, "Thanks, honey. Maybe you'll tell him that when you get home."

"I sure will," Jill said, sounding better.

"Are you okay, now?"

"I think so."

"If you want to call again, just call."

"I will."

"Don't forget."

"I won't."

"Bye-bye, sweetheart. I love you."

"I love you, too, Mom. Bye."

Chris hung up the phone, all the while looking at Gideon with eyes still moist with tears. "She's special."

"Damn it, I know that," Gideon said crossly. He was feeling shut out. "What's wrong out there?"

"She's lonesome. They're not what she's used to. She wished I'd gone with her."

Gideon stared at her for another minute before snatching up the phone. By the time he was done with his call, he was feeling defiant. "That's what I should have done in the first place," he told Chris.

Her mouth was agape and had been since the start of his call. "You made reservations to fly to Phoenix?"

"For two." His finger wagged between them. "You and me. I can't take this sitting around, worrying about her. We're leaving at dawn tomorrow, we'll be there by noon, so we'll have the rest of the day to pack her up and take her off and decide what we want to do for the rest of the week. I vote for the Grand Canyon. I've never been there. Jill will love it. And there are some great places to see along the way. Then we can fly home on Sunday."

Chris couldn't believe what he'd done. More than that, she couldn't believe the feeling she saw in his eyes. "But—but you have work," was all she could manage to say.

"I have Johnny, and even if I didn't, work'll wait. We're right on schedule, even a little ahead at the Rise, which is the one project I've been worried about. I could use a vacation."

"You took one in February."

"So did most of my men, so it didn't matter then, and we're only talking two days here. I deserve it." Scowling, he stuck his hands on his hips. "I should have suggested this when the plans were first made. It would have made things a whole lot more enjoyable for all of us. But I was afraid to say anything, because Jill's not my daughter, she's yours, and I'm not even your husband. But damn it, if we're gonna be a family, we're gonna be a family. That means good times and bad. It means we stick together. It means we share things." He held up a hand and arched a brow in warning. "Now, if that's not what you want, I think you'd better tell me right away, because if it isn't, I'm not the guy for you. If it is, let's get married—now. I have no intention of sitting at home by myself for the next three years until Jill goes off to college and you decide you're lonesome. Either you want me or you don't. Either you love me, or you don't. I've waited almost forty years for a woman as warm and giving and bright and sweet and sexy as you, and I can't wait any longer. I just can't." He took a deep breath. "So, what'll it be, Chris? Do we get married, or do we call the whole thing off?"

Chris eyed him askance. "You're giving me an ultimatum?"

"That's right," he said, returning his hand to his hip. "Not only that, but I want an answer now. And don't tell me that I'm rushing you or pressuring you, because you either feel it here—" he knocked a fist to his heart "—or you don't. If you love me, and you know I love you, we'll be able to handle anything that comes up with Jill." His face went beseeching. "Don't you see, it's the love that counts?"

At that moment, Chris would have had to be blind not to see, ignorant not to know, heartless not to feel. Gideon Lowe, master-builder, macho flirt, notorious bachelor, rabid Celtics fan, was also a man of sensitivity and insight. If she'd ever wanted a stepfather for Jill, she couldn't have asked for a better one. But Gideon was more, even than that. Far more. He was kind and caring and generous. Yes, he'd upset the applecart of her life, but in such a way that the apples would never taste as sweet without him. When she was with him, she felt the kind of wholeness she'd seen in her parents. If she'd ever wanted a lover, she couldn't have asked for a better one. And if she'd ever wanted a husband...

"Yes," she said softly, and went to him. "I see. I do see." She slipped her arms around his neck, leaning into him in such a way that their physical fit was as perfect as everything else. "The love's there. Let's do it."

Gideon's eyes lit up in the endearingly naughty way that she loved. "*Do* it?"

She grinned, feeling, with the commitment, suddenly happier and more light-headed than she ever had before. "Get married." She paused. Her grin tilted. "And the other, too."

He didn't need to hear any more. Scooping her up in his arms, he made for the stairs.

"Put me down, Gideon Lowe," she cried, laughing. "Put me down. I can walk. This is embarrassing."

He didn't miss a step. "Embarrassing? It's supposed to be romantic."

"It's totally tough and macho."

He did stop then, just shy of the top step, and met her gaze. "The irony of that is really too much."

"What irony?"

"Crosslyn Rise. I went into the project to shake the image."

"What image?"

"Brawn versus brain. And here I am, carting you off to bed like the best of my big-rig buddies." His grin grew wicked. "Know something?" When she shook her head, he said, "This is the *smartest* damn thing I've ever done in my life." Still grinning, he took the last step.

THE DREAM COMES TRUE

1

Eight people sat around the large table in the boardroom at Gordon Hale's bank. They comprised the Crosslyn Rise consortium, the men and women who were financing the conversion of Crosslyn Rise from an elegant, singly owned estate to an exclusive condominium community. Of the eight, seven seemed perfectly content with the way the early-morning meeting was going. Only Nina Stone was frustrated.

Nina hated meetings, particularly the kind where people sat at large tables and hashed things out ad nauseam. Discussion was part of the democratic process, she knew, and as a member of the consortium, with a goodly portion of her own savings at stake, she appreciated having a say in what was happening at Crosslyn Rise. So she had smilingly endured all of the meetings that had come in the months before. But this one was different. This discussion was right up her alley. She was the expert here. If her fellow investors weren't willing to take her professional advice now that the time had finally come for her to give it, she didn't know why in the world she was wasting her time.

Nina's business was real estate. She was the broker of record for Crosslyn Rise, the one who would be in charge of selling the units and finding tenants for the retail space. It was mid-May, nearly eight months since ground had been broken, and the project was finally ready to be marketed.

"I still think," she said for the third time in thirty minutes, "that pricing in the mid-fives is shooting low. Given location alone, we can ask six or seven. What other complex is forty minutes from Boston, tucked into trees and meadows, and opening onto the ocean? What other complex offers a health club, a catering service, meeting rooms and even guest rooms to rent out for visiting friends and relatives? What other complex offers both a marina and shops?"

"None," Carter Malloy conceded, "at least, not in this area." Carter was the architect for the project and the unofficial leader of the consortium. As of the previous fall, he was married to Jessica Crosslyn, who sat close by his side. Jessica's family had been the original owners of the Rise. "But the real estate market is lousy. The last thing we want is to overprice the units, then have them sit empty for years."

"They won't sit empty," Nina insisted. "Trust me. I know the market. They'll sell."

Jessica wasn't convinced. "Didn't you tell me that things weren't selling in the upper end of the market?"

"Uh-huh, but that was well over a year ago, when you were thinking of selling the Rise intact, to a single buyer. Selling something in the multiple millions was tough then. It's eased up, even more so in the range we're talking." She sent her most confident glance around the table. "As your broker, I'd recommend pricing from high sixes to mid sevens, depending on the size of the unit. Based on other sales I've made in the past few months, I'm sure we can get it."

"What kind of sales were those?" came the quiet voice of John Sawyer from the opposite end of the table.

Nina homed in on him as she'd been doing, it seemed, for a good part of the past hour. Of all those in the room, he disturbed her the most, and it wasn't his overgrown-schoolboy look—round wire-rimmed glasses, slightly shaggy brown hair, corduroy blazer with elbow patches and open-necked plaid shirt—that did it. It was the fact that he was sticking his nose in where it didn't belong. He was a bookseller, not a businessman. He knew nothing about real estate, and though she had to admit that he usually stayed in the background, he wasn't staying in the background today. In his annoyingly laid-back and contemplative way, he was questioning nearly everything she said.

"Three of those sales were in the eights, one in the nines, and another well over the million mark," she told him.

"For properties like ours?" he challenged softly.

She didn't blink. "No. The properties were very different, but the point is that, A, this community is in demand, and, B, there is money around to be spent."

"But by what kinds of people?" he countered in the slow way he had of speaking. "Of course, the superwealthy can spend it, but the superwealthy aren't the ones who'll be moving here. They won't want condo living when they can have ten-acre estates of their own. I thought we were aiming at the middle-aged adult whose children are newly grown and out of the house and who now wants something less demanding. That kind of person doesn't have seven or eight hundred thousand dollars to toss around. He's still feeling his way out from under college tuitions."

"That's one way of looking at it," Nina acknowledged. "Another way is that he now has money to spend that he hasn't had before, precisely because he no longer has those tuitions to shoulder. And he'll be willing to spend it. As he sees it, he's sacrificed a whole lot to raise his family. Now he's ready to do things for himself. That's why the concept of Crosslyn Rise is so perfect. It appeals to the person who is still totally functional, the person who is at the height of his career and isn't about to wait for retirement to pamper himself. He has the money. He'll spend it.''

''What about the shopkeepers?'' John asked.

''What about them?''

''They don't have it to spend. If you set the price of the condos so high, the rental space will have to be accordingly high, which will rule out the majority of the local merchants.''

''Not necessarily.''

''You'll give them special deals?''

''The rental space doesn't have to be that high.''

''It can't be anywhere *near* that high—''

Her eyes flashed. ''Or you won't move in?''

''I won't be *able* to move in,'' he said calmly.

With a glance at his watch, Gideon Lowe, the builder for the project, suddenly sat forward. ''I don't know about you guys, but it's already nine. I'm losin' the best part of my day.'' He slanted a grin from Nina to John. ''How about you two stay on here and bicker for a while, then give us a report on what you decide at the meeting next week?''

Nina didn't appreciate the suggestion, particularly since she suspected that Gideon's rush was more to see his wife than his men. She couldn't blame him, she supposed; he'd been married less than a month and was clearly in love. His wife, Christine, was doing the decorating for Crosslyn Rise. Nina liked her a lot.

Still, this was business. Nina didn't like the idea of staying on to bicker with John Sawyer when she wanted an immediate decision from the group. Keeping her voice as pleasant as possible, given the frustration she was feeling, she said, ''I think this is something for the committee as a whole to decide. Mr. Sawyer is only one man—''

''One man,'' Carter interrupted, ''who is probably in a better position than any of the rest of us to discuss the money issues you're talking about. He's our potential shopkeeper.''

Jessica agreed. ''Maybe Gideon is right. If the two of you toss ideas back and forth and come up with some kind of compromise before next week, you'll save us all some time. We're running a little short now. Carter has an appointment at nine-thirty in Boston, I have one in Cambridge.'' Murmurs of agreement came from around the table, along with the scuffing of chair legs on the highly polished oak floor.

''But I wanted to go to the printer with the brochure,'' Nina said, barely curbing her impatience as she stood along with the others. "I need the price information for that."

Carter snapped his briefcase shut. "We'll make the final decision next week." To John, he said, "You'll meet with Nina?"

Nina looked at John. The fact that he was still seated didn't surprise her at all. The consortium had met no less than a dozen times since its formation, and in all that time, not once had she seen him in a rush. He spoke slowly. He moved slowly. If she didn't know better, she'd have thought that he didn't have a thing in life to do but mosey along when the mood hit and water the geraniums in the window box outside the small Victorian that housed his bookstore.

But she did know better. She knew that John Sawyer ran that bookstore with the help of only one other person, a middle-aged woman named Minna Larken, who manned the till during the hours when John was with his son. Nina also knew that the boy was four, that he had severe sight and hearing problems and that her heart went out to both father and son. But that didn't make her any less impatient. She had work to do, a name to build and money to make, and John Sawyer's slow and easygoing manner made her itchy.

Typically, in response to Carter's query, John was a minute in answering. Finally he said, "I think we could find a time to meet."

Forcing a smile, Nina ruffled the back of her dark boy-short hair and said in a way that she hoped sounded sweet but apologetic, "Wow, this week is a tough one. I have showings one after another today and tomorrow, then a seminar Thursday through Sunday."

"That leaves Monday," Carter said buoyantly. "Monday's perfect." Putting an arm around Jessica's waist, he ushered her from the room.

"Carter?" Nina called, but he didn't answer. "Jessica?"

"I'll talk with you later," Jessica called over her shoulder, then was gone, as were all of the others except John. Feeling thwarted, Nina sent him a helpless look.

With measured movements, he sat back in his chair. "If it's any consolation, I don't like the idea of this any more than you do."

She didn't know whether to be insulted. "Why not?"

"Because you're always in a rush. You make me nervous."

She *was* insulted, which was why she set aside her normal tact and said, "Then we're even, because you're so slow, you make *me* nervous." But it looked as though the group would be expecting some sort of decision from John and her, and she couldn't afford to let them down. There were some important people among them. Impressing important people was one way to guarantee future work.

Hiking her bag from the floor to the table, she fished out her appointment book. "So, when will it be? Do you want to make it sometime next Monday, say late morning?"

John laced his fingers before him. "Next Monday is bad for me. I'll be in Boston all day."

"Okay." She flipped back a page, then several more. The seminar would be morning to night, and draining. No way could she handle a meeting with John on any of those days. "I could squeeze something in between three-thirty and four tomorrow afternoon."

He considered that, then shook his head. "I work then."

"So do I," she said quickly, "but the point is to fudge a little here and there." She ran a glossy fingernail down the page. "My last showing is at seven, but then I have a meeting—" She cut herself off, mumbled, "Forget that," and turned back one more page. "How about later today?"

When he didn't answer, she looked up. Only then did he ask, "How much later?"

She studied her book. "I have appointments through seven. We could meet after that."

He freed one of his hands to rub the side of his nose, under his glasses. When the glasses had stopped bobbing and his fingers were laced again, he said, "No good. I'm with my son then."

"What time does he go to bed?"

"Seven-thirty, eight."

"We could meet then. Can you get a sitter?"

"I can, but I won't. I have work to do in the store."

"But if you don't have a sitter—"

"I live on the second floor of the house. If I'm downstairs in the store and he cries, I can hear it."

She sighed. "Okay. What time will you finish your work?" It occurred to her that she would rather meet with John later that day, even if it meant cutting into the precious little time she had to herself, than having the meeting hanging over her head all week.

"Nine or ten."

"We could meet then. I'll come over."

He eyed her warily. "Isn't that a little late for a meeting?"

"Not if there's no other time, and it looks like there isn't."

His wariness persisted. "Don't you ever stop?"

"Sure. When I go to bed, which is usually sometime around one or two in the morning. So—" she wanted to get it settled and leave "—are we on for nine, or would you rather make it ten?"

"And you work all day long?"

"Seven days a week," she said with pride, because pride was what she felt. Of six brokers in her office, her sales figures had been the highest for three years running. Granted, she didn't have a husband or children to slow her down, but the fact remained that she worked hard.

"When do you relax?"

"I don't need to relax."

"Everyone needs to relax."

"Not me. I get pleasure in working." She held her pen poised over the appointment book. "Nine, or ten?"

He studied her in silence for a minute. "Nine. Any later and I won't be thinking straight. Unlike you, I'm human."

His voice was as unruffled as ever. She searched his face for derision, but given the distance down the table and the fact of the glasses shielding his eyes, she came up short. "I'm human," she said quietly, if a bit defensively. "I just like to make the most of every minute." By way of punctuation, she snapped the appointment book shut, returned it to her bag and hung the bag on her shoulder. "I'll see you at nine," she said on her way out the door.

There was no sound behind her, but then, she hadn't expected there would be. John Sawyer would have needed at least thirty seconds to muster a response, but she'd been gone in fifteen. By the time the next fifteen had passed, her thoughts were three miles down the road in her office.

Within fifteen minutes, after stops at the post office and the dry cleaner, she was there herself. Crown Realty occupied the bottom floor of a small office building on the edge of town. The brainchild of Martin Crown, the firm was an independent one. It had the advantage over some of the larger franchises in its ties to the community; the Crown family had been on the North Shore for generations. Over and above two local restaurants and a shopping mall, the family assets included the weekly newspaper that made its way as far as Boston. In that weekly newspaper were real estate ads that would have cost an arm and a leg elsewhere. The money saved was tallied into profits, and profits were what interested Nina Stone the most.

Nina had plans for the future. She was going to have her own firm, have her own staff, have money in the bank, stability and security. She'd known this for ten years, the first four of which she'd spent in New York. Four years had taught her that as tough as she was, New York was tougher. So she'd moved to the North Shore of Massachusetts, where the living was easier and the market was hot. For six years, she'd doggedly worked her way up in the world of real estate. Now the end was in sight. With one more year like the ones behind her and a respectable return on her investment in Crosslyn Rise, she'd have enough money to go out on her own.

Having a solid name, a successful business and scads of money meant independence, and independence meant the world to Nina.

"Hi, Chrissie," she called with a smile as she strode through the reception area. "Any calls?"

"Pink slips are on your desk," was the receptionist's reply.

Depositing her bag, Nina snatched them up, glanced through even as she rearranged them in order of importance, then settled into her chair and reached for the phone. The first and most urgent call was from a lawyer whose client was to pass papers on a piece of property that morning. At his request, the meeting was put off for an hour, which meant that Nina had to shift two other appointments. Then she returned calls to a seller with a decision on pricing, an accountant trying to negotiate his way into prime business space and a potential buyer who had heard a rumor that the price of the house she was waiting for was about to drop.

Nina was on the phone chasing down that rumor when a young woman appeared at her door. Lee Stockland, with her frizzy brown hair, her conservative skirts, blouses and single strand of pearls, and the ten extra pounds she'd been trying to lose forever, was a colleague. She was also a good friend, one of the best Nina had. Their personalities complemented each other.

Nina waved her in, then held up a finger and spoke into the phone. "Charlie Dunn, please."

"I'm sorry, Mr. Dunn's not in the office."

"This is Nina Stone at Crown Realty. It's urgent that I speak with him." She glanced at her watch. "I'll be here for another forty-five minutes. If he comes in during that time, would you have him call me?"

"Certainly."

"Thanks." She hung up and turned to Lee. "Maisie Stewart heard that 23 Hammond dropped to eight-fifty." She swiveled in her chair. "It wasn't in the computer last night. Have you seen anything today?"

"Nope."

Nina brought up the proper screen, punched in the listing she wanted and saw that Lee was right. She sat back in her chair. "If word of mouth beat this computer, I'll be furious. Charlie knows the rules. Any change is supposed to be entered here."

"Charlie isn't exactly a computer person."

Nina tossed a glance skyward. "Do tell. He claims you can't teach an old dog new tricks, but I don't agree with that for a minute. What you make up your mind to do, you do." With barely a breath, she said, "So, what did the Millers think of the house?"

Lee took the chair by Nina's desk. "They weren't thrilled to see me rather than you, but I think they liked it. Especially her, and that's what counts."

Nina nodded. "I know him. He'll see every little flaw and be tallying up how much it will cost to fix each one. Then he'll balance the amount against the price of the house and go back and forth, back and forth until someone else's bid is accepted and it's too late. Then we'll start right back at the beginning again." She sighed, suddenly sheepish, and fiddled with her earring. "Thanks, Lee. Jason is a pain in the butt. I really appreciate your taking them out."

"You appreciate it?" Lee laughed. "I'm the one who appreciates it. If it weren't for the clients you give me, I'd be twiddling my thumbs all day."

Nina couldn't argue with that. As brokers went, Lee was an able technician. Given a client, she did fine. But she didn't know the meaning of the word 'hustle,' and hustling was the name of the game. Nina hustled. When she wasn't showing a potential buyer a piece of property, she was meeting with a seller, or phoning potential others with offers of appraisals, or organizing mailings to keep her name and her business in the forefront of the community's mind.

Lee didn't have the drive for that, and while once upon a time Nina had scolded her friend, she didn't any longer. Lee was perfectly happy to work less, to earn less, in essence to serve as Nina's assistant, and Nina was grateful for the help. "You're a lifesaver," she said. "The Millers insisted on going early this morning. I couldn't be two places at once."

"Speaking of which," she gave a pointed look at Nina's bright red linen dress, "I take it that's your power outfit. How did it go at the bank?"

Nina's mouth drew down at the corners. "Don't ask."

"Not good?"

"Slow. Sl-ow." She began to pull folders from her bag. "Let me tell you, working with so many people is a real hassle. To get one decision made is a major ordeal."

"Did they like the brochure?"

"I think so, but I never got a final judgment on it, because they got hung up discussing the pricing of the units."

"What did they decide on that?"

Nina's phone buzzed. *"Nothing,"* she cried, letting her frustration show. "They want me to meet with this one guy—" She picked up the phone. "Nina Stone."

"Ms. Stone, my name is Carl Anderson. I was given your name by Peter Serretti, who worked with you on your new computer system."

Nina remembered Peter clearly. He had indeed worked with her, far more closely than she had wanted. Long after she learned to operate the system, she'd been plagued by phone calls from Peter asking her out. So now his friend was calling. She was immediately on her guard.

"Of course, I remember Mr. Serretti. What can I do for you, Mr. Anderson?"

"I'm actually calling from New York. My wife and I are both in education. We'll be moving to Boston in August. We were thinking of buying something on the North Shore. Pete said you were the one to talk with."

Nina felt an immediate lightening of her mood. "I'm sure I am," she said with a smile for Lee, who had settled into her chair to wait. "What kind of place are you looking for?"

"A condo. Two to three bedrooms. We have no children, but have a dog and two cars."

Nina was making notes. "Price range?"

"Two-fifty, three hundred tops." He rushed on apologetically. "We just can't handle anything more than that. When we visited Pete, we were impressed with the North Shore. If I'm totally out of my league, tell me."

"You're not, not at all." Crosslyn Rise was out of the question, both in terms of price and availability, but there were other options. "There's an older three-bedroom condo on the market for two-ninety-five, and several more updated two-bedrooms in the same range. But there's a new complex that you should probably see. It's in Salem, near the harbor, and it's beautiful. About half of the units have been sold, but there are still some wonderful three-bedroom ones that would fall within your range." She described the units, at times reading directly from the promotional packet that Lee had smoothly slipped her.

Carl seemed pleased. "We thought we'd drive up Friday and spend Saturday and Sunday looking. Would that be all right?"

"Uh, unfortunately, I'll be at a seminar all weekend—" her eyes met Lee's "—but one of my associates could certainly show you as much as you'd like to see." She frowned when, with a helpless look, Lee gave a quick shake of her head.

"Pete recommended you," Carl insisted. "He said you knew what you were talking about. I had an awful time with a broker here when we bought the place we're in now. She messed up the Purchase and Sales agreement, and we nearly lost the place."

Nina loved hearing stories like that. "I don't mess up Purchase and Sales agreements."

"That's what Pete said."

"Is this weekend the only time you can come?"

"This is the only weekend my wife and I are both free."

"Then let me suggest this. I'll go through all the listings, come up with everything I think might be worth seeing, and my associate will do the showing." Lee was still looking helpless. "You and I can talk first thing Monday morning when I'm back in the office. I'll be able to handle things from there."

Carl Anderson seemed satisfied with that. After taking note of his address and phone number, plus additional information regarding what he wanted, Nina hung up the phone. Her eyes quickly met Lee's. "Problem?"

"I can't work this weekend," Lee said timidly.

"Oh, Lee. You said you could. I've been counting on you to cover for me while I'm away."

"I can for Thursday and Friday, but—" she hesitated for a split second before blurting out "—Tom wants to go to the Vineyard. I've never been to the Vineyard. He's already made reservations for the ferry and the hotel, and he's talking about lying on the beach and browsing through the shops and eating at terrific restaurants—" She caught her breath and let out a soft, "How could I say no?"

Nina felt a surge of frustration that had nothing to do with work. "You can't. You never can, to Tom. But it's always last minute to a dinner or a movie or a weekend away. Why doesn't he call sooner?"

"He just doesn't plan his life that way. He likes spontaneity."

"Baloney. He just can't make any kind of commitment. He goes here, goes there, calls you when he gets the urge. He uses you, Lee."

"But I like him."

"You're too good for him."

"I'm not," Lee said flatly. "I'm twenty-eight, and I've never been married. I'm not cute like you, or petite, or blue eyed. I can't wear clothes like you do or polish my nails like you do. I'm not aggressive, and I'll never earn much money, so I'm not much of a bargain. But Tom is good to me."

Nina died a little inside. Each time she heard a woman use those words, no matter how innocent they were, she thought of her mother. So many times Maria Stone had said the same—*but he's good to me*—and for all the men who'd been "good" to her, she had ended up with nothing. Nina ached at the thought of that happening again, particularly to someone she cared about, like Lee.

Coming forward on the desk, she said with force, "You're not a lost cause, Lee. You're attractive and smart and warm. You're the one who taught me how to cook, and arrange flowers, and save bundles by shopping in the stores *you* found. You have lots to offer a man, lots more than me. You don't need to stoop to the level of a Tom Brody. If you want male company, there are plenty of other men around."

"Fine for you to say. You attract them like flies, then you swat them away."

"I do not."

"You're not interested in a relationship."

"I'm not interested in marriage, and I'm not interested in being kept, but I date. If an interesting guy comes along and asks me to dinner, I go."

"When you have time."

"Is there anything wrong with that?" Nina asked more gently. They'd had the discussion before. "Work means a lot to me. It's my future. At this point in my life, the investment I make in it means a whole lot more than the investment I might make in a man." Under her breath, she muttered, "Heaven only knows the return stands to be better."

Lee heard the low muttering and sighed. "Speak for yourself. Those of us who aren't so independent are looking all over for Mr. Right, but I think all the Mr. Rights are taken."

"Just wait. Give all those Mr. Rights a chance to divorce their first wives, then they'll be yours for the taking. I'm told they're far better husbands the second time around."

"I want Tom first. I think I have a chance with him, Nina. I really do."

But Nina knew more about Tom Brody than she let on. She had seen him in action against her boss years before, when he'd tried to renege on an agreement that was signed and sealed. "He's not right for you, Lee. He's a huckster with his eye out for the fast lane. When he hooks onto it, he'll be long gone. What you need is someone softer, slower, less driven." The image that popped unbidden into her mind made her snort. "You need a guy like John Sawyer."

"Who's John Sawyer?"

"A member of my consortium. He's invested in the Rise, but he's not a businessman, at least, not in the strictest sense of the word. He sells books. He's a thinker."

Lee arched an interested brow. "Married?"

"His wife died. He has a little boy who's four."

Lee's interest waned. "Oh. I'm no good with kids. I don't think I want to get into that. Forget John Sawyer."

Nina's thoughts flipped back to the meeting earlier that morning, then ahead to the one to come later that night. "I wish I could. The man might prove to be the biggest thorn in my side since Throckmorton Malone." Throckmorton Malone was a perennial house-shopper. He found a house he liked, put down a deposit, started bickering with either the builder or the owner or the owner's agent about the smallest, most insignificant details, then pulled out of the deal after handfuls of others who might have been interested had been turned away.

"No one could be that big a thorn."

Nina sighed. "Maybe. Still, this one could give me gray hair. He thinks we're pricing the units too high. He thinks he knows the market. Worst of all, the rest of the group thinks he knows what he's talking about, so they're making me meet separately with him to try to come to some sort of compromise."

"That's not so bad. You can convince him to see things your way."

"Yeah, but he's so—" she made a face as she searched for the word, finally exploding into a scornful "—*blah*. He's so calm and casual and unhurried about everything. He has all the time in the world to mull over every little thing. What ought to take five minutes will take fifty with him. Just looking at him frustrates me."

Lee showed a hint of renewed interest. "He's good-looking?"

"Not to *my* way of thinking. He's too bookish. I mean, we're talking thin and pale. Drab. Boring."

"Is he tall?"

Nina had to think about that, then think some more. "I don't know. I don't think so. Funny, I've never really noticed. He's that kind of guy, blink and you miss him." She frowned. "Mostly when I see him he's sitting down. Everyone else get up to leave, he stays in his seat. He doesn't move quickly. Ever." She sighed. "And I have to meet with him at nine o'clock tonight. Who knows how long he'll drag out the meeting." She grimaced. "Could be he'll put me to sleep."

"That'd be novel." They both knew Nina rarely slept. She had too much energy to slow down for long.

With a glance at her watch, Nina was out of her chair. "I'm meeting with the Selwyns at the Traynor cape in five minutes. Gotta run."

"About this weekend—" Lee began.

"Not to worry," Nina assured her. Taking a file from the corner of the desk, she slipped it into her bag. "I'll get someone else to cover."

"I'm really sorry. I hate letting you down."

Turning to her, Nina said in earnest, "You're not letting me down, at least not about filling in here. You have a right to a life, and if you haven't been to the Vineyard, you *have* to go. I just wish you weren't going with Tom.''

''I'll be fine. Really.''

''Famous last words,'' Nina said softly, gave Lee a last pleading look, then murmured, ''Gotta run.''

2

Nina's day was busy enough to prevent her from giving the impending meeting with John much thought until she returned to her office at seven, with all other appointments behind her and two hours to fill before nine. Filling them wasn't the problem. She had more than enough paperwork to do, and if she finished that, there were phone calls to make. But the urgency wasn't the same as it would have been at the height of the workday. So her mind wandered.

She thought about Crosslyn Rise, and how pretty the first of the units, nestled in among trees at the duck pond, were beginning to look. She thought about the brochure she had so painstakingly put together with the artist who'd drawn pictures of the Rise, and the printer, and the fact that she felt it should already be in circulation. She thought about the pricing, the arguments both ways, her own conviction and John's. She thought about his slow, slow way of thinking and talking and her own preference for working more quickly. The more she thought about those things, the more frustrated she grew. By the time she finally got into her car and drove to The Leaf Turner, she was spoiling for a fight.

The house stood close to the center of town and was a small white Victorian, set in relief against the night by the glow of a street lamp that stood nearby. The second floor was dark, the first floor lit. Walking to the front door as though it were the middle of the day and she were out shopping for a book, she turned the brass knob and let herself in.

"Hello?" she called, closing the door behind her. When there was no response, she called again, in a more commanding tone this time, "Hello?"

"Be right there," came a distant voice, followed after a time by the leisurely pad of rubber-soled shoes on the back stairs, which was followed, in turn, by John's appearance. At least, it was the appearance of someone she assumed to be John. His face was partially hidden behind the carton he was carrying, a carton that looked to be heavy from the way he carefully lowered it to the ground. When he straightened, he looked her in the eye and said in that slow, quiet way of his, "You're right on time."

For a minute, she didn't speak. The man who had emerged from behind the carton had John's voice and features, but that was the extent of the similarity to the man with whom she served on the Crosslyn Rise consortium. This John's face wasn't pale, but flushed with activity and shadowed with a distinct end-of-the-day beard. This John's face slightly shaggy brown hair was clustered into spikes on his forehead, which glistened with sweat. As she watched, he mopped a trickle of that sweat from his temple, displaying a forearm that was leanly muscular and spattered with hair.

"I aim to please," she said lightly, but she couldn't take her eyes from him.

This time he ran the back of his hand over his upper lip. "I'm short of space up here, so the courier service puts deliveries in the basement. I've been carting books around, trying to get things organized. If I'd realized I was going to build up a sweat, I'd have showered and changed."

"No problem." She was still wearing the red dress she'd had on since dawn. "It's the end of the day. Besides," she added in an attempt to set the tone for their meeting, "we won't be long enough to make it worth the effort. I'm sure we can hash out our differences in no time."

He responded to the suggestion with a nonchalant twitch of his lips. "I don't know about that, but you're welcome to try." Leaning over, he slit the carton open with a single-edged blade, set the blade back on the counter and pulled the flaps up. "Go ahead. I'm listening."

He was wearing the same plaid shirt he'd been wearing that morning, only he'd paired it with jeans. They fit his lean hips so familiarly that his shoulders looked broad. She hadn't expected that. She had thought he'd be spindly under his corduroy blazer. She had also thought he'd be weak, but from the looks of the carton he'd been carrying—and the fact that, though sweaty, he wasn't winded in the least—she'd been wrong. She could see strength in his forearms, in his shoulders, in the denim-sheathed legs that straddled the box as he began to unload it.

Straightening with an armful of books, he looked at her. "I'm listening," he said again, and the mild derision in his eyes wasn't to be mistaken. Only when she saw it, though, did she realize something else.

"You're not wearing your glasses." She'd never seen him without them before, had simply assumed they were a constant.

"They get in the way sometimes."

"Don't you need them to see?"

"When I'm reading. Or driving. Or thinking of doing either." Turning away, he hunkered down by a low riser near the cash register and began to stack the books, turning one right, then one left, alternating until his arms were empty. When he was finished and stood, she realized yet another thing. Though he wasn't tall by the standards of men like

Carter Malloy and Gideon Lowe, in relation to her own five foot two, he was long. She guessed him to be just shy of six feet.

"Something wrong?" he asked with maddening calm.

She felt a warm flush creep up from her neck, all the more disconcerting because she wasn't normally one to blush. Rarely did things take her by surprise the way John Sawyer's physical presence had. "No, no. It's just that you look so different. I'm not sure that if I'd walked in here cold, I'd have connected you with the man at the bank."

He considered that for a minute, then shrugged. "Different circumstances. That's all. I'm still the same guy you're gonna have to give a slew of damn good reasons to before I'll agree that those condominiums should be priced out of sight."

His words stiffened her spine, counteracting any softening she'd felt. "Out of sight? A million dollars would be out of sight. Not six hundred thousand."

"You were arguing for six-fifty to seven-fifty."

"The local market supports that."

He held her gaze without a blink. "Are there any other condominiums—not single-family homes, but condominiums—selling in that range around here?"

She didn't have to check her listings. At any given time, she knew the market like the back of her hand. "No, but only because there haven't been any built that would qualify. Crosslyn Rise does. It's spectacular."

He rubbed the bridge of his nose. "Is that reason to price it so high that no one will be able to enjoy it?"

"Plenty of people will be able to enjoy it."

"Not at that price, and if the condos don't sell, you can kiss the shops goodbye. No merchant—least of all me—wants to open up in a ghost town."

"It wouldn't be a ghost town," Nina scoffed, but softly. He'd raised a good point, namely the connection between sales of the condos and success in renting out the shops. Granted, the shops would hardly be relying on the residents alone; none would survive without the patronage of the public, for which purpose public access had been carefully planned. But the public wouldn't be coming to shop if the rest of the place looked deserted.

Returning to his carton, John bent over and filled his arms a second time with books.

Helpless to look away, Nina noticed the way his dark hair fell across his neck, the way the plaid shirt—darkened in random dots of sweat— stretched across his back, the way his fingers closed around book after book. Those fingers were long and blunt tipped. Rather than being delicate, as she'd have assumed a bookworm's to be, they looked as sturdy as the rest of him. She had the sudden impression that his laid-back manner hid a forbidding toughness. If so, she could be in for trouble.

Wanting to avoid that, she gave a little. "Okay. We could set a limit at seven. The smaller units could be in the low sixes, the larger ones closer to six-ninety-five."

John gathered books into his arms until he couldn't hold any more, then moved to the riser and arranged a second pile beside the first.

"John?"

"You're still a hundred grand too high. There's no need to price gouge."

"There's need to make a profit. That's the name of the game."

"Maybe your game," he said complacently, and returned for a third load.

"And not yours? I don't believe that for a minute. You put your own good money into the consortium, and from what I hear, there isn't a whole lot more where that came from."

One book was stacked on another. He neither broke the rhythm nor looked up from his work.

"The only reason," she said slowly, hoping that maybe a man who spoke slowly needed to hear slowly in order to comprehend, "why a man stakes the bulk of his savings on a single project is if he feels he has a solid chance of getting a good return."

John straightened with the last of the books. "Exactly."

She waited for him to go on. When he simply turned and began arranging a third pile by the first two, she moved closer. "The higher we price these units, the greater your return will be. The difference of a hundred-thousand over two dozen condos is two-and-a-half million dollars. That spells a substantial increase in our profit." She frowned. "My Lord, how many of those books do you have?"

"Twenty-five."

"And you really think you'll sell twenty-five at $22.95 a pop? I could believe five, maybe ten or twelve in a community this size. But twenty-five? How can you be so optimistic about books and so pessimistic about condos?"

Taking his time, he finished stacking the books. When he was done, he stood, wiped his palms on his thighs and gave her a patronizing look. "I can be lavish with books because the publishers make it well worth my while. When they're trying to push something, they offer generous deals and incentives. They're pushing this book like there's no tomorrow."

"It stinks."

He shrugged. "Sorry, but that's the way the publishing world works."

"Not the deals. The book. It stinks."

"You've read it?"

For the first time, she had caught him off guard, if the surprised arch of one brow meant something. "Yes, I've read it."

"When? I thought you worked all the time."

"I never said that."

"Sure sounded it from the way you were standing at the bank this morning struggling to squeeze in a single meeting with me."

"This week's worse than most because of the seminar. It's four intensive days—"

"Of what?"

"Classes on commercial real estate transactions. In the past year or two, I've been doing more with stores and office buildings. I've been wanting to take this seminar for six months, but this is the first time it's been offered at a time and place I could handle."

He gave her a long look. "Funny, I assumed you could handle most anything."

"I can," she said without flinching. "But it's a matter of priorities. Let me rephrase what I said. This is the first time the seminar's been offered at a time and place that work into my schedule without totally screwing up everything else."

He gave that brief thought. "So, when do you read?"

"At night. Late."

"When you can't sleep because you've got yourself wound up about everything you should be doing but can't because no one else is awake to do it with you?"

She was about to summarily deny the suggestion when she realized how right he was. Not that she intended to tell him that. "When I can't sleep, it's because I'm not tired."

The look in his eye was doubtful, but he let her claim ride. "And you didn't like this book?"

"I thought it was self-indulgent. Just because an author writes one book that wins the Pulitzer Prize doesn't mean that everything else that author writes is gold, but you'd have thought that from the hype the book was given. So I blame the author for her arrogance and the publisher for his cowardice."

"Cowardice?"

"In not standing up to the author and sending her back to rewrite it. The book *stinks*."

John pondered that. After a minute, he said, "It'll make the bestselling lists."

"Probably."

"And I won't lose a cent."

Given deals and incentives and bestselling status, he was probably right, she mused.

"Out of curiosity, if nothing else," he went on leisurely, "people will buy the book. No one will be broken by $22.95. Readers may be angry, like you are. They may feel gypped. They may even tell their friends not to buy the book, and I may, indeed, have two of these stacks standing here three months from today, just as they are now. But one disappointing book won't hurt my business." His eyes took on a meaningful cast. "At Crosslyn Rise, on the other hand, a thirty-three percent sell rate will hurt and hurt bad."

Nina shook her head. "The analogy's no good. You're comparing apples and oranges—sweet apples and moldy oranges, at that. Crosslyn Rise is quality. This book isn't. No one who buys into the Rise will ever say that it wasn't worth the money. In fact, some of the sales will probably come about by word of mouth, people who buy and are so excited that they spread the excitement."

"People who are stretched tight financially may not be able to feel much excitement."

"People who are stretched tight financially have no business even looking at the Rise, much less buying into it."

John's eyes hardened. "You're tough."

"I'm realistic. The Rise isn't for first-time home owners. It isn't for twenty-five-year-olds who've just gotten married and have twenty thousand to put down on a mortgage that they'll then pay off each month by painstakingly pooling their salaries." She held up a hand, lest he think her a snob. "Listen, I have properties that are less expensive, and I have clients who are looking for that. But those clients aren't looking for Crosslyn Rise, or if they are, they should be awakened to the rude realities of life."

"Which are?"

"Everything costs. *Everything.* If you don't have money in your pocket to pay for what you want or think you need, the cost comes out of your hide and is ten times more painful."

Her words hung in the air. Even more, her tone. It was hard and angry, everything Nina was accused of being from time to time by one detractor or another whose path she crossed. Now she held her breath, waiting for John Sawyer to accuse her of the same.

He didn't say a word. Instead, after studying her for what seemed an infinite stretch, he turned away, bent and swept up the empty carton, and forcibly collapsed it as he walked from the room.

She waited for him to return. Gnawing on her lower lip, she kept her eyes on the door through which he'd gone. His footsteps told her that he'd taken a flight of stairs, leading her to guess he'd returned to the basement, but all was still. She shifted her bag from the left shoulder to the right, shifted her weight from the right foot to the left, finally glanced at her watch. It was after nine-thirty, getting later and later, and they hadn't reached any sort of agreement on Crosslyn Rise.

"John?" she called. When the only thing to greet her was silence, she let out a frustrated sigh. Wasted time drove her nuts, and this meeting spelled wasted time in capital letters. She and John Sawyer had some very basic differences. He was relaxed and easygoing, she was driven. Neither of them was going to change—not that change was called for. All that was called for was some sort of compromise recommendation for the pricing of the units at Crosslyn Rise.

At the sound of a quiet creaking over her head, she looked up. He must have gone upstairs, she realized, probably to check on his son, and she couldn't begrudge him that. It would have been nice if he'd said something, formally excused himself, told her he'd be back shortly, rather than just walking out. She hadn't associated relaxed and easygoing with rude before, nor had she associated rude with John. Slow, mulish, even naive, perhaps. But not rude.

He didn't like her. That explained it, she guessed. The hardness that came to his eyes from time to time when he looked at her spoke clearly of disapproval, which was all the more reason why she should finish her business and leave. She wasn't a glutton for punishment. If he didn't like her, fine. All they needed was to come up with a simple decision, and she'd be gone.

The creaking came again from upstairs, this time more steadily. Soon after, she heard footsteps on the back stairs, but they went on longer than they should have. It didn't take a genius to figure out that he'd gone on down to the basement, and in the wake of that realization, she realized something else. She didn't like John Sawyer any more than he liked her.

Annoyed, she stalked toward the back room, turned a corner until she saw the stairs and called out an impatient, "I haven't got much time, John. Do you think you could come up here and talk this out with me?"

"Be right up," he called nonchalantly. She could well have been the cleaning lady, for all the attention he was giving her.

Spinning on her heel, she returned to the main room of the shop, where, for the first time, she took a good look around. The bookstore took up the entire front portion of the house. Working around tall windows, a fireplace that looked frequently used, a sofa and several large wing chairs, bookshelves meandered through what had once been a living room, parlor and dining room. The overall space wasn't huge, as stores went, but what it lacked in size, it made up for in coziness.

Antsy, Nina began to prowl. Passing a section of reference books, she wandered past one of history books, another of fiction classics, another of humor. As she wandered, her pace slowed. That always happened to her in bookstores and libraries. Whether she intended to or not, she relaxed. Books pacified her. They were nonjudgmental, nondemanding. They could be picked up or put down with no strings attached, and they were always there.

At the shelves holding recent biographies, she stopped, lifted one, read the inside of its jacket. She liked biographies, as was evidenced by the pile of them on her night shelf, waiting to be read. Tempted by this one but knowing that she didn't dare buy another until she'd made some headway with the pile, she replaced the book and moved toward the front of the store. At the cookbooks, she stopped. One, standing face front, caught her eye, a collection of recipes put together by a local women's group. She took it from the shelf and began to thumb through.

"Don't tell me you cook."

Nina's head flew up to find John's expression as wry as his voice, but neither of those things held her attention for long. What struck her most was the surprise she felt—again—at the way he looked. Tall, strong, strangely masculine. She hadn't expected any of those things, much less her awareness of them. The relaxation she'd felt moments before vanished. "Yes, I cook."

He turned to put down another carton where the first had been. Looking back at her, his eyes were shuttered. "You work, you read, you cook. Any other surprises?"

At least they were even, she mused. He surprised her in not being a total wimp, she surprised him in being a businesswoman who cooked. She still didn't understand his dislike for her, but there was no point in pursuing it. Their personal feelings for each other didn't matter. If Crosslyn Rise was the only thing they had in common, so be it.

"It's getting late," she said with studied patience as she watched him bend in half and slash the new carton open. "Do you think you could take a break from that for a few minutes so that we can settle the matter of pricing?"

Straightening slowly, he slipped the blade back onto the counter. In measured cadence, he said, "I've been listening to everything you've said. You're not swaying me."

"Maybe you're not listening with an open mind."

He gave the possibility consideration before claiming, "My mind is always open."

"Okay," she said in an upbeat, "why don't you run *your* arguments by me again?"

He arched a casual brow. "Would it do any good?"

"It might."

After studying her for several long moments, he bent to open the box and began to unload books.

"John," she protested.

"I'm getting my thoughts in order. Give me a minute."

Tempering her impatience, she gave him that. During its course, he carried half a dozen books to one shelf, half a dozen to another. She was beginning to wonder whether he was deliberately dragging out the time, when he came to face her. His skin wore the remnants of a moist sheen, but his eyes were clear.

"I believe," he said slowly and quietly, "that we should keep the pricing down on those units because, one—" he held up a long, straight finger "—we stand a good chance of selling out that way, which in turn will make the shops more appealing both to shopkeepers and to the general public—" he held up a second finger, "two, we'd attract a better balance of buyers, and three, the profit will be more than respectable." He dropped his hand and turned back to the box of books.

"Is that it?"

"That's enough." Hunkering down, he started to fill his arms. "Didn't I win you over?"

"Not quite."

With a sidelong glance, he shot back her own words. "Maybe you're not listening with an open mind."

"I always have an open mind."

"If that were true, you'd have already given in. My arguments make sense."

"Mine are stronger."

"Yours have to do with profit, and profit alone."

She wanted to pull her hair out. "But profit is what this project is *about*!"

"Right, and you could blow it all by getting greedy. The entire project will be jeopardized if we overprice the goods."

"Okay," she said with a sigh, "if the units aren't snapped up in six months or so, we can reduce the price."

He shook his head. "That smacks of defeat, and it'll taint the whole thing. The longer those units sit empty, the worse it'll be." He sighed patiently. "Look, the duck pond will be completed six months before the pine grove, and the meadow six months after that. If we don't sell the duck pond first thing, there's no way the pine grove will sell, and if the pine grove doesn't sell, forget the meadow."

"Okay," Nina said, trying her absolute best to be reasonable, "how about this. How about we price the duck pond in the sixes, then move up into the sevens as we move toward the meadow."

"How about we price the duck pond in the fives, then move up into the sixes as we move toward the meadow." He reached for more books.

Bowing her head, she squeezed her eyes shut and pressed two fingers to her brow. "This isn't going to work."

"It'd work just fine if you'd listen to reason."

Her head came up, eyes open and beseeching. "But I'm the *expert* here. Pricing property is what I do for a living! If I was off the wall, I wouldn't be as successful as I am!"

Arms filled with books, John straightened and gave her a look that was shockingly intense. "You're successful because you push with such force and persistence that you wear people down. But you're barking up the wrong tree when it comes to me. I'm not the type to be worn down."

Nina stared up at him, stunned by the vehemence of his attack and its personal nature. She couldn't believe what she'd heard, couldn't believe the anger that had come from the quiet, contemplative, laid-back bookseller. Swallowing something strangely akin to hurt, she said, "Why do you dislike me? Have I done something to offend you?"

"Your whole *manner* offends me."

"Because I work hard and earn good money? Because I know what I want and fight for it? Or because I'm a woman?" She took a step back. "That's it, isn't it? I'm a strong woman, and you feel threatened."

"I'm not—"

"Don't feel singled out or anything," she said quickly, and held up a hand. "You're not alone. I threaten lots of men. I make them feel like they're not fast enough or smart enough or insightful enough. They want to put me in my place, but they can't."

John's look was disparaging. "I wouldn't presume to know where your place is, and I doubt you do, either. You want to wear the pants in the family, but you're so busy trying to get them to fit that you blow the family part. How old are you?"

"It doesn't matter."

"It does. You should be home having babies."

She stared at him in disbelief, opened her mouth, closed it again. Finally she sputtered out, "Who are you to tell me something like that? You don't know anything about me. You have no idea what makes me tick. And even if you did, these are the 1990s. Women don't stay home and have babies—"

"Some do."

"And some work. It's a personal choice, one for *me* to make."

"Clearly you have."

"Clearly, and if you were any kind of a man, you'd respect that choice." She was suddenly feeling tired. Hitching her bag to the other shoulder, she headed for the door. "I think we've reached a stalemate here. I'll call Carter tomorrow and let him know. There's no way you and I can work together. No way."

"Chicken."

She stopped in her tracks, then turned. "No. I'm being practical. My standing here arguing with you is an exercise in futility. My arguments won't change your mind, any more than yours will change mind. We're deadlocked. So we'll have to do what I wanted to do from the start, let the whole committee hear the arguments and take a vote. And we'll chalk up this time to—to—client development."

"What does that mean?"

"That some day when you're selling this house and you want the bitchiest broker to get the most money for you, you'll give me a call." With that, she tugged open the door and swept out into the night. She was down the wood steps and well along the front walk before she heard her name called.

"Nina?"

"Save it for the bank," she called back without turning, raised a hand in a wave of dismissal and rounded her car.

"Wait, Nina."

She looked up to find John eyeing her over the top of the car.

"Maybe we should try again," he said.

"It'd be a waste of time." Opening the door, she slid behind the wheel.

He leaned down to talk through the open window. "Why don't you give me some time to think."

With one hand on the wheel and one on the ignition, she said, "Buddy, you could think till the cows come home and you wouldn't see things my way."

"Maybe we could meet halfway, you'd come down a little, I'd come up."

That was the only thing that made any sense, she knew, but the idea of meeting John Sawyer again didn't appeal to her in the least. "Why don't you suggest that next Tuesday at the meeting?"

"They're expecting a recommendation from us."

"We can recommend that the consortium take a vote." She started the car.

"Look," he said, raising his voice so that its even timbre carried over the hum of the engine. "It doesn't matter so much to me if they think we couldn't come to some kind of consensus. Hell, I'm just a bookseller who's trying to make a little money by investing in real estate on the side. But you're supposed to be the master of the hard sell. I'd think you'd want to impress those guys at that table in any way you can."

She did. No doubt about it. Staring out the front window into the darkness with both hands on the wheel, she said, "If we can agree right now to go with figures halfway between what you want and what I want, we've got our consensus."

"I think we ought to discuss it."

"That's the only solution."

"I still think we ought to discuss it."

Earlier, she had thought him mulish. She thought it again now. John had to be one of the most stubborn men she had met in years. Turning her head only enough to meet his gaze, she said, "That sounds just fine, only there's one small problem. We went through the whole week this morning, and the only time we both had free was tonight. Now tonight's gone. So what do you suggest?"

"We find another time."

She shook her head. "Bad week."

"Then the weekend."

"I told you. I have a seminar. It runs from nine to five every day, and I'll have to allow an hour before and after for travel."

"So you'll be home by six. We can meet then."

Again she shook her head. "I'm moving a week from Monday. Every night after the seminar is reserved for packing. I have to get it done."

"I'll help you pack."

Like hell he would. Eyes forward, she set her chin. "No."

"Why not?"

"Because I can do it myself."

"Of course you can," he said indulgently. "But I can help. I'm not the scrawny weakling you imagined I'd be."

Her eyes shot to his. "I never said—"

"But you thought. So you were wrong. And I can help you pack."

"You can *not*. I don't want your help. I don't *need* your help."

He was silent then, his expression a mystery in the dark. Finally, sounding even-tempered and calm, the John she'd known from the bank, he said, "Tuesday morning before the meeting. I'll meet you at Easy Over at seven-thirty. We'll talk over breakfast." Before she could say a word, he gave the side of the car a tap and was off.

"John!" she called after him, but she might just as well have saved her breath. He didn't move quickly, but he moved smoothly, covering the distance to the house and disappearing inside without a glance behind.

3

Nina prepared carefully for breakfast Tuesday morning. After wading through her wardrobe and discarding anything red, purple or lime green, she chose a beige suit that was as reserved as anything she owned. That wasn't to call it conservative. The blazer was nipped in at the waist over a skirt that was short and scalloped, exposing a whisper of thigh with every move. In an attempt to tone that down, she left the matching, low-cut gauzy blouse in her closet in favor of a higher necked silk. With a single strand of pearls around her neck and pearl studs at her ears, she felt she looked as traditional as it was possible for Nina Stone to look.

Her goal was to impress John Sawyer—not in any sort of romantic way, because she *certainly* didn't think of John that way, but in a business way. Normally she dressed in the bright, chic, slightly funky style that had become her trademark; clients came to her because they saw someone who was one step ahead of the eight ball. Somehow she didn't think that was where John Sawyer wanted to be, but she wanted him to be on her side when it came to marketing Crosslyn Rise, so it behooved her to impress him.

She arrived at Easy Over, a light-breakfast and lunch place not far from the bank, at seven-thirty on the dot. When she saw no sign of John, she took a table, ordered a pot of coffee and waited. He arrived five minutes later, wearing loose khaki pants, another plaid shirt, a slouchy brown blazer and glasses. Looking slightly sleepy, he slid into a chair.

"Sorry," he murmured. "Had a little trouble getting out." His eyes fastened on the coffeepot. "Is that fresh?"

She nodded, lifted the pot and filled the cup waiting by his place. "Anything serious?"

"Nah." He took a sip of coffee, then a second before setting down the cup, sitting back in his chair and catching her eye. "That's better. I didn't have time for any at home."

"What happened?"

He took another drink, a more leisurely one this time as though he were just then settling in to being his normal slow self. "My son isn't wild about the sitter. He didn't want me to leave."

"I thought kids nowadays were used to sitters. Don't you have one every day?"

"He likes the afternoon ones. They're high school girls with lots of energy and enthusiasm. For morning meetings at the bank, I have to use someone else. She's kind enough, and responsible, but she doesn't relate so well with him."

"He must be very attached to you."

"I'm all he has."

Nina thought about the boy's mother, wondered how she had died and whether the child remembered her. She wasn't about to ask John any of those things, though. They weren't her business.

"What'll it be, folks?" the waitress asked, flipping the paper on her pad and readying a pen.

Nina didn't have to look at the menu. She'd been at Easy Over enough to know what was good. "I'll have Ronnie's Special. Make the eggs soft-boiled, the bacon crisp and the wheat toast dry. And I'll have a large TJ with that." She watched the waitress note everything, then turned expectant eyes toward John.

He hadn't opened the menu either, but he seemed thoughtful for a minute. "Make that two," he paused, "only I want my eggs scrambled, my sausages moist and my rye toast with butter."

"Juice?" the waitress prompted.

"OJ. Large." Still writing, the waitress ambled off. John turned placid eyes on Nina. "For a little girl, you eat a whole lotta food."

"I have to. I rarely make it to lunch, and dinner won't be until eight or nine tonight."

"That's not healthy."

She shrugged. "Can't be helped. I'm into my busiest season. If I don't make the most of it, it'll be gone, and then where will I be?" With the reminder, she pulled up the folder that had been waiting against the leg of her chair, set it down in front of her and opened it up. "I spent awhile yesterday working with figures." She lifted the first sheet from the folder, but before she could pass it to him, he held up a hand.

"Not yet."

"Not yet?"

"Not before breakfast." He settled more comfortably in his seat. "I can't deal with business before breakfast."

"But this is a *business* breakfast. That means we eat while we talk."

His gaze touched the clean white Formica surface before him. "We haven't got any food yet. Let's wait on business."

Nina wanted to say that if they did that, they would not only be wasting good time, but if she had to go past Plan A to Plan B or C, they might well run *out* of time before they reached an agreement. She wanted to say that first thing in the morning was the *best* time to discuss business, while they were the freshest. She wanted to say that they were due at the bank at eight-thirty, which, given John's tardiness and the time they'd already spent in chitchat and ordering, left them not much more than forty-five minutes.

She didn't say any of those things, because John's eye stopped her. She saw something in them, something strong enough to penetrate his glasses, something with a quiet but forceful command. She also saw that his eyes were amber, then looked more carefully and didn't see it at all. She remembered it. It must have registered on her subconscious the last time she'd seen him.

Carefully, with her heart beating a hair faster than it had been moments before, she set down the paper, sat back in her chair, crossed her hands in her lap and wondered what they would talk about in the time before their food arrived. There were a million things she could ask him, things she was curious about, like his wife and his son and his interest in books. Only none of that was her business.

She was used to talking. She *always* talked. Her role in life was to keep things moving, to win people over, to make sales. But she didn't know what to say to John.

She was beginning to feel awkward—and annoyed at that—when he asked, "Did you get your packing done?"

Relieved, she nodded. "Most of it."

"I trust you had other people to help you."

"No."

He arched a questioning brow and shook his head.

She shook her head right back.

"No stream of admirers dying to show off their muscles?"

His tone was deferential, his expression benign. Still she had the feeling that somewhere inside he harbored a grudge. "No stream of admirers. No men at all. Why would you think that there were?"

"You're an attractive woman. You must have men all over you."

"I'm an *independent* woman. I couldn't bear to have men all over me. I told you I didn't need anyone's help."

"You told me you didn't need *my* help."

"Then you took it too personally. I didn't—don't—need anyone's help. When I do, I hire it and pay for it. By check," she tacked on, just so he didn't think she was trading her body for something. Men tended to think that way, and she hated it. The few men—precious few men— she'd been with in her thirty-one years had known that she gave because she felt affection and attraction, and because she knew they wouldn't demand anything more. They never did. She was as free as a bird, and glad of it.

"Where are you moving to?"

"Sycamore Street."

His brow flickered into a frown. "I go down Sycamore all the time. I don't remember seeing any For Sale signs—or were you able to get an inside scoop and snatch something up before it hit the open market?"

There it was again, the deferential tone, the benign look, the little dig underneath. Looking him straight in those amber eyes of his, she said, "I'm not buying. I'm renting the second floor of a duplex, and, yes, I snatched it up before it hit the market. That's one of the perks of being a broker, and it's perfectly legal."

She had been direct enough to issue a challenge and expected him to meet it. Instead, he simply looked surprised. "You're renting? I'd have thought a successful woman like you would be living in a spectacular house on a spectacular piece of land with a spectacular view of the ocean."

"I'm not that successful. Not yet." But she intended to be. One day, she'd have enough money to buy anything her heart desired. "Where I live right now isn't as important as saving as much money as I can."

"You put a whole lot into Crosslyn Rise."

"No more than you." They'd each seen the figures.

"That's a whole lot."

She thought about the sum. "Uh-huh."

"And you want to open your own business."

Her brow went up. "Who told you that?"

"Carter," he answered factually. "When the consortium was forming. Just like he told you about me. So when do you think you'll do it?"

"I don't know. It depends on how much money we make on Crosslyn Rise and how soon." Her hand went to the first paper on her pile, but before she could address herself to its contents, the waitress placed a large glass of tomato juice in front of her. She smiled her thanks and opened her mouth to speak to John when he stopped her with a hand.

"Not yet. I need food first."

"There's food," she said, pointing to his orange juice. "Drink up, then I'll talk."

Rather than taking a drink of the orange juice, though, he drained the last of his coffee and refilled the cup. "Aren't you happy at Crown?"

After a moment's consideration, she gave a one-shouldered shrug. "As happy as I'd be working for someone else, but I've always wanted to be on my own."

"Independent."

"That's right."

"So you can rake in the most bucks?"

She raised her chin. "It's not as much the money as the freedom. I don't like having to answer to someone else."

"Marty Crown's a nice guy."

"A very nice guy. I could have done a lot worse picking a boss." Not that she'd left that to chance. Before moving up from New York she had researched each and every real estate agency in the North Shore area. She'd picked Crown for its reputation, its connections and Martin.

"Does he know your plans?"

"No, and I'd rather he not," she advised, sending John a look that said she was trusting him to keep her secret. "I've done well for Martin in the six years I've been here. He's made good money from my sales, and I don't begrudge that. It's the way things work. He gets his share in exchange for giving me a forum to work and to learn. I'm a much better broker now than I was when I came. Whether I have Martin to thank for that, or myself, isn't important. What's important is that if I can take out of Crosslyn Rise double what I put in, I'll be in great shape to make my move." Feeling that to be as smooth a segue as any, she once again fingered the top sheet in her file.

Once again John stalled her. "That's a lot of money," he said with thought-filled preponderance. "I'd have thought you could pretty much set up a real estate brokerage wherever you wanted with little more than a telephone."

"Not the kind of brokerage I want," she said, and let her dreams momentarily surface. "I want something classy. I want to either buy a house and do it over, or rent the best commercial space available. Then I want to decorate with the best furnishings, the best window treatments, the best artwork. I want a secretary, a sophisticated telephone system to make certain parts of my work easier, a computer setup to handle the latest programs and handle them well. I want to design a distinctive logo and stationery, and I want to advertise." She took a breath. "All of that costs money."

"I'll say," John said, and sat quietly back, studying her as though she were something foreign that he couldn't quite understand. "Couldn't you start small? Do you need everything all at once?"

"Yes. That's the whole point. Real estate agencies are a dime a dozen around here. Granted, some are better than others, and those stand out. But for a new one to spring up and attract enough of a clientele to be successful, drastic measures are called for. From the very first, my agency has to be different. It has to attract attention. I think I can do it if, A, my offices are elegant, B, my staff is courteous, hardworking and smart, and, C, I advertise like hell."

"Your staff?"

She sent him a dry look. "I'm not doing all the work on my own.

That would be suicide. The whole point is to have people who are answerable to me, to teach them and train them, let them do their work, then take *my* cut in the profits. Isn't that the way successful entrepreneurs do it?''

John didn't answer. He took a slow drink of his juice, set it down, then pushed his utensils out of the way when the waitress delivered plates filled with eggs, meat and toast.

Mindful that once they had food in their stomachs, John would be willing to talk business, Nina began to eat. She cracked her eggs, scooped them from the shell onto the wheat toast, gave them a light sprinkling of salt.

John's fork seemed stuck in the first of his scrambled eggs. "I'm surprised," he said unhurriedly, "that you want to set up business around here. If the goal is to make money and buy your freedom—"

"Not buy. Ensure."

"Ensure. If that's what you want, wouldn't you be better in a large place where, by virtue of sheer numbers of people, the market would be more active?"

"I've been there. I didn't like it."

"Why not?"

"Too impersonal. I may be hard, driven, aggressive, ambitious, even ruthless—people have called me all those things—but I like being able to greet the local grocer by name and have him greet me the same way. Besides," she added with a glance out the window, "I do love the ocean."

John followed her gaze briefly before returning to her. "When do you have time to see it?"

"I see it. Here and there. Coming and going." She nudged her chin toward his plate. "Eat up. Time's passing."

"Ever spend a day at the beach?"

"A day? No. An hour or two, maybe. Any more and I get itchy."

"You never wanted just to lie out on the sand for hours listening to the sound of people and the surf?"

"No. There's too much to do."

He took a bite of his eggs, then swallowed. "That's sad."

"Maybe for you. Not for me. I'd much rather get brief glimpses of the ocean lots of different times in the course of a day, know that it's there, even listen to it at night at the same time that I'm getting something else useful done, than sit doing nothing on the sand."

He looked baffled. "But don't you ever just want to go out and enjoy it for itself, rather than as an accompaniment to something else?"

"Why should I? It's the best accompaniment in the world. It makes anything else I'm doing that much nicer."

"That's sad," he said again, and Nina found herself getting irked.

"I don't see *you* with a tan."

"I haven't had time yet this spring. But I will. You can count on it. As soon as lessons let up a little for my son, we'll be hitting the beach."

Nina was about to ask what lessons he meant, when she caught herself. The child had a handicap. She didn't want to put John on the spot. Besides, his personal life wasn't her affair.

With a tolerant shrug, she said, "Different strokes for different folks. What works for you doesn't necessarily work for me, and vice versa. It's no big thing, John. Really." He didn't believe her, but that wasn't her worry. Crosslyn Rise was. "Listen, I'd really like to get to those papers." She glanced at her watch. "We have to be at the bank in less than half an hour."

"How was your seminar?"

"My seminar was fine." She put her hand on the top paper. "What I have here is my personal recommendation. I've broken the project down by size and expected date of completion—"

"Did you learn a lot? At the seminar."

She paused, stared, nodded. Then she patted the paper. "The more I thought about it over the weekend, the more I realized that we hit on something good last time we talked. The idea of—"

"Was it worth the four days?"

She took a breath for patience. "I'd say so."

"You're a better broker for it?"

"I'm more knowledgeable." She took another breath. "The idea of pricing the units progressively—"

"Don't you ever get tired?"

She pressed her lips together. "Of work? I told you. I love my work."

"But don't you ever get *tired*?"

"You mean physically fatigued?"

"Mentally fatigued. Don't you ever want to stop, even for a little while?"

"If I do that, it'll take me longer to reach my goal."

"What about burnout?"

"What about it?"

"Doesn't it scare you?"

"Not particularly. If I get where I'm going, I'll have plenty of time to take it easy, without the risks."

"What are the risks?"

"Of taking it easy now?" She didn't have to take time to think. She lived with certain fears day in, day out. "Loss of sales. Loss of reputation. Loss of status in the agency. There are other brokers out there just dying for my listings. If I'm not around, if I'm not working, if I'm not on top of things, if I'm not getting results, I lose.''

In a rare instance of expressiveness, his mouth twisted in disgust. ''I get tired just listening to you.''

''Then don't,'' she snapped. ''Don't ask me questions, and you won't have to listen to my answers. All I want—'' she slapped the paper beside her plate ''—is to come to some sort of decision here!''

John stared at her. She glared back. Gradually his stare softened into study, and before she knew it, she felt the same kind of quiet force emanating from him that she'd felt before. As had happened then, her heartbeat picked up, all the more so when his amber eyes began a slow, almost tactile meandering over her face. She felt their touch on her cheeks, her nose, her chin, then her mouth, where they lingered for a while to trace the bow curve of her lips.

The indignation she felt moments earlier was forgotten, pushed from mind by a strange, all-over tingle. ''John?'' Her voice wobbled. She cleared her throat. ''I, uh, really think we should talk.''

He wasn't done, though. His gaze dropped to her throat, touching the smooth skin there before slipping down over silk to the gentle swell of her breasts.

Even sitting, she felt weak in the knees, which made so little sense at all that a flare of pique shot through her. *''John.''*

His eyes rose. ''Hmm?''

''I *need* to show you my *papers*.''

''What papers?''

She rapped the folder. *''These.''*

He looked at the folder, then looked back at her. Along the way, his mouth hardened. ''You won't let it go, will you?''

''Let it go? But this is why we met!''

He said nothing, just stared at her. Not even his glasses diffused the strength of that stare.

She felt penetrated. ''Wasn't it?''

Slowly he shook his head.

''Then why?''

''To have breakfast.''

''You insisted on this meeting just for *breakfast*?''

Slowly he nodded.

''But *why*? You could have had breakfast for less money and with less hassle if you'd stayed home with your son. Why on *earth* did you drag me out here if you didn't have any intention of discussing Crosslyn Rise?''

''We'll discuss Crosslyn Rise. When we're done eating.''

''So what do I do until then?'' she asked in exasperation.

"You slow down. You take a deep breath. You look out that window and watch the sea gulls. You have a second cup of coffee and take the time to smell the brew." His voice lowered, growing sharper and more direct. "You're rushing your way through life, Nina. If you're not careful, the whole thing will be over and you won't know what in the hell you've missed."

Incredulity holding her mute, Nina stared. She had to take a deep, deep breath and give a solid swallow before she was able to say, "Last time I looked, this was my life. Seems to me I should be able to do what I want, and if that means rushing, I'll rush."

His voice came out gentler than before, but no less direct. "Not with me, you won't."

She sat back in her chair. "Fine." Two could play the game. She hadn't wanted this breakfast, anyway. All along, she had wanted the committee to take its vote. "Fortunately, I won't *be* with you beyond this meeting." She smiled. "Take your time. Eat. I'll just sit here and enjoy the scenery."

She worked hard at doing that. After an eternity, with barely ten minutes until they were due at the bank, John invited her to show him the papers she'd brought. Staying calm, patient and professional, she went through them. With surprising ease, they came to an agreement on the third of her plans. Together they walked to the bank.

Sixty minutes later, when Nina returned to her office, she was like a steam kettle ready to blow. Slapping the folder sharply on her desk, she squeezed her eyes shut, put her head back and let out an eloquent growl. Its sound brought Lee in from next door.

"How'd it go?"

"Don't ask."

"Which plan did he go for?"

"C, damn it."

"And the consortium agreed?"

Nina nodded. Seconds later, she threw a hand in the air. "Don't ask me why I didn't argue more. I should have."

"Plan C is just fine."

"It's not aggressive enough."

"So why *didn't* you argue more?"

"Because—because—" she struggle for the words, finally blurting out, "because John Sawyer wore me down, that's why."

"I thought he was *blah*."

"He is."

"But he wore you down." Lee grinned in a curious kind of way. "That's a change. Usually it's the other way around. You must be losing your touch.'' When Nina gave her a dirty look, she said in an attempt to appease, ''Sometimes the most blah people can be forceful, just because they take you by surprise.''

But it wasn't that, Nina knew. It was John's persistence, his molasses-slow approach and a doggedness that was built of reason. His will was stronger than she'd expected, and, as fate would have it, his will coincided with that of the majority of the consortium.

Not for the first time, Nina vowed that she would never again involve herself in a project where decisions were made by committee. Unfortunately, she was stuck with this one to the end. ''Crosslyn Rise may be the death of me yet.'' Snatching up the pink slips that were waiting, she flipped sightlessly through, then flattened them back on the desk. ''The *worst* of it is that they want me to keep working with him. Can you believe that? They see him as kind of a lay advisor. So even though consortium meetings won't be held more than once a month through the summer, they're expecting John and I to meet once a week.''

''That shouldn't be too hard.''

''It's a royal waste of time, a total frustration.'' She sent a beseeching look skyward. ''Someone up there better help me out, or I'll be a raving lunatic by the time summer's done.'' Eyes dropping back to the desk, she sighed. ''At least I can give the printer the go-ahead to print those brochures.'' Moving the folder aside, she drew up a pad of paper. At the top, she wrote Call Printer. ''I want to have an introductory Open House over the Fourth of July weekend, something with lots of hoopla to launch the selling campaign.'' To the list, she added, Call Christine, then Call Newspaper. Her pen went back to the Christine part. ''*If* the model apartment is ready. Chris was aiming for the first of the month. It'll be impressive.'' Looking at Lee, she asked, ''Have you been up there lately?''

Lee shook her head. ''I'm waiting for you. Maybe today, after lunch?''

Something about the way Lee mentioned lunch gave Nina pause. She dropped her eyes to her desk calendar. Catching in a breath, she said, ''Lunch! That's right!'' She had forgotten all about it. With a grin, she looked up. ''Happy birthday, Lee.''

Lee blushed. ''Thanks.''

''I'm sorry. Wow, I should have been thinking about that when you first walked in here, but I've been so annoyed all morning. Hey, how does it feel to be twenty-nine?''

''You've been there. How did it feel to you?''

''I don't know. It came and went so fast, I think I missed it.'' For a split second, she remembered what John Sawyer had said, then pushed her mind on to more meaningful things. "So, we'll go out for lunch to celebrate. Any other plans?"

"I'm meeting my parents in town for dinner."

"Nice," Nina said with enthusiasm, though she couldn't help but wonder about Tom Brody. If there was something real going on between Tom and Lee, he should have been the one to take her to dinner on her birthday.

As though reading her mind, Lee said, "Tom and I celebrated last night." She touched her earlobe. "See?"

Nina was a stickler for her own appearance, dressing for the part she wanted to play. She carefully shopped for clothes and accessories, and wore them unselfconsciously once they were hers. There, though, her interest in fashion ended. She was far more apt to notice the overall effect of a person's clothing than the details of it. That was why she hadn't noticed Lee's earrings before.

Looking back, she didn't know how she'd missed them. They lit up Lee's ears in a way that neither gold, silver nor neon enamel could. "Wow," she breathed, coming out of her chair for a closer look. "Those are *gorgeous*."

"They're three-quarters of a karat each. Tom said to make sure I insured them."

Nina wanted to say that if Tom Brody had style, he'd have given her a year's worth of insurance along with the gift. But Tom had flash, not style. There was a difference.

"Definitely insure them," Nina said. She didn't add that that way Lee would be sure to have something of value when Tom left her behind. Nina wasn't a spoiler. But she felt awful. "It's too bad he can't join you tonight. Has he ever met your parents?"

"No. He has to be in Buffalo. It's just as well," Lee reasoned indulgently. "My parents would be looking Tom over as husband material, and that kind of pressure is the last thing Tom needs. He has enough pressure with work."

Nina felt momentarily chilled. Making excuses for a man was a sure sign that a woman was giving more than she was getting. But before she could say that, Lee made for the door.

"Martin is having a root canal. I told him I'd cover for him. He has some people coming in from the Berkshires. Their daughter is starting at Salem State in the fall and they want to buy a condo for the four years she's here."

Nina was hearing that same story more and more often. She supposed that if she had kids she'd want to do the same thing, since, given rents versus tax benefits and property appreciation, it made sense. Of course, she didn't have kids, so it was a moot point.

"How about I make reservations for twelve-thirty?" she asked.

"Sounds great," Lee said. "I'll be back here by twelve. See you then."

Nina waved a goodbye, then looked again at her desk calendar. The fact that she'd forgotten about lunch was nothing new. At the end of a given day, when she looked over her program for the next one, business appointments were the things she saw. Fortunately, she didn't have anything that would conflict with Lee's birthday celebration. She liked Lee a lot. She felt good about taking her out.

She was also grateful for the opportunity to eat, since she hadn't had much of the breakfast she had so glibly ordered at Easy Over. John had distracted her. Even when he'd been leisurely eating his own food, she hadn't eaten much. He made her stomach jump.

Annoyance, she told herself. Annoyance and irritation. John was the kind who, in his innocent way, gave people ulcers.

Actually, it was a wonder he was so calm, given the problem he had with his son. It couldn't be easy for him raising a child alone. She wondered about the extent of the boy's problems, wondered what kind of schooling those problems entailed. She wondered whether John ever got frantic, threw his hands into the air and gave up. Some parents did that when confronted with a frightening situation. Her mother had, more than once.

Something nagged in the back of her mind. Lifting the collection of pink slips that she'd barely seen earlier, she set one after another aside until she came to the one that had caused the nagging. It was a message from Anthony Kimball, the medical director of the Omaha nursing home where her mother lived. The call had come in promptly at nine that morning. The message requested a callback.

Lifting the phone, Nina punched out the number that she knew by heart. "Dr. Kimball, please," she asked. She gave her name, then waited while the call was transferred.

"Nina?"

"Yes, Dr. Kimball. I got your message. Is something wrong?" It wasn't often that Anthony Kimball called her, and when he did, there was usually a problem.

"I'm not quite sure. Your mother had some sort of seizure during the night. Her blood pressure fell dangerously low. We have her stabilized now, and there doesn't seem to be any other side effect from whatever the seizure was, but I thought you ought to know. This may be the start of the weakening that we've been expecting."

Nina swiveled her chair away from the door and bowed her head. "Is she comfortable?" she asked quietly.

"As far as we can tell."

"Is she aware of anything?"

There was a pause, then a quiet, "I don't believe so."

Nina sighed. "I guess we should be grateful for that." She pressed a hand to her eyes. "This weakening. Once it begins, does it go fast?"

"I can't tell you that. Every case varies. It could take one month or ten, but you may want to come out here to see her within the next few weeks."

Nina didn't have to look at her calendar to know that the next few weeks were fully booked. This was her busy season. A trip to Omaha would take precious time, not to mention a toll on her emotions. Seeing her mother was always painful. "Why don't I talk with you next week and see how she is then," she suggested. "If she stays stabilized, I'd rather wait a bit before coming out."

The doctor agreed to that, as Nina knew he would. Though the home was the finest Nina had been able to find, it wasn't unlike others in its overriding concern with money. Nina paid well for the service of having her mother cared for. As long as the checks kept coming, Anthony Kimball and his staff were content.

Hanging up the phone, Nina felt the same hollow ache she felt whenever she thought of her mother. Such potential gone to waste. A beautiful woman now a vegetable. She wished she could credit the damage to a disease like Alzheimer's, but her mother's mind hadn't fallen victim to anything as noble as that. She'd taken drugs. Bad drugs. Too many drugs. Rather than dying of an overdose, she had lived on, simply to languish in whatever position her attendants arranged her.

Nina was the one who felt the pain of it all. She was the one who felt the remorse. She couldn't say that she felt a loss, because her mother had never been hers to enjoy, but there were times, once in a very great while, when she thought of what might have been if things had been different way back at the start.

But they wouldn't be—couldn't be—and thinking about it only caused pain. One of Nina's earliest lessons in life had been that the only sure antidote to pain was activity. It was a lesson she still lived by.

4

Sunday was moving day. Nina completed all her weekend showings on Saturday and was up with the sun the next morning to pack the last of her things. Rather than pay a formal moving service, when she had so little of intrinsic value to move, she had hired two young men to help. Between their muscles, the small pickup truck one of them owned and the promise of a generous check for the job, they had successfully transferred her meager furnishings and not so meager personal belongings from the old apartment to the new one by noon.

Shortly after, Nina went to work, first pushing the furniture over or back until the positioning was perfect, then opening carton after carton in an attempt to see what was where. She was standing in the midst of chaos, feeling vaguely bewildered, when she heard a call from downstairs.

"Hello?"

She tried to place it, but she wasn't expecting any guests. "Yes?" she called back without moving.

"It's John Sawyer, Nina. Can I come up?"

"Uh—" she looked around, bewildered, "—sure." John Sawyer? Downstairs? She hadn't seen hide nor hair of him since the Tuesday before, and though she told herself to be grateful, more than once she had wondered where he was. The consortium wanted them to work together, but since she wasn't thrilled with the idea, she'd decided to leave the initiative up to him. She hadn't expected that he'd seek her out in person, much less at her home, much *less* at the home whose exact address he couldn't possibly have known.

Yet John Sawyer it was emerging from the stairwell wearing a T-shirt, jeans and sneakers. His hair was mussed, his nose and cheeks unexpectedly ruddy. He looked fresh and carefree, neither of which she was feeling at that moment, and as if that weren't bad enough, the first thing he did after he came to a halt was to give her an ear-to-ear grin.

John had never grinned at her before. She'd caught a twist of the corner of the mouth once or twice, but never a full-fledged grin. The surprise of it had her insides doing little flip-flops, to which she responded by frowning.

"How did you find me?"

"Your car. You said you were moving to Sycamore Street. There aren't many houses here with bright red BMWs in the driveway."

For reasons unknown to Nina just then, she felt suddenly defensive about the car. "It's not new. I bought it used and had it painted. Some people think it's pretentious to have a car like that when I live pretty modestly, but the fact is that it impresses clients. They like riding around in it."

John studied her, his grin softening into something curious. "Don't you?"

"Don't I what?"

"Like riding around in it."

"I suppose." She frowned again. "What are you doing here?"

"Helping." He stuck his hands into the back pockets of his jeans, a gesture that should have been totally innocent. Given the way his T-shirt tightened over his chest, though, it wasn't. Nina felt a corresponding tightening in the pit of her stomach.

"I told you I didn't need help," she snapped, scowling now.

"Everyone needs help." His eyes skimmed the sea of cartons on the floor. "This place will be a mess until everything's unpacked. Why be burdened doing it after work every day this week, when between the two of us, we can get it all done now?"

He had a point, though she wouldn't concede it. "I'm sure you have better things to do with your time."

"Actually, I don't. J.J. and I were at the beach this morning, but he's gone off for the afternoon with friends, and the store is closed, so I really do have time to waste. I'm in the mood for unpacking." Shifting his hands from his pockets to his hips, he looked around at the cartons. "Where should I begin?"

"Uh—" Nina tried to concentrate, but all she could think about was that she hadn't showered, that she hadn't put makeup on and that between her ultrashort hair and the loose shirt and jeans she wore, she looked more like a boy than a girl. She felt embarrassed. "Uh, really, John, there's no need—"

"Where?" he repeated. Stepping over one carton, he peered down to look at the writing on the side of another. The words *living room* had been crossed out and replaced by *dining room*, but that, too, had been crossed out. *Bedroom* was the word that seemed left, though even from where she was, Nina saw through the open flaps of the box that it contained pots and pans.

"I've used these cartons lots of different times," she explained, wringing one hand in the other. "I kind of gave up on marking things this time, which is why everything's mixed up out here."

"No sweat," John said, lifting the carton. "This looks like it goes in the kitchen.'' He hitched his chin toward the back of the house. ''That way?''

''Uh-huh.''

Carrying the carton, he passed her, went through the dining room and into the kitchen. Within minutes, she heard the clattering of pots and pans being stacked. Wondering where he was putting them, she followed the noise to find him on his haunches before one of the kitchen cabinets. ''I don't know if this is right, but at least they'll be out of the way. If you find in a week or a month that you want them elsewhere, it'll be easy enough to move them.''

''That's fine.''

''Why don't you go back into the other room and sort through the rest of the cartons. If I carry stuff into the bedroom, you can organize things there, while I finish up here.''

She tried again. ''John, this really isn't necessary.''

''Of course, it's not. But it helps, doesn't it?''

Given the direct question, she couldn't lie. ''Yes, but—''

''Unless there's stuff here you don't want me to see.''

''There isn't, but—''

''Or you're expecting someone else and my being here will embarrass you—''

''I'm not and it won't, but—''

''Then there's no problem.''

''There *is* a problem,'' she cried, driven by exasperation to a semblance of her usual force. ''I told you this last week. If I wanted help, I'd hire it.''

He looked up at her. ''And pay for it. With a check. Yes, I did hear that.''

''Well, I meant it.''

His eyes held hers for a time before he returned them to the task at hand. He had barely set another pot into the nest of them in the cabinet when he looked up again. ''This is free, Nina. I'm not asking for payment of any kind, and if you offered, I'd give it back. I'm doing this as a friend. You won't owe me anything.''

She felt color warm her cheeks. ''I know that.''

''I'm not sure you do,'' he said with a frown. ''You've made it clear that you prefer to hire and pay people when you need things done. But when you get someone who's willing to help for free, the only reason I can think of why you'd turn him down is that either you can't stand his company or you're afraid there's a price.'' His words came slowly but steadily, one sentence flowing gently into the next. ''Now, I know we haven't necessarily hit it off on a personal basis, so it may well be that you can't stand my company, and if that's the case, just tell me, and I'll leave. On the other hand, if you're afraid there's a price, I'm telling you there isn't. I'm offering my services free and clear of return obligations." He paused. "Do you believe me?"

After a minute, she said a quiet, "Yes."

"Then why don't you let me help." It was more statement than question. "Come on, Nina. Go with the flow. I'm here and I'm willing. Use me."

Use me. It was usually the other way around, where relationships between men and women were concerned. But he'd said the words himself. He'd offered them. Freely. Just as he was offering his help. "Are you sure you don't have anything else to do?"

"I'm sure."

As he sat there on his haunches looking up at her, it struck Nina that he wasn't bad looking. Not bad looking at all. Actually, rather good-looking, even with those glasses perched on his nose. With his longish hair, his light tan, and his T-shirt and jeans, the glasses made him look oddly in vogue.

Which was a surprising thought, indeed.

"Fine," she said, and headed for the front room before she had a chance to regret the decision. "I'll sort through the cartons. Come back in when you need another one."

With a certain amount of kicking and shoving, she had cartons separated into groups by the time John returned. As promised, he carried everything for the bedroom into the bedroom before continuing with the kitchen.

For one hour, then a second, they worked straight. Nina was back to being her usual efficient self, in part to keep her mind occupied and away from the fact of John's presence in the other room. Come the time when they were both unpacking cartons in the living room, that became more difficult. He was never out of sight. She was highly aware of him. Adding to the problem, most of the cartons contained books, so John's progress slowed. For every four that he placed on the shelf, there was one that he wanted to discuss.

She tried to keep moving. She tried, even when she was giving her opinion of one book or another, to keep unloading others and lining them up on the shelves. But the questions he asked were good ones, often ones that required thought, and she found her own progress slowing down right along with his. She found herself curious to know *his* opinions.

Nina had never thought of herself as an intellectual. She had a college degree more out of practical necessity than love of learning. John, on the other hand, was an intellectual. It was clear in the way he looked and acted, not to mention his occupation, and to some extent, she had assumed that given this difference between them, they would have trouble communicating. To her surprise, they didn't. He didn't make obscure references to classical writers or philosophers. He didn't pick apart books along the lines of arcane theories. He offered honest, straightforward thoughts in honest, straightforward English. Pleasantly surprised, she indulged herself the discussion, letting her defenses down, enjoying the talk for talk's sake.

Engrossed as she was in it, she was taken off guard when, in the midst of a discussion of James Joyce and his wife, Nora, John said, "Have you had lunch?"

Sitting cross-legged on the floor, she straightened, looked at him, swallowed. Dragging herself back from a pleasant interlude to the present, she glanced at her watch. "It's after three."

"I know. I'm starved. Did you have anything?"

Silently she shook her head.

"I'll go get something." Coming to his knees, he fished his keys from his pocket. With another smooth motion, he was on his feet. "You'll eat, won't you?"

"I don't need—"

"Are you hungry?"

"I wasn't planning to—"

"Lobster rolls?"

Her mouth watered. "Only if I pay."

He thought about that for a minute. She was prepared to dig in her heels and insist that that was the only way she'd eat anything he brought, when his mouth quirked. "Okay."

He was *quite* good-looking, she realized with a start. Dragging her eyes from his, she looked around for her purse. Unfortunately, it was directly behind him. The only footpath through the cartons took her by him with mere inches to spare. His flesh was warm from work. She felt that warmth, smelled its scent, and where she should have been repelled, she wasn't. John Sawyer smelled healthily male. Attractively male.

Convinced that the tension of the move was jumbling her mind, she quickly found her purse and fumbled inside her enough money to cover sandwiches and drinks. John took the money.

"You do know," he said, and eyed her straight on, "that I'd never allow this if it weren't for the big deal you made about not wanting my help to unpack. The way I see it, your treating me now is payment for my work, so we're even. Got that?"

His gaze was so strong and his voice so firm that all she could do was manage a quiet, "Uh-huh." If he had asked her to say anything else, she'd have been at a loss. Fortunately, he didn't. Tucking the money into his pocket, he went off down the stairs.

During the time he was gone, Nina was a whirling dervish of activity. Bending over and around repeatedly, she emptied two full cartons of books, then moved on to her stereo equipment. She tried not to think about anything but the work she was doing, and to some extent she succeeded. Only intermittently did images flash through her mind— John's long arms flexing under the weight of cartons, John's shaggy hair spiking along his neck, John's very male, very alluring scent—but she pushed them away as quickly as they came.

She had a rack of CDs filled and was halfway through a second when he returned.

"This is a treat, let me tell you," he said with a smile as he began to unload the bag he carried. Shifting a carton from the low coffee table onto the floor, he spread out not only lobster rolls, but cups of potato salad, ears of corn and soda. "Take-out for me is usually McDonald's."

Instinctively Nina knew that the choice had nothing to do with money. "That's what your son likes?"

"He *loves* it. He'd be happy to go there every day of the week if I let him."

"What does he eat?"

"A hamburger, a small bag of fries and a milk shake. He doesn't always make it through the shake, but he devours the rest. For a little guy, he always amazes me."

"He's four?"

John nodded. Sitting down on a nearby carton, stretching his legs comfortably before him, he took a bite of a lobster roll, closed his eyes, chewed softly and neatly. "Mmm," he said with feeling, "is this good."

Nina, too, took a carton as a seat. Using one of the plastic forks that had tumbled from the bag, she sampled the potato salad. "So's this." She took another bite, all the while thinking about her curiosity and the fact that maybe, now that she and John were friends, she could ease it. It seemed she'd been wondering about certain things for a long time.

Shooting for nonchalance, she took a sip of soda, then said, "Tell me about your son."

John's glasses might have hidden the flash of wariness in his eyes had she not been watching him closely. Clearly he guarded his son. She wondered if he'd tell her to mind her own business—one part of her was telling herself that very same thing—and felt deeply warmed when, instead, he said in a low, slow voice, "J.J.'s a sweet little boy who's had a rough go of it in life."

"When did his mom die?"

"When he was one. He doesn't remember her."

"Is that good or bad?"

"Good, I guess. He doesn't know what he's missing."

Nina wanted to ask how the woman had died, but didn't. It was enough that John had agreed to talk about his son. "I'm sure you give him twice the love."

"I try," he said thoughtfully, and took another mouthful of lobster roll. After he'd swallowed, he said, "It's hard sometimes knowing if what I'm doing is right. Normal guidelines don't fit when it comes to J.J. He's a special child."

Eating her own lobster roll, she waited for him to go on. As curious as she was, she didn't want to sound nosy. Surprisingly the silence wasn't awkward. She ate patiently, wondering about all those ways in which J.J. might be special.

Finally John raised his eyes to hers. "What have you heard about him?"

"Just that he has vision and hearing deficiencies."

"That's pretty much it. He wears glasses and hearing aids." With the words, John looked momentarily in pain. "God, it hurts to see him sometimes. My heart aches for the poor little kid. He didn't ask for any of this."

"What caused it?"

He thought about that for a minute, then shrugged. "No one knows. He was born that way."

"Did you know right then?"

He shook his head. "Things seemed fine at the beginning. By the time he was six months old, I could tell that he wasn't responding to sound. It was when I brought him in to be tested that they detected the problem with his eyes. Unfortunately, there wasn't much of a medical nature that they could do about either. They wouldn't even fit him for glasses until he was close to a year. He'd have just dragged them off."

"They must help."

He nodded. "A lot. He reads."

"At four?"

John shot her a quintessentially parent-proud grin. "Nothing's wrong with his mind. He's a bright little kid."

"I'm sure," Nina said.

"I wasn't. Given all the other problems, I'd been told there was a possibility that he'd be retarded. Thank goodness that isn't so. I mean, how much should the child have to take?"

"But you'll be putting him in a special school." That was what she'd been told, the major reason John had invested in Crosslyn Rise. Handled wisely over the years, the profit he stood to make would cover the high cost of that special school.

"I have to. What hearing he has is negligible. He has to learn how to sign, how to read lips and how to talk."

"That'll all start next year?"

"It all started as soon as we diagnosed the problem. He and I work with a therapist every morning, and in the afternoon he's in a play group with children like him. Their parents are trained like I am. The learning for these kids has to be continuous." His eyes widened and he shot a hurried glance at his watch. The abrupt movement, coming from him, took Nina by surprise. Seeing the time, he let out a breath. "I'm okay. He's with one of those other families today, but I still have a few minutes."

"Oh, John, I feel guilty. It can't be often that you get a free afternoon like this, and to blow it away unpacking my things. I'm really sorry."

He regarded her strangely. "Don't be. If I hadn't wanted to do this, I wouldn't have. You didn't exactly invite me." He paused. "You didn't exactly *want* me. I inflicted myself on you, so you don't have anything to feel guilty about." He paused again. "Besides, I got a lobster roll out of it. And some interesting conversation." His voice lowered. "I like you better when you're talking books than when you're talking real estate."

"The feeling's mutual," Nina said, then regretted it the moment the words were out because, behind his glasses, John's eyes darkened. "You're not as bad as I thought you'd be," she added quickly, lest he think she was being suggestive in any way, shape or form.

His eyes remained dark. They dropped to her mouth.

"I think," she babbled on, "that when you only see a person in one context, say for matters involving a business deal like Crosslyn Rise, you get a very narrow view." Her voice seemed to be fading, like the rest of her was doing. Fading, weakening, feeling all warm and trembly inside. "It's nice to know you like lobster rolls."

John's brows drew together in a brief frown before he managed to drag his eyes back to hers. "I do," he said quietly. "But I'd better go, I think." He stood.

Simply so that she wouldn't feel so overwhelmed, Nina stood, too. "Thanks." She waved a hand in the vague direction of the food, then broadened the gesture. "For everything."

He walked slowly to the door, one hand deep in his pocket reaching for his keys, his head slightly bent.

Nina was suddenly nervous. "John? I didn't upset you, asking about your son, did I?"

"No, no." He pulled the keys from his pocket, but he didn't turn.

She moved closer. "I was curious. That's all."

They keys jangled in his hands. "People are."

She moved closer still. "You must be a very good parent. I'm beginning to feel a little humbled."

"That makes two of us."

She frowned. "Two?"

Slowly he turned, and what she saw in his eyes took her breath away. His voice was low, still slow but nowhere near as smooth as it usually was. "I thought I was immune to women like you. I thought that there was no way a woman with a fast-driving career could turn me on, but I was wrong."

A tiny voice inside Nina told her she ought to be angry, to either lash back or turn in the opposite direction and run, but that voice was drowned out by the sound of her pulse beating rapidly, hammering her feet in place on the floor.

His hand shaped her cheek, then slid along her jaw until his fingers were feathered by her hair. "Tell me not to want to kiss you," he said.

But she couldn't. As outlandish as it seemed, given that John Sawyer was the antithesis of the kind of man she usually liked, she wanted his kiss. Maybe, deep down inside, she'd been wanting it since he'd shown up at her door that afternoon wearing a T-shirt that made his chest look heart-stoppingly hard and broad. Maybe she'd been wanting it even longer, since the night she'd shown up at his store and seen him sweating. There was something about sweat that blew the intellectual image. Sweat was earthy and honest. Sweat was intimate. Given the right chemistry between a man and a woman, it was a powerful aphrodisiac.

Whether she wanted it to be so or not, Nina had to accept that the chemistry between John and her was right. There was no way her body was letting her move away from his touch, no way it was letting her evade him when his head slowly lowered and his mouth touched hers.

He gave her one kiss, then a second, then a third. Each one lasted a little longer than the one before, each one touched her a little more deeply. He seemed to be savoring her, reluctantly, if his words were to be considered, but savoring her nonetheless. His lips were firm, knowing, increasingly open and wet. His kisses were smooth as warm butter and ten times more hot.

By the time the last one ended and he raised his head, Nina's breath was coming in short, shallow wisps. Her eyes were closed. She felt miles and miles away from everything she'd always known, transported to a place where kisses touched the heart. She'd never been there before.

"I shouldn't have done that," he said quietly.

She opened her eyes to find his face flushed, his eyes serious. "Probably not," she said softly.

"You're not my type."

"Nor you mine."

"So why did it happen?"

She tried to think up an eloquent answer, but for all the hard selling she'd done in her day, she was without one. The best she could do was to murmur, "Chemistry?"

After a minute's thought, he said, "I guess." As though the admission were a warning, he passed his thumb over her lips—moist now, warm and naturally rouged—before letting his hand fall to his side.

"I didn't come here for this," he said gruffly. "I hope you know that."

She did. Somehow, with John, it wouldn't have occurred to her otherwise. He wasn't a wily sort of man.

"I'm not looking for anything," he went on, still in that same gruff voice. "I don't have time for this kind of thing. Between the store and my son, I have all I can handle."

"Hey," she said, taking a step back, "I'm not asking for anything." It sounded to her as though he thought she was, or would. "It wasn't *me* who started that kiss."

"You didn't tell me to stop."

"Because I was curious about it. But it's no big thing. It's over and done. Curiosity satisfied. Period."

He thought about that, then nodded. But he didn't turn to leave. Instead, he looked thoughtful again. Then, in a low voice, he said, "Was it good?"

She took a deep breath. "You don't really want to know."

"I want to know."

"It won't help the situation."

"I want to know."

"It'll only make you angry, because the last thing you want is for someone like me to say it was good."

"Was it?"

"John," she pleaded, "why don't you just leave it be?"

"Because I want to know," he said with the stubbornness of a child. Nina had the sudden fear that he would stand there asking until she told him the truth.

Staring him in the eye, she said, "Yes, it was good. It was very good, and I'm sorry it ended. But it had to, because it wasn't right. We're totally different people with totally different wants and needs. You can't understand why I talk so fast, and I can't understand why you talk so slow. I want to make money, you want to meditate on the beach." Her hands went in opposite directions. "Worlds apart, John, we're worlds apart."

"Yeah." His amber eyes moved over her features. "It's too bad. You're awful cute."

She snorted. "Cute is what every woman over thirty wants to be."

"Over thirty?"

"Thirty-one, to be exact."

His mouth quirked at the corner. "I wouldn't have guessed it."

That quirking annoyed her. She didn't like being laughed at. "Well, now you know, and since you do, you can understand that I mean all I say about what I'm doing and where I'm going. I'm not some cute little pixie fresh out of college trying to make it big. I've had years of training in my field, and now that I'm on the verge of getting where I want to be, I'm not letting anyone stand in my way." She stole in a breath and raced on. "So if you think that I'm going to think twice about that kiss, that I'm going to look for a replay or want something *more*, you're mistaken. I'm off and running, and you'll only slow me down. I won't let that happen."

Having said her piece in a way that she felt was forceful and clear, she stood her ground with her jaw set, waiting for John to do his thinking thing then come up with a rejoinder. Not more than thirty seconds had passed, though, when, with a start, he glanced at his watch.

"Damn," he muttered, "I'm late." Raising his arm in a wave, he was fast out the door, taking the stairs at a speedy trot. Nina had never seen him move so fast, but it made sense that if he did it for anyone, he would do it for his son, and she was glad. From what he said, the boy had precious little going for him but a good brain and a loving dad.

Standing there amid the cartons in the living room that didn't feel quite hers yet, Nina's mind traveled back in time to when she'd been four herself. She hadn't had any obvious handicap. Her vision had been fine, along with her hearing, and her mind had been sharp—too sharp, in some respects. Even at that age she had wondered why she didn't have a father. Even then she had known something was wrong when she'd heard gruff voices coming from her mother's room late at night. Even then she had known that the bruises on her mother's face and arms and legs weren't normal.

She sighed. Ignorance would have been bliss back then, but what was done was done. She'd overcome those things that had darkened her early years and was now well on her way to having the security she wanted. Okay, so once in a while she wished things were different. Once in a while she wished *she* had someone rush home to her the way John Sawyer had to his son. But life wasn't perfect, she knew. No one had everything. So if she didn't have that special someone who cared, she had a growing career and a growing name and lots of respect along the way. She could live with that. She had no other choice.

Come eight o'clock that night, she wasn't thinking of choices. Having unpacked the very last carton, the only thing on her mind was soaking in a hot, hot bath. Stripping out of her shirt and jeans, she started the water and returned to the bedroom for a robe, when the phone rang.

Absurdly, her first thought was that the phone would also be ringing at her old apartment, jangling through rooms now empty and forlorn. Remembering the good two years she'd had there, she felt a twinge of sadness.

Her second thought was that Lee was calling in to report on any activity that had taken place at the office that day. Shrugging into the robe, she reached for the phone.

"Hello?"

"Nina?"

It was a man's voice. Though she hadn't ever heard it before on the phone, she knew instantly whose it was. Thoughts of him had been hovering at the back of her mind since he'd left her house in such a rush.

"Hi," she said cautiously.

"It's John."

"I know."

The line was silent for a time before he said, "I, uh, just wanted to apologize for leaving so abruptly. Time had gotten away from me and J.J. was due home."

"Did you get back in time?"

"Almost."

"No?"

"They were waiting out front in the car."

"For long?"

"Three or four minutes. I'm usually on time. They were starting to worry."

"How about J.J.?"

"He was okay."

"Did he have fun?"

"I think so. Sometimes it's hard to tell whether he had a good time or he's just real happy to be home. One thing's for sure. He ate enough. He was wearing mustard, fruit punch and chocolate all over his shirt."

"Oh, yuck." She thought about single parenthood, and a sudden fear struck. "Are you the one who has to do the wash?"

"You got it."

"Oh, *yuck.*"

"Actually, given all I've had to clean up in the last four years, the dribbles from a picnic lunch are a snap."

Nina found herself picturing those other things. "You changed diapers?"

"All the time."

"What a good father. And husband. Your wife must have appreciated that." Once the words were out, she held her breath.

"Actually," he said after a brief pause, "she took it pretty much for granted. It was part of the bargain we made. I wanted the baby. She agreed to carry it if I was willing to take the responsibility for its care once it was born."

"That's awful," Nina exclaimed without thinking, then she did think and regretted the outburst. If John had adored his now-dead wife, the last thing Nina wanted to do was criticize her. "I mean, I suppose people do what's right for them. Did it work for her?"

"Not particularly. She went right back to work the way she planned, but she felt guilty, and she resented that."

"Oh, dear."

"Yeah." He paused. "Well." Another pause, then a new breath. "Anyway, I'm used to doing everything for J.J. It's kind of fun. Gives me a real sense of self-sufficiency."

Nina thought about that. "Do you cook?"

"Nothing gourmet, but he doesn't mind that. He's big on things like BLTs, and PB and Fs."

"PB and Fs?"

"Peanut butter and fluff sandwiches. Not quite the kind of meal you make, I'm sure."

Remembering the exchange they'd had over cookbooks in his store, Nina felt sheepish. "I don't really do that much."

"Ha," he scoffed. "I'm the one who unpacked your kitchen today. I saw that wok and that clay pot and that fondue dish."

"Those are all for fun. I don't use them often, except maybe for the wok. When I want a quick meal and don't feel like a frozen dinner, I stir-fry something up. I'm pretty good at it, actually. I've found some good recipes. I'll make you something sometime, if you'd like."

For the third time in the conversation, words had slipped from her mouth that she hadn't consciously put there. The idea that John Sawyer, whom she worked with but with whom she didn't have another thing in common except a love for reading, should want to come back to her house—for dinner, no less—was ridiculous. Surely he'd see that.

"Yeah," he said, "well, maybe." He paused. "So. Did you finish with the rest of your things?"

Feeling as though she'd been eased from a precarious place, she said, "Sure did. I'm feeling it now."

"Sore?"

"Mmm. I was just about to get in the—oh, hell! Hold on! I forgot about the water!" All but dropping the phone on the floor, she raced into the bathroom in time to watch the first of a steaming waterfall cascade over the edge of the tub. Frantically twisting the taps, she turned off the water, pulled out the plug, then reached for the towels she'd so recently hung on the nearby bar. "Good show, Nina," she muttered to herself as she mopped up the spillage. When she had the worst of it absorbed, she dropped the sodden towels into the sink, replaced the plug with just enough water left for her bath and returned to the phone.

"I can't believe I did that," she said without prelude. "A fine thing it'd be if the first night I'm here, I send water dripping onto my landlord's head."

"All cleaned up?"

"Enough." Thinking of the still-damp floor, she sighed. "I'd better go finish. Thanks for calling, John. And thanks again for your help. It was nice."

Some time later, lying in the tub with the heat of the water seeping into her tired limbs, Nina realized that it had been nice, both his help and his call. He was a nice man. A *sexy* man. All wrong for her, of course, and there was no point in even *thinking* of a repeat of that kiss. Still, he was nice to be with—which was what she told Lee the next morning when she was asked about the car that had been parked behind her car that Sunday afternoon.

"I was going to stop in and see how you were doing," Lee explained, "but when I saw that, I figured you already had a guest. I never thought it'd be John Sawyer." Her eyes narrowed in play. "Is there something you haven't told me?"

"Nothing at all," Nina said, cool and composed from the top of her shiny black hair to the toes of her shiny purple shoes. "John Sawyer is someone I work with. He knew I was moving, so he stopped by to help."

"I thought he drove you nuts."

"He does when it comes to work. But he's good for lifting cartons. So I used him." More pointedly she said, "That's what you have to learn to do. Turn the tables on Tom. Use him for a change, rather than the other way around."

"I'm not moving."

"Then use him for something else. Ask him to bring the wine and dessert if you're the one who's cooking dinner. Ask him to give you a lift to the service station when you have to pick up your car."

Lee wrinkled her nose. "I don't think he'd appreciate that."

"Probably not." Her voice gentled. "He does things on his terms, and his terms alone. That's not good. It's not fair."

Lee shrugged. "Maybe not, but that's the way it is."

Not for me, Nina thought. *Never for me.* She had her work. It, and the reward it brought, were all she needed.

With that reminder, she swiveled around to face her computer, punched up the current listings and got busy.

5

Out of sight was not out of mind. Nina tried not to think about John. She tried not to think about the way he looked or the way he acted. Mostly she tried not to think about the way he kissed, but it didn't work. Memory was insidious, wending through her mind in brief but potent flashes.

She hadn't had a kiss like that since...she'd *never* had a kiss like that. In her experience, men kissed women either rapaciously, showing their hunger and proud of it, or timidly, showing their fear, hoping to pass it off as sensitivity. John hadn't kissed her either of those ways. His kiss had been forceful in a quiet, thoughtful way, which was pretty much how he was himself. He'd known what he was doing. His mouth had conveyed the attraction he felt. The fact that the attraction was unbidden made it all the more special.

But it was over, and she had put it from her mind, so she immersed herself in her work for all she was worth. It wasn't hard, since she loved what she did. And there was plenty to keep her busy. If she wasn't out showing a piece of property, she was working with the newspaper on fresh copy or doing paperwork for an impending sale or tracking down a competitor with a co-broke offer. When she was in the office, her phone was forever ringing.

None of those calls were from John. As the week wore on, during those brief in-between times when she thought of him, she began to wonder why he hadn't called. He had been so persistent at first that they discuss Crosslyn Rise, and though the decision on pricing had been made, the consortium had very clearly asked them to continue to work together.

She wondered whether he was as bothered, after the fact, by that kiss as she was.

She wondered whether he was embarrassed. Or disappointed. Or disgusted.

She wondered whether he hated her.

By Friday afternoon, she'd just about had it with the wondering. Picking up the phone, she punched out his number.

He answered, his voice deep and pleasantly resonant. "The Leaf Turner."

"John? It's Nina. Am I getting you at a bad time?" Heart pounding, she waited.

His voice came back a little less deep than it had been. "No, not at all. There's actually a comfortable lull here right now. How are you?"

She chose to believe he was pleased that she'd called. "Fine," she answered lightheartedly. "And you?"

"Can't complain."

"How's J.J.?" she asked, knowing it was the one thing that would guarantee a positive response.

"Great. The girls took him out for ice cream. He loves that."

"Girls, plural?"

"Two. Twins. What with J.J.'s problems, I like knowing there are two of them, so that one can keep an eye on him at any given time. You know how baby-sitters can be."

Actually she didn't. An only child herself, she'd never had a baby-sitter, but had been left with a neighbor or, at a frighteningly tender age, alone. Her mother hadn't had the money to pay a sitter. By virtue of that same fact, when Nina had been old enough to work, she had by-passed baby-sitting in favor of a supermarket job with more regular hours and higher pay. It hadn't mattered that the supermarket didn't hire kids under fifteen. She had talked them into hiring her. Even back then, she'd had a persuasive mouth.

"Do they talk on the phone a lot?" she asked.

"It's not as much that, as getting distracted cooking pizza or watching television. Actually, these two are pretty responsible. And they think J.J. is adorable."

"I'll bet he is," Nina said, because if he looked anything like John, she was sure he was. "Did you get all the mustard and stuff out?"

"The what? Oh, that. Pretty much."

Again she pictured him doing the wash and felt admiration. He was a good father. A good man.

Aware of the silence, she cleared her throat and said, "Uh, I'm actually calling about work, John. I picked up the finished brochures from the printer today. They're the ones we'll be handing out at the open house, and then, after that, in the office to anyone interested in Crosslyn Rise. I thought you might like to see them."

"That would be nice," he said with what she could have sworn was a touch of caution.

"I'll be working most of the weekend, so I'll be in and out, but I have to man the front desk at the office Sunday morning from ten to twelve." She had thought it all out. Her calling him was a business move. She didn't want him thinking it was anything else. Hence, the office. "Do you want to stop by then?"

After a pause, he said, "I could do that."

"You could bring J.J. if you want." He certainly didn't have to hire a sitter for something as innocent as a brief office meeting. "We won't be long. You'll probably want to take the brochure home to study. I'll be passing out copies to all of the members of the consortium at our next meeting, but I thought you might want to see it before then. There may be some things that you think are stronger or weaker, that we can compensate for in person at the open house."

"Okay. I'll drop by."

"Sometime between ten and twelve?"

"Uh-huh."

She shrugged. That was that. "See you then."

She told herself that it was nothing more than another business meeting and probably wouldn't last longer than two minutes, still she took care in dressing, again passing over some of the more outlandish of her outfits in favor of a relatively sedate slacks set. Granted, the pants were harem-style and the top short and loose, but the color was moss green, the neck barely scooped and the sleeves as voluminous as the legs.

Well, hell, he didn't expect that she'd dress like a schoolmarm, did he? At least, the outfit wasn't neon pink, like some of hers were, and her nails weren't red now, but beige.

Ten o'clock came and went. She talked with a couple who walked in off the street, people who thought *maybe* they'd look for something new but *only* if they could sell their old place and what were their chances of that. Ten-fifteen became ten-thirty. One of Martin's clients came by to drop some papers he'd signed. A potential buyer called to check on the time of another open house. Ten forty-five passed and eleven arrived.

She was beginning to wonder whether he'd forgotten, when, shortly before eleven-thirty, he came leisurely through the door. He was alone; she felt an unexpected stab of disappointment at that. But the disappointment was brief, because he looked so good. His hair was damp, freshly combed back over his ears and down over his nape. He was wearing a white shirt—open at the neck, with the sleeves rolled—and a pair of jeans that looked relatively new. She wondered if it was his Sunday best.

When he planted himself directly before her desk, she smiled. "You've been at the beach again." His skin had a golden glow, a bit of new color over what she'd seen the week before.

He nodded. "This morning. J.J. is still there."

Her face dropped. "Oh, I'm sorry, John. I didn't mean to drag you

away from him. This wasn't so important. We could have done it another time.''

"You didn't drag me away. He's with friends. He's happy."

"The same friends who took him out last week?"

He shook his head. "Different ones. They have a daughter with special needs. She's just about J.J.'s age. They're in the same play group."

"Do all the children in the play group have similar handicaps?"

"Roughly."

"How many children?"

"Twelve."

She was stunned. "And they all live around here?" She couldn't
imagine so many four-year-olds with similar problems in the immediate
area. As populations went, the local tally was low.

"No. Some of them come from pretty far, which means that we go
pretty far to see them in return. But it's worth it. Socialization is critical,
but it's hard for kids like these to get it through regular channels. I tried
J.J. in a local play group when he was two. I figured that he was doing
all the same things the other kids were, playing with blocks and all. But
he wasn't talking. Since he couldn't hear, he couldn't react to the other
kids the way they expected. And he made the mothers nervous."

Nina thought that was awful. "Screw *them*."

He gave a lopsided grin that created a dimple in his cheek—and sent
a ripple of awareness through Nina. "I felt the same way. Actually, I
felt worse. I was furious. Then I thought about it, and I talked it over
with J.J.'s therapists, and the way we reasoned it out, it wasn't so awful.
Those women were nervous because they didn't know how to communicate with J.J. They kept expecting him to be just like their own
kids, only he wasn't. Isn't. And it didn't matter how angry I got, no
way was that experience going to be positive, and that's the name of
the game. So now he's with people who understand him. They understand me. We've all been through the same things. We help each other."

"Like watching kids at the beach?"

"Like that."

Nina reached for the brochure that she'd tucked safely to the side.
"You'll probably want to take this and leave, then." She held it out,
trying to be a good sport. "It's a beautiful day for the beach. You'll be
anxious to get back."

He closed his hand around it, but rather than turning away, he arched
a questioning brow toward the chair by the desk. She was surprised,
and delighted. With an enthusiastic, "Please," she watched him lower
himself into the chair, stretch out his legs and open the brochure.

He really *was* handsome, she decided again. He wasn't urbane or
sophisticated looking, certainly not slick, still he was handsome. Today

there was something western about him. With his fresh jeans and his damp hair and the color the sun had painted on his skin, he looked like a cowboy newly off the range and showered. With high-heeled boots, the picture would have been complete. Then again, she preferred his deck shoes, particularly the way he wore them without socks. She wondered what his ankles were like, whether they were as well formed as his hands and wrists, and half wished he'd cross one of his legs so she could see.

But he didn't. Looking perfectly comfortable as he was, he took his time reading the copy, studying the drawings, closing the brochure to look at the piece as a whole. "This is very professional," he said at last.

She felt inordinately pleased. "Thank you. Do you think it'll impress the people we want to impress?"

"It should." He turned to the last page, where the price guides were listed. "I was wondering whether they'd get these right."

"You mean, you were wondering whether I'd hike those prices back up between the time the consortium voted and the printer printed?" She couldn't quite tell if he was kidding. Rather than overreact if he was, she kept her voice light. "I wouldn't do that, John."

He shrugged. "You never can tell with typos."

"There aren't any typos in that brochure. Not a single one. I've been over it with a fine-tooth comb dozens of times. It's perfect."

Taking several more minutes, he looked through it again. Then, unfolding himself from the chair, he stood. "I like it, Nina."

She hated to see him leave so soon. "I thought maybe you'd have some suggestions."

"This is pretty much a *fait accompli,* isn't it?"

"Yes, it's all printed, but that doesn't mean we can't approach things differently when we're talking with clients, if you think a different approach is called for." She was feeling a little foolish, because he was right. The brochure was done and printed. Everything major was correct. To change something small and reprint hundreds of copies would be an absurd expense.

Still, the consortium wanted them to work together.

Eyes on the brochure, he said, "Why don't I take this home and read it again—" his voice dropped and slowed "—when I'm not so distracted by the piles of soft stuff you're wearing." With each of the last words, his eyes rose a notch until finally they met hers. "I'll call you if anything comes to mind."

She swallowed. "That sounds okay."

He nodded. Raising two fingers in a wave that could have been negligent, bashful or reluctant, he left.

* * *

Nina made a point not to wait for his call. She figured that after the way she'd invited him over when she could as well have put the brochure in the mail, a little aloofness was called for. So she ran around as usual, confident that if he called the office, she'd get his message, and that if he called her at home, he'd keep calling until she was there.

It wasn't until Thursday night that she picked up her phone in response to its ring and heard his voice. "I still think the brochure is fine," he said after the briefest of exchanged hellos. "But I thought maybe we could go up to the Rise and take a look around. I haven't been there in a while. If you're looking for the reaction of an everyday Joe, I'm your man."

Not even at the beginning, when Nina had broken into cold sweats over John's pokey ways, had she thought of him as an everyday Joe, and she certainly didn't now. He was different. He marched to his own drummer. She did concede, though, that of all the consortium members, he was probably the one to give the most off-the-cuff response, so she supposed in a way he was right.

"Okay. When can you go?"

"Tomorrow morning, actually, but I know this is pretty last-minute for you. You probably have appointments all over the place."

She did. She didn't have to dig out her appointment book to know that, and when she did open it, she saw that her schedule was even worse than she'd thought. But John was free, and he was right. They really should get up to see Crosslyn Rise.

"I may be able to shift things around," she said, her mind already at work. "Can you give me half an hour to find out?"

"Sure. I'll call back."

During the next thirty minutes, Nina phoned four clients, one other broker and Lee. By the time John called back, she had cleared a two-hour stretch starting at ten. They agreed to meet then.

No matter how frequent a visitor Nina was to the Rise, she was always amazed at the progress she found with each return. Most impressive this time was the mansion. It had long since been scooped clean of its innards, with little left but structural elements such as the grand staircase and period details like ceiling moldings and chair rails. Renovation was well under way. Woodwork that had been stripped and sanded was now being stained. Walls were being modified, doorways shifted from one spot to another. From the large first-floor room that would serve as an elegant paneled meeting-room-lounge-library, to the large back room that would be a health club, to the totally modernized kitchen, the two private dining rooms, and the charming suites on the second floor that could be rented out to guests, the place was suddenly taking on the feel of something on the verge of being real.

"Does this ever look different," John said as he stood with his head tipped back to take in the height of the huge front hall. "Very nice."

He wasn't bubbly. His voice was as quiet as ever. But Nina, who had studied his face closely in the recent past, could read the subdued excitement there. Taking excitement from that, she waved him on. "Come." She led him from one room to the next, pausing in the middle of each, letting the feel of the place seep in. At spots where there was active construction going on, they had to watch where they stepped and moved, and at those times, John either went first and took her arm to guide her by or cautioned her to take care.

Nina had never been one to cling to a man, but John's touch felt good. Particularly on bare skin. In deference to the June warmth, she had worn a sundress. It was bright yellow, actually little more than a long tank top that, once hiked up at the waist by a wide leather belt, grazed the top of her knees. She had also worn flats for the sake of walking, and the overall effect was to make her feel that much more delicate next to John, who, wearing jeans and an open-necked shirt—a horizontally striped one this time—looked surprisingly rugged.

She stayed close, under the guise of safety, until they reached the outdoors and the danger of flying wood chips was gone. She would have given him more room then, but he didn't move away. He stayed close by her side during the walk down the path toward the duck pond, where the first of the near-completed condos were.

"Such a gorgeous place," he said. "I don't know how Jessica was ever able to give it up."

"She had to. She couldn't keep it as it was, and we couldn't find a single seller who could afford the whole thing. So rather than seeing it broken down by a developer who didn't care a whit about the glory of the Rise, she decided to form the consortium and be the one to call the shots."

"Does she call them, or does Carter?"

Nina looked up to find a mischievous smile touching his mouth. Her gaze lingered on his mouth for a minute before she said, "Jessica does. Carter gives her input, and he runs the meetings, but in the end the decision is hers." She returned her eyes to the path.

"They seem happy."

"They are."

"I think she's pregnant."

Nina's eyes flew back to his. This time John seemed totally serious. "How do you know?"

"She has that look."

"You mean, radiance? For heaven's sake, John, that's a crock."

"It is not."

"When a woman is pregnant, she feels sick. Then fat and clunky. There's nothing radiant about being that way."

"Fine for you to say," John said, kicking aside a fallen twig. "You've never been pregnant. You don't know what the feeling's like."

She laughed. "And you do? I hate to tell you this, John—"

"I remember when my wife was pregnant," he said quietly. Coming to a stop, he looked off in the distance, seeing not the duck pond but another time years before. "She wasn't real happy about it, but I was. I thought it was a miracle, the idea of this little life growing inside her. Long before the baby moved, I could see the changes in her body. First her breasts, then her waist, nature doing its thing in a totally generic way. Maybe she was too close to be able to appreciate it. I was just that little bit removed, so I could see things in a broader scheme. Then, when I felt the baby move in her stomach, everything that had been so broad seemed to focus in on the fact that it was my child growing there." His breath caught on the intake. Seeming surprised by his own words, he looked quickly at Nina. "Sorry. I get carried away. It was an incredible experience."

Standing still beside him, she felt goose bumps running up and down her arms. "You make it sound incredible." And she could almost believe in radiance, because she could have sworn that was the look she had seen on John's face for the few seconds before he'd caught himself.

The look she saw now was more earthy, and there was no way his glasses could mask it. His eyes were on her goose bumps. "Cold?"

"No."

Lightly, starting at her wrists, he ran his hands up her arms. They stopped just shy of her shoulders to gently knead her skin. He watched their progress, first one, then the next. "It's too bad you don't want to have kids. You'd make a pretty mother."

Her skin felt hot where he touched it, and the heat was stealing inside. "People would have trouble telling me from the kids," she managed to say, though her voice was meager.

"Pregnant, I mean. You'd be pretty pregnant."

Her heart was racing. "Maybe more substantial."

"No." His eyes touched her breasts, which rose with each shallow breath she took. "You're substantial now. But it's different when you're pregnant. Not just added weight. Something else." His eyes slipped to her stomach, caressing it through the thin jersey material, causing the same kneading sensation that was so seductive on her arms. She could barely move, barely breathe. Slowly, searing a path along the way, his gaze rose and locked with hers. "I keep thinking about you, Nina. I don't want to, but I do."

At the reluctant admission, she started to shake her head, but he made a shushing motion with his mouth and that stopped her. His voice was low, slow and sandy. "I keep remembering that kiss. It was so good. The only problem was that nothing touched but our mouths."

"I know," she whispered.

While his hands kept up their gentle motion, his thumbs slid sensuously up and down under the thin straps at her shoulders. "I keep wondering what it would be like to touch other places. I lie in bed at night imagining. It's not fun."

She swallowed. "Because you don't want to like me?"

"Because I get hard."

Her breath caught in her throat and stayed there despite the wild skittering of her pulse. She gave a short, sharp shake of her head.

"What?"

"Don't say things like that," she begged.

"Because it embarrasses you?"

"Because it excites me."

The flare in John's eyes told her what her words had done. His thumbs began moving more widely, stroking her skin in small patches that inched downward, under the edge of her dress, over the starting swell of her breast.

"I want to touch you more," he said. With the lightest pressure, he brought her arms just that tiny bit forward to angle her body better for his seeking thumbs. They stroked deeper, even deeper, under her bra now, moving toward the center of her breasts.

Her nipples tightened. "John," she whispered weakly. Heat seemed to be gathering and pooling not only in her breasts, but down low. She clutched his hips for support.

"Let me," he whispered back, as his thumbs reached their twin goals. He circled them once, touched their tips, then moved back and forth in a gentle rubbing.

Catching in a small cry, Nina bit her lip. But the feeling in her breasts was still too intense, so she closed her eyes and dropped her head back.

With a low groan, John caught her to him. His hands left her breasts and circled her, drawing her fully into his body at the same time that his mouth came down on hers. He kissed her long and deep, first with his lips, then his tongue. Wrapping her arms around his neck, she sought his firmness. Opening her mouth wide to his, she tasted his hunger. There was nothing in him that was either rapacious or arrogant. He kissed her like a man who simply needed to be closer.

And closer he brought her. His arms swept over her back, one lower, one higher, pressing her into him at every point. His strength came at her through his thighs, his chest, his arms, made all the more enticing to her by the faint tremor that spoke of his restraint.

When he finally tore his mouth away, his breathing was ragged. Dragging his arms from around her, he took her face in his hands. "What the hell am I going to do with you?"

She didn't know what to say.

"Can you feel how much I want you?"

She hadn't been that long without a man that she didn't know the meaning of the hard presence against her stomach. Unable to take her eyes from his, she nodded.

"So?" he asked in frustration.

"So I don't sleep around."

"Me, neither."

"I don't take making love lightly."

"Me, neither.

"So we can't do it. We're all wrong for each other. We don't even like each other. And we have to work together."

He looked at her for a long time, his amber eyes dark and hungry still. "You're right." His thumbs skimmed her cheeks. "But all that doesn't take the wanting away. I haven't wanted a woman—"

He was cut off by the intrusion of a loud voice on the approach. "Okay, you guys, I think you'd better break it up."

Nina's head shot around as quickly as John's, and she found herself staring into the amused eyes of Carter Malloy, who was coming from the direction of the duck pond. Stopping not far from them, he said, "I think there's something about the air out here. It makes you forget that just anyone could be walking through. Fortunately for you, it's me. I understand these things."

Nina knew her cheeks were red, but she didn't say a word either in defense of herself or protest to John when he slowly released her.

Carter scratched the back of his head. "I nearly lost it with Jessica, just about a year ago, not far from where you stand." He paused, looking from Nina's face to John's. "I think the ducks were less embarrassed then than you two are now."

Nina took a deep, faintly shuddering breath. "You should have called from way back on the path."

"I did."

"Oh."

John had his hands on his hips. "You should have called a second time."

"I did. But, hey, now that you're awake and aware, I'll just be moving along." He gave them a grin and started off. "Catch you later."

He'd gone a good ten yard when Nina called, "Carter, is Jessica pregnant?"

He stopped in his tracks and turned, wearing a guarded look. "Where did you hear that?"

"Is it true?"

Taking a deep breath that straightened his back and expanded his chest beneath the blazer and shirt he was wearing, Carter allowed himself a slow smile. "Yeah, it's true. She miscarried in January, so we've been cautious about saying anything. But she's almost into her fourth month. Things look good this time."

Forgetting her embarrassment, Nina burst into a grin. "Hey, that's great. I knew she wanted a baby."

"We both do."

"How's she feeling?" John asked.

Carter shimmied a hand. "Sometimes nauseous, sometimes not. The doctor says the sickness is a sign that the baby's really settling in, which is good news after the first one. We're keeping our fingers crossed."

"I'll keep mine crossed, too," Nina said.

John put a thumb up and said in a very male way, "Good goin', Carter."

Carter tossed him a macho smile before turning and continuing along the path.

Watching him go, Nina murmured under her breath, "Are you going to say, 'I told you so'?"

"Of course not. The important thing is that it's true."

"Mmm. She did tell me she wanted a baby. I'm excited for her."

"Excited about the baby?"

"Excited because she's getting what she wants. I don't know enough about babies to get excited about them."

"Don't have any friends with kids?"

"A few. But I've never been terribly involved. I'm too busy with work. My friends seem to know that. When they meet me for lunch, it's without the kids." She allowed herself a glance at John. "Which is another reason why you and I are no good. You have a kid. I wouldn't know what in the devil to do with one."

John didn't say anything. He stood there, looking down at her, looking *into* her, seemingly, for something she was sure wasn't there. Looking back at him, all she could see was the random brush of his hair on his brow, the lean contour of his jaw, the straight slash of his nose, the tightness of his lips. It was a face that drew her even when she told herself that it shouldn't.

Finally he raised his head and looked away. "We'd better get going."

Nodding, she started off toward the duck pond, but the glow that had earlier been on the day was gone. In its place was a tension that began in the body and ended in the mind, causing an awkwardness that was underwritten with need.

They walked through the condominium that was to be the model, then through two others. Nina pointed out various features and options, just as she might have if John had been an interested buyer. They avoided looking at each other, avoided standing too close, but that didn't ease the wire that seemed strung taut between them. Whatever the distance, it hummed.

By the time they returned to the mansion, Nina was feeling strung out, herself. She was only too glad to put together a hasty goodbye to John, climb into her car and drive off. She wasn't used to confusion. Hitherto in her life, she had been the sole master of her fate. Now, though, it seemed she was losing control, if not of her fate, then of *something*.

She wished she knew what that something was.

She wished she could stop it from slipping away.

She wished she didn't feel hot, then cold, light, then dark, good, then bad.

Mostly she wished she understood what she was feeling for John. He wasn't like any man she'd ever known. He was maddeningly laid-back, but she respected him. He saw the world differently from her, but she trusted him. She liked him, but she didn't.

And she wanted him. Wanted him. He haunted her for the rest of the day and all that night. She lay in bed wide awake, remembering how he'd kissed her and held her, how safe she'd felt, how valued, how hot and needy. The need returned, making her flop one way then the next, but no position was better for the aching within. *I lie in bed imagining,* he'd said, and she imagined him imagining. She also imagined him hard, and the fever built.

She slept for an hour, then awoke, slept for another, awoke again. When her skin grew damp in the warmth of the night, she sponged herself off, but no sooner did she return to bed than she was sweaty again.

By dawn, she was fit to be tied. No man, *no man*, she vowed, could do this to her. No man was worth it. She had her life, and it was free and independent, just as she wanted. Once she had her own agency, that independence would increase. She was well on her way to where she wanted to be. She didn't need any man, *any man*.

Then, at eight o'clock, her doorbell rang. Sticky, tired and more than a little cranky, she plodded down the stairs. "Who is it?" she yelled through the wood.

"John," he called back.

Moaning softly, she put her forehead to the worn pine. It was cool, with a faint musty scent that took her out of time and place, but the relief was short-lived. John was on the other side. She didn't know what to do.

His voice came more quietly, as though he'd moved closer. "Open the door, Nina. We need to talk."

"I don't think," she said, squeezing her eyes shut, "that this is the best time."

He didn't answer. Had he been another man, she might have wondered if he'd left. But this was John.

After a minute, he spoke again, still quiet, still close. "Nina? Open the door, Nina. Please?"

She might have had a comeback had it not been for his tone of voice. Not even the thickness of the door could muffle the quiet command. But there was something else there, something even more potent. Beneath the quiet command was a hint of pleading.

Fearing she was making a huge mistake but helpless to avoid it, she gave a tiny sound of frustration, took a small step back and opened the door a crack.

6

John pushed the door open only enough to slip through. Watching him from the corner by the hinge, Nina felt beset by every one of the wild imaginings she'd tried to stifle through the night. The fact that he wore a T-shirt and shorts didn't help any. The sight of leanly muscled legs spattered with warm brown hair stirred the fire inside her to a greater head.

"I brought donuts," he said quietly, but his eyes hadn't risen above her neck.

She was in the short nightie that she'd put on in the wee hours, and wore nothing beneath it. "I was in bed," she said, feeling the need to explain. She wouldn't normally have answered the door dressed that way. But she felt reckless, at the end of her tether. "It was a bad night."

At that, he did raise his eyes. He'd left his glasses at home, and it struck her that he looked every bit as sweaty as she felt. His hair was damp and disheveled, his skin moist. "I ran." His eyes were intent, the deepest, richest amber she'd ever seen. "I thought we could talk."

"I don't know if I can." Her need was written all over her face, she knew, but she couldn't erase it.

John seemed to see it, consider it, fight it—with about as much success as she had. After an eternity of searing silence, he muttered, "I don't want these." Dropping the bag of donuts onto the stair, he reached for her.

Coming up against his body, winding her arms around his neck, feeling him lift her nearly off her feet, Nina felt the first relief she'd had in hours. She sighed his name and held tighter, burying her face against his neck.

For the longest time, they stood like that, holding each other tighter, then tighter still, making no sounds but those of quickened breathing and the occasional whimper or moan. Nina might have stayed that way forever if it wasn't for the gradual awakening of her body to the one molding it. She began to move against him in small ways to better feel him, and when that wasn't enough, she started to use her hands.

John's own hands made slow sweeps of discovery over her back. She could tell the instant he knew for sure she was bare under her nightie by the sharp catch of his breath. Fingers splayed, his hands stole up the back of her thighs to her bottom.

"Tell me to stop if you don't want this," he said in a gravelly voice she'd never heard before. It was laced with raw need and was a stimulant in itself.

"I want it," she breathed frantically. Exploring the lean line of his hips, she pushed her fingers over his thighs. The hair there abraded her palms delightfully. "I need it," she confessed just as frantically, then let out a cry when he touched the fire between her legs. "Help me," she begged, and to convince him, she worked her fingers up under his shorts. He wore cotton briefs, but they were stretched taut.

Clearly he didn't need any convincing.

Before she had any inkling of what he was doing, he slid his hands under her thighs and lifted her. When her legs were cinched around his hips, he covered her mouth with his and devoured it whole as he started up the stairs. He didn't stop until he was in her bedroom, where he lowered her to the rumpled sheets and crouched over her.

His voice a rough burr, he drew up her nightie. "I haven't been with anyone since my wife. Do I need a condom?"

Nina helped him pull the thin fabric over her head. As soon as one hand was freed, she reached for him. "It's been longer than that for me," she whispered hurriedly as she tugged at his shirt. It was over his head in an instant, revealing a chest that was well formed and tapering. A wide wedge of hair narrowed, arrowlike, toward his fly. She reached there and touched him. "No condom."

John lowered his zipper and shifted to thrust both shorts and briefs aside. "Babies?"

"I take pills," she gasped, then, "Hurry, John, hurry." His large hand swept her under him, and no sooner did she open her legs when, like a heat seeker, he was in. Stunned by the force of his impaling, she cried out and arched up.

"Nina—"

"No, no, it doesn't hurt, it feels good, so good."

But that penetration, that first feel of his masculine strength, was only the beginning. What he proceeded to do then nearly blew her mind. He stroked her inside and out, using his hands, his mouth, his sex. He nipped, he laved. He quickened the pace and the force when her breath came more quickly. At times his movements were rhythmic, at times less so. At times he filled her to the utmost, withdrew nearly all the way, then reentered with a sharp pulsing burst that she might have feared was climactic if he hadn't continued right on again.

Hungry for everything he gave her, she touched him wherever she could, but the heat he stoked in her soon drove everything from her mind except the release coming on. She erupted with a vengeance, throbbing against him for what seemed an eternity. Lost on the other side of rapture, she wasn't able to separate her climax from his until she finally returned to consciousness enough to feel the last of the spasms shaking his body.

Slowly, breathing hard, he lowered himself over her. After a long minute, he rolled to his side and drew her along, still inside her.

She looked into his eyes, and for a minute she couldn't speak. Something caught at her throat, something deep and emotional, something she couldn't—didn't want to—understand. Making love with John had been the experience of a lifetime.

As the minutes passed and she regained her poise, she let a smile soften her lip. "Who'd have guessed it?" she finally whispered.

His brow creased in a frown that was here and gone. "Guessed what?"

"That slow, quiet, thoughtful John Sawyer was a crackerjack of unleashed virility in bed."

His cheeks were already flushed, but she could have sworn they grew more so. "I was inspired."

"You certainly were." Her smile faded. She touched his face. "That was special."

He gave a slow, thoughtful nod. "Are you sure I didn't hurt you?"

"Do I look hurt?"

He shook his head. Slowly. "You look well loved." He touched her lips, which were still warm and swollen, then her cheek, then her hair. "How can hair that is shorter than mine be feminine?"

"It's not real hard to have hair shorter than yours," she quipped, and buried her fingers in the thickness at his nape, "but I like it."

"You didn't at first."

"I didn't like much about you at first. You were slowing me down."

"I still am. It's become my cause."

She assumed he was teasing and teased him right back. "It won't work."

"Sure, it will. You're not rushing off to work right now, are you?"

She shook her head. "I don't have to be in until ten."

"If you had to be in at nine, would you be rushing?"

"Maybe." She grinned. "I suppose it would depend on how forceful that *thing* you're anchoring me here with is. Doesn't feel too forceful right now."

He grinned back. "Give it a minute."

"You think so?"

"I know so."

She waited a minute, during which time she touched his chest, tracing the hair there, teasing his nipples. "Hmm," she said, clamping her thigh higher around his when she felt him growing inside her, "I think you may be right."

"Of course I'm right." He caught her mouth and ate at it gently, then less gently as his hunger grew. Fluidly he rolled to his back, bringing her up to straddle him. His eyes were focused on her breasts, which were warm and rose tipped. After guiding her hips for a deeper joining, he left her to her own devices there and touched her breasts.

Nina watched the long fingers she admired curved around her flesh. She watched them trace her shape and weigh her fullness. She watched them knead, then rub her nipples into hard beads, then draw her forward to meet his mouth. The sight of his tongue dabbing the tip of her breast with moisture that his finger then spread, was nearly her undoing. Closing her eyes, she began to move on him, shifting forward, then back and around, feeling him grow and grow inside her until he was rising to meet her thrusts.

He brought her to a first climax by tugging her nipples into elongated points. He brought her to a second one by finding the hard bud between her legs and stroking it to fruition. He brought her to a third one by rolling her over and plunging into her with the kind of savagery she'd never have expected from him, but which drove her wild. By the time he'd emptied himself into her, their bodies were slick and spent.

For a short time, they lay limp and quiet, and at first, Nina enjoyed the closeness. Then her mind clicked on. Slowly picking up speed, it ran her through what had happened, painting pictures of what it meant, and she grew frightened. She had enjoyed herself too much, far too much. John Sawyer as a lover could be habit-forming. But she didn't have room in her life for a relationship. She didn't have time for a man like John. She had places to go. She couldn't be tied down, *wouldn't* be tied down, not even by her own desires.

"Gotta get up," she murmured from against his chest.

His arm tightened around her. "No, stay."

"Gotta get to work."

"Call in. Get someone to cover."

"I can't."

"I have a sitter till noon."

A sitter. The word represented one of the major differences between Nina and John. Flattening a firm hand on his chest, Nina ignored the lure of damp, warmly furred male flesh and levered herself up. Seconds later, she was out of bed, headed for the bathroom.

"Nina?" John called.

"I have to shower," she called back.

"Put it off."

"I can't."

She turned on the water. As soon as steam rose from it, she stepped under and began to soap herself. She worked methodically, the same way she always did. If certain spots were more sensitive than usual, even tender, she ignored that. She went on to her hair, scrubbing it hard, then rinsed, turned off the water, reached for the towel and began to rub herself dry. By the time she returned to the bedroom, John was propped up against the brass headboard, looking extraordinarily masculine against her bright pink sheets. Everything in the room was bright pink for that matter; still he didn't look foolish. Just masculine.

Ignoring that, too, she took underwear from a drawer and put it on, then a pair of silk walking shorts and a matching silk blouse, both in fuchsia. After hooking a pair of turquoise spangles onto her ears, a matching necklace around her neck and a belt around her waist, she stepped into strappy sandals. Then she shook her head, vigorously, peered into the mirror over the dresser and finger-combed her hair.

"Nina."

She looked over at John in surprise. She hadn't forgotten he was there—no way could she do that—but he'd been so still for so long that his voice, strangely sharp, startled her.

"Is that it?" he asked. His face was expressionless, his eyes level.

"What?"

"We make love, you get up and leave?"

Opening her makeup case, she began to smooth moisturizer onto her face. "I have to work."

"I want to talk."

Eyes on her own reflection, she shook her head. "Can't do that now. Maybe another time."

"When?"

She shrugged. "I don't know. I'll have to see when I'm free."

"You can be free any time you want to."

"I cannot. I have clients to service."

"So what about me?"

Her voice was low, her fingertips busy dabbing eye shadow onto her lids. "Seems to me I just serviced you."

John swore. Kicking back the sheet, he rolled to his feet and came to stand over her. Looking in the mirror, Nina caught sight of his nakedness for an instant before her own body blotted out the image, and not a moment too soon. Naked, he was stunning.

"Don't use that word with regard to what we did."

She forced a shrug, hinting at a nonchalance she didn't feel, and went on with her makeup.

"Damn it, Nina, didn't that *mean* anything to you? I mean, you're the very first woman I've been with—wanted to be with—since the debacle of my marriage, and you say that you haven't been with any other man, yet you can just climb out of bed, get dressed and move on?''

"I have work to do," she said quietly. "I take it seriously."

He rubbed a hand along the back of his neck. She could see that much. Even barefoot, he stood tall over her. Warily, with half an eye, she watched him, waiting for him to move or speak. With the other half, she finished her makeup. He hadn't said anything by the time she snapped her blusher shut and zipped it back into the bag, but he was giving her a baleful stare.

"Okay," she said, turning to him in concession, "so I'm a cold, hard bitch who's in a rush to get back to work. You can think it. You can *say* it. You knew it before this ever happened."

"Didn't this mean anything?"

"Of *course* it did. I told you, I don't play around, and I *haven't* been with a man in years. But just because we made love doesn't change anything. You still have your priorities, and I have mine. Neither of us is going to change. You knew that, John. We both knew it. That's why doing this was so stupid."

"So why did we?"

She tried to find a sensible answer, but the only thing she could come up with was, "Because we couldn't *not* do it. There's something chemical between us. It was building up and building up. This was inevitable." She turned away to reach for the purse that matched her outfit. "Dumb, but inevitable."

He stuck his hands on his lean hips, totally unselfconscious, seemingly unaware of the magnificent picture he made. "And you're sorry we did it?"

She hung her head and fingered the purse. "No. I enjoyed it."

"But you'll just turn and walk away from it?"

Her eyes shot to his. "What would you have me do?"

"Stay here. Talk to me."

"There's no *point*. What's done is done. Now I'm getting back to my life."

"You work too hard."

She made for the door. "What else is new?"

"You looked awful when I walked in here," he said, following her through the apartment.

"That was because of you. I didn't sleep last night. I kept thinking of *you*." As indictments went, it was a revealing one, but her step didn't falter.

"And you think you can stop now?"

"I'm sure as hell going to try."

"How?"

"By *working*." She reached the head of the stairs, and without a pause, started down.

"You won't be able to," he called from the top.

"Yes, I will."

"What we've done just now will haunt you."

"I won't let it."

"You can't even *look* at me!" he shouted.

Nina hadn't ever heard him shout before. The sound shook her from the top of her head to the tips of her toes, but it wasn't enough to make her turn. Lest she be stopped cold like Lot's wife, she hauled open the door and fled without a single glance back.

Nina was determined to do just what she'd said, to get back to work as though nothing as earth-shattering as making love with John had ever happened. Neither John nor his gorgeous body nor his masterful way of loving was going to sidetrack her from her goals of making money, making a name and making a fully independent way of life for herself.

So she poured herself into work more single-mindedly than ever that Saturday. It wasn't until after nine that night that she returned to her apartment, and she was off at seven the next morning to drive to Hartford for a one-day seminar. She was exhausted by the time she returned, feeling hot and sweaty and achy, just as she had on Friday night. Knowing John was the culprit and determined to push him from her mind, she refused to answer the phone—which rang repeatedly through the evening—and instead set herself up with a particularly tricky and, therefore, demanding book of figures relating to home mortgage options, shifting interest rates and tax plans. She worked at it until two in the morning, when a combination of exhaustion and an upset stomach got to her. Fortunately, exhaustion was the stronger of the two. She was asleep soon after her head hit the pillow.

At nine the next morning, Lee popped into her office. "Been here long?" she asked.

Nina looked up from the papers she'd been poring through. "Since eight. I'm off to show 93 Shady Hill in a couple of minutes."

Lee came closer to the desk. "You sound funny."

"Funny?"

"Tired. You look it, too. Pale."

Nina put down her pen. "I think it's a stomach bug or something. Don't come too close." Though she'd tossed the warning off half in jest, Lee backed up to the door.

"Whatever you have, I don't want. I'm making dinner Friday night at Tom's place for us and three other couples."

Nina lowered her head but not her eyes. "You're what?"

"Three other couples, and I know you're going to say that I'm crazy," she rushed on, "but I want to do it, Nina. Tom didn't ask me to. I offered."

"But he's left you sitting home alone for the past two weekends while he's off playing in New York—"

"Chicago, and it's business."

"Both weekends, *all* weekend?"

"Yes, and he was thinking of me. I showed you the scarf he brought me after last weekend. This weekend he sent flowers. It's not like he's off with another woman or anything." At Nina's dubious expression, she insisted, "He's not. Tom loves me."

Gently Nina said, "He loves what you do for him, and you love belonging."

"So, what's wrong with that?"

"Nothing—" She was about to add an "except" and then go on to say more, but caught herself. Much as she hated to see Lee hurt, she hated even more bad-mouthing Tom all the time. Lee was hooked on the man, so Nina was damned either way. It was a no-win situation. She *hated* no-win situations. Particularly when she was tired. "Listen," she said, forcing a smile, "maybe it'll work out. Maybe I'm all wrong, a cynic to the core." She tried to draw the last, but the draw went flat.

"You *must* be feeling lousy," Lee commented, eyeing her strangely. "We've been arguing about Tom for months, but you've never given up before."

"I'm not giving up. Just taking a breather. You'll hear from me again."

After a minute, softly, a bit worriedly, Lee said, "Are you sure it's just a bug that's getting you down?"

Nina touched the face of a pink slip that lay separate from the rest. "A bug and my mother. She's not doing well."

"Have you talked with her doctor?"

Setting her pink slip aside, she began to gather up her papers. "A few minutes ago. She seems to be having these little seizures. Her condition fluctuates."

"Maybe you should go out to see her."

The doctor had suggested the same thing. Again. "How can I go out there," Nina said, scooping the papers into a folder, "when there's so much to do here? This fluctuating could go on for a while. It's not even like she'd know I was there."

"But she's your mother—"

"And I do all I can. She's in the best possible place, totally at my expense, and I don't mind that. But in order to do it, I have to work. Bills don't get paid by flying all over the country." Setting the folder aside, she reached for her bag and stood.

"It's just Omaha."

"And I'll *get* there. Right now, things are buzzing here. The momentum is on. Business is great. As soon as there's a lull, I'll be on the first plane west." Holding a palm out she said, "I'm coming through the door. Move, or I won't be responsible for my germs."

Lee moved, and Nina was on her way.

The germs lingered through the rest of Monday and Tuesday, alternately leaving Nina crampy, then not. By Wednesday, she acknowledged that what was ailing her didn't have much to do with John, other than to kill any thought of sex she might have had. That was why, when John showed up at her door on Wednesday night, she opened it.

Under the light of the porch, he looked furious. "I've been trying to reach you all week. Didn't you get my messages?"

Feeling guilty and sad, then angry at herself for feeling either, not to mention the heartthrobbing that the mere sight of him caused, she said, "I've been busy."

"So busy that you couldn't return a single phone call to the man you took to bed last Saturday?"

"It was the other way around. You took me to bed."

"Want to argue about who was willing?" He barely paused, something that unsettled her even more than his words. John took his time, always took his time—unless he was upset. "You look like hell."

"Thanks."

"I'm serious." His fury faded some as he studied her face, and his voice, more tentative now, touched her heart. "Are you all right?"

She swallowed. "I'm fine. Just busy."

"What you're doing isn't healthy—"

"Just for a little bit. This is the height of the season. Come next fall—"

"Next fall! You can't keep up this pace till then!"

"I've done it every other year. This one's no different, except that this time the end is in sight. If Crosslyn Rise comes through the way I want, by next summer I'll be out on my own. Then I'll have other people to do the running through the height of the season."

"If you're still alive."

"I'll be alive."

He was quiet then, looking at her, pensive in the way she'd come to find both comforting and provocative. Since she wasn't feeling up to provocative, she took advantage of comforting until he ended it by saying, "What about us?"

"What about us?"

"Can I see you?"

She shook her head. "I need some space."

"How much?"

"I don't know."

"Look, I'm not asking you to give up your work."

"You were last Saturday—"

"Because it was so nice holding you that I didn't want you to leave. But I thought about it after that, and you were right. You had previous appointments, and you hadn't known I was coming. So all I want now is to arrange a time when you *do* know I'm coming."

"John," she whined in frustration, "you don't *like* me."

"I don't *want* to like you. There's a difference."

"If you don't want to like me, what are you doing making a date with me?"

"Trying to find out why I like you, even if I don't want to. That was what I wanted to talk about in the first place on Saturday morning, before we got sidetracked."

Nina saw a complicated discussion on the horizon, but she was in no more of a mood for it than she was for a sixteen-ounce steak. Her stomach was feeling weird, which was how it had been feeling on and off for too long. She would see a doctor if she had the time, but she didn't have the time. Work came first. Everything else would have to wait.

"Can we save this for another time, John?"

"Sure, if you can tell me when."

"I don't know when. If you call tomorrow, I'll check—"

"I call and you're out, and you don't return my calls."

"I'll return your call this time," she said earnestly. She *really* wanted to go upstairs and lie down. "Better still, I'll call you." She was ready to promise almost anything to get him to leave. Feeling worse by the minute, she was using every bit of her strength not to let it show.

Apparently she succeeded, because he looked calmer. "Will you?"

She nodded. "First thing tomorrow, once I get into the office. I'll call and we'll arrange a time. Okay?"

He thought about it for a minute, then nodded. "I'll be waiting."

His eyes fell to her mouth, and for a minute she thought he was going to kiss her before he left. One part of her wanted that more than anything; his kiss was a balm, able to make her feel good. Then again, when his kiss was over and done she always felt worse, and she didn't need that now. She was feeling awful enough without any help from John.

For whatever his reasons, he took a step back, turned and slowly went down the walk to his car. Taking only distracted pleasure from his tight-hipped walk, Nina closed the door and leaned against it for a minute before making her way upstairs.

Despite the earliness of the hour, she went right to bed. She was hurting too much to do anything else. It occurred to her that maybe people were right and she did need more sleep, and though, given her druthers, she'd rather be working, she figured she'd give it a try.

Sleep came sporadically. She dozed, only to awaken to a knotting in her stomach a few minutes later. After tossing and turning, she dozed again, but less than an hour later she was awake. Her stomach was feeling worse, aching almost steadily. Not one to take pills, she sipped water, then a little ginger ale, but nothing seemed to help. After a while, she slept, only to wake up this time in a sweat with the realization that the ache in her stomach had become a pain.

She began to grow frightened. She didn't have time to be sick. She couldn't *afford* to be sick. Desperately seeking an explanation for what was happening, she thought back on anything she had eaten that might have upset her, but what little she'd had in the past few days had been light and bland. Sipping more ginger ale, she lay down again, but the pain grew worse. Try as she might, no amount of rearranging of her body seemed to ease it.

She began to wish she had seen a doctor. She began to wonder if she should now. But other than her gynecologist, she didn't have one, hadn't ever needed one. Besides, it was after eleven. She couldn't be calling a doctor now. If worse came to worst, first thing in the morning she could make some calls and get a name.

That decided, she managed to sleep for a bit, only to rouse with a sharp cry as an acute pain suddenly tore through her insides. Clutching her stomach, she struggled to sit up, but she couldn't seem to catch her breath.

Fear gave way to terror. Something was very, very wrong. She didn't know what it was, didn't know what to do about it. Worse, she didn't think she would have been able to do anything if she *did* know what to do. She couldn't stand up straight. She could barely move.

Fighting panic, she picked up the phone by her bed, and with shaky fingers, punched out John's number. The phone rang twice before it was answered, but she didn't hear a voice.

"John?" she cried feebly. "Are you there, John?"

After a minute, she heard a groggy, "Nina?"

"Something's wrong," she cried in short, staggered bursts. "Awful pain. I don't know what to do."

His voice came stronger, all grogginess gone. "Where's the pain?"

"My stomach. I wanted to wait. But it's getting worse. I've never had this before."

"Is it cramps?"

"No. Pain. Sharp pain." She was bent in two trying to contain it.

"Which side?"

"I don't know. All over. No, more on the right."

He spoke firmly, exuding a gentle command. "Listen, babe, I'm gonna run next door for a sitter—"

"It's two in the morning. You can't—"

"Can you make it down to the front door?"

"I don't know. I think so."

"I want you to go there, unlock the door and wait for me. I won't be more than ten minutes."

"Oh, God, John, I'm sorry—"

"Go downstairs and wait."

"Okay." Trembling, she hung up the phone. Then, fearful that if the pain got worse she wouldn't make it, she stumbled out of bed and headed for the door. She stopped against the doorjamb, doubled over in pain, caught her breath, then stumbled on. Reaching the stairs, she sat on the top step and, one by one, eased herself down. She barely had time to unlatch the door at the bottom before she crumpled back onto the lowest step, in excruciating pain.

She must have passed out, because the next thing she knew, John was crouching down by her side. "Nina? *Nina.*"

His hand was cool against the burning on her forehead, her cheek, her neck, but it was the worry in his voice that reached her. She forced her eyes open. "I'm okay," she said, but even her voice was far away. Her insides were on fire, hurting like hell. With an anguished moan, she closed her eyes against the pain.

"You'll be fine," John said as he lifted her. The words came through a fog, the same way as the feel of his arms did. What was happening inside her body seemed to be putting distance between herself and the world. But trust was an intuitive thing. She trusted John. For that reason, as soon as she was in his arms, as soon as she felt him start to carry her out to his car, she yielded her well-being to him and turned her own focus to fighting the intense pain that was eating her alive.

Wakefulness came to Nina in fits and snatches over the course of the next few days. She seemed able to grasp at consciousness only briefly, enough to find out what had happened and ease the fear in her mind before yielding to the effects of anesthesia, painkillers and illness. At times when she woke up, there were doctors with her, poking and prodding, asking her questions that she had barely the strength to answer. At times there were nurses bathing her, shifting her, checking the fluid that ran from bottles, down thin tubes, into her veins.

At times John was there. Of all the faces she saw in her daze, his was the clearest. Of all the things she remembered hearing, his words were the ones that registered.

"You had a ruptured appendix," he told her during one of those first bouts with wakefulness.

"Ruptured?" she whispered, dry mouthed and groggy.

He was sitting close by the side of the bed and had her free hand in both of his, pressed to his throat. "But it's okay now. You'll be just fine."

Another time, when she awoke to find him perched on the side of the bed by her hip, she asked in a croak, "What did they do?"

He smiled crookedly. "Took out your appendix. Cleaned up the mess in there. Sewed you back up."

Moving her hand to her stomach, she felt what seemed like mountains of bandages. "So much stuff here."

"It'll come off soon. How do you feel?"

"Hot."

"That's the fever. They're giving you antibiotics. It should help pretty soon. Are your hurting?"

"A little. And tired."

Brushing her cheek with the back of his hand, he said, "Then sleep."

Given the quiet command and the warm assurance of his body close by, she did, and those hours of sleep were the best. When she awoke alone, there was an emptiness along with the pain and the heat, and she sought sleep again as an escape. Aloneness was bleak, strangely frightening. Given that she'd spent so much of her life alone, that would have mystified her if she'd been in any condition to analyze it. But she wasn't.

For nearly three days, she was in a limbo of fever and pain. Slowly, on the morning of the fourth, she began to emerge from it. The doctors were the first to visit, in the course of making their rounds. Then the nurses came in to do their thing. And then John.

She was awake this time when he appeared at the door. His face brightened when he saw that her eyes were open.

"Hey," he said, coming inside, "you're up."

"Finally." Her voice was still dry, weak and hoarse, and she was feeling more feeble than that, but the sight of him pleased her.

"You look better."

"I look awful."

"You've been up looking at yourself in the mirror?" he teased.

But she nodded. "They made me get out of bed."

"That's great," he said with enthusiasm, then grew more cautious. "How was it?"

"Terrible. I can't stand up straight."

"That'll come."

"I got dizzy. I nearly passed out, and that was just between the bed and the bathroom. It's discouraging."

"Were you expecting to get out of bed and dance a jig?"

"No, but I thought I'd be able to *walk*, at least. I mean, I've been lying here doing nothing for three full days—"

"Doing nothing?" His brows went up for an instant. When they came down, his expression was dark. "Babe, you were fighting for your life. It was touch and go for a while there. Didn't they tell you that?"

"Doctors exaggerate things."

"Not this time," John said, and his face underscored the words. "You've been really sick, Nina. They wanted to know if there were any close relatives who should be notified."

That sobered her a bit. "What did you tell them?"

"What Lee told me."

"Lee?"

"I called your office Thursday morning to let them know you wouldn't be in, and she was the one who called back. She's been in a couple of times, but you've been asleep." He settled gently on the side of the bed and said in a quiet, compassionate voice, "She told me about your mother. I'm sorry, Nina. I didn't know she was so sick."

Nina closed her eyes. "She's been sick for a long time."

"That's what Lee said."

He grew quiet, giving Nina the opportunity to go on, but she wasn't up for that. During the past few days, on those occasions when she'd woken up alone, she had thought about her mother more than she might have expected. She was feeling very strange about some of the thoughts she'd had, particularly now, knowing how sick she had been herself.

"Want to sleep?" John whispered.

She shook her head and whispered back, "I'm okay," but she didn't open her eyes.

He took her hand. "You can sleep if you want. I'll be here when you wake up."

"You've been here a lot."

"Whenever I could."

"You shouldn't have."

"This is important."

"But you have other things—"

"I have backup. Right now, this is where I want to be."

At the words, she felt a slow knot form in her throat. Turning her head away, she murmured, "I'm sorry."

"What for?"

"Being a pain in the butt. You've got more important things to do than sit here with me. You should be home with J.J."

"J.J.'s with a sitter. He's fine."

She squeezed her eyes shut. "He's with a sitter too much lately, and all because of me. First I drag you out in the middle of the night, then you feel you have to stay here—"

He touched her lips, stilling her words. "Thank God you did drag me out in the middle of the night. If you'd waited for morning, it might have been too late. And as for my staying here, I don't have to. I want to. Think of me as your warden. I'm gonna make sure you don't do too much too fast."

Her warden. She didn't know whether he was that or something else, but she did know that he was special. Lee might have stopped by to visit, but she'd left. Her other friends had sent cards and flowers, even called. But John had come. Time and again, he'd come. And stayed.

Feeling suddenly weepy, she tried to turn over onto her side, but the attempt brought a wince. John's hands were there, then, helping her, propping pillows behind her to give her support. "Okay, now?" he asked, leaning over her shoulder.

She nodded. Seconds later, she felt him brush at the tears escaping from the corners of her eyes.

"Ah, Nina," he whispered.

"I'm okay," she whispered back. "I'll just rest for a while." Taking his hand from her cheek, she tucked it inside hers, between her breasts. "Rest for just a little while," she murmured, and let herself go to sleep.

John was there when she woke up, then again later that night, then the next morning. He helped her out of bed and into the bathroom, then back into bed. He sat close beside her when she ate Jell-O, then later, custard, then later, a soft-boiled egg. He left for a little while at the end of the day but was back after he'd put J.J. to bed, then sat with her until after eleven.

By the Tuesday morning, her sixth in the hospital, she was finally feeling better. The intravenous solutions had been replaced by oral antibiotics, her stitches by tape. She was still sleeping on and off through the day, but she was beginning to think about work more and more. There was so much she wanted to do. Each day she lazed around in the hospital was another day wasted.

"When can I go home?" she asked the doctor after he checked the incision and her chart and appeared pleased with both.

"Another two or three days."

"*Two* or *three*?" That surprised her. "But I'm fine now. I'm up and around. The worst of the pain is gone, and without any medication for it." One of the first things she'd done was refuse painkillers. She hated being doped up.

"But there's still the danger of infection," the doctor pointed out. "Your body's suffered a trauma. You need to be monitored for that. And you need rest."

"I can get rest at home."

"But will you?" He was middle-aged, with a pleasant manner, a gentle sense of humor and particularly expressive eyes. Those eyes were now filled with an I-know-your-type look, for which she had only herself to blame. She had told him about her work. In the telling, some of her compulsion must have come through. "You live alone. There'll be no one to keep tabs on how much you do or don't do."

"I'm a big girl. I can keep tabs on myself."

"But will you?"

"I'll rest."

"With a pen in one hand and the phone at your ear?" he chided. "No, I'd rather you stay here a little longer."

"But there's a shortage of beds," she argued, having read that time and again in the paper.

"Not for sick people, there isn't."

"I'm not sick."

"You were. More sick than some. And it didn't help that you were run-down." He looked about to scold her for that. Instead, he simply said, "I'm not sure I can trust that you'll rest at home."

Though she was beginning to tire, Nina wasn't giving up the fight. "I'll rest better there than here. Sleeping was fine here when I was half out of it, but now I wake up with every little noise in the hall, and then you guys come at me at six in the morning—"

"You're still weak, Nina. You need watching."

A low voice came from the door. "What if I were to watch her?"

Nina turned her head to find John there, and felt a little more peaceful than she had moments before. He did that to her, had a way of making her feel safe. It had to do with his confidence, she guessed, and that air of quiet command. He would argue with the doctor. He knew how much better she was feeling.

Responding to his question, the doctor said, "Can you do that?"

"If she's at my house, I can."

His house? But that wasn't what Nina had in mind. Not at *all*. "Uh, wait a minute, John. That would be tough."

"Why so?" he asked, approaching the bed. "I have a perfectly good guest room with a perfectly good bed. You can sleep in it just as well as you can sleep in your own bed, and there wouldn't be the hospital interruptions.''

There wouldn't be a telephone, either, Nina knew. Nor would she feel comfortable having people stop by from the office with updates on work. Nor would she be able to call clients. John would never stand for that.

"I could make sure you eat," he went on, "and I'd be able to see if you were worse and get you back here in time." His gaze shifted to the doctor. "Would you let her leave if she stayed with me?"

The doctor didn't have to give it a second thought. "Sure."

His easy agreement infuriated Nina. "That's ridiculous," she said, but more quietly. She was beginning to fade and was appalled by it. Before she totally lost her strength, she said to John, "What about J.J.?"

"What about him?"

"He'd see me."

John considered that. "Yes."

"But you don't want that."

"Uh, listen," the doctor interrupted, "this is sounding like a private discussion." To John, he said, "If you want her, she's yours, but not until this afternoon. I want to do a final blood workup before I discharge her. Why don't you leave word at the desk when you decide what to do. I'll be on the floor for most of the morning."

"Dr. Caine?" Nina called weakly. She wanted to go to *her* home, not John's. She didn't want to owe him a thing. And she wanted to be free to work.

"I'll be back," the doctor said from the door and disappeared.

She took in a big breath and let it slowly out, sinking deeper into the pillows as she did.

"You're feeling tired, aren't you?" John asked.

She wanted to argue, but couldn't. Silently she nodded.

"Caine says it'll be that way for a while."

She wanted to ask—indignantly—when John had spoken to Dr. Caine, but it was a foolish notion. John had brought her to the hospital on that nightmare of a night. He'd been the one to tell the doctor what she was feeling, since she was unconscious. He'd been the one in the waiting room while she was in surgery and the one in her room when she woke up. Of course, he'd spoken with the doctor. Naturally the doctor trusted him.

So did she, but going to his house involved matters beyond trust. It involved an intrusion in his life that was different from the time she'd hitherto taken up. It involved meeting J.J.

As though reading her mind, John carefully lowered himself by her side. "I've thought about this a lot, Nina. The idea of your coming home with me isn't out of the blue. If you're leaving the hospital, you need to be with someone who can take care of you."

"I can take care of myself."

"Maybe in a few days. But not now. At least, not very well. You need to rest. You don't need to be thinking about making a meal when you're hungry or answering the door when the bell rings or doing work. Work will wait," he said with subtle emphasis. "It'll wait till you're well."

In other circumstances, Nina would have argued up a blue streak about that. But either she was simply too weak to argue, or his slow, confident tone was too persuasive. So she let it go for the time being. At the moment, the issue of work didn't seem quite as important as the one of John's son.

"What about J.J.?" she asked again, very softly. "If I were to stay at your place, what would you tell him?"

"Just what I've been telling him all week, that you're a friend who's sick."

"I'll be in the way there."

He shook his head. "You're not demanding. You barely let me do things for you here. I can't imagine you turning into a spoiled witch once we leave."

"But there's *J.J.*"

John's eyes searched her. "You seem hung up on that. He's just a child."

"Just a child? He's *your* child, and he means the world to you. You didn't want me to meet him—"

"Whoa. You said that before. What makes you think it?"

"You always get a sitter when you see me."

His lips grew wry. "Because what I'm thinking of doing when I see you isn't exactly appropriate for a child, any child, to see."

"But that Sunday when you came by my office for the brochure, you could have brought him, still you didn't. You left him with friends at the beach."

"Because he was having fun."

"If he'd started to cry when you left, would you have brought him?"

John was contemplative for a minute. "Maybe." Slowly he added, "But maybe you're right, in a way. I want to protect J.J. from hurt, so I've kept our lives—his and mine—very simple. My job is perfect for that. I haven't brought strangers around often, and in particular, I haven't brought women. I haven't wanted to confuse him."

"If you bring me home now, he will be confused."

He thought about that. "I can explain that you're a friend."

"But I'll be there, in your house, then when I'm better, I'll be gone. Won't *that* confuse him?"

"I'll explain that you're better."

Nina wasn't expressing herself well, and the more she tried, the more frustrated she grew. Closing her eyes, she sighed. "Oh, John."

"What?" he asked with such gentleness that the words, sounding fragile and meek, spilled out.

"I'm awful with kids. I don't know what to do, and J.J.'s not just any kid. He's special. But what if I do something wrong? What if I *say* something wrong?" In the silence that followed, she dared open her eyes. John's were every bit as gentle as his voice.

"You'll be at my place to rest, not to perform," he said, and gave a sad smile. "Besides, you don't have to worry about saying the wrong thing to J.J. He won't hear you, anyway."

Feeling John's sadness, she closed her eyes. From within that cocoon of darkness, she heard his low-spoken words. "I'd like you to meet him, Nina. I'd like him to meet you. It's time."

She wasn't quite sure what that meant, but somehow it didn't seem important. If John wanted her, truly wanted her to recuperate at his home, she'd go. There was a danger in it. She would have to be careful not to compromise her own independence in any long-term way. But she was sick. And he was offering. And there was a small part of her— call it expediency or curiosity or just plain old selfishness—that wanted it, truly wanted it, too.

7

The doctor did his workup and was sufficiently satisfied with Nina's condition to release her into John's charge late that afternoon. Wearing the loose sundress and sandals that Lee had brought by earlier in the day, she walked slowly to the elevator, holding lightly to John's arm.

"Just your speed, eh?" she teased.

"I'm not complaining." He studied her face. "Are you okay?"

"Uh-huh." But she wished it was true. Her legs felt weak, and since she refused to walk hunched over, her incision pulled. The doctor had promised that both the weakness and the pulling would get better each day, but she was impatient. She wasn't used to being sick. The thought of being slowed down frustrated her.

Nonetheless, by the time the elevator ride was done and they had crossed the parking lot, she was grateful to sit. Easing herself gingerly into the car, she put her head back against the seat and worked at regaining her breath.

"You're pale as a ghost," John observed the instant he joined her. "Are you sure you don't want to go back in there?"

She shook her head. The *last* thing she wanted was to go back in there. She had places to go and things to do, and though she would rather be heading for her own home, given the doctor's stubbornness, John's home would have to do. At least she'd be able to sleep when *she* wanted to, then use the rest of the time to think. John might not allow her to spend hours on the phone, but she would be able to do some creative planning and write out instructions for Lee regarding Crosslyn Rise.

"I'll be fine," she said in a thin voice. "I'm just not used to being upright for so long."

"Try this." Gently he eased her down so that her head was braced in the fold of his groin. "Better?"

She sighed against his thigh. "Much."

Putting the car in gear, he started off. "You were lying this way when I drove you in last Wednesday night. Do you remember?"

"No. That whole time's a blur."

He stroked her hair. "I was scared."

"Did you guess what was wrong?"

"Uh-huh. That's why I was scared. It used to be that once an appendix ruptured, the person was gone. I figured yours had ruptured, but I didn't know when. It must have been right before you phoned me."

She shivered.

"Cold?"

He was already reaching to lower the air conditioning when she shook her head. "Just remembering. The pain was so awful. I've never felt anything like it."

"Thank goodness you knew to call me."

She thought about that, just as she'd done more than once while lying in her hospital bed. She could have called Lee. She could have called Martin. She could have called 911. But she'd called John. She hadn't seriously considered any other option. And while one part of her—the part that had built a life on the concepts of independence and self-sufficiency—resented it, she had to accept the practical fact that of all the people she knew, John had the coolest, calmest head on his shoulders.

Reaching for his hand, she tucked it under her chin. "I haven't thanked you. You came. You knew what to do and did it. You saved my life."

He cleared his throat. "All we need now are a few violins—"

"I mean it, John. I'm very grateful."

"Good. Then you can show your gratitude by being a good girl over the next few days and staying in bed."

"*Staying* in bed?"

"At least at the start."

She settled in against his thigh.

After a short silence, he said, "What? No argument?"

"I'm too tired," she said in a feeble drone, answering the very question she kept asking herself. Going with John this way was against all she stood for, but the circumstances were mitigating. "I didn't realize it at the hospital. I just wanted to get out." After a minute, she said, "Now I just want to rest."

"Then rest. We'll be there soon."

She let the hum of the car and the strength of John's thigh lull her. "Get me up before we reach your street?"

"Why?"

"So your customers don't see me drag my head from your lap and think awful things."

He chuckled. "I'll get you up. But watch what you say, or you'll get me up, too. Then the customers will really have a show."

Had she been feeling well, Nina would surely have marveled that the bookish John Sawyer was into double entendres. Had she been feeling well, she would have been turned on by it. But she wasn't feeling well. Sex was the last thing on her mind. Or nearly. She couldn't resist a smile at the image of the proper bookseller, improperly aroused, escorting her across the front lawn.

In no time it seemed, John was nudging her awake. "Rise and shine," he whispered, and helped her sit up as he turned onto his street. Seconds later, he turned into his driveway and pulled directly up to the side door. Though Nina guessed that he normally parked by the garage that stood well behind the house, she didn't argue. Walking through the hospital had exhausted her. She was still feeling the drain.

With John's help, she eased herself from the vehicle. As they walked toward the door, her heartbeat quickened. She wanted to attribute it to the weakness of her limbs, and that might in part have been true. But she was also nervous.

"What will he be doing now?" she asked in a whisper. "Does he watch TV?"

John didn't have to ask who she was talking about. "Sometimes. But I think he's out." He pulled the door open.

"Out?"

"With the girls."

"Oh." She was relieved, then again, disappointed. Starting up the stairs with John's arm in light possession of her waist, she said, "I'm beginning to think he's a phantom. He's never around when I expect him to be."

"He'll be back," John said with certainty, and tightened his arm when she seemed to lag. "Maybe these stairs weren't such a good idea," he muttered.

"I'd have had stairs at my place, too," she said, huffing more with each step. "Once I get to the top, I'll be fine."

"Once you lie down you'll be fine."

She agreed with him there. With little more than a vague impression of lots of browns and blues, she let him guide her past the living room and down a hall to the very last room. It too was blue, blue and white, not quite masculine, not quite feminine, not quite decorated, but simple and sweet. The one thing that interested her most though was the bed. It was a double, had two fluffy pillows and was covered with a quilt that had already been turned back. Desperate to lie down, she crossed to it, sat on its edge and, bracing her stomach with an arm, carefully lowered her head to the pillow. John lifted her feet behind her.

She sighed and close closed her eyes. "Ah, that's better."

"You're sweating."

"I'm okay."

"Is there a nightshirt with the clothes Lee picked up?"

"Should be." She heard him take the bag from his shoulder and drop in onto a chair, then unfasten it and rummage through.

"This is pretty," he mused dryly.

She managed to lift her head and open an eye, but what she saw didn't please her. Lee had packed her skimpiest nightie. She couldn't possibly wear it, not with a little boy running around.

With a moan, she returned her head to the pillow. "I'm okay like this for now." She'd worry about nightwear later.

But John had other ideas. Without a word, he left the room, returning moments later with a shirt of his own. "Assuming this reaches your knees, it'll be loose and soft and decent," he said, and began to unbutton it.

Nina was too weak to protest when he helped her off with the sundress and on with the shirt. She managed some of the buttons while he did the others, then, while she lay down again, he rolled up the sleeves. After surveying his work and judging it acceptable, he flipped a switch on the wall. A soft whir of air drew Nina's notice to the ceiling, where a fan had gently started to turn.

"Nice," she said with a small smile, but what was nicer was the clean way she felt in John's shirt, the way the mattress molded to her body as the hospital one had never done, the freshness of the linen by her cheek. "I think I'll just rest awhile now," she murmured and, within minutes, dozed off.

When she awoke, she was disoriented. At first she thought she was at the hospital, but the smell wasn't right, too pleasant, not antiseptic at all. Then she thought she was at home, but the sound wasn't right, too smooth, almost a hum, like the fan she had always wanted but didn't yet have. Then she remembered where she was and slowly opened her eyes.

Before her, standing nearly at eye level little more than an arm's length away, was J.J. Sawyer. He had thick shiny hair that was a shade lighter in color than his father's dark brown and fell over his forehead in full bangs, skin that was smooth and gently tanned, a small nose and serious mouth. Barefoot, he was wearing a faded T-shirt over denim shorts. His limbs were slender though not skinny. In fact, while she had expected him to look frail, that wasn't the case. Had it not been for the thick glasses he wore and the hearing aids on each ear, he'd have looked like anyone's rough-and-tumble, normal healthy four-year-old son.

Feeling an unexpected tug at her heartstrings, Nina smiled. "Hi," she said. She didn't move other than to lift a hand and flex it in a small wave.

He waved back, but, with the movement of her hand, his attention had been drawn to her wrist. She followed the line of his gaze to the identification band the hospital had put there. She hadn't thought to take it off. Holding her arm out, she let J.J. take a closer look.

He turned the band slowly, first one way, then the next.

Had she been able, Nina would have slipped it off and given it to him, but by design it was too small to slip off. Shooting for second best, she mimed cutting through the band with scissors. She pointed to him, then to the door, then repeated the cutting motion.

J.J.'s eyes, magnified by the glasses, rose to hers. She raised her brows in invitation, smiled, nodded and made the cutting motion again. Without a sound, he turned and scampered from the room.

Only then aware of the quickening of her pulse, Nina took a deep, steadying breath. Either she'd gotten her point across, or she'd sent J.J. off to his father with reports of a real weirdo in the spare room. But, what the hell, how was she supposed to know what a four-year-old did? All kids used scissors, didn't they? Or was it only ones older than four? She tried to remember what *she'd* been doing at that age, then decided against it. Nothing about her childhood had been normal.

Before she could give it another thought, J.J. ran back into the room, carrying a pair of small, blunt-tipped scissors. Feeling victorious that she had made herself understood, Nina held out her wrist. "Can you do it?" she asked, pointing from him to the bank, to the scissors and back.

Opening the scissors, he slipped them under the band and tried to cut, but the plastic resisted the dull blades.

"Try again," Nina coaxed. Giving him a thumbs-up sign in encouragement, she pushed the band deeper into the jaws of the scissors. He made another single slash with the scissors, but to no avail. His brows came down, his small mouth thinned.

Feeling his frustration, Nina held up a finger to tell him to wait, then pushed the band even deeper into the scissors and made a series of repeated movements with her fingers. He took the hint. Using smaller cuts, he finally managed to pierce the plastic. Once that initial piercing was done, the split grew longer with each cut.

Though he was the one making the effort, Nina was the one who had worked herself into a cold sweat of determination by the time the scissors finally made it all the way through. "Good boy!" she said with a grin.

J.J., too, was grinning when he looked up at her.

"Thank you," she mouthed, and his grin widened, then his eyes followed suit when she offered him the band. "It's yours if you want it. You earned it."

He couldn't have heard her words, wasn't even looking at her face at the moment she said them, so he couldn't possibly have read her lips, but the excitement she saw in his eyes was an eloquent as could be.

Nudging the band into his hand, she nodded. He took it, turned and ran from the room.

Again Nina felt the race of her heart and concentrated on slowing down. J.J. had done the work, but she was exhausted. Pathetic as it was, it was a fact of life, for this day at least. If she rested today, surely she'd feel stronger tomorrow.

But she had barely closed her eyes when the patter of small running feet returned. J.J was back, one hand holding her band, the other closed into a fist. Squatting down by the side of the bed, he put the band between his feet, opened his fist, rearranged its contents, then stood and offered her the five jelly beans that lay carefully cupped inside.

Nina hadn't eaten much in the past week. Her stomach was just getting back to normal. Sweaty jelly beans weren't the kind of food that the doctor would have necessarily recommended. But she grinned at J.J., put on an honored look and, one by one, telling him how good each was with the roll of her eyes, ate the beans.

"Dee-licious," she said with a final eye roll. Then she settled into a smile and gave him a silent but exaggerated, "Thank you."

With a grin, he retrieved the band from where it had been safely resting and ran from the room again. She half expected him to be back seconds later with something else, but he wasn't, and it was just as well. She was feeling tired again.

Gingerly rolling over, she pulled the sheet up to her chest, closed her eyes and slept. This time when she awoke, the room was bathed in the early-evening sun and the eyes she looked into were John's.

"Hi, there," he said. He was sitting on the side of the bed. She wondered how long he'd been there.

"Hi."

"Sleep well?"

"Mmm-hmm."

"Feeling better?"

"For now." Wryly she added, "In five minutes, I'll be tired again."

"That'll pass."

"I hope so."

"Are you hungry?"

"No. I had a snack last time I was up. Five jelly beans."

"So I was told."

"He's sweet, John. So sweet."

"I think so."

"Does he look like his mom?" Other than the hair, she didn't see the resemblance to John, though that could well have been due to the discrepancy in size and age.

John thought about it for a minute, finally saying, "It's hard for me to tell. When I see J.J., I see J.J. He has a way about him that's all his own, maybe because of the problems, I don't know. But I've never done much comparing of him either to other children or to adults."

"He's bright and quick. He knew just what I was saying."

"About the bracelet?"

"He told you?"

"Showed me. Made me tape it together so he could wear it." His eyes rose and went past her. "Speak of the devil." He gestured with his hand and spoke with the same kind of exaggerated mouth movements that Nina had used. "Come on in."

Too content lying where she was to turn, Nina asked, "How good is he at that?"

"At lipreading? He gets short things, simple things, far more than a normal four-year-old would get but far less than he will in a year or two or three." Scooping the boy onto his lap, he said, "J.J., this is Nina." Then he snickered. "It'd help, of course, if he were looking at my lips, but he's too busy looking at you. Not that I blame him," he added under his breath.

Nina gave the child the same kind of small wave that she'd given him before. With his smaller hand—circled now with the taped plastic band—he returned it. Then she looked at his mouth, which was surrounded by a faint orange ring. "Is that spaghetti sauce I see?" She ran her finger around her lips.

Carefully, J.J. put the tips of his baby fingers together and drew them apart with the faintest of spiraling motions. John made a different motion, bringing one hand down from his mouth, palm up, into the other. Tipping his head back, J.J. gave him a grin.

For Nina's benefit, John explained. "He signed 'spaghetti.'" He repeated the motion J.J. had made, doing it more neatly so that she could see. "I praised him back in sign."

Nina was impressed. "Does he sign a lot?"

"About as much as he reads lips. We work on both with the therapists, and I reinforce it at home. Spaghetti's one of his favorite things. He eats it a lot, so he has the sign down pat." He paused, leaned over, planted a kiss on his son's forehead. "Overall, he does damn well at it, for a four-year-old."

Nina felt a touch of envy for the love passing from father to son. Then she thought of something else and felt a shaft of timidity. "Does he get frustrated with people who don't sign?"

"He gets frustrated when he wants something and can't make himself known, but every kid does that. As far as signing goes, he only gets frustrated when someone who doesn't sign gets frustrated with him.''

"Do his sitters sign?"

"A little. The girls do it more than the grown-ups. They think it's a game." Snorting, he nuzzled the top of J.J.'s head. "They wouldn't think it was such fun if it was their only means of communication." Leaning sideways, he signed something to J.J., who promptly nodded. In the next instant, John lowered him to the floor and stood. "He's going to help me bring in your supper."

Nina pushed herself up on an elbow. "John, I can go into the kitchen.''

"Not tonight."

"I can do it," she insisted. With her mind clear and her body newly rested, she was uncomfortable in the role of the helpless patient.

"Why should you try, when I can bring it in here?"

"Because you shouldn't be waiting on me."

"Yes, I should. That was the whole point in your coming here. It was the only condition the doctor let you out."

"But I don't want—"

"Tough," he cut in with uncharacteristic sharpness. "It's done." Following J.J.'s lead, he left the room.

Nina didn't resume the fight when he returned with a dinner tray. She only made it through half of the spaghetti and sauce he'd given her, and even less of the salad, before she felt too tired to go on. "I'll have more later," she said, putting her head onto the pillow as soon as he removed the tray. To her chagrin, she fell asleep.

She awoke once not long after that to find J.J. in pajamas, playing on the floor with a brightly colored plastic tow truck and two matching cars. His small head, hair clean and damp, was bent in concentration, and from time to time a low, flat sound came from his throat, clearly an imitation of the truck's roar. She wondered if he ever heard the real thing, or simply felt the vibrations. She wondered if he heard anything at all. He wasn't wearing his hearing aids. She wondered what a totally silent world might be like.

Loath to disturb him, she simply watched for a short time until her eyes felt heavy again. Then, bidding him a silent good-night, she went back to sleep.

When she awoke at eleven, John was sitting in the nearby chair, reading a book. After seeing her to the bathroom and back, he made her a frothy milk shake that she was sure he'd slipped an egg or two into, but she didn't complain. It was cool and tasty, smooth going down. Feeling comfortably full, she went back to sleep.

* * *

When she awoke the next morning, J.J. was on the floor again, this time perched on his heels, reading a book of his own. From what Nina could see, it contained far more pictures than words, but he turned the pages in order and seemed engrossed in what he saw.

She rolled over and stretched, but he couldn't hear the rustle of the sheets. So she ruffled his hair. At that he looked up. Seeing her awake, he jumped up and, leaving the book on the floor, ran for John.

She was sitting on the edge of the bed when he arrived. "Did you have him standing guard?" she teased.

The only answer she got was a shrug. His gaze was fixed on her face. "How did you sleep?"

"Soundly. It's peaceful here."

He continued to study her, finally deciding, "You look better."

"It's about time."

"Want some breakfast?"

For the first time since she'd taken sick, she said. "Just a little." But "just a little," as interpreted by John, turned out to be nearly as large a breakfast as Ronnie's Special at the Easy Over. She came nowhere near finishing. "You're trying to fatten me up," she complained. "Much more of this and my clothes won't fit."

"You're clothes don't fit now. You've lost weight."

She guessed it was true, though her stomach still felt puffy near the incision. "Maybe I could get dressed today and see."

But John shook his head. "Tomorrow."

Figuring that he was taking his orders from the doctor, she didn't argue. But she wasn't beyond bargaining a little. "How about the newspaper, then? I haven't seen one in a week."

He considered that for a minute, then used the tip of his sneaker to gently nudge J.J., who had returned to his book. A brief sign sent the boy scurrying off.

Nina repeated the sign, a double snapping of the heels of her hands with her fingers aimed in opposite directions. "Newspaper?"

"That's right."

She filed the information. "How do you say 'thank you'?"

John mouthed the words.

"In sign," she prompted dryly, and repeated the sign when he showed it to her, then used it when J.J. ran back in, the proud bearer of the morning paper.

Unfortunately, she wasn't as proud of herself when, barely halfway through the paper, she set it aside, slid down on the pillows and fell back to sleep.

The pattern repeated itself through all of Wednesday. She woke up feeling bright eyed, only to wither after a brief time. Fighting it seemed to do no good. Her body had a will of its own.

"Is this normal?" she asked John later that day. Back in bed, feeling as though she'd run a marathon rather than just taken a shower, she was discouraged.

"Perfectly normal," he said, flanking her hips with his hands.

"But I wasn't this tired in the hospital."

"You were, but you didn't think anything of it. Here, you keep thinking you should be up and around."

"I should be."

He shook his head in the slow way that was an answer in itself.

"I should be," she insisted. "When I stop to think about the work I'm missing—"

"Lee is covering for you."

"I know, but I should be doing it."

He pulled back a little, and his look grew dark. "That's exactly the kind of argument that nearly got you killed. If it hadn't been for your compulsion to work, you'd have seen a doctor earlier and gotten by with a simple appendectomy. Instead, you let it go, so you ended up going through ten times more danger and pain. Stick inconvenience in there wherever you want. If you're missing work, it's your own fault."

"But what about Crosslyn Rise?" she asked more meekly. She always felt bad when John raised his voice or spoke more quickly than usual, which was what he was doing then. "We've come so far with it, and it's almost there. If we're launching the marketing program with an open house on the Fourth—"

"That's barely two weeks off, Nina," he interrupted more calmly but with no less force. "You can't hold it then. Put it off a month."

"A *month*!"

He gave a slow nod. "Carter and Jessica have no problem with that."

"You talked with them about my work?" Not wanting to sound annoyed after all he'd done, she spoke with care, but John must have sensed some of what she was thinking, because he came back firmly.

"It's my work, too, and Carter's and Jessica's, and of course I talked to them. They've been worried about you. You're part of the team."

"Part of the team, that's right, and I have no intention of letting down on my end. I can plan the open house, John. Right from this bed I can plan it. Assuming Christine gets the finishing touches done on the model condo, I can handle it. There's nothing much to putting a few ads in the paper, sending around a few invitations, making a few phone calls to get interest humming."

John turned sideways, looking back at her over a shoulder. "And what about standing on your feet for hours on end talking with lookers, not to mention giving tours of the grounds?''

"I can have other people do that."

"Wait a month."

"But the Fourth is a perfect weekend."

"People go away on the Fourth. Wait a month."

"People go away in *August*."

"So wait until Labor Day."

"Impossible."

"Then the last week in July."

"How about the weekend after the Fourth?"

"The last week."

"The next to last week." Wrapping her arms around her middle, she slid lower into the sheets. "And that's as much as I'll give."

Silently he stared straight ahead while she studied his profile, trying to guess at his mood. She knew she irked him at times, particularly when it came to work, but she didn't want him angry.

Anger wasn't what she saw when he turned his head, but rather a trace of amusement. "I'm surprised you gave that much," he mused. "I expected more of a fight."

In another day and age, she might have said something clever, clicked her heels and walked out of the room, but she wasn't up to any of that. "Believe it or not," she said with a sigh, "I don't love fighting even when I *do* feel good."

"Which you don't right now."

"Weak, just weak. Damn it."

Taking a deep breath, John straightened his arms on either side of her again. Looking deeply into her eyes, he said with exquisite gentleness, "Is it so awful to be weak once in a while?"

"I *hate* being weak," she ground out, feeling that hatred in her very marrow.

"But once in a while? Not all the time, just once in a while?"

Nina shut her eyes against the flood of memories that his words brought back. *Once in a while, that's all, I'll just see him once in a while. I can't not see him at all. He's too good to me for that. I need him, Nina. I do.*

"Nina?"

Feeling a great wave of sadness, she opened her eyes to John. At first she didn't think she had the strength to answer. Then she saw the concern—and question—in his eyes and knew that, given all he'd done for her, the least she could do was to tell him the truth.

Quietly, soberly, almost frailly, she said, "My mother used to ask me that, whether it was wrong to be weak once in a while. Her weakness was men. She loved being held by them and kept by them. She didn't demand anything except that they give her enough to get by, and for years, that's what she did. She got by. She got *us* by. We never had anything extra, and that was okay by me, except that she was never around, and that *wasn't* okay, because I wanted her. When I was old enough to ask her to get a real job with regular hours, she said she couldn't. So-and-so was too good to her. She couldn't give him up. We used to fight about it, more when I got older and the so-and-sos kept changing. I'd tell her she was weak, and she'd say that was okay. Then I started seeing the bruises, and I'd tell her she didn't have to stand for that, but she would. She'd take it over and over again. Then she started in with the pills—''

Nina swallowed hard and, with the motion, felt suddenly more tired than ever before. Wearily she turned her head to the side.

John touched her hair. ''Were they painkillers?''

''All drugs are, in the broadest sense.''

''She moved from one to the next?''

''Right on up the scale.''

Gentle fingers brushed Nina's scalp, soothing her, silently giving her strength. ''Was it an overdose that finally did it?''

''Mmm-hmm. Not enough to kill, just to permanently disable.'' Thoughts she'd had in the hospital came back to her, thoughts about illness and death, friends, relatives. In a shaky whisper, she said, ''I should see her. She's lying alone. I hated lying alone when I was sick. But she is, all the time. I should see her.''

''Do you often?''

She shook her head. ''Too far away. Too much work.''

''Too many mixed feelings.''

She met his gaze. ''How did you know?''

''It follows from things you've said. You wanted her there and she wasn't. You asked her to change, and she wouldn't. You've made your life the antithesis of what hers was.'' He paused, his thumb tracing small circles on her temple. ''Were you around when it got bad with the drugs?''

''Yes. I was in school, and working.''

''Where was your father?''

Feeling the same old pain she'd lived with for years, she raised a single shoulder all the way to her ear. Slowly it slid back into place.

''Don't know?''

She shook her head.

''Do you know who he is?''

After a pause, she shook her head again.

Silently John slipped his arms beneath her and brought her up into his embrace. She went limply at first, until the need he felt took her, too. Aloneness was a painful thing. Holding and being held by another person offset that pain. Wrapping her arms around his waist, she clutched at bunches of his shirt.

At first he said nothing, and that was fine. Nina was content to listen to his heartbeat, to let it lull her and offer a comfort of its own. As though she had unburdened herself of a secret that had been weighing her down for years, she grew increasingly relaxed and mellow.

His breath was warm against her hair. "Loving a man doesn't have to be a weakness."

"It's not the loving that's bad," she breathed, "it's the depending. Men meant everything to my mother. When none of them wanted her anymore, she was broken."

"So you never want to depend on a man."

"Mmm. Right."

"You want to be self-sufficient."

"Mmm-hmm." She took in a deep breath, enjoying as much the feel of John as his scent. "I won't let myself get in that bind. Not ever."

Having said that, she felt better. She had warned John. She'd been as blunt as she could be. If he wanted to nurse her, that was fine. If he wanted to wait on her and play guardian, that was fine. She couldn't deny that the coddling was nice, given that her health wasn't yet up to snuff. But once she was well, she would be on her own again.

It was good that he understood that.

8

The following morning, while John and J.J. were at the therapist's office, Lee came to visit. Wearing the sundress she'd worn home from the hospital—and having polished her nails, which made her feel greatly improved—Nina had progressed to sitting in the den. John didn't know that yet. She planned to surprise him with her strength when he returned at noon.

"Cute place," Lee said with a cursory sweep.

Nina thought so. She had wandered around herself, for the first time, just before Lee had arrived. There were two bedrooms in addition to the one she was in, a large kitchen, a living room, and a dining room that had been converted into the den in which they sat. Nothing was "decorated," yet everything had a lived-in look that gave a feeling of warmth. She liked that far more than she was willing to admit to Lee. So she said simply, "It's clean and functional. Nothing fancy. Definitely a man's place."

Lee nodded. She looked vaguely at the walls, then the floor, then at Nina. "So. How are you feeling?"

Nina couldn't miss the awkwardness in her friend. Unsure as to its cause, she went along with the game. "Better today. I was beginning to wonder when I'd revive. It seems like forever since I've been at work."

"It's only been a week. You still look peaked."

Nina didn't like the sound of that. Lee was usually more complimentary than not, certainly more encouraging. Something was odd. "My coloring will pick up. I may go out into the backyard later." John would never allow that, but she rather liked the idea. "So," she said, affecting her business tone of voice, "tell me what's happening at the office. Did you have any luck with the Donaldsons?"

Lee opened her briefcase. "Uh-huh. They're interested in buying."

"They are? That's great!"

Lee didn't seem terribly excited. As she busied herself looking through a pile of papers, she said, "Uh-huh. They'll be coming back with a bid later this afternoon. Four o'clock, I think it is."

"Terrific. It's been a long time that they've been looking. I'm thrilled we were finally able to please them."

"Uh-huh."

"Thanks, Lee. I really appreciate all you've done." The fact was that, at Nina's insistence, Lee would get the full commission, so it wasn't work done for free. Still Nina was grateful. By ably taking over for her, Lee was keeping her professional reputation intact. "I know how much work you've put in, not only in this case, but with all of the others this past week. You've been a good friend."

Eyes still inside her briefcase, Lee shrugged. "I have plenty of time. It's nice to be able to fill it."

That sounded odd, not like the Lee Nina knew at all. Lee wasn't one to fill every minute, the way Nina did. Though she always helped Nina out when asked, she didn't actively look for work. She had always preferred a slower pace.

Nina's mind took off in all sorts of different directions until she caught herself and asked outright, "What's wrong, Lee?"

"Nothing."

"Something is. You don't sound like you."

"I'm fine."

"You're *not*."

Retrieving her hands from the briefcase and dropping them into her lap, Lee hung her head. "You're right." Timidly she looked up, her eyes filled with tears. "Tom's moving. He's getting rid of his place here and moving to Chicago. He says it's an official transfer, but I think he's taking a whole new job. And he's not taking me. It's over, he says. It was nice, but it's over." Pulling a tissue from her sleeve, she pressed it to her nose. "You were right, Nina. You had him pegged."

Heart aching, Nina reached for her arm. "Oh, Lee…"

Sniffling around the tissue, Lee said, "You were right. You knew. And you tried to tell me, but I wouldn't listen. I thought this was it. I really did. I refused to see the truth about those long weekends away. You were that much more realistic than me."

"I just didn't want you hurt."

"You saw it coming."

"I'm jaded, but that's not always so good."

"It sure has worked for you. You're not dangling at the end of Tom Brody's line. He's a rat. All men are rats."

"Not all," Nina said. She was thinking of John, of how giving and undemanding he had been. She was lucky. Strangely so. "You'll find someone else, Lee. Someone better." She squeezed Lee's hand and continued to hold it while Lee cried for a minute longer. "Now that you're free and looking around, you'll see possibilities where there didn't seem to be any before." Unexpected things happen. Nina knew.

Not that *she* was looking for a man to marry, the way Lee was. "You'll do fine."

"But I'll miss him."

"I know. But you'll keep busy. I have plenty for you to do, if you want it."

After a bit, Lee stopped sniffling. "I want it," she said with resignation.

"Good," Nina said gently. "Let's talk about Crosslyn Rise."

For the next few minutes, they did just that. Determined to take Lee's mind off Tom, Nina gave her a long list of calls to make regarding a planned launch for the next-to-last week in July. She had calls to make herself, though she didn't rush to make them the minute Lee left. Instead, indulging herself in the tiredness she felt, she turned the stereo on low to a classical station, stretched out on the sofa with her head on the soft leather cushion and took a nap.

The slam of a door woke her. She opened her eyes to see J.J. dash through the room, followed at a more sedate pace by John, who stopped the instant he saw her. "Who let you out?"

"Me." She punched up the cocoa-colored cushion under her head, but made no move to rise. From her vantage point, John was looking tall, dark and handsome. She was in no rush to change the view. "It got a little claustrophobic in the bedroom, and Lee was stopping by, so I figured I'd entertain her in style. How did everything go this morning?"

"Fine." With a slowness that came across as caution, he asked, "How did it go with Lee?"

"Really good. I gave her lots of work to do. There's not a whole lot left for me."

Seeming satisfied with that, he slipped into a chair and stretched out his legs. He was wearing shorts. Nina liked his legs. They were well formed, snugly muscled and just hairy enough.

"Did you tell her about the change in dates for the open house?" he asked.

She dragged her eyes up. "Uh-huh."

"Any problem?"

"No. She'll go along with whatever I say. My worry is more with the consortium. I feel like I'm letting them down."

"You've been sick. They would never hold that against you."

"But I've been telling them that the Rise would be on the market as of the Fourth."

"So you'll tell them differently now."

"I hate to lose those few weeks of potential selling."

"Will it really make a difference in the long run?"

"I suppose not," she conceded, then shifted her gaze to J.J. when he returned to the room. As though he'd plum run out of steam, he was walking slowly, had his thumb in his mouth and was carrying a battered teddy bear. There was something so forlorn looking about him that Nina couldn't resist holding out an arm. Without the slightest hesitation, he went to her.

Drawing him in by the waist, she said, "That's a sad-looking teddy." She fingered the bear's worn nose.

"Not sad," John informed her. "Well loved. His mother gave him that teddy not long before she died."

Nina sucked in a breath. "Does he know?"

"That it was from her? Probably not. But it's special to him. He doesn't love any of his other animals the way he does this one."

Feeling a deep ache for the little boy who would never know his mother, Nina tightened her arm around his waist. He kept up his sucking without complaint.

"What happened, John?" she asked softly. She alternately touched the bear, then the small warm fingers clutching its neck. When silence continued to come from John's direction, she raised her eyes to his. "Tell me about her."

Sitting back in the chair, he crossed an ankle over his knee. Though the pose was relaxed and his voice slow, it lacked the ease that would have normally been there. "We met in Minneapolis. I had a store there, pretty much like the one I have here. Jenna was a market analyst who had just been transferred out from New York."

He rubbed his ankle with the pad of his thumb. After a long minute, he went on. "She wasn't thrilled about the move. Even though she was high up in the office bureaucracy, she felt it was a step down. But the money was good, and she figured that if she was patient, she'd move even higher, and then, if she wanted, she could move out again, preferably back to New York. From the beginning, I knew that was what she wanted, but somehow, when we started seeing each other and then got closer, it didn't seem real."

Breaking away from Nina, J.J. crossed to the television and turned it on. With the sudden blare of sound, John jumped up, tapped the boy on the shoulder and motioned him to turn it down, which he did. John turned it even lower, then turned off the stereo, leaving little to interfere with their talk.

Nina was just noticing that the program was *Sesame Street* and that an interpreter was signing in a corner of the screen, when J.J. returned to her side. Thumb back in his mouth, arm around his teddy, he climbed onto the sofa to sit in the curve of her body.

John was quickly alert. "Is he hurting you?"

"Of course not." She ran a hand down the back of J.J.'s head, over thick, silky hair. "He's so little."

"But your stomach—"

"Is fine. He seems tired."

"He'll take a nap after lunch."

Nina nodded and looked at John expectantly. Apparently satisfied that she was comfortable, he returned to the chair. This time, his legs remained sprawled.

"I'm listening," she prompted.

Though his eyes settled on her, she was sure he was seeing another woman in her place. "I thought maybe she'd change. Even when I convinced her to have the baby, I thought she'd change. I thought for sure she'd take a look at the little kid who was her own flesh and blood, and melt."

Nina didn't know how Jenna hadn't. The little kid who was her flesh and blood was a heart stopper. "Did she have a problem right from the start?"

John nodded. "She resented him. He wasn't any bigger than a peanut and he didn't say a word, but he made her feel guilty about the time she spent working. Unfortunately, her work meant everything to her." He frowned down at his hands. "When we found out about the ears and the eyes, she couldn't take it. Just couldn't take it. It was like he had been declared a troublemaker, so she washed her hands of everything to do with him. She started working longer hours, started taking overnight trips whenever she could. She always brought him things— little cars, balloons, teddy bears—but she figured that the less she had to see him, the better."

"What about *you*? Didn't she want to see *you*?"

The bleakness of his expression said it all. Still he added, "By that time, there wasn't much left between us."

The quiet sounds from the television filled the ensuing silence. Like a puppy snuggling in, J.J. turned sideways to lay his head on Nina's thigh. She ran a hand back and forth on his warm little shoulder, but her eyes were on John. Needing to know, she asked softly, "How did she die?"

He looked off toward the window. "She was driving home very late one night after a three-day symposium, fell asleep at the wheel and hit a tree. Death was instantaneous. No other cars were involved."

Without conscious effort, Nina drew her legs up, tucking J.J. closer to her. "Tragic," she whispered, and felt a private chill. Many a time she had returned late at night from exhausting multiday seminars. More than once, she had stopped for coffee or rolled down the window to stay awake.

John stared broodingly at the floor. "It was a waste. Our marriage wasn't any good, so we'd probably have gotten divorced, but that's the least of it. She had potential. I hated what she did—hated the way she did it with such single-mindedness—but she was good at it. A lousy mother, but good at her work."

The grudging respect was clear in his voice. In turn, Nina respected him for it. Given the way Jenna had left him and his child, he could have easily been filled with scorn.

"You must have loved her once."

He thought about that for a while. "I did, in a dreamlike kind of way. She was like a butterfly, beautiful but elusive."

"Do you miss her?"

He shook his head, and as though the bubble of the dream had burst all over again, his voice leveled. "Like I said, we'd have ended up divorced if she hadn't wrapped herself around that tree. She wasn't an easy person to live with. She was always on, always thinking work. She was always wondering who else in the office was doing what and getting where, and how it would affect her. Her mind was always working on ways she could get ahead. Work was her be-all and end-all, her raison d'être. As time went on, it only got worse."

"*I'm* not that bad," Nina said with feeling, then caught herself, realizing what she'd done. Defensively she said, "You compare us. I know you do."

His eyes held hers steadily. "Do you wonder why?"

In an attempt to be fair, she shrugged. "I can see some similarities. She worked a lot, I work a lot. She was trying to get ahead, so am I. But I'd never have done what she did. I'd never have turned my back on a child. Or a husband. There are responsibilities involved when you marry and have kids. You shouldn't do either, if you want to work."

"It's all or nothing, then?" John shot back with startling speed. "Either you marry and have kids, or you work? No middle ground?"

"Sometimes no, sometimes yes. It depends on where you are in life. I'm at the work stage. I'm not saying that I'll never get married and have kids, just that I wouldn't take on either of those now."

"You couldn't compromise? You couldn't make time for all of it?"

"There are only so many hours in a day, and you're the one who's been telling me I work too much. Where would I find the time to give to a husband or kids?"

He remained quiet.

"Where?" she demanded. If he was putting her on the spot, she could do the same to him.

"You make time for what you want," he stated in a voice that was deafeningly clear. "You give a little here, give a little there. It may mean that one thing or another takes longer to achieve, but it all comes out in the wash.''

"'One thing or another,'" Nina echoed. "You mean work. If a woman is willing to sacrifice her career, she can have the husband and kids.''

"She doesn't have to sacrifice the career," he insisted, "just defer the ultimate gratification. And that doesn't mean there isn't gratification along the way, simply that the achievements may not be as high until the kids are grown and out of the house.''

"She's an old lady by then.''

"No way." He sat back and linked his fingers, seeming more relaxed, as though confident he had the argument won. "Take that woman. She had kids in her mid-twenties. They're out on their own by the time she's fifty. Fifty is not old.''

"It's too old to start building a career.''

"She's not starting. She started years ago. She may have taken a leave when the kids were babies, but after that she worked part-time, maybe full-time as the kids got older. Okay, so she didn't go running off on business trips, or push past a forty-hour week, and maybe that held her back a little. But look what she *has*. She has a solid career. She has a solid marriage. She has kids who probably give her more satisfaction than anything she does at work. And she's only fifty.''

With barely a breath, he raised a hand and went on. "Then again, take the woman who put her career before everything else. She got out of school, entered the marketplace and worked her tail off. She started climbing the ladder of success, and the drive became self-perpetuating. The higher she climbed, the higher she wanted to be. The more money she earned, the more she needed. There was always something more, always something more.''

"Her being a woman didn't help," Nina put in. "A woman has to work twice as hard.''

To her surprise, John agreed. "You're right. And that made her all the *more* determined to make it. So she put off thoughts of getting married, since she didn't have time for that. And she put off having kids, because she didn't have time for *that*. Then she reaches her mid-forties, when theoretically she should be up there on the threshold of the president's office, only there are suddenly four other candidates vying for the job and one of them is the new son-in-law of the chairman of the board. So she misses out. And then what does she have?" He raised a finger. "She doesn't have the corner office." Then another. "She doesn't have a husband." Then a third. "And her childbearing years are gone." He dropped his hand to his lap. "Do you think she's happy?''

His eloquence left Nina momentarily speechless.

"She's alone, Nina," he said more quietly. "She's alone, and she's getting older, and she's beginning to wonder what she'll do with herself if she ever has to retire. Happy? My guess is she's scared to death."

Tearing her eyes from his, Nina looked down at the floor. Aloneness was something that had flashed through her mind more than once when she'd been in the hospital. Different people had dropped by to visit, but John had been a constant in her life. Without him, she would have felt very much alone.

She wondered what, if anything, her mother felt sitting in that nursing home day after day. The doctors had said that she didn't know who or where she was, or who came and went, but Nina had always had a niggling fear in the back of her mind that maybe it wasn't so. Over the years, she had successfully kept the fear hidden in a dark corner of her mind. She was a lousy daughter.

Feeling suddenly very much an imposter in a haven she didn't deserve, she looked at John. "Why am I here?"

He frowned. "What do you mean?"

"From the beginning, I reminded you of Jenna. I'm everything you had once and couldn't stand. I'm a repeat of a mistake. So what am I doing here, interfering with your life?"

"You're here because I want you here."

"But why?"

"Because I like you."

"But I'll only cause you grief."

"Maybe not."

"What does *that* mean?" she cried.

John didn't answer for a while, but sat quietly, eyes downcast, brows drawn together, and Nina didn't prod. She was feeling tired again. Turning her head into the cushion, she closed her eyes.

His voice came gently. "I like you, Nina. Yes, you're right, you did remind me of Jenna, but only at the start and only with regard to work. In other ways, you're different. She was tall, blond and green eyed, you're blue eyed, dark and petite. She dressed to fit in, you dress to stand out. She smiled on cue, you smile whenever you want to. You're your own person far more than she ever was."

Nina had opened those blue eyes and was looking at him, feeling a longing that was only in part physical. "But I love my work."

He nodded. "Yes, you do."

"And you hate that."

Again he nodded.

"So why are you *bothering* with me?"

"Because," he said with a somber look and a surprising lack of hesitancy, "I like you enough to care. I'm not sure I felt that way about Jenna. I may have loved her once, but I didn't like her. When she was barging headlong toward self-destruction, I did nothing to stop her."

"You were busy with J.J."

"True, but I could have tried more if I'd cared. Then again, Jenna was a hard woman. She wouldn't have listened. Once she set her mind to something, she wouldn't budge." His eyes softened a fraction. "You're not as hard. As determined as you are, you still listen."

She gave a small self-conscious laugh. "I haven't exactly had much choice lately."

"Even before you got sick, you listened. You didn't want to work with me, but you agreed to do it. You made time for it even though you said you couldn't. Besides that, you're more sensitive than Jenna ever was. You feel badly when I have to get a sitter for J.J. in order to see you. You worry that you're going to do something wrong when it comes to him. Look at you," he said with the hitch of his chin, "you've been touching him in some small way, just like a seasoned mother, ever since we got back, and I don't think you even realize it."

Startled, Nina shot a glance at J.J., who was curled up in the curve of her body. Her hand was on his arm, the backs of her fingers brushing ever so lightly over the baby-smooth skin.

When she returned her gaze to John, he was looking satisfied. Pushing out of his chair, he bent over her, putting his mouth by her ear. "Not bad, for someone who doesn't know what to do with kids." On his way to straightening, he scooped J.J. up. "Lunchtime, my man," he said.

J.J., who had neither heard him nor seen his lips, made a loud sound in protest and started to squirm. John immediately set him on his feet and hunkered down before him. "Time for lunch," he mouthed clearly. He tapped his wrist with a finger, then mimed bringing food to his mouth.

J.J. looked questioningly back at Nina.

"She'll come, too," John assured him with a nod, gave him a pat on the bottom and stood. To Nina, he said, "Want to?"

"Sure. What are we having?"

John caught J.J.'s eye. "What do you want to eat?" he asked slowly, signing along with the words.

J.J. made the sign for spaghetti.

John shook his head. "We had that for supper last night."

J.J. made a stirring motion with one hand, then tapped the back of his fist with two fingers.

Again John shook his head. "Mashed potatoes alone aren't enough."

J.J. drew large twin arches in the air.

John chuckled. "Not McDonald's. How about a surprise?" He

formed two fingers of both hands into curved Vs, put the fingertips together, then drew them apart with a look of surprise.

J.J. said something that wasn't any kind of word Nina had ever heard but sounded agreeable nonetheless, particularly when he clapped.

"Okay," John finger-spelled, then repeated the gesture for Nina. "I would have spelled out 'bologna,' except that it's too hard a word for him to read. Is bologna okay for you?"

"It's my favorite," she said with a smile, feeling warm and amenable and all kinds of other nice things. The rapport between John and his son was delightful. Being part of their group, undeserved though it was and brief though it would be, was an honor.

After lunch she napped, then John surprised her by suggesting that, while J.J. was with his sitters and he was at work, she sit out in the backyard. "Great minds think alike," she said. "I told Lee I wanted to sit there, but I didn't think you'd let me."

"You look too pale. You need some color." The corner of his mouth turned wry. "We wouldn't want people to think you've been sick, now, would we?"

"Certainly not," Nina said, but no sooner was she settled in a chaise lounge, in the dappled sun that danced through the oak boughs, when she thought of what he'd said. He'd been facetious, of course. But, in fact, the rest of the world was waiting. She did have to get back to work.

She'd have to discuss that with John, she knew, but she wasn't looking forward to it. He would tell her she wasn't well yet, and she would feel obligated to say she was getting there fast, and it would go back and forth, as arguments went. In the end, he would wear her down, simply because she wasn't feeling up to par. So, valid or not, he'd have made his point.

Telling herself that she had time to spare, she didn't say a word for the rest of that day. Rather, she lay in and out of the sun for several hours, dozing at some points, watching J.J. play at others. For a time, curious to see what he was doing and how, she sat on the edge of his sandbox and helped him make sand castles. She had as much fun with the sand as she did with J.J. and didn't feel either bothered or frightened to be left alone with him when his sitters went back inside for cold drinks. He was a gentle little boy with the calm temperament of his father. With simple hand motions and facial expressions, she found she could communicate with him just fine.

For dinner, John grilled swordfish steaks, and though J.J. wasn't wild about his, Nina ate every bite. J.J. was wild about dessert, though, a chocolate cake that John had bought at the bakery that morning, and while Nina was watching him eat, John got up to do the dishes. When she offered to help, he refused.

"I didn't insist that you come here, just to put you to work."

"I'm not helpless," she protested.

"But you've been sick."

She wanted to point out that anyone who was well enough to sunbathe and build sand castles could probably handle a few pots and pans, but she didn't. Anyone who could handle a few pots and pans could probably do the cooking as well, which meant that she really should be heading home. But she wasn't ready for that just yet. John kept telling her that she was weak, that she needed more rest, that she had to take it slow if she wanted to regain all her strength. She chose to believe him.

The believing was all well and good on Saturday. John was in the bookstore all day. J.J. was in and out with sitters. Nina slept a bit, read a bit, boiled up chicken breasts and made chicken salad sandwiches for lunch as a surprise for John.

He was furious. "I don't want you working."

"But I'm feeling stronger, and I'm bored. Honestly, John, what I did was no effort. I'm standing better and walking better. Besides, I have all afternoon to rest."

The look he gave her said that she'd better do just that, but she noticed with satisfaction that he ate every last bite of his sandwich before he returned to the store. Buoyed by that, she did rest awhile. When she woke up, she finished the book he had given to her to read, then went back into the kitchen and cooked up a batch of chocolate chip cookies.

J.J. Sawyer might have had vision and hearing problems, but nothing was wrong with his sense of smell. The cookies were still in the oven when he followed his nose there. He was positively ebullient when she let him peek through the glass.

John's sense of smell was nearly as keen. At the first lull in business, he too materialized in the kitchen, where, hands on his hips, he surveyed the scene. Two fifteen-year-old girls, J.J. and Nina were sitting at the table having an orgy of cookies and milk.

"Better hurry," Nina warned. "They won't last long."

"Should I ask who made them?"

"No."

Eagerly standing up on his chair, J.J. held out a half-eaten cookie to his father. "Are they good?" John asked in sign.

Nodding vigorously, J.J. continued to hold out the cookie until John reached for it, and, with a mischievous grin, he promptly stuffed it in his mouth.

"You devil," his father said, and reached for a cookie of his own. He made a show of taking a bite and thinking about the taste, before downing the rest of the cookie in one large bite.

"You're as bad as he is," Nina said as she rose from the table. Taking J.J.'s eyeglasses from his nose, she washed a chocolate streak from one lens, rinsed and dried both, then carefully slipped them back on. She bent over to study her handiwork. "Better?" Her eyes shot to John's. "How do I sign that?"

He showed her. She repeated the two-part gesture to J.J., who returned it. Eminently pleased with herself and the situation, she took up a napkin, filled it with cookies and handed it to John. "For work," she said.

In a typically John way, he looked at the cookies, looked at her, then slowly took the small bundle. "Thanks," was all he said before he returned to the store.

Nina thought a lot about that "thanks" during the rest of the day. Even more, she thought about the look that had gone with it, because it hadn't held gratitude so much as puzzlement, even frustration, if she guessed right. But what could she tell him? She liked to bake so she'd baked cookies, which was no more than she might have done if she had been home and snowed in on a winter weekend with no hope of getting to work.

Maybe he was thinking that she wanted to impress him.

Maybe he was thinking that she wanted to impress J.J.

Maybe he was thinking that she was well enough to leave.

She was. She really was. Come Saturday night, when she stayed awake through the entire movie he rented, she knew it. Come Sunday morning, when she put on the bathing suit he'd picked up at her apartment and spent the day—albeit restfully—at the beach with J.J. and him, she knew it. Come Sunday evening, lolling around on the sofa, trying to read but thinking instead about the irresistible lure of John's body, she knew it.

John knew it, too, because shortly after she said good-night and stole off to her room, he appeared at her door. Little more than a shadow in the night, he crossed to the bed and sat down. No longer a shadow then, he took her in his arms.

Senses that had been gradually reviving over the course of the past few days came fully awake. With a soft moan, Nina slid her arms around his neck. He was so wonderful to hold, so solid, so gentle, virile in everything from his shape to his scent. She felt so alive, restored, whole in mystifying ways.

"I missed this," he murmured. "All the time you've been here, I've wanted to hold you. It was toughest at the beach today. You looked so pretty.''

She swallowed against a swell of emotion.

''You want to leave.''

''I don't, but I can't stay. I'm getting better. Every day.''

For the first time, he didn't refute her argument. Instead, he said, ''It's a rat race out there. You don't belong in it.''

''I do. It's where I've always been.''

''Only because you had no other choice. But you do now. I want you to stay here, Nina. I want you to stay here with me.''

Her heart contracted. ''Oh, John.''

''What does that mean?''

''I *can't*. I can't just give up everything I've spent a lifetime working for.''

Pulling back, he took her face in his hands. ''I'm not asking you to give everything up, just to add some things. You've been happy here. I know you have. You made up your mind that you couldn't work, and you were happy here.''

''But now I *can* work. Maybe not full-time yet, but certainly half-time.''

''So go to work from here.''

''I can't.''

''Why not?''

Unable to resist, she touched his mouth. ''Because I'd feel guilty. I've always been independent. I come and go as I please. I can't be doing that from your home. Especially now.''

''What does that mean?''

Her fingers moved aside. Inching up, she touched her lips to his, simply because she needed to feel him that way. When she drew back, she knew that what she was about to say was the frightening truth. ''Now I'd be tempted, so tempted to play with you. I'd be tempted to lie around reading all night, or spend the afternoon making sand castles, or bake us all into obesity. It's been nice here, so nice, but I have to leave. If I don't, I won't get where I want to be, and if I don't get where I want to be, I might come to resent you, and I'd never want to do that, John.''

Amber eyes alive in the dark, he moved his gaze around her face. He followed the eye motion with that of a hand. His voice was low and sandy. ''It isn't right that it should be one or the other. You'll be hurt, Nina. I don't want that.''

''No hurt,'' she said, but the accompanying shake of her head was cut short when his hand slipped lower to her neck, then lower still to the budding swell of her breast. She bit down on her lip to stifle a moan.

"You like that?" he whispered. His large hand circled her, moving inward in slow, concentric rings.

"Oh, yes," she whispered back. "You have a way with my body."

"At least I have that."

"You have more—" she began, but the words died when he touched one taut nipple. Another moan came from her throat, this one slipping free into the air.

"Do I hurt you?"

"Only by making me want more."

"Your stomach—"

"No, no." Covering his hand, she pressed it close. "You set me on fire."

The night hid his expression, but the catch of his breath told of what she'd missed. Gently he lowered her to the bed. His mouth followed, capturing hers in a kiss that opened gently, as did her body. Taking advantage of that opening, his hands loved her breasts through the silk of her thin nightie. She felt herself swell to his touch, felt the ache of wanting in her nipples, then lower. Arching upward, she tried to bring him down, but he held himself steadily over her while his hands continued their sweet torture.

The doctor had told her, before leaving the hospital, that her body would tell her when sex was okay. At the time, she'd felt numb and sore. Passion had seemed a distant phenomenon, not the least bit appealing to her bruised and mending self.

Five days of rest and tender care at John's hand had made a world of difference. Though she could feel the intermittent tugging in stomach muscles that contracted with desire, the sensation blended in with her need.

"I want you," she whispered, and slid her hands down his thighs. She was making the upward journey to his groin when he caught her hands and pinned them by her shoulders.

Holding both wrists, he seduced her mouth with a series of deep soul kisses. Then he worked his way down and applied that devastatingly capable mouth to her breasts. From one hard tip to the other he moved, using his tongue, his teeth, his fingers. The wetter her nightie grew, the hotter she grew inside.

When he slipped his hand under the shirt and touched her between her legs, she cried out.

"Hurting?" he asked in concern.

"With need." She grabbed his wrist to stop him. "Make love to me, John." She arched toward his hips but was only able to make the briefest, glancing contact with his erection when he pinned her down.

"It's too soon."

"No. No. I want you inside."

"Too soon," he repeated, and levered himself up enough to return his hand to her cleft. "This way," he whispered, taking her mouth in an enveloping kiss at the same time that his fingers found their way to her darkest heat.

She was lost then. The best she could do was to flex frantic fingers on his back while he built the fire inside her to an explosive level. He stroked her inside and out, up and down, back and forth, until her shallow breathing caught and she was shot to the pinnacle of orgasmic release.

Her return to reality was a slow one. By the time she could finally open her eyes, she was being cradled against John's supine body. The pervasive weakness she felt told her that, much as she wanted to make love to him back, she wouldn't be doing it that night.

Her "Oh, John" was a soulful sound.

Silently he stroked her hair.

Gradually the trembling of her body eased, leaving a great fatigue in its place. "I want... I want..." The words were slurred, the thoughts behind them muddled.

It wasn't until dawn Monday, when she woke up wanting John and finding herself alone in bed, that those thoughts jelled.

9

By the time she heard waking sounds in the rest of the house, Nina had dressed, gathered her belongings and packed her small bag. As soon as those other sounds moved into the kitchen, she headed there, too.

John was at the stove frying eggs. At the sight of him, she felt an ache start inside. It had nothing to do with her recent surgery and everything to do with her growing feeling for the man she had to leave.

She hadn't been standing at the door for more than a few seconds when he looked her way, not the least bit startled. She guessed that he'd been expecting her.

Returning his attention to the eggs, he scooped one onto a plate, added a piece of toast and set the breakfast in front of J.J., who was on his knees on a chair at the table.

Looking at the little boy, Nina felt another ache. She had growing feeling for him, too, and that was even more surprising than the other. She had liked John for a while now; in the past ten days, her feelings had only intensified. J.J., on the other hand, had been a stranger up until the Thursday before. Stranger? *Alien being* was more apt. He was a child and he had problems. She had never lived with a child before, let alone one with problems. It hadn't been anywhere near as bad as she'd thought it would be.

Sliding into a chair beside the little one, she stroked his head in wordless "good morning." When he grinned up at her, she grinned back. When he picked up a piece of his toast and offered it, she shook her head and the ache inside grew.

"You're leaving," John said quietly.

She nodded. "I have to."

He could have argued, she knew, but he didn't. They had been through the arguments and exhausted each one. Nothing had changed.

"Will you have breakfast first?"

Though she wasn't terribly hungry, she wasn't denying herself a few last moments of the particular pleasure of being with J.J. and John. "Only if you have enough."

"There are two more eggs here. We'll each have one. Same with the toast."

Clearly he hadn't made extra, hadn't expected that she'd eat. "Oh, no," she said quickly, "you have them. I didn't mean to take—"

He interrupted her with a level stare and a firm, "We'll share. I don't mind. One egg is more than enough for me, and even if it weren't, I don't mind giving a little."

The emphasis on the last few words and the message therein was mirrored in his look. He was saying that life didn't have to be all or nothing, that he was more than willing to compromise if she was.

But she wasn't. Though she nodded yes to the egg and accepted the plate he offered without a word, she felt guilty. She couldn't compromise. She *couldn't*. For too long, she had wanted her independence. With Crosslyn Rise about to go on the market, she was coming close to her goal, too close to give it up.

But what she was giving up on the other end—that was where it was starting to hurt. Her feelings for John were strong and growing more so with each day. To stay would be asking for trouble. Already she wanted things she couldn't have.

I want to make love to you. I want to spend the night with you. I want to stay here forever. Those were the words she might have said if she hadn't been so spent from his loving the night before. Then again, if she'd been in full control of her senses, she wouldn't have said them at all. Leading John on, giving him cause to hope for something that couldn't be, would be cruel.

Did she mean the words? Yes. That was what she'd realized at dawn, why she knew she had to leave. She did want all those things. But she wanted her self-sufficiency more. In her mind—right or wrong—to be dependent on John would be a sign of weakness. She prided herself on being stronger than that.

"Are you going right back to work?" he asked quietly.

She pushed at the deckled edge of her egg. "Tomorrow, I think. I'll get home today, maybe make a few calls. As soon as I get tired, I'll stop." Unspoken was the fact that as long as she felt all right, she'd keep at it. John knew she would. He had experience with her type.

He bit hard into his toast, chewed, swallowed, took another bite.

"We have a consortium meeting next week," she said in an open-ended kind of way. When he didn't respond, she said, "Will I see you before then?"

He shrugged. "Do you want to?"

She was asking herself the same question. On one hand, the thought of not seeing him at all was bleak. One the other hand, perhaps a clean break was for the best.

But they were friends, weren't they? And they'd just come through a harrowing experience together. Surely he'd want to know that she was all right. "I think I'd like to talk. You know, see how things are going here and all."

"Then why don't you call when you have time." With barely a break, he said, "Eat your egg. It's getting cold."

At first she thought he was talking to J.J., but J.J.'s egg was gone. Seconds later, J.J. was gone, too, off to play in his room.

Nina ate her egg. Not at all hungry for the toast, she held it out as a peace offering to John, but he shook his head, so she put the plate down. He was angry. Maybe hurt. Maybe disdainful again. He wanted her to stay, and she wouldn't. She wouldn't meet him halfway. He had a right to be upset, she supposed, after all he'd done for her.

But that was exactly the kind of thinking that could get a woman into trouble, she knew. So, rather than apologize or try to explain things she'd already tried to explain more than once, she said, "I'd better call a cab, I guess."

John's reaction was fast and furious. "You don't need any damn cab. I'll drive you home." With the scrape of his chair, he rose from the table and carried the plates to the sink.

She met him there. "Let me do that. You can take care of J.J."

"J.J.'s all ready to go," he said, and began loading the dishwasher.

"Then do something else. Let me *help* for a change."

He rounded on her with such suddenness that she took a startled step back. "I don't need your help. I don't need *anyone's* help. You're not the only one who likes to be independent and self-sufficient."

Feeling duly chastised, she said a quiet, "I know. I was just trying to help. You've done so much—"

"And I never asked for a thing in return. I never *expected* a thing in return. So don't feel you owe me, because you don't. I did what I wanted to do, what *I* wanted to do."

When he turned back to the sink with a vengeance, Nina silently withdrew from the room. She got her bag, dropped it by the door, then, without conscious intent, found herself looking in on J.J. He was standing in front of a low bookshelf, on the top of which was a large drawing pad. With crayons from a nearby box, he was making random marks on the pad.

Approaching, she saw that the marks weren't random at all, but his version of letters. There was a wide assortment of them in various shades and sizes, but her eyes were drawn to two deep blue ones, bolder and more distinct than the others, two *J*s.

Grinning, Nina pointed to them. "Look at that. Good boy, J.J." Remembering what John had done, she signed the word "good," then clapped her hands together. Then, while J.J. was beaming with pride, she took a bright pink crayon and wrote her own name. "*N-I-N-A.*

Nina." She pointed from the name to herself and back several times, then gently tipped up J.J.'s chin to see if he understood. "Nina," she mouthed, pointing again to herself.

He repeated the mouth exactly.

"Good boy!" she signed, then arched her brows and pointed questioningly at herself.

He mouthed her name a second time, this time pointing to her as he did it.

Grinning widely, she grabbed his hand, brought it to her mouth and gave it a smacking kiss. Then she hauled him in and gave him a full-fledged hug while he giggled and squirmed. She'd miss him, she knew.

But she'd miss his father even more.

Her apartment was quiet, the same yet strange. She wandered from room to room, trailing her fingertips over the furniture, trying to reacquaint herself with possessions that were familiar, until she realized that she was the one that was strange. She had been away for a week and a half. A week and a half. Not much. Then again, a long time.

John had insisted on stopping at the market on the way for fresh food so that she wouldn't have to go out, but the emptiness she felt wasn't from hunger. She climbed into bed, thinking that maybe after a nap she'd feel more like herself. When an hour passed and she couldn't sleep, she got up, opened her appointment book and picked up the phone.

Work was what she needed, she knew. It had always been her greatest source of satisfaction. It was what made her tick.

Sure enough, after calling first the office, then several clients to tell them she was back on track, she was feeling fuller. Liking that feeling, she made more calls and would have made even more if she hadn't been legitimately tired by then.

This time she slept, and when she woke up, she made more calls. When she ran out of calls to make, she dialed John's number, only to hang up before the phone had rung. Calling him so soon after she'd seen him was a weak thing to do. She was fine on her own, just fine.

As though to prove that to herself, she grabbed pen and paper and began to organize her thoughts for the rest of the week. With each note she took and each list she made, she felt more convinced that what she was doing was right. Work was *definitely* what she needed. It was the best medicine money could buy.

The following morning, telling herself how great it was to be out and moving around on her own once again, she drove to the office. She didn't stay long, only long enough to let everyone know she was back and ready to work. Armed with a computer printout of the latest listings, she spent the rest of the morning viewing the new entries. By then, to her chagrin, she felt drained. So she went back home, changed out of her dress into shorts and spent the afternoon lounging on the living room sofa, feeling blue.

That was why she didn't call John. She refused to go running to him when she was down. She could pick herself up. She always had before, and she would again.

Wednesday morning, things were better. Feeling just that little bit stronger, she took several clients out for showings. By noon, though, she'd had it. She slept most of the afternoon away, picked at the dinner she had halfheartedly cooked, then spent the evening trying to get into one of the books she had brought home from John's. But she was distracted. She kept thinking of him, wondering what he was doing and whether he was thinking of her—then chastising herself for the thoughts. She'd made her choice. She would just have to live with it.

And damn it, if he wanted to talk with her, *he* could call.

Thursday morning, after showing two clients five separate pieces of real estate with little more than a nibble of interest, she went out to Crosslyn Rise. She needed uplifting. Crosslyn Rise could give her that.

The mansion was moving along nicely. It occurred to her that with the open house pushed back those two extra weeks, something impressive might well be done here. Her mind shifted into gear, turning the possibilities around and around. Pulling a notepad from her bag, she jotted down some ideas.

Then she headed for the duck pond, where the first cluster of eight condominiums was nearing completion, and she was struck, truly struck, by the beauty of the place. The outside hadn't changed drastically since she'd seen it last. She still loved the modified Georgian design, the hints of pillars and balconies, the sloped roofs that hid rear skylights, the cedar shingles painted taupe with cream trim. But something was different. Lowering herself to the ground with her back braced against a tree, she pondered that difference.

After a long time, during which she stretched her legs out in the sun, followed the antics of an occasional duck and breathed deeply of air redolent with the smell of grass, new wood and nature, she realized that it was the trees. With the start of summer, they were fuller and richer than they had been. And the lawn. Sod that had been put down where men and machines had mangled the earth had taken root and was now a deep, healthy green. And the shrubbery. Christine had worked with a landscaper on that, and between them, they had created a masterpiece of color and texture. As the icing on the cake, the greenery worked.

For the first time, Nina wished she could afford one of the units herself. There was something so peaceful about the place. Everything that had been done was of high quality and refined—everything Nina might have let herself dream of owning, but hadn't. She'd always had other dreams. They came first.

Sitting there in the sun, though, lulled by the smells of the outdoors and the sounds of the ducks and the nearby ocean, she didn't want to think about those other dreams. She just wanted to *be*.

Which, to her surprise, was exactly what she proceeded to do for what had to have been nearly half an hour, before two people emerged from the model condominium and approached her.

Tipping her head back against the bark of the old maple, she grinned. "Hey, you guys, what's been goin' on in there?"

Christine shot her husband a mischievous look. "Nothing much—"

"—through no fault of mine," Gideon cut in. "But Chris is all business when it comes to this place. She wants everything done, and done right, in time for your show."

"How are you feeling, Nina?"

Other than squinting against the sun, Nina didn't move. "Fine. Lazy. This place is like a drug. I'm in awe that you both manage to get work done here. Every time I come, I get sidetracked."

This time, the mischievous look Chris sent Gideon was reflected right back. "We know the feeling," she said, then took a deep breath and tore her eyes from his to look at Nina again. "You're looking good. It's hard to believe you went through what you did only two weeks ago."

"I had good care. I was lucky."

"John was pretty worried about you," Gideon said, more serious now. "When he called to tell us you were sick, he was upset."

Nina chuckled. "He was laying it on thick, so none of you would dare ask me when I'd be getting back to work."

"He was right about the open house, though," Chris put in. "It can just as easily wait until the end of the month."

Gideon draped an arm around his wife's shoulder. To Nina, in a conspiratorial voice, he said, "Especially since the fabric of the living room furniture in the model came through wrong. Chris has been sweating bullets about that. With the few extra weeks, it'll be fixed."

"So. Are you guys buying one of the units?"

They exchanged a meaningful look. It was Gideon who said, "We've been sorely tempted. It'd be a gorgeous place to live in. But Chris's daughter is still in high school. It wouldn't be fair to uproot her and tear her away from her friends—''

"And then there's this little matter of Gideon's dream," Chris put in, looking up at him again. "He's been waking up in the middle of the night with the notion that once Jill graduates we should sell his place in Worcester, buy land somewhere and build a spectacular house of our own."

"It's not a notion," Gideon argued. "It's a full-fledged plan. I can picture the whole house. Hell, I've got the basics already down on paper. It may take us a while to get it built, but when it's done, it'll be super."

He kissed Chris lightly on the lips and looked as though he wanted to do more, when Chris offered a soft, "If we don't get going, we'll be late." To Nina she said, "We're meeting Carter and Jessica for a late lunch. You know that Jessica's pregnant, don't you?"

Nina nodded. "I'm thrilled for her."

"So are we." As they started off, she added, "Listen, I'll give you a call in a day or two. Don't work too hard, Nina. We want you well."

Nina raised a hand in a wave, then let if fall to her lap as Chris and Gideon went farther up the path toward the mansion. She was thrilled for them, too. They were clearly so pleased to be together, so very much in love.

Sitting there, she felt a smidgeon of envy. Christine Lowe had it all— a husband, a daughter, a career. Jessica Malloy was on her way, too. Gideon and Carter were both fine men.

So was John. Fine, and kind, and smart, and sexy.

Feeling, at the very moment, an intense urge to touch him, she moaned aloud. She hadn't seen him since Monday morning. She missed him. Indeed, she'd been missing him all week. It occurred to her that the idea of making a clean break had sounded good but it wasn't much fun.

She deserved a little fun once in a while, didn't she? A little fun wouldn't be compromising her independence, would it?

Determined to call him that night, she pushed up against the tree trunk, returned to her car and drove home. By the time she got there, she knew that a call wouldn't be enough. She wanted to see John. Just a short visit. A drop-in visit. Just to see how he was getting on. And how J.J. was getting on. She could say hello, then leave with her sense of independence and self-sufficiency intact.

She went shortly after seven. The Leaf Turner was closed then, dinner would be over, and though there was a chance that John might have taken J.J. out for ice cream, she figured that with his bedtime approaching, they'd be back soon.

Her heart did a soft flip-flop when she saw the car parked back by the garage. Driving up to the side door, she rang the bell, then stuck her head inside. "John?" she called. Hearing no response, she went up the stairs.

She found them in the bathroom. John was giving J.J. a bath, though it was questionable who was the wetter of the two. For a minute she just stood at the door and watched. They were an adorable pair, playing under the guise of rinsing. Aside from the sounds that weren't quite like those of other children, J.J. looked like a happy, normal child. But it was to John that her eye kept returning. He looked wonderful, pleasantly wet and mussed, capable, strong. Thanks to the water, his shirt and shorts were clinging to his body more lovingly than they might otherwise have done. To her hungry eyes, he looked extraordinarily masculine.

Suffused with a warm glow inside, she asked, "What's going on here?"

John's head flew around at the sound of her voice. His sudden movement alerted J.J. to her presence. Though the child wasn't wearing his glasses, he must have recognized her overall color and shape, because with the splash of water and a nasal squeal, he began to jump up and down.

"Easy," John said, turning quickly back to him and grabbing an arm. "You'll slip if you're not careful." He said it more to himself, because with one hand on J.J. and another groping for a towel, he couldn't sign. Not that that would have worked, anyway. J.J.'s eyes were riveted to Nina.

Nina was the one who grabbed the towel and shook it open. "Lift him out," she said, "and I'll wrap him up." John did that, and within seconds, J.J. was enveloped in a warm terry-cloth cocoon. Nina gave him a hug, only to pull quickly back when he complained in the most vociferous of ways. "Oops, what'd I do?"

"You wrapped up his arms," John explained quietly. "He can't communicate without them."

J.J. had already set about remedying the situation by pushing his way out of the towel. Then his little arms reached for her and his little body followed close by. Even if Nina had been wearing her fanciest dress rather than shorts and a T-shirt, she wouldn't have minded the dampness or warmth. Grabbing J.J. around the bare back and bottom, rocking him from side to side, she felt she was holding something more valuable than any property title that had ever passed through her hands. He was precious. He was alive. He was a special, special little boy.

Her eyes rose to John, who was standing near where she knelt. He was regarding her somberly, seeming unsure as to what to make of her arrival.

"I just wanted to stop by and say hi," she explained softly. "To see how you are."

"We're fine," he said as somberly as he was looking. "We weren't the ones who were sick."

"Well, I'm fine, too," she said, but no sooner were the words out than J.J. pulled back and began making sounds. His small hand was at work finger-spelling something, but far too quickly for her to follow, even if she had known the manual alphabet, which she didn't. Something about the sounds, though, the repetition of the syllables, began to ring a bell. Not knowing whether to believe what she was hearing, she looked wide-eyed up at John, who explained.

"He wrote your name for the therapist. She had him practice finger-spelling it, but he wanted to say it, too." Begrudgingly, Nina thought, he added, "It isn't often that he voluntarily speaks. You should feel honored."

"I do," Nina breathed. Looking back at J.J., she grinned and nodded vigorously, then gave him another hard hug, followed by a kiss, followed by, "*Very* honored."

John didn't sound terribly impressed. "It's nice you stopped by so he could try it out on you. He's been asking all week where you were."

She raised stricken eyes to John's, but he turned on his heel, muttering something about getting pajamas, and left the bathroom. Holding J.J. back, Nina put a finger to the tip of his nose, mouthed, "Thank you," then, tucking him into the curve of her arm, pulled the plug on the water in the tub. When he reached over to take out his rubber duckie, she saw an ugly scrape on his elbow. Forming her mouth into a dismayed "Oh," she took the arm in her hand. "Boo-boo?"

J.J. nodded and signed something that she couldn't understand. She was telling herself that she'd have to learn more signs, when John returned.

"He did that yesterday. Came fast off the slide and scraped it. It hurt."

Gently Nina lifted the scraped elbow and put a feather-light kiss to it. "I'm sorry."

Retrieving the towel, John began to dry J.J.'s back. "It's part of growing up."

"It must hurt you, too, when it happens." She could feel the sting herself.

"Uh-huh."

Little by little, J.J.'s small body disappeared into his pajamas. Sitting back on her heels, Nina watched. She half wished she had someone to take care of like John had J.J. She didn't have the time, of course; still there had been something nice about that warm little body snuggling close.

With a flurry of hands, John and J.J. began to talk to each other. Nina waited patiently, wishing she knew more about signing, making up her mind to learn. Finally John looked at her.

"How long were you planning to stay?" he asked in a neutral tone of voice.

Wanting to stay awhile, but, thanks to that neutral tone, unsure of her welcome, she shrugged. "Did you have plans?"

"J.J. wants you in on a good-night story. He wants you to hold the book and turn the pages, while I sign."

"I'd love to," she said with pleasure. John might not have been thrilled to see her, but if J.J. was, that was a start. She'd steal time with John any way she could.

The next fifteen minutes were near to heaven. Sitting on J.J.'s bed with the small child nestled close to her side, Nina watched John sign the story of *The Little Engine That Could* as she read it aloud. She knew the story. Her first-grade teacher had loved it, and she had loved her first-grade teacher, so she'd always remembered the book.

She wondered whether John had chosen it for a reason. With its theme of the small engine that, against all odds and by dint of sheer determination, made its way over the mountain to deliver toys and games to the little boys and girls on the other side, it suggested to J.J. that he could do whatever he wanted if he was determined enough.

It suggested the same thing to Nina.

She was still thinking about that when the book was over. A sleepy J.J. gave her a big hug and a kiss, then turned to his father. Not wanting to intrude on their private good-night, Nina quietly left the room. She was leaning against the wall in the hall, with her arms wrapped around her middle, when he joined her.

His look was quelling. "He wanted to know if he could go in and see you in the morning. I had to explain that you wouldn't be here." Without giving her a chance to reply, he took off down the stairs.

Silently she followed. He had a right to be upset on J.J.'s behalf, she knew. But she would have liked it if *he* had been pleased to see her.

He hadn't said a word to that effect. Nor had anything in his look said that he was glad she had come—except maybe for his surprise when he'd first seen her, maybe there had been a little pleasure in that.

He went straight on into the bookstore, to the cartons stacked there, waiting to be unpacked. "It's hard for a kid to understand why someone he likes is there one day and gone the next."

"I know."

His gaze was cutting. "You should, if what you told me about your mother was true."

"It is. But I didn't think J.J. would make such a close tie in such a short time."

"Neither did I, or believe me, I'd never have let you stay here. But it worked between you and him. You're so totally without preconceptions about what a little boy his age should or should not be doing that you accept him completely. He senses that and responds." Swearing under his breath, he pounded the seam of the top box with a fist. Without benefit of a knife, he slipped his fingers into the small slit he'd made and pulled the carton open.

"I'm sorry," she said, and meant it. "But I'm not sorry you had me here. You were right. I couldn't have gone home. I was too weak at the beginning."

She waited for him to pick up on the suggestion and ask how she was feeling now. Instead, he pulled books from the carton and stalked off toward a far shelf. Several minutes later, after he'd taken his time putting those books in the appropriate spots, he was back for more.

"I talked with Christine and Gideon today," she said lightly. "They agreed about postponing the open house. Chris was actually relieved, because some of the furniture for the model didn't come in right, and with the extra time, she can have it done over. She wants everything to be perfect." The last sentence was spoken more loudly to follow John down another aisle with another arm load of books.

Again he was several minutes arranging the books on the shelves. By the time he returned, Nina was growing uneasy.

"Aren't you going to talk to me?"

He was loading his arms a third time. "When you say something worthwhile. So far, all I've heard is babble." Off he went.

"It'd help if you'd stop working and look me in the eye," she called, growing annoyed. She waited until he returned before muttering, "And you tell me *I* work too much."

"These books have to be shelved." Tossing one empty carton aside, he started in on the second.

"Right now?"

"Is there something more worthwhile I should be doing?"

"Talking with me."

"Worthwhile, I said. There's nothing worthwhile in what we have to say to each other."

"There might be, if you could stop running back and forth with those books."

His answer to that was to head in a different direction with a new arm load.

"John! *Please!*" On impulse, she took right off after him, following him down a short aisle and around a corner. "I want to talk with you."

He was already putting one book after another in line. "What about?"

"You. How you've been. What you've been doing."

"Well," he said, raising the last six books and wedging them in a bunch onto the shelf, "I've been fine and doing all the same things I always do, so that'd be a pretty worthless conversation." He turned to leave.

"John," Nina cried, unable to take any more of his running. *"Don't!"*

Her cry must have reached him, because he stopped in his tracks. At first his body was straight. With an expelled breath, it seemed to sag a little. Cocking a hand on one lean hip, he hung his head and stood, silent, with his back to her.

She wanted to reach out and touch him, but didn't dare. Nor, though, could she let him go. More quietly, a little desperately, she said, "Talk with me. Just for a minute. Please?"

At first, she thought he'd refuse. When she was about to repeat her plea, even to intensify it, he straightened his spine and turned slowly. Spreading his arms along the bookshelf at shoulder height, he leaned back against the books and looked her in the eye.

"What did you want to say?"

She saw it then, saw hurt in his eyes, saw confusion and vulnerability and wanting. Long fingers clenched around her heart. She let out a small breath, then swallowed.

"I'm listening," he said evenly.

Swallowing again, she started toward him. Guilelessly, thinking only to tell him what she was feeling, she said, "I've missed you."

"You could have called to tell me that."

"I didn't know it until tonight."

"It just—" arms still outspread, he snapped his fingers "—came to you?"

"Seeing you." Stopping before him, she raised a hand to his face. "I've never missed anyone before." She brushed the wayward hair from his brow, but it fell right back in the way she loved. Entranced by that and by a tug she felt inside, she rasped a palm over the shadow of his beard, touched fingertips to his chin, then his mouth. Unable to help herself, she went up on tiptoe.

"Nina—"

"Don't move," she said in a hoarse whisper, and before he could say another word, she put her mouth to his. It was a simple touch at first, a sweet homecoming that was repeated with additional little touches and tastes. "I've missed you," she whispered again, going up this time for a deeper kiss. His lips resisted. She stroked them gently, traced them with the tip of her tongue, nipped at them until they began to soften. When he opened them enough to allow her entrance, she slipped her tongue inside. He tasted wonderful, so warm and exciting, so like John that when he began to respond to her kiss, she gave a totally helpless moan.

Startled by the sound, she dropped back to her heels. Watching her, John's eyes were alert. They seemed to question and warn, but she was beyond answering and heeding. The only thing she was capable of doing was touching him in response to a clamoring need inside. Raising trembling hands to his shoulders, she tested his strength there before moving inward to the buttons of his shirt.

"Nina, what—"

"Shh. Let me." One by one, she released the buttons, finally spreading the still-damp material to the sides. From the first time she'd seen him bare, she had known he was beautifully made, but memory paled before the real thing. Slightly awed, she caught her breath. Her hands skimmed lightly over his skin, over the cording of muscles higher up, over the wedge of hair that tapered toward his belly, over the dark, flat nipples that grew hard and tight. He was warm and gentle yet masculine through and through. Unable to deny herself the pleasure she leaned forward and put her mouth where her hands had been.

He whispered her name. She shushed him again, this time against the soft hair that swirled over the swells of his chest. She pressed her lips to one spot, put her tongue to another, dragged her teeth over a third. Only once did she stop, with her ear to the rapid thud of his heart and the pad of her thumb on his nipple, but if what she was doing excited him, it excited her as well. While her mouth continued its loving sport, her hands fell to the snap of his shorts.

Again he whispered her name, this time taking his arms from the shelves and framing her head. Still she hushed him. She kissed him lightly, one spot to the next on his chest, while she unzipped him and slipped her hands inside. He was hard and hot, a binding brand against her palm. She traced his length, curved her fingers around him and drew him up, then repeated the stroking until he began to shake.

"Oh, Nina, that feels good."

It was all she needed to hear. Working her way down from his breast, she kissed a trail over his navel to the thick nest of hair that flared at his groin. When she opened her mouth on the velvet tip of his sex, he tried to pull back.

"I'll come, baby, I'll come." His voice was a tortured moan, the sound of a man in the deepest stages of want.

The sound excited her beyond belief. Defying the hands that clenched and unclenched around her head, she loved him in ways she'd never loved a man before, and when his release came she stayed with him, showing him without words how much he meant to her.

Between harsh gasps, he whispered her name. His body seemed held erect by nothing more than the wild trembling that shook it. As the trembling eased, he slid down down until he was kneeling, face-to-face with her. Hands in her hair, he looked at her for the longest time until, brokenly, he said, "No one's ever done that to me before."

"Then it was a first for us both," she whispered back.

His thumbs brushed her cheekbones, his lips caught hers. He drew her against him, only to ease her back in the next breath and tug her shirt from her shorts. "I need to feel you against me," he whispered as he unhooked her bra, and in the next instant he pushed her shorts to her knees and drew her in close again.

Nina couldn't contain the bubble of desire that swelled from her throat into a ragged moan. Large, capable hands covered her back, then her bottom, then worked their way to her breast and her belly.

"Does it hurt?" he asked by her ear, fingering the scar that was still too new to have faded.

Her breath was warm against his neck. "Once in a while, just a pinch."

"Can I make love to you?" he whispered.

"I wish you would," she whispered back.

Very gently then, with a care that brought tears to her eyes and small sighs of pleasure to her lips, he lowered her to the carpet, removed her shorts and his, and filled the place inside that had been wanting him so. Though he held his weight off her stomach, his penetration was deep. He let her set the pace, but he was attuned to her every need. When she grew hotter and her body began straining toward his, he used his fingers to help her to a stunning climax. His own followed soon after, leaving them in a limp tangle of arms and legs.

Snuggling closer into his embrace, Nina whispered a broken, "Oh, John, I was beginning to think you hated me."

He took a long, deep, shuddering breath. "Not hated. Loved. Love, present tense. I love you." Her fingers flew to his mouth, but the words were already out. Taking her wrist, he anchored her hand on his chest. "I do, Nina, and it's hell. I want to be with you all the time, but you have this thing for independence. I've been in agony all week, waiting for you to call."

Shaken by the depth of his feeling, by the intensity in the amber eyes that peered down at her, by the intensity of all *she* was feeling inside in the wake of his declaration, she managed a meek, "You could have called me."

"No. I insisted you come here from the hospital, and while you were here, I insisted you lie around and be coddled. I couldn't insist anymore. You wanted to fly. It was your turn to take the initiative."

She remembered words that had been spoken in anger and frustration on the day she'd left. "You said you were independent and self-sufficient, too."

"I am," he said quickly, then slowly to a more pensive pace, "but it's not how I want to live my life. I don't see anything weak about wanting a woman the way I want you. I don't see anything weak about wanting to sleep with a woman, or talk with her over breakfast and dinner, or take her to the beach, or eat the chocolate chip cookies she bakes. I don't see that I'd be losing anything by committing myself to you—" he took a deep breath, but when he went on, his voice was harder "—unless you don't make the same kind of commitment in return. I can't live the way I have been this week, Nina. I can't live in a vacuum, thinking of you, wondering, worrying, wanting. I can't sit around waiting for you to call when you chance to get a free minute. And I can't put J.J. through that."

Hearing his words, feeling the beat of his heart and the warm draw of his spent body, Nina was in heaven and hell at the same time. "What are you telling me?"

He was awhile in answering, and during that time, she had the awful feeling that he was savoring the last bits of pleasure before it all fell apart. She was feeling nervous when he finally took a deep breath and spoke.

"I'm saying," he began slowly and with conviction, "that I've been down this road before, only this time there's so much more of my heart involved that I can't, just can't take the risk. I love you, Nina, but if you don't love me back, if you can't marry me and move in here with me and cut back on your work so you can be a wife to me and a mother to J.J., I don't want it." He took another breath, a more labored one this time. "I guess maybe it is all or nothing. I can respect your work. I'd be the first to insist that you keep it up, and if you had an appointment at dinnertime once in a while, I certainly wouldn't complain. But work can't come first in your life. I have to. That's the only way it can be with me. I'm sorry."

Nina wanted to cry. Exerting the utmost control not to, she carefully pushed herself up. "Then—"

"Either we do it my way, or not at all," he said, rising to look her straight in the eye. "Either you love me, or you don't. Either we're together the way we should be, or we break it off. Cold turkey. Over. No phone calls. No visits. No 'maybe, if we find the time.'"

"But...that's not fair."

"Maybe not to you. You'd be just as happy to let things ride for years. But I can't do it. I feel too much."

She was incredulous. "You love me so much you'd give me up in a minute? That doesn't make any sense, John!"

The only response he made was a slow shrug.

"John," she pleaded. When he didn't answer but simply sat there staring at her, she was suddenly lashed by conflicting emotions. She wanted to rant and rave, to hit him, to knock some sense into him; at the same time, she wanted to throw herself into his arms and beg him to hold her, to love her, to keep on loving her while she did what she had to in life.

Overwhelmed and confused, she did the only practical thing she could at that moment. She reached for her shorts and pulled them on to cover her nakedness that had felt so right such a short time before.

"You're leaving then?" he asked.

"I have to. I can't think. I feel confused. I don't know what to do. I need time."

"I don't have time, Nina," he said in a grim voice. "The longer this goes on, the more it hurts."

"Loving shouldn't hurt."

"But it does."

She knew she should argue or plead or throw herself at him and make love to him again and again, until she was so firmly entrenched under his skin that he wouldn't be able to shake her no matter how hard he tried.

But she had too much dignity for that. Pushing her feet into her sneakers, concentrating on willing away the tears that seemed bent on pooling in her lids, fighting the odd sense of near-panic gripping her insides, she stood, straightened her T-shirt and started walking toward the door.

One word from John and she would have stopped. But that word didn't come, so she continued on out into the warm summer night and drove home, shivering all the way.

10

Nina went to work the next morning, but her heart wasn't in it. She hadn't slept well and was feeling tired and sore and, in general, disinterested in anything to do with real estate. When, after four hours of moving in and out of the office with and without clients, she'd had enough, she prevailed on an accommodating Lee to take over the few appointments she'd made for the afternoon.

Back in her apartment, she was at loose ends. There wasn't anything she wanted to do there, and though she was tired, she couldn't sleep. No sooner did she close her eyes than images appeared behind her lids that kept her awake—John standing on the beach looking out to sea, or kneeling by the tub bathing J.J., or lying naked from the waist down on The Leaf Turner's carpet, between the shelves for Self-Help and Romance. Each image brought back a memory in vivid detail. Each one haunted her.

The one image that kept returning, though, the one that haunted her the most, was the scene in J.J.'s bedroom. She was on the bed with J.J. tucked up against her. A large book was open on their laps, but their eyes were on John, who was telling the story with his hands.

Over and over Nina saw that scene, each time struck by something different. Once there was the warmth—maternal, if she dared use that word to describe what she felt—of holding J.J. in her arms. Another time there was the magnitude of her feeling for John, the sense of trust and respect and attraction that she'd never felt for any other man. Yet another time—and repeatedly—there was the totally unexpected contentment of being a part of an intimate family scene.

John had said that loving her hurt. In those long hours at home, she came to feel the hurt herself. He had given her a glimpse of something she had never expected to experience, and where once ignorance had been bliss, she was ignorant no more. She knew the pain of tasting something exquisitely sweet.

But wasn't independence sweet? Wasn't self-sufficiency? Wasn't freedom?

The more questions she asked herself, the more confused and unhappy she grew. Friday night passed on leaden hands creeping around the clock. By the time Saturday morning arrived, she was feeling no more like going to work than she had the day before, and that unsettled her all the more. She loved her work, at least, she always had. Now, somehow, it seemed inconsequential.

What she wanted to do was to see John, but she couldn't.

Nor could she call a friend. Or take a drive. Or go to the beach. Or the supermarket. Or a movie. She couldn't do anything frivolous, not when she was confronting the most momentous decision she'd ever had to make in her life.

What she did, acting on an instinct that was so nearly subconscious that she couldn't possibly give it much thought, was to pick up the phone and call first the airport, then Lee, then pack a small bag and head for Omaha.

Within minutes of her arrival at the nursing home where her mother lived, Anthony Kimball strode out to greet her. "I'm glad you're here, Nina," he said. After shaking the hand she offered, he guided her down the hall. "I wasn't sure you'd gotten my message. When you didn't return the call—"

"What call?"

"The one I made this morning." He frowned. "You didn't get the message?"

"No." She felt the rise of a cold fear inside. "Is she worse?"

He nodded. With quiet compassion, he said, "It won't be long now. It's good that you've come." At her mother's room, he opened the door. With a sense of dread, Nina stepped inside and moved toward the bed. The tiny figure that lay there seemed little more than a skeleton under a token blanket of skin.

Nina was horrified. "She's so thin."

"The last few months have been hard for her."

"But she doesn't know that," Nina said a bit frantically.

"No."

The reassurance was welcome but brief. The very same instinct that had put Nina on the plane that morning was telling her that, as the doctor had said, her mother's death was at hand. And though she had never been close to Maria Stone, though Maria had let her down again and again, though there had been times when Nina had actually hated her, blood was thicker than water. Maria, for all her weaknesses, was still her mother.

Nina didn't realize that the mournful sound she heard came from her own throat until the doctor touched her shoulder. "If you'd rather wait in my office—"

"No," she said and, though determined, her voice was thin, "I want to stay here with her."

She did just that. Sitting in the chair that the doctor brought to the side of the bed, she held her mother's frail hand, studied her expressionless face, stroked her thin gray hair and pretended that things had been different.

Hours passed, still she stayed in that chair. After a time, though, she stopped pretending, because memories started coming from nowhere at all, memories that she hadn't known she had for events she hadn't known she'd lived through. She remembered being very little, falling off a curb and skinning her knees, then being held by a woman with the same delicate profile as this woman on the bed. She remembered fishing funny little noodles out of a soup that she loved, while the woman who had made that soup, a woman with the same bow-shaped mouth as this woman on the bed, looked on and laughed. She remembered the sound of that laugh, and the smell of perfume. She remembered the way that smell had clung to her after she'd been hugged tightly by a woman with slender, fine-shaped hands that, in a healthier time, could well have been those of this woman on the bed.

There had been good times, she realized with a start. There had been some smiles between the frowns, only she'd been so overwhelmed by the need to survive in those frightening times that she'd forgotten them. They had been lost, probably would have been lost forever, had she not, through the force of fate, taken the time out to spend these last hours with her mother.

She wondered at the solace she might have had over the years if she'd taken that time sooner. She wondered whether she would have felt less anger toward Maria and less pity for herself. She wondered whether she might have been more complete a woman. For so long, she had believed that she'd risen way above anything her mother had been. Suddenly she wasn't so sure. Her mother had given her life, then in her own way and working around her own limitations, had loved her. Nina hadn't given anyone life or love. She had been too wrapped up in her own drive to prove that she didn't need either.

But she'd been wrong. Sitting there by her mother's bedside, holding tightly to the hand that had long ago held hers, Nina understood things about herself that she would never have considered before. As the hours wore on, as Maria's skin grew more waxy and her breathing more shallow, Nina was humbled.

Anthony Kimball stopped in before he left for the day. Nurses checked in and out, monitoring Maria's state at the same time that they offered Nina hot coffee and snacks, most of which she refused. She felt a great emptiness inside, an emptiness that wasn't totally foreign to her, but she wasn't hungry. All she wanted to do was to sit by her mother's side, to talk softly on the chance that she could be heard, to warm Maria's cold hands, to let her presence be felt.

She never knew if it was. Shortly after dawn the next morning, when the sun rose with a joy Nina didn't feel, Maria took a last breath and slipped away.

Nina had her buried later that afternoon under a pretty dogwood in a small cemetery on the outskirts of town. After thanking the priest for his kind words and Anthony Kimball for his kind care, she took a cab to the airport. From there, just as her flight was being called, she phoned John.

As though he'd been waiting, he picked up after the very first ring. "Hello?"

With a fast indrawn breath, she said a timid, "John?"

His voice softened. "Nina. Ah, Nina, thank goodness you've called. I've been so worried. Are you in Omaha?"

She nodded, then realized he couldn't see, and said a small, "Uh-huh."

"How is she?"

"Gone. Early this morning—" Her voice cracked. She pressed a hand to her mouth.

"Oh, God, baby, I'm sorry."

"Maybe—" she cleared her throat of the tightness there "—maybe it's for the best."

"Maybe," he said quietly.

"But it's hard—" Again her voice cracked.

"Are you all right?" he asked very softly.

"Uh, I think so." She gulped in a breath. "John?"

"Yes?"

"I'm coming home now. I want—I need—you. Can you—"

"What time? What flight?"

She gave him the information, then hung up the phone and, brushing the tears from her eyes, boarded the plane. She didn't cry during the flight. Nor did she eat or sleep. She felt in a state of suspended emotion, too tired to think or feel, but waiting, holding herself together as best she could.

The plane was fifteen minutes late in landing, which was late indeed, given that it was due in well after eleven Boston time. Putting the strap of her overnight case on her shoulder, Nina followed the rest of the passengers down the aisle of the plane. Passing through the jetway, her throat began to tighten. By the time she made it into the terminal, her eyes were filling up again. Her step slowed as she looked around. She swallowed. She said a silent prayer.

Then she saw John. He was standing off to the side, out of the path of the passengers. Wearing his glasses and a somber expression, he looked tense.

Slowly she started toward him. Her heart was in her mouth, ahead of every other one of the emotions that were clogging her throat, but she kept her feet moving, kept her composure intact. Only when she stood directly before him, when she could feel the warmth, the strength and caring that were hers for the taking, did everything she'd been keeping inside swell up and spill over. Wordlessly she slipped her arms around his waist, buried her face against his throat and began to cry.

At what point his arms closed around her she didn't know, though she felt his support from the start. She cried softly but steadily, unable to stem the tears, barely trying. She cried for her mother, for the years and the love that had been lost, and when she was done crying for those things, she cried for all she'd put John through.

His collar was damp from her tears by the time her sobs slowed, and by then, the strain of the past thirty-six hours was taking its toll. Bone weary, she mustered scattered bits of strength to raise her eyes to his and utter a whispered plea. "Take me home?"

Something in her tear-damp eyes must have elaborated on the request, because, without a word, John slipped an arm around her waist and helped her out the door to the car. Once inside, he brought her close to his side. Then he drove straight to the small white Victoria that he called home, led her upstairs and, with the most heartrendingly gentle kiss, put her to bed.

The sky was newly pink in the east when Nina opened her eyes again. Though her memory of the night before was vague, she knew instantly that she was in John's home, in John's bed, wearing another one of John's large shirts. John wasn't as decently dressed. Bare to the hip, at which point he disappeared under the sheet, he was propped on an elbow, watching her. His expression didn't give away anything of what he was thinking.

The lack of knowing, the fear that brought, dashed all remnants of sleep. With a nervous half smile, she said, "Hi."

"How are you feeling?" he returned without any kind of smile.

She was quiet for a minute, looking into his eyes, wanting to melt into him but knowing it was time to talk. So she said, "Sad. Happy. Scared."

"That's a lot. Want to run through them for me one by one?"

Thinking about what she wanted to say was difficult. For a minute, her throat knotted and she thought she might cry again. Determined to be stronger than that, she forced the words out. "Sad, because she's gone and I never really knew her. Happy, because being with her Saturday taught me something that I might not have otherwise known. Scared, because I know where I want to go now, but I'm not sure I'm worthy of it.'' Her voice broke, still she went on. ''I've been blind about lots of things.''

''Like what?'' he asked, his eyes level.

''Like her, and the fact that she loved me, even though she was so screwed up she couldn't show it much of the time.

''That happens to lots of parents.''

''I know. But I didn't know it when I was growing up, so I got bitter and angry and blamed her for everything that was missing in my life.'' Her voice dropped. ''But I was the one responsible for lots of those things being missing.''

''What things?''

''A home and family. Close relationships. I set out to become independently rich, which was something my mother had never been. I was sure that would be a panacea, and I wasn't letting anyone or anything get in my way. Work would fill up my life, I thought. I thought being busy and successful would be enough. But it isn't.''

''How do you know?''

''Because,'' she searched helplessly for the words, ''it just isn't.''

''Why not?''

''Because—'' she wished she could say what she was feeling, but the emotions were so strong, so momentous, so frightening ''—it's not the same.''

''The same as what?''

''*Being* with people.''

''Being?''

''Living with people.''

''As in cohabitating?''

''*Loving* people.''

John was very still. His amber eyes grew darker, more alert than before. ''Are you in love?'' he asked softly.

Eyes large and locked with his, she nodded.

''With me?''

Again she nodded.

For the first time, she saw a softening of his expression. ''For a lady who can talk up a storm when she wants to make a sale, you're sure having trouble with this.''

''That's because it's so important.''

''Is it?''

She nodded. ''More important than anything I've ever said or done before in my life.''

"So. Tell me what you're thinking. Just spit it out."

Taking courage from the gentleness of his face, she said, "I'm thinking that I don't want to be like that lady you once described. I don't want to wake up one day and be alone and empty and too old to have kids." She took a tremulous breath. "I'm thinking that I love you, and want to live here with you and be a mother to J.J. and maybe be a mother to kids we could have. I mean," she hurried to add, "I don't know anything about changing a diaper or making a bottle, but I could learn, if you wanted more kids. But you may not. J.J. is special, and he takes twice as much love."

"I've got more than that," John said softly. Cupping a hand to her face, he rubbed his thumb over her lips. "I've got more than enough for you and him and a bunch of others."

"I want a bunch. That's what I want."

"What about work?"

"I'll work. Just not all the time."

John looked skeptical. "Will that be possible?"

"You were the one who said it was."

"But is it for you? You love your work. It's been your life for so long—"

"Until I met you. It hasn't been the same since. Nothing's been the same since."

He grinned then, the grin she found so sexy, the one that could make her insides go all hot and soft. "I like the sound of that. Now, if I could just hear those other little words again."

She knew which ones he wanted. Swallowing down the last of her fears, she said, "I love you."

"Again."

They came more easily this time. "I love you."

"One more time."

She grinned. It was a snap. "I love you."

Shifting under the sheets, John rolled over so that his long body fit hers. Linking their fingers on either side of her head, he effected a slow undulation of his hips. "Now if we could have the words with a little kiss, then a little touch, then a little—" A loud sound in the hall cut him off. "Damn," he muttered, rolled off Nina and yanked the sheet up to cover her completely. "J.J.'s up."

"He's saying 'daddy'?" she whispered from under the sheet. Her hand was on his hip. She left it there.

"Yup." The door opened and his voice picked up. "Hi, sport, how're you doing?" From under the sheet, Nina could feel the movement as he signed. Seconds later, she felt a small bundle hit the end of the bed, but it slid off nearly as quickly, followed by the patter of small feet leaving the room on the run. "Smart kid," John muttered. "He saw your clothes. He's off to the guest room." Leaning close to the sheet, he warned, "Last chance, Nina. If he finds you in my bed, there's no going back. I can still make up some excuse for your clothes—"

Her hand slid over his hip just far enough to make him jump. "What excuse will you give for this?" He was still fully aroused.

"Uh, he doesn't have to, uh, see that. Damn it, Nina, don't play with me now. Are you staying, or aren't you? I have to know for sure."

"For J.J.?"

"For *me*. He'll have his own life, and I want mine. I want you in it. What do you say?"

"I may be a lousy wife."

"I'll take that chance."

"I may be a lousy mother."

"No way. Come on, Nina. Is it a yes?"

Beneath the sheets, Nina was flying high as a kite. "I need the magic words."

"I love you."

"Again."

"I love you!"

"Louder."

"I love you!"

The shout was barely out when the patter of feet announced J.J.'s return. "Didn't find her?" Nina heard John ask. She felt movement, then all was suspiciously quiet until, with a gleeful guffaw, J.J. pulled back the sheet and jumped on the bed. John caught him seconds before he would have pounced on Nina's stomach, but she was up and laughing, being hugged by them both in no time flat.

Never before had she felt so happy, so whole, so loved.

Epilogue

The sun was warm on their skin, but it felt good. The winter had been a long, snowy one. Spring had finally come.

Leaning back against John, whose body was a more comfortable chaise than any other she had ever tried, Nina took a deep, deep breath and let it out in an appreciative, "Mmm, does this feel good?"

His mouth tickled her ear. "The sun or me?"

She hooked her arms around his thighs, which rose alongside her hips. "Both. This is an absolutely gorgeous spot."

They were at Crosslyn Rise, sprawled on the lawn that sloped toward the sea. Behind them, on the crest of the hill, stood the mansion, its multichimneyed roof, newly pointed bricks and bright white Georgian columns setting it off against a backdrop of evergreen lushness and azure sky. To the left and right were more trees, many newly budded, and beyond the trees, grouped in clusters, were two dozen condominiums, all finished, all occupied, all spectacular. Before them, at the foot of the hill, was the small marina with its pristine docks and proud-masted yachts, and the row of shops that included an art gallery, a clothing boutique, a sports shop, a video store, two small restaurants, a drugstore and The Leaf Turner.

"Are you sorry we didn't buy a place here?" John asked.

"Not on your life. It's enough that you have the bookstore. Besides, I love the Victorian, especially now." As soon as John had moved the Leaf Turner to Crosslyn Rise, they had repossessed the first floor of the house. What with the professional expertise of Carter Molloy and Gideon and Christine Lowe, they had renovated the place into something neither one of them had dared dream of. Nina might have done even more—finished the attic as a playroom for J.J. or built on an attached garage—had not John been vehement that the bulk of her Crosslyn Rise profit was to go into an account in her own name. He didn't care if it sat there untouched for years, he told her, just so long as she knew it was there, for her, should she want or need it.

He understood where she'd come from. He was special that way.

But then, she mused, lazily shifting her bare feet in the warm, soft grass, he was special in lots of ways. Like his concern for her. There was times when she could swear that his only goal in life was to make her happy.

"Are you sure," his deep voice came now, "that you wouldn't like to rent a small space here for you?"

"Can't do," she said with pride. "We're leased to one-hundred-percent capacity."

"But when something opens up."

"Nope. I'm happy where I am." She was still at Crown Realty, with Chrissie handling her pink slips and Lee, albeit engaged to a wonderful guy now, backing her up.

"You don't ever think about having your own agency, not even for a minute, for old times' sake?"

Tipping her head against his arm, she looked up into his face. How many times she'd seen those strong features in the past two years, seen them in every light and mood, and it seemed that she only loved each one more. "When do I have time to think about having my own agency? My life is so full." Full as opposed to busy. There was a difference.

"But you wanted to be independent."

"I am. I work when I want and come home when I want." She touched his cheek. "It's a pretty nice deal." She paused. "Why don't you look convinced?"

"I just worry sometimes. I think back to when I met you and remember all the things you wanted—"

"What did I want?" she cut in to ask in a rhetorical way. "I wanted my own business, but that doesn't mean anything to me now, because I have enough else to do that I don't want the responsibility. I wanted lots of money, and I have it, right in the bank."

"You wanted freedom—"

"Which is just what I've got. You've made me free." The words had slipped out on their own, but she thought about them for a minute, finally saying a soft and knowing, "It's true. I used to think that loving meant being a slave to another human being. But loving you isn't that way at all. You make me feel whole and important and secure. You give me strength to do new things." With a mischievous grin, she said, "I've bloomed."

Chuckling, he moved his hand over the flaming orange tunic that covered her belly. "Just a little, but it's in there."

Covering his hand, she held it fast where it was as she looked up into his eyes. "I'm so excited," she whispered, barely able to contain it.

"Not scared?"

"Sure, scared."

"But you've been a super mom to J.J."

"J.J.'s a big boy." Her eyes took on an added glow. "He's doing so well. I'm so proud of him.'' The special school he was at—the one John had financed with his share of the profit from Crosslyn Rise—was doing wonderful things for him. He had lots of friends. He was reading, writing, signing, lipreading, even talking in his way. He, too, was blooming. ''But a little baby, a little baby is different.''

''We'll do it together,'' John said with quiet confidence.

Doing things together was pretty much the story of their marriage, which was another reason why Nina hadn't once felt that she'd given something up in teaming with John. He was an able man, an able father and husband. He had been just as self-sufficient, as she before they'd met, and he could easily be self-sufficient, as could she. The fact that they chose to share whatever load it was they were bearing at a given time, was a tribute to their mutual respect and love.

In the months since they had been married, Nina had done something she had sworn never to do. She had grown dependent—dependent on John for his love. But while once that would have terrified her, it didn't now. She trusted him. She knew beyond a shadow of a doubt that she would always have his love.

Feeling happy and hopeful, if hopelessly smitten with the man holding her, Nina gazed out over the picturesque scene ahead and sighed in utter contentment. ''There's something about this place. Carter said it once, and I think it's true. There's something in the air here. Crosslyn Rise is a charm. Look at Carter and Jessica and how happy they are with that beautiful little girl of theirs.'' She grinned. ''I'm glad they bought the unit in the meadow. It's perfect for them.''

John kissed the top of her head, then murmured into her hair, ''It seems right to have a Crosslyn still here.''

''Mmm. Even though they spend weeks at a time with Carter's folks in Florida. I understand it's a fantastic place that Carter bought for them.'' She took a quick breath. ''And speaking of fantastic places, the one Gideon is building in Lincoln is going to be *incredible*—'' savvy broker that she was, she couldn't resist tacking on a self-righteous ''—even if he did overpay for the land.''

''He has the money. Crosslyn Rise did well for him.''

''In many respects—money, reputation, love. They're so happy, he and Chris. I love seeing them together.''

John flashed his wristwatch in front of her nose. ''Is it time?''

She shook her head against his chest. ''We have another five minutes.'' Since the Crosslyn Rise consortium had formally disbanded, the three couples—the Malloys, the Lowes and the Sawyers—had taken to getting together once a month or so. Sometimes it was for dinner, sometimes for a show, sometimes for an evening of general playing at one or another of their homes. On this particular day, they were having an impromptu lunch at one of the small restaurants on the pier. Nina was looking forward to it.

Even more, though, she was looking forward to spending the rest of the day with John. Though he was working full-time in the store now that J.J. was in school, he had arranged to have Minna Larken cover for him that afternoon. Likewise, Nina had scheduled all of her appointments for the morning. So they were free. Nina had her monthly checkup with the doctor, which John refused to miss, but after that they were heading into Boston for several hours of walking and shopping and sipping cappucino in sidewalk cafés. They would pick J.J. up at school on the way home.

It was a wonderful life, Nina mused, and all because of John. Shifting impulsively to face him, she slipped one arm around his neck. "Do you know how much I love you, John Sawyer?"

The question alone was enough to bring pleasure to his face, which, in turn, enhanced hers. "I think so," he answered with a soft half smile, "but I wouldn't mind if you told me again."

She didn't have to. Slipping her other arm around his neck, she gave him a long, breath-robbing, arm-throbbing hug that said it all.